ANDREW M. GREELEY

PATIENCE OF A SAINT

Futura

A Futura Book

First published in Great Britain in 1987 by
Macdonald & Co (Publishers) Ltd,
London & Sydney
This Futura edition published in 1988

Published by arrangement with Warner Books, Inc.,
New York.

All characters in this publication are fictitious and any resemblance to real persons, living or dead, is purely coincidental.

ISBN 0 7088 3582 1

Reproduced, printed and bound in Great Britain by
Hazell Watson & Viney Limited
Member of BPCC plc
Aylesbury Bucks

Futura Publications
A Division of
Macdonald & Co (Publishers) Ltd
Greater London House
Hampstead Road
London NW1 7QX
A Pergamon Press plc company

For Pastora Cafferty and her preparations for the Fifth Star

A Literary Note

At the time I write this novel there are two Chicago newspapers, the *Tribune* and the *Sun-Times,* both on what Red Kane would call the "Rive Droite" of the Chicago River. One could write many splendid novels about either of them, not all necessarily scurrilous.

However, for the purposes of this book I have created a third Chicago paper, the *Herald Gazette,* located it on the "Rive Gauche" and transferred to its ownership the United of America Building. None of the journalists who work at this illustrious, if altogether imaginary, paper are based on actual living human beings in Chicago. If any readers think they see themselves in the sundry characters that inhabit the Herald Gazette Building, the explanation is either coincidence or paranoia.

I add this note, not to fend off libel suits, but to remind the folks who might want to see themselves in a novel that they are not nearly as interesting as my imaginary reporters. Moreover, this is not a novel about Chicago reporters (though many interesting such novels could be written, not all of them scurrilous), but about one man's desperate flight down the days and down the years.

All the other characters are also products of my imagination, as are the events of the story.

If this be interpreted as meaning that I think I can create more interesting Chicago journalists than God has, all I can say in reply is that God doesn't seem to have been working very hard at it lately.

My love is like a mare among the chariots of Pharaoh.

—*Song of Songs 1:9*

On State Street, that great street,
I just want to say
They do things they don't do on Broadway,
Say,
They have the time, the time of their life,
I saw a man, he danced with his wife,
In Chicago, Chicago, my home town.

—Fred Fisher
"Chicago"

Nigh and nigh draws the chase
With unperturbèd pace,
Deliberate speed, majestic instancy;
And past those noisèd Feet
A Voice comes yet more fleet—
'Lo! naught contents thee, who content'st not Me.'

—Francis Thompson
"The Hound of Heaven"

Until the day breathes cool and the shadows lengthen, roam, my lover, like a gazelle or a young stag on the mountain.

—*Song of Songs 2:17*

I am man and he is not. So no argument or suit between the two of us is possible.

—*Job 9:32*

And Jacob wrestled all night with the angel of Yahweh. When the angel saw that he could not throw Jacob he smote him in the hollow of his thigh.

—*Genesis 32:24*

You duped me, O Lord, and I let myself be duped. You were too strong for me and you triumphed. All the day I am an object of laughter. Everyone mocks me....The word of God has brought me derision and reproach all the day....But then it becomes like fire burning in my heart, imprisoned in my bones; I grow weary holding it in. I cannot endure it.

—*Jeremiah 20:7–9*

...the Holy Ghost over the bent
world broods with warm breast and with ah! bright wings.

—Gerard Manley Hopkins
"God's Grandeur"

"Woman, you'd try the patience of a saint!"

—Irish Adage

PATIENCE OF A SAINT

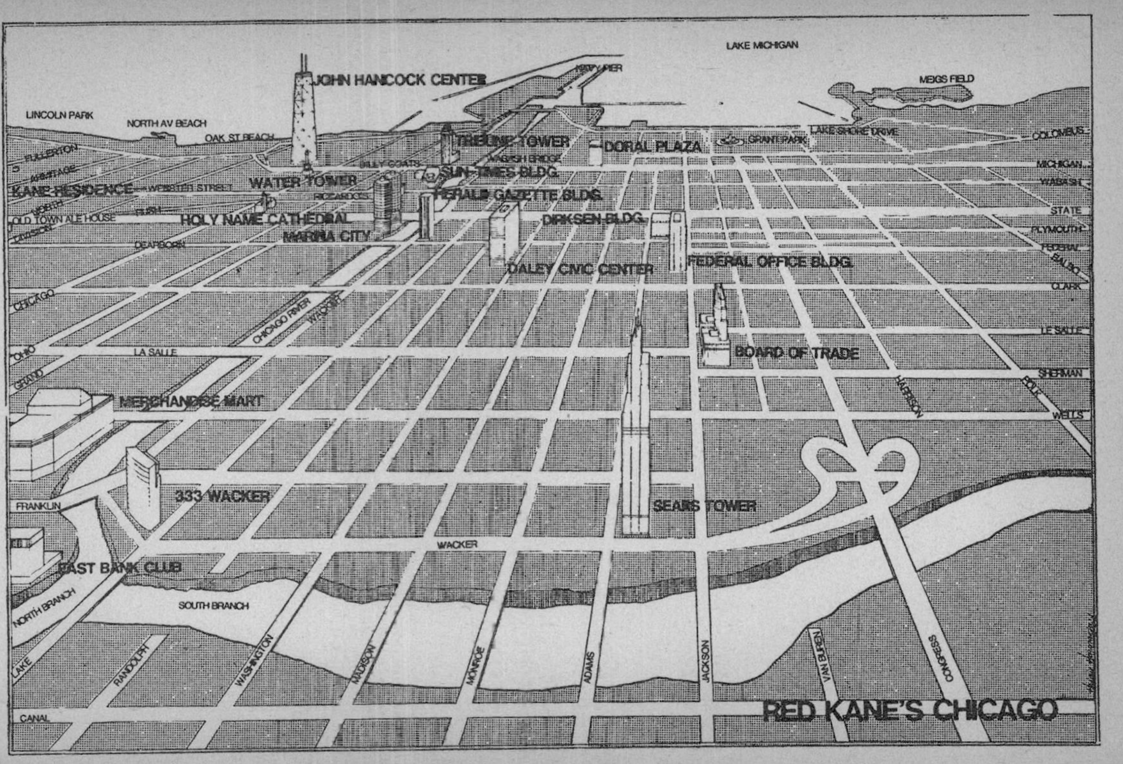
RED KANE'S CHICAGO
LAKE MICHIGAN
MEIGS FIELD
NAVY PIER
JOHN HANCOCK CENTER
LINCOLN PARK
NORTH AV BEACH
OAK ST BEACH
TRIBUNE TOWER
DORAL PLAZA
GRANT PARK
LAKE SHORE DRIVE
COLUMBUS
MICHIGAN
WABASH
STATE
PLYMOUTH
FEDERAL
BALBO
CLARK
LE SALLE
SHERMAN
POLK
WELLS
FULLERTON
ARMITAGE
KANE RESIDENCE
WEBSTER STREET
NORTH
RUSH
OLD TOWN ALE HOUSE
DIVISION
DEARBORN
WABASH BRIDGE
BILLY GOATS
SUN-TIMES BLDG.
WATER TOWER
RICARDO'S
HERALD GAZETTE BLDG.
HOLY NAME CATHEDRAL
MARINA CITY
DIRKSEN BLDG.
DALEY CIVIC CENTER
FEDERAL OFFICE BLDG.
CHICAGO
CHICAGO RIVER
WACKER
OHIO
LA SALLE
GRAND
BOARD OF TRADE
HARRISON
MERCHANDISE MART
333 WACKER
SEARS TOWER
FRANKLIN
EAST BANK CLUB
NORTH BRANCH
SOUTH BRANCH
LAKE
RANDOLPH
WASHINGTON
MADISON
MONROE
ADAMS
JACKSON
VAN BUREN
CONGRESS
CANAL

Prologue

"God screwed me," Red Kane insisted, staring glumly at the Mexican American Christmas crib on the coffee table.

"Typical," replied the priest. "Long history of that sort of thing. You are not the first and, unless I underestimate the proximity of the End of the World, you won't be the last person to undergo a life-transforming religious experience."

"I'm going along in the middle years of life...."

"Like Dante...," the priest observed helpfully.

"A lot older than Dante," Red continued, thinking that what he was about to say would make a great column—if he were still writing columns. "I'm a success at my career, not at the top, but a hell of a long way from the bottom...."

"Irish Royko," said the priest.

Outside the dirty window of the Cathedral rectory large snowflakes were drifting lazily down Wabash Avenue, laying the groundwork for a half foot of snow that was supposed to come before morning.

"I'm a virtual stranger to my three teenage children; I have a bad relationship with my wife, whom I love, a good relationship with my mistress, whom I don't love; I haven't spoken to my boss in six months...."

The votive candle in front of the crib had burned down to the wick. Like Red Kane it seemed disposed to be snuffed out.

"Deservedly," the priest agreed.

"Most of my colleagues hate me, I'm two years behind on the delivery of my novel, I drink too much but I'm not overweight, I smoke too much but the doctor says my heart is in better shape than it ought to be...."

"Topflight condition compared to most Chicago Irish journalists." The little priest stared at a piece of paper that had somehow come into his hand.

"I am, in other words, a typical American male of my generation."

"Living a life of noisy desperation." He rotated the paper so that he could puzzle over it from another angle.

"Thurber," Kane murmured, dismissing the interruption. "Anyway, I wasn't all that happy, but I was surviving."

"Make a good column." Shrugging his shoulders, the little priest made another note on the paper with a pencil stub and stuffed it back into the pocket of his clerical shirt.

In the distance the Cathedral choristers were working their way through a polyphonic version of "The First Noel."

"Now I have nothing—no job, no wife, no mistress, no family, no friends, my parish priest sends me to a psychiatrist who wants to lock me up...."

"A veritable modern Job."

"...And it's all the Lord God's fault."

"Absolutely. The Lady God, I always say, tries the patience of a saint."

"I'm not a saint."

"I suspect She has other plans for you."

"What the hell does She...He...Whatever...see in me?"

The little priest blinked his nearsighted eyes. "Hard to tell. Historically God's taste has been somewhat questionable. Strange people...your man Peter, for instance, he was a loudmouthed braggart too...."

"I'd like to get drunk," Kane said, with a heavy sigh. "Except all the fun has gone out of drinking."

"The unkindest cut of all."

The votive light died a quiet death.

"Shakespeare. Julius Caesar....Monsignor, what the hell did I do wrong?"

The priest shrugged. "I dunno, Red. Should have stayed off that Road to Damascus, I suppose."

Book ONE

Heat
Light
Fire
God of Abraham, God of Isaac, God of Jacob,
Not of philosophers and scholars.
Certainty, certainty, heartfelt joy, peace,
God of Jesus Christ,
God of Jesus Christ,
My God and Your God...

—Blaise Pascal
November 23, 1654
(found, after his death,
on a piece of parchment
sewn into his clothes)

I

Wacker Drive is not exactly the Road to Damascus. Nonetheless, it was on Wacker Drive that the Lord God hit Red Kane over the head with a cosmic baseball bat.

Or so it seemed to Red afterward.

"I was minding my own business," he told the little priest in the Cathedral rectory six weeks later. "The Feast of All Saints, Anno Domini 1983, I'd been to Mass, and I was minding my own business."

Indeed the Lord God assaulted him just as Red was noting lackadaisically the similarity between the color of a new glass skyscraper and his wife's ice green eyes.

"There I was, on the Rive Gauche of the River at the corner of Wacker and Wacker—you know, right at the fork in the River where the street slants southward along the South Branch?—blameless as a newborn child. God snuck up behind me when I wasn't looking."

"Typical," the little priest sighed again.

Moreover, the Lord God used the same one-two punch with which he had done in Saint Paul. The latter worthy was knocked from his horse perhaps by a lightning bolt. Red Kane, not having a horse, was bowled over by a large Cadillac limousine that narrowly missed him as it made a rapid right turn against a red light and sped away at high speed.

"Eileen!" Red cried as he jumped out of the path of the car, lost his balance, and fell with considerable lack of dignity on his rear end.

Harv Gunther, he thought to himself as he scurried across the street and leaned against the concrete guardrail above the Chicago River, sweating profusely and gasping for breath. A warning to leave him alone.

His life did not pass in review as it is supposed to at times when sudden death threatens. As he tried to slow down the panic in his breathing beneath the aloof green ice of the building across the street, the last few hours of that morning did slip by his mind, reprimanding him for his wasted life.

Appropriately enough it was the Feast of All the Saints. He had been walking back to the Herald Gazette Building from Mass at Old St. Patrick's on Canal Street across the river. He had not walked over to Old St. Pat's to fulfill his November first obligation but to mark the fifteenth anniversary of the death of his younger brother, Colonel Davitt Kane (West Point '53), in an ambush near Hue in Viet Nam. Perhaps Dav's wife Gerry, remarried now to one of Dav's West Point classmates who was a general in Germany, and their older kids would shed a tear or two. Certainly Red's other brother, the sometime Monsignor Parnell Kane, would not remember and would not waste a tear even if he did.

At first he considered writing the column for today's paper about Dav. The deadline had closed in inexorably on him yesterday afternoon and he could find not a glimmer of an idea. His parched throat had demanded a stiff shot of Jameson's. He'd typed out the lead sentences of the column. "Fifteen years ago today Jane Fonda's friends in the Viet Cong blew up my brother. He was driving a jeepload of crippled Vietnamese kids to a hospital. Ms. Fonda's friends proved they were not biased against Americans. They blew up the kids, too."

Then he decided that such Irish sentimentality was a sign of the brain softening with age. So he'd gone after Jane Fonda, one of his all-time favorite targets, for exploiting The People with her exercise book: It was designed to enable women to remain sex objects.

Red felt that somehow he had partially avenged his brother. He realized sadly as he tossed the printout on the desk of the op-ed page editor, the way he would throw a poisoned bone to a rabid dog, that Dav would have thought it uncharitable. Dav was the only one of the three boys who had not studied to be a priest and the only one that might have made a good priest.

So, instead of writing a column about Dav, he had gone to Mass today in memory of his brother, not sure Dav would still need his prayers, not sure there was anyone to hear his prayers, and not sure that what he was doing was prayer.

The Cathedral was closer than Old St. Pat's, but he had not wanted any of the older women employees of the *HG*, the only ones who worried about Holy Days of Obligation in the modernized Catholic Church, to see him at Mass. His reputation as a "fallen away" had been too carefully cultivated to be given up so easily. Moreover, if the pious women of the *HG* saw him in the Cathedral they would undoubtedly begin praying for him again, and Red did not need THAT.

Finally, he would have to see his brother-in-law the Cathedral Rector at a family party that night. One encounter a day with the Monsignor was more than enough.

Sitting in the pew, he at most directed a few distracted reflections vaguely upward, "to whom it may concern."

He was very careful not to think about his own death, a subject that would force him to double the number of Jameson's, neat, he would have to drink before the day was done.

He confidently expected that the Mass—or Eucharist, as his kids called it—would be lifeless and dull. The handsome young priest, however, by his own admission inspired by the solid phalanx of statues that lined either side of Old St. Pat's—"Black, Hispanic, Native American, Italian, Swedish, German even," a gesture toward Mary and Joseph, "two Jewish saints"—preached a brisk and incisive homily (the name for sermons these days) about the achievement of sanctity through generosity and kindness in everyday life—almost as if he knew that it was a memorial service for Dav. Instead of indulging in a tear or two, partly for Dav but mostly for himself, Red was forced to consider how he measured up to the criteria of the homily.

Not very well. Perhaps guilt would be a better reason for getting drunk that afternoon than self-pity. He could not afford to be too drunk. Then he would miss the Ryan party and they would have an opportunity to talk about him and about how his wife had had to marry him because he had made her pregnant. Eileen had never told them, of course. But whatever their weaknesses, the Ryans could count. They had doubtless noted that the day of his son's birth was August 22, precisely nine months after the murder of John Fitzgerald Kennedy.

As the young priest worked his way through the Mass, Red found himself distracted, not unpleasantly but dangerously, by the most serious temptation in his life—an overwhelming instinct to fall in love with his wife again. Eileen, as always, was the temptress—subtle, low-keyed, and devastating. Would the woman never learn that their infrequent love affairs meant more agony for both of them?

A touch more affection in the sometime end-of-the-day, routine kiss, a more loosely wrapped towel emerging from the shower, a bra strap falling off her shoulder as she vigorously brushed her gleaming black hair and hence the revelation of more of a sumptuously jiggling breast: Ah, the woman knew all the tricks of issuing an invitation to temptation!

Moreover, she'd lost seven or eight pounds, a feat she could accomplish, much to Red's chagrin, almost at will. Such an achievement made her already delectable body even more appealing—as it was designed to do. Since infidelity in Eileen's case was unthinkable, he was obviously the target.

He endeavored to banish from his mind the obscene image of his wife's bobbing breasts and disturbingly svelte waistline. Surely it was not an appropriate picture for the canon of the Mass—or the Eucharist, as they called it now. The good Lord forgive her for her tricks and traps. He forced himself to think of her patient and patronizing sigh, a hint that he had once again been a feckless boy child. The sigh often drove him to furious, if unexpressed, anger.

Now it sufficed only to diminish somewhat the love that insidiously crept into all his lustful feelings for her. It did not, however, diminish the lust at all, for which God forgive her again.

And He Himself knows how often her breasts, wondrous and insidious spheroids, have been my downfall before!

It would be, he was certain, his last love affair with his wife. It would fail as all the others had. Better, to quote one of his favorite aphorisms (which he with deliberate falsehood attributed to the Bible), not to try at all than to try and fail.

There was enough in his life to be guilty about or, alternatively, to feel self-pity about, depending on his mood. In addition to the usual messes he had created through unkindness and selfishness, Great Western Books had threatened that if his novel, two years late, was not on their desk by January 1, they would sue to recover the advance.

Also, he should move his ass and pursue the leads he had in the Gunther case, as the sterling investigative reporter he was alleged once to have been would have done when he was hungry for a Pulitzer.

He had already used some of the money for John's education. A lot left over, but not enough to pay it all back. It would be embarrassing to have to ask Eileen for help. She would give it, of course, without a word of protest. They never argued about money—or about anything else. To argue was to talk, and they had both avoided talk for twenty years. Eileen's anger, as he had once claimed the seventh wonder of Chicago, had disappeared from her personality. All that remained were gentle reproofs, a mild and patient form of nagging, and an occasional brisk session of lovemaking, when Red was able to participate in such activity. She was never unreasonable and never overtly domineering.

"I was thinking of making a down payment on a house at Grand Beach, Red; do you mind?" she had said.

"Gosh no. Near the family?"

"You don't have to see them. The house is a decent distance away. They do like you, Red. Want to drive down and look at it?"

"Sure. Not this Sunday though."

He most certainly had not wanted to be in the same resort community as his relatives and promptly swore that he would never visit the damn place. Like most of his other promises, he had violated that one in a few months. Actually came to like the house, though he would never admit it to her.

Eileen was almost always right. And she never said "I told you so." Nor did she ordinarily make the same mistake twice. Except in her persistence in her love for Red.

He never asked stupid questions like "Can we afford the house?"

Surely they could, or Eileen wouldn't have been buying it.

They had separate checking accounts, separate budgets, separate financial lives, though not yet separate beds.

Well, she had a budget. They avoided conflict by not buying anything for which one needed to ask the other's money.

Red had written the monthly checks for their house on Webster till the second year of Eileen's private practice. Then she said one morning at breakfast—a chance meeting—"I can take over the mortgage payment now, Red."

"Fine," he'd said, and that was that.

Stop thinking about Eileen, you dummy. You don't care what she meant by that one sentence in the feature story.

I will think about something simple and unmysterious. Like why I haven't finished my novel.

He found the protagonist loathsome, a bleary-eyed drinker and lecher behind whose mask as a comic commentator on the passing parade hid self-disgust and despair. How could you write a novel about a failed reporter, an incompetent father, and an unfaithful husband?

About Red Kane, in other words.

Better perhaps to try a fictional account of the life of Harv Gunther. That name reminded him of his friend and mentor and hero Paul O'Meara, who, more than twenty years ago, on a snowy night in January of 1963, had walked across the Wabash Avenue Bridge to meet a friend from the *Sun-Times* and was never seen again. Red, several sheets to the wind, saw him disappear into the blizzard. Joe Crawford waited on the other side till nine o'clock. The next morning he called Red. As soon as Red heard Joe's voice, Red knew that Paul had disappeared from the face of the earth and that not even his dead body would ever be found.

Red had sworn he would hunt down those who killed Paul if it was the last thing he ever did. After three weeks of blind alleys he gave up. Dav would never have given up. And Dav would have finished the novel. And Dav would have gone after Gunther a couple of months ago. And Dav...

But why bother with comparisons?

The young priest, a brown-haired, brown-eyed Irishman with a quick politician's handshake, smiled at him as he walked out of church. "Hi, Mr. Kane. I remembered your brother at Mass."

How the hell did he know that?

"Keep working at it and you might make pastor," Red replied, not unkindly.

"I AM the pastor," said the young priest.

Red edged away from him toward the Adams Street Bridge over the river, lighting his inevitable cigarette. The skyline along the river seemed to change every time he walked through this part of the city. Wacker Drive on its north-south leg was now even more striking than the Magnificent Mile. The Skidmore, Owings & Merrill Canyon he'd called it in the column in which he'd attacked the Sears Tower, the Merc, and the Gateway Center. He grinned to himself. It was a great column. He could still remember it.

"The carpetbaggers who run this city's cultural life are fond of telling one another in whispers of hushed surprise that Chicago is an exciting city. Ask them what they mean and, if they recognize that you exist—they have a hard time seeing native Chicagoans, the little men who aren't there—they'll cite the glass and steel monstrosities in the SOM Canyon along the river.

"Actually, Chicago is a lot less exciting than it used to be. We haven't had a really good gang shoot-out in a long time, or a major police scandal, and the last presentably sized riot was more than ten years ago.

"If they want excitement they should try the Robert Taylor homes or Cabrini-Green, where the last Mayor—what was her name anyway?—lived for a few publicity-hungry days.

"In Robert Taylor and Cabrini-Green they would have an experience like exploring the upper reaches of the Amazon. Lots of thrills and the danger of being killed any moment.

"That's what excitement means, isn't it?"

Someday he'd write a column comparing the Skidmore Canyon favorably with Madison Avenue in New York. Long ago it had been ordained by Chicago readers that it was perfectly all right for Red Kane to argue both sides of the street.

Satisfied with himself, and impressed by the cut of the canyon against the sky, he crossed the street and lit another cigarette. He had finally given up telling himself that he should quit smoking. He had also begun to smoke again at home, despite Patty's and Kate's cries of outrage.

He shouldn't have been surprised that the priest remembered Dav. Probably a seminary contemporary of his other brother, the sometime Monsignor Parnell Luke Kane. Hero's death on All Saints' Day would stick in his mind. He'd ask Monsignor Ryan about him tonight.

The hell I will. Then he'd know I went to church.

Red walked toward the Herald Building. He paused for a final consideration of the 333 Wacker Building. Hell of a name for a building. Wacker Drive, hell of a name for a street. A long time ago, some group of folksingers had done a record about "Wack, Wack, Wacker Drive." Lousy record. Except for one song, "Dick the Magic Mayor, he lives in City Hall" to the tune of "Puff the Magic Dragon."

Why did the old man have to go and die on us? He was great copy. Imbeciles ever since.

Red had baited the Mayor constantly and the old man had fought back. Bitter enemies, everyone said. Yet after all the sizzling columns Red had written in the summer of 1968, the old man had phoned him in the evening of the day of Dav's death.

"Sis and me and the kids want to tell you how sorry we are for your trouble." The age-old Irish line at a wake.

And all Red could say in return was, "We're grateful for your sympathy," the equally age-old Irish response.

Just as Red, who had cried three or four times in his life since his father's death on Memorial Day 1937, had wept on the bitter cold December day when he told the Daley family that he was sorry for their troubles. Everyone wept that day, so Red didn't figure it counted.

1968—Kennedy and King and Dav had all been killed. A few days after Dav's death the country was given Richard Milhous Nixon as a consolation prize, so that it would know that no matter how bad things were they could always get worse. If it was fifteen years since Dav's death, it must have been fifteen years since Nixon was elected.

A month for anniversaries. November 22 would be the twentieth anniversary of Jack Kennedy's murder and of the first time he and Eileen made love.

Another month and it would be Christmas. He would go into his usual Christmas funk, drowned in self-pity and booze. The day after Christmas would be the twentieth anniversary of Eileen's telling him she was pregnant. She had waited till then so as not to spoil Christmas.

"Only one night of lovemaking!" he had exclaimed in dismay, thinking at first that there had to be someone else, though he knew that was absurd.

John Patrick Kane was born on August 22, 1964. At least, Red reflected later, it had been a spectacular night of love that had produced John Patrick. For a virgin Eileen had learned quickly, almost instantly. The way she learned everything else.

At the thought of Eileen, he abruptly ended his reverie and returned to the 333 Wacker Building. Of all the reasons in his life for guilt and self-pity and fury, Eileen was the most important.

And hence the one he tried to think about as little as possible.

He certainly would not fall in love with her again, no matter how insidious her seductions became. No way! All right, she had great breasts, the best he'd ever seen. But Red's prudery—the other side of his fascination with female flesh—could be depended upon to help him to look the other way. Well, some of the time.

He had blasted the 333 Wacker Building in his column for two reasons: The nitwits who wrote architecture criticism for all three papers liked it and they hadn't been right since the Chicago Fire. Worse still, the architect was from New York. In the world view of Red's column, everything from New York was effete, sick, demented, vulgar, and tasteless. One of the secondary reasons that Wilson Allen had given for firing him a couple of months ago was that many Jewish readers complained that Red's criticism of New York was proof that he was anti-Semitic.

Having had several Jameson's to loosen his tongue for the argument, Red had responded that in fact he wasn't anti-Jewish at all, but anti-Italian, and that there were more Italians in New York ("By a factor of two, asshole") than there were Jews. Poor Wils was speechless, as he always was when he permitted himself to be caught in a face-to-face confrontation with the "Poor Man's Mike Royko."

Pauper's Mike Royko, actually.

Quite apart from the necessities of turning out a column every day, Red liked the 333 Wacker Building, an elegantly carved slab of green ice mirroring the city beyond the river—which most great Chicago architects tried to ignore—and reflecting the cotton-candy white clouds that were marching across the blue sky in orderly ranks toward the lake. On this first day of November, he imagined the saints passing in neatly disciplined columns before the divine reviewing stand.

The building made him think again of Eileen, the cool, green-eyed, and elegantly carved mystery woman with whom he shared a bed every night, although not much else besides sleep happened in that bed. He would have believed twenty years ago that it would have been impossible to lie next to that tightly packed body and those lush breasts and not want to fuck her. Now he knew that it was possible and even easy.

Not that she was a bad lay (though he would not dare use the word with her). Much better than Melissa Spencer, Red's mistress. Eileen's approach to sex, on the rare occasions that they did make love, was relaxed sensuality. Melissa concentrated intensely on performance, as if she were an Olympic diving queen being watched by judges who would hold up score numbers after the tango was over.

When Eileen had told him calmly that she was pregnant but that he did not have to marry her—meaning every word of it—he replied, his hands sticky with sudden sweat, his stomach queasy with fear but also with anticipation, "I want to marry you. You're the most perfect woman I've ever known." The first sentence was dubiously honest. The second was the absolute truth. Then and now. Unfortunately, perfection in a wife did not make for a successful marriage when a husband was afraid of women.

He sighed a loud, west-of-Ireland sigh and turned away from the green glass building. He would have to start his drinking at the Old Town Ale House early, call Eileen, and tell her that he would meet her at the party later on in the evening.

Eileen's green eyes: the granite eyes of a determined, utterly rational lawyer; the weary emerald eyes of a patient and long-suffering housewife; the wanton turquoise eyes of a violently aroused lover; the smoky aquamarine eyes of the fey witch girl he sometimes thought was the real Eileen.

The one sentence that had jumped out of the page in the feature article on her in the *Sun-Times* continued to haunt him. What could she have meant?

He turned his head for a final look at the green skyscraper. Its graceful sweep was somehow similar to the graceful sweep of her warm and lovely breasts. The Holy Ghost...with warm breast and with ah! bright wings.

That's when the Lord God intervened.

Later Red would insist to his priests and his psychiatrist that first he experienced a moment of terror—confusion, chaos, disorganization; then, before he could cry out desperately for help, he heard a whooshing sound in the air behind him, like someone swinging a mighty two-by-four. Or an outsize baseball bat. There was a transient instant when he knew something was going to happen, that he might be well advised to duck, and that it wouldn't do him much good to try.

Then time stood still, the whole of eternity filling a single second and a single second filling the whole of eternity. He was opened up like a lock on the Chicago River and everything flowed into him, the 333 Wacker Building, the city, the blue sky, the lake, the world, the cosmos. With them there came a love so enormous that his own puny identity was submerged in it like a piece of driftwood in the ocean. The invading love was searing, dazzling, overwhelming. It filled him with heat and light, fire that tore at his existence and seemed about to destroy him with pleasure and joy.

The flaming, cosmic passion that had invaded him both threatened to deprive him of life and bathed him in an extraordinary peace. Redmond Peter George Kane SAW.

What did he see? They would ask him when they wanted later to institutionalize him.

He SAW.

What?

The unity of everything in the universe and his own place in that unity, the certainty that everything would be all right.

Red knew at that moment of body-rending joy and peace that it WOULD be all right. Afterward, when he wanted to believe that he had been deceived and that everything would most definitely not be all right, the afterglow of certainty would not relinquish its hold on him.

Time and space dissolved at the corner of Wacker and Wacker. The man who was Red Kane dissolved with them. A creature who used to be Red Kane was now dancing merrily on a flaming sea of ecstatic love. That creature was part of the sea on which it danced and had only a body and a three-piece, slightly frayed, and more-than-slightly unpressed gray suit in common with what had once been Red Kane.

Then the sea calmed down and the flames died out. Eternity slipped out of time. The cosmos retired to its proper place. The veils fell back into place.

Redmond Kane stood on the corner of Wacker and Wacker, hot tears pouring down his face, not because his brother Colonel Davitt Kane was dead.

But because he himself was still alive.

2

Mike Royko, of all people, was the first one to encounter the new Redmond Kane. He was walking across Wacker Drive on Wabash, toward the same bridge to the Sun-Times Building on which Paul O'Meara had disappeared long ago.

Red cut across the street to intercept him, with the buoyant steps of a man about to congratulate a new parent. Royko looked surprised and a little dismayed. The most he and Kane ever exchanged were brief grunts of recognition.

"I haven't seen you lately, Mike," Red said, not altogether truthfully because they had seen each other on opposite sides of Ricardo's during one of Red's infrequent visits to that hangout of the journalistic establishment. "I wanted to tell you how great those baseball play-off columns were. The big difference between Cubs fans like you and me and White Sox fans is that we're at least neutral when the Sox are playing for the championship. Sox fans would actively cheer against us if the positions were reversed. Damn it, I wish I had written those columns."

Greater compliment no one could pay.

Mike could not have looked more surprised if the Archangel Raphael had apprehended him on the Wabash Avenue Bridge on the Feast of All the Saints. He waited for the punch line—there was always a punch line with Red Kane.

Red went on to commend him on his columns about the fancy haircuts that some of the machine aldermen were sporting, saying that aldermen with twenty-five-dollar haircuts were more of a problem than corrupt aldermen.

His rival decided to accept the possibility that for once in his life Red Kane was actually playing it straight and gracefully acknowledged the compliment, even beaming a little with pleasure, like a cautious elf who has had a surprisingly pleasant word from a troll. Then he slipped away as though he had encountered a dangerous madman—or a totally transformed Red Kane, who might be even worse than a dangerous madman.

Wait till the crowd at Ricardo's hears this, Kane chuckled to himself.

He met Wilson Allen coming out of the elevator on the editorial floor of the Herald Gazette Building, Wils's suit, shirt, tie, and shoes a color-coordinated symphony in gray. His principal qualification as editor was that he had marginally more sex appeal than Jim Hoge of the *Sun-Times*. Wils fit the current fashion for Chicago editors as if he'd been designed for the part: tall, youthful looking, handsome, WASP. Allen Wilson was to editors, Red had said on Channel 2 after he was fired, what Ronald Reagan was to politics—the triumph of media image over substance. He looked like an editor in the same way the Bears' sometime quarterback Bobby Douglass looked like a quarterback, even though he had the lowest completion percentage in the NFL. He was to editing what Rock Hudson was to masculinity—whatever else you might say, he had all the right moves. Winston Bradford, the president of the conglomerate that owned the *Herald*

Gazette, wanted three things in an editor, a clean-cut movie-star face, razor-cut blond hair, and a name like his own in which the first and last words were interchangeable.

"You mean Wilson Allen and Bradford Winston, don't you?" interviewer Walter Jacobson had said.

"That's what I said; and, you know, Allen Wilson really has been working hard to learn more about Chicago. He's only been here two years and he's made it to Halsted Street already. You can't blame him for not going any farther. He didn't want to get lost the first time out."

On this Feast of All the Saints, Red felt great compassion for Wils. His older boy, a rugby star at a prep school in New England, had been stricken with leukemia.

"How's the boy doing, Wils?" he asked sympathetically, as if they had not been separated by a wall of silence for the past half year.

Allen recoiled as though he had been blindsided by Mean Joe Green, examined Red's face for a hint of a cruel joke, and then said very carefully, "It looks like he's going into a remission. They can do wonders with chemotherapy these days. The doctors say the odds are on his side, but you never know...."

"No one realizes what it's like unless he's been there," Red said gently. "We went through a scare a couple of years ago when there was a possibility that our Johnny had bone cancer. Eileen and I are praying for you and Madge and the kid."

Which was not strictly true. Red certainly hadn't prayed for him; and, while Eileen might well have, she had never mentioned it to Red. The sentiment, however, was accurate. Now, at any rate.

"That's very kind of you, Red," the editor replied, genuinely moved. "He's receiving the best medical treatment money can buy, but it's all in the hands of God."

Ah yes, I've heard of Him.

"We'll keep up the prayers." Red patted his boss's muscular arm. "Let me know how it goes."

Wilson Allen was so astonished that he did not ask why it had taken Red three weeks to offer sympathy and support.

Red walked through the newsroom to his desk, whistling

"When Irish Eyes Are Smiling," the first time in the memory of humankind that he had whistled anything.

The editor before Wilson Allen was, according to Red, the most brilliant designer of newsrooms in the world; it was a shame that he couldn't read or write. Awed by the *Washington Post*'s newsroom—as depicted in *All the President's Men*—he had been determined to preside over an even more attractive layout and thus prove he was a better editor than Ben Bradlee. Hence the plastic cubicles that separated some of the staff from the rest of the staff were painted blue and pink. For purposes of sexual differentiation, according to Red. And the crimson carpet was so thick that you needed snowshoes to traverse it. Red contended that the general effect would have reminded you of a high-class Swedish bordello, except the combination of noiseless word processors and sound-absorbing walls and ceilings made you think you were in a cathedral and ought to fall on your knees in prayer.

Ben Hecht would vomit.

A line of motionless word processor screens marked Red's path as he weaved his way to his own cubbyhole. It would have been much better in the old days, when the typewriters would have stopped clacking.

Being nice to Wils wasn't even hard, he thought as he slipped into his chair. "Didn't see you in church, Amanda," he said in a stage whisper to the *HG*'s food editor, a Catholic woman of his generation and the old school.

"I went last night," she said as though Santa Claus had appeared and asked her the same question.

"Tsk, tsk, getting liberal, it seems to me. Are you sure it counts? Not even a venial sin to sneak it in the night before?"

"Oh, no." She returned to her word processor, doubtless processing an article about food processors.

What the hell is happening to me? They are looking at me like I'm drunk, but I'm either a mean drunk or a sad drunk, never a happy drunk. A happy Red Kane is impossible.

And now it almost seems that I was never unhappy. Something strange happened out there on Wacker Drive. Maybe I'm dying. Maybe I'm losing my mind.

I don't care. I like it. I'll enjoy it while it lasts.

Bring Eileen a bouquet of roses tonight.

Then he felt a momentary sadness—how many other nights had he thought of such a gift and dismissed it with a quip like, "Let her bring me a bouquet; she makes more than twice as much as I do."

All right, he thought crisply, *I'll bring her two tonight. Eventually, given a long-enough life, I'll catch up.*

That thought struck him as hilariously funny. So he laughed. All the word processors in his area stopped blinking. Red Kane never laughed in the newsroom.

Automatically he dialed—the *HG* had dial phones to save money—Harvard Gunther's number. Why? Had he not given up on the Gunther case because it was too much work?

He put the receiver down. Was he going after Gunther again because he wanted revenge? Red's stepfather had put a bullet through his head in 1942 because of an unfair prosecution by Gunther when he was a young prosecutor. In the back of Red's mind there lurked a hunch that Gunther might have been involved in Paul O'Meara's disappearance.

Settling grudges, he decided, didn't matter, but a story to which the public had a right did. The Gunther file was open again, despite the threats the old man had made in their last conversation. And despite the limo on Wacker Drive.

Red had once written in his column that when Gunther finally was unable to pay protection money to the Grim Reaper and went to his eternal reward, such as it might be, his survivors would have to build a urinal for a headstone because so many Chicagoans had sworn that they would befoul his grave.

The editor had killed the lead, of course. Red had changed it to "put a barbed-wire fence around the grave to keep out those who will want to dig it up to make sure that Harvard is dead." The editor, long before Wils, had passed it without a word.

Harvard had stopped him on the street the next day to say that he had heard about the original lead and thought it was wonderful and he was having designs for such a tombstone prepared.

Red hesitated before he dialed Harv's private number. Gunther had warned him off last time with verbal threats. And now there was the hint that he could wipe Red off the face of the earth if he wanted to. Ought he to run the risk of a confrontation? Backed into a corner, Harv could be very dangerous. Who was Red Kane, at his age in life and with a wife and family that could be vulnerable, to take on that evil old man?

Much to his own surprise, he dialed the number. The sultry voice at Gunther's end of the line pretended not to know who he was but assured him she would tell Mr. Gunther that he had called.

If Red Kane thought of himself as the last of the Irish journalist drunks in Chicago, Harv Gunther was the last of the robber barons, the last and the greatest. Harv, who was now over seventy, was a crook not because it was in his interest to be a crook—he was one of the wealthiest men in Cook County—but because it was in his nature to be a crook. Not to have a piece of the action in every major money-making scheme that slipped down LaSalle Street would be a threat, an intolerable threat, to Harv's existence. These days, slick entrepreneurs dealt Harv in at the beginning on the assumption that if he were left out he could hurt them and that if he were inside he could help. So great was the Gunther legend that he hardly had to do a thing to earn his money. His presence in the list of investors on a new project guaranteed that the various approvals required from government agencies would quickly fall into place. And his absence would raise questions of what was the matter with, for example, a new high-rise condo/office combination or a new sports arena. If Harv wasn't involved it wasn't going to make money.

His involvement rarely cost him a penny. He'd have his money back even before ground was broken.

A tall, stooped man with an egg-bald head and vast shaggy eyebrows, Harv Gunther looked like a dissolute Merlin who had run away from King Arthur's court with all the crown jewels in a shopping bag and the Holy Grail thrown in as a bonus. Harv's father had worked in the mills—South Works, not Republic—and Harv claimed special friendship with Red because their fathers had both been millhands.

Red wrote a column about that too, pointing out that Harv's father had been a foreman who took bribes from workers during the Depression so that they wouldn't get laid off and who spied on union organizers in his free time.

The son far excelled the father, though his beginnings were humble enough as a bagman for a crooked State's Attorney and a go-between for bribing judges and juries. As government became more complicated in the 1950's and the services purveyed by businesses to the government more lucrative, Harvard Gunther forsook petty corruption for influence peddling. He knew how to get things done in the increasingly confusing maze of government agencies, starting with minor favors like changing a zoning regulation, on up to major favors like airport concessions. He was adroitly subtle at hinting what size of campaign contribution would be required as payment, or what cut of a deal the relevant politician would want in return. Naturally, there was also a cut for Harv.

Suppose that you were responsible for snow removal and knew that, since the Bilandic Blizzard swept the Lady Jane into office, no administration dared to be without fallback snow removal contractors. Suppose also that you needed money for your reelection campaign—or just needed money. You would convey to someone the notion that the city might contract with him for snow removal if there were certain contributions made or if certain considerations were given with regard to investment opportunities. Then that someone would subcontract snow removal to those who had the actual equipment—at ten percent less than the city paid him. His profit could be defended in the name of administrative overhead. And his generosity to your campaign or a cut of a lucrative real estate deal could not be linked to his snow removal contract.

Not if Harv Gunther was the go-between, it couldn't.

There were several younger generations of wheelers and dealers in Chicago. None of them could hold a candle to Harv. Some of them did time in the slammer. Harv was never once brought to trial, save on a federal income tax rap in the fifties, and that was thrown out of court.

He was a free man because he managed to make himself indispensable to every mayor and governor that Chicago and Illinois had known for thirty years, because he was too smart to take needless risks, because he was a master of bribe and blackmail, and because he was ruthless against those who threatened him.

The days were over when Harv might have your legs broken or acid thrown in your wife's face, or make your star witness disappear like he was a magician. He had too much power now to need to threaten violence. His mild hint to Red earlier in the year that Eileen's practice might suffer if Red pushed his questions was more of a test of Red's nerve than anything else.

Yet if Red did get too close, he might disappear on the Wabash Avenue Bridge as Paul O'Meara had.

"The way she's keeping crooks out of jail, Harv," he had laughed in the old man's face, "you'd probably hire her if we ever got an indictment against you."

They had both laughed together at that.

Gunther wore thousand-dollar suits now, a considerable improvement over the thirty-five-dollar shiny double-breasted black suits, off the rack at Goldblatt's, that he'd sported when he was bustling around traffic court fixing tickets and selling ration stickers during the war. He was conveyed around town in a Mercedes limousine that was a cut or two above the Cottage Grove streetcar. He was on all the major cultural and charitable boards in the city—art, opera, music, ballet—and had funded a chair at the Northwestern University Hospital. His wife, who lived in the family home in Lake Forest while Harv occupied a two-floor co-op on the Gold Coast, served on several hospital boards and appeared frequently, with her long stringy gray hair, on the social pages of the Chicago papers.

Harvard Princeton Gunther was wealth, power, prestige; a man to be admired, respected, and feared; exactly what his father had in mind when that poor Anglo-Saxon immigrant had named him after not one but two universities. And because he was all these things, he was now a distinguished civic leader.

He was also a two-bit crook, a little smarter than the others and a little more vicious. He was, as Red had called him in a column, a WASP mafioso who had no business walking the streets with decent men and women.

Harv had found that amusing too. Wanted to know how Red could pick out the few decent ones who were on the streets of Chicago.

Red had two leads on Gunther, only one of which the old man knew. The first was a simple and elementary land clearance scheme on the South Side in which an alderman who was a crony of Harv's had directed the contract, through his influence on a council subcommittee, to a demolition company in which Harv had a substantial ownership. The money involved was peanuts, but the alderman and the contractor had been greedy and the city agency either stupid or venal. The demolition had been done effectively enough, but the city had been overcharged by about ten percent. The alderman, under pressure from the feds, had whispered some things to the grand jury. And one of the feds, after a little too much to drink at Billy Goat's, had whispered the story to Red.

The Justice Department was debating an indictment. Harv had hired Washington attorneys with strong Justice ties to contend that the indictment would never stand up because the evidence was simply not strong enough (Red learned that the fee of the Washington lawyers was half a million, for a few phone calls). The local U.S. Attorney, a man who Red said reminded him of the cowardly deputy sheriff in Gary Cooper movies, much preferred cases against ex-basketball stars like Hurricane Houston, whom Eileen was currently defending, than crusades against powerful members of the Establishment like Harvard Gunther and was not pushing Washington for a decision. The bet was that it would all quietly be dropped without a word leaking to the press.

Only Red Kane knew the other lead.

3

Red was running for his life, frantically trying to climb out of the deep black waters of the river, but the waters were thick and muddy, and the bank was far away. The masked warriors who were chasing him were drawing closer. Their furious drums were demanding his death. With the strength born of despair, Red pushed his way through the muck and stumbled weakly toward the bank. He seized the dead branch of an overhanging tree. It broke. A woman was there extending her hand. It was Eileen, ready now to save him. He grabbed her hand and her face changed. It was no longer Eileen but someone else...Rita Lane! She pushed him back into the river. The masked gunmen who were following him had changed into ugly, hammerheaded fish—piranhas!

As Red watched in horror they began to eat away his leg.

He would wake up, convinced still that he had lost his left leg in the dark waters of the Rio Negro. Desperately he would clutch for his leg. It was still there. He would shake his head, grope around, brush against Eileen, and realize that he was safe in their bedroom on Webster Avenue in Chicago, seven thousand miles from the Rio Negro and its piranhas.

The dream had come almost every night since, several months before his excursion on the Wacker Drive Road to Damascus, Red had made a hasty trip to Brazil.

Beside him Eileen would be sleeping peacefully. In his dream he must have converted her into Rita Lane—fearful that his wife might turn into a madam who sacrificed teenage girls to rich men's twisted lusts.

Red would shiver. He didn't really think, even unconsciously, that Eileen was that kind of a woman, did he? Of course not.

Before he fell back to sleep, he would mentally review the Rita Lane file.

Last spring, late May, six or seven weeks before his slapstick public fight with poor Wils Allen, he was hanging around Billy Goat's on a Friday afternoon, trying to think of a good reason for not going to Grand Beach and a Ryan family outing on the weekend. Billy Goat's was not exactly Red's favorite place. First of all, it was adjacent to the Lower Level of Michigan Avenue, whose depressing gloom touched at raw superstitious nerves in Red's soul. Stealing one of Paul O'Meara's lines and elaborating on it, he claimed that after dark, the Lower Level became a tributary of the River Styx. "That fella Charon paddles his canoe filled with a shipment of lost souls along here every night; I'm afraid some night he'll pick me up by mistake because I look like I belong on the boat."

Many was the night when, staggering out of Billy Goat's, too much of the Drink having been taken, Red, frightened by his own joke, ran up the steps to the Michigan Avenue bus shivering with terror and swearing that he would never touch a drop again.

The promise rarely lasted more than a few seconds after the bus picked him up.

Second, he found the know-it-all cynicism, which was *de rigueur* there, even among the youngest of the New York punks, most of whom had never heard of the River Styx, to be offensively idiotic. God knows, he would tell himself, I've spent fifteen years at least hiding behind the mask of comic cynicism. Still, as one of the certified old-timers of the Chicago media, he knew about the cops and the pols better than anyone else did. There were honest cops, even in the days of Black Jack Carmody, and honest pols, even in the days of Sewer Pipe Ed Kelly. Angles in Chicago were always tricky, always involved, always a little bit different from what they seemed. When some punk six months out of Columbia journalism school figured he had Eddie Vrdolyak's motives summarized in two sentences, it made Red want to vomit.

Worse still, reveling in cynicism at Billy Goat's was an excuse among the younger generation for not working. If everything was already figured out, then there was no point in digging for a story. Personally—he thought, and soon he would do a column saying so, that Eddie Burke, the junior partner of the two Eddies, was much better copy than Fast Eddie Vrdolyak. He was more cunning politically, more ruthless, more politically intelligent, and more likely to surround himself with extremely able staff.

Red had pushed some of the stringers and bureau chiefs of the East Coast newspapers to take a good hard look at Eddie Burke. None of them paid any attention. "He's Fast Eddie's straight man," sneered Moses Mayo, a sleazy type from the *Time* empire. "Why write about a ventriloquist's dummy?"

Red had composed mentally the lead for his own column on Burke. "The mayor is the first generation in his family in politics. That makes it a little tough when you're up against somebody like Eddie Burke, whose family was in politics 3,000 years ago, when the Celts were still living in trees and painting themselves blue."

"Mr. Kane?" A trim young woman approached him gingerly. Dressed in a neatly tailored charcoal-gray suit, self-possessed, clear brown eyes and long brown hair, she was entirely too much like Eileen for him to make a pass.

"That's my name. And yours?"

"I'm Fran Hurley, from the Los Angeles Times Syndicate...." She hesitated.

"Sure." Red patted the barstool next to him. "Sit down, order yourself something. It's always a pleasure to have a drink with a first-rate professional."

The young woman blushed pleasantly. "Thank you very much, Mr. Kane."

"Unless I remind you of your grandfather, you'd better call me Red. Your series on the Andes was wonderful. Made me want to visit those awful places."

"On the whole I'd rather be in Billy Goat's." She pointed at Red's Jameson's. "I think I'll have one of those. I hope you'll forgive me for having it on the rocks. I wonder if I might give you something, Mr. Kane." She hesitated and flushed slightly, another Eileen-like trait. "I wouldn't bother you, but you have such a fine reputation for ethical integrity and professional competence...."

"Don't believe all you hear about me," he said lightly. The girl's admiration tore at his gut. Fifteen years ago that reputation was deserved. Now it was like his marriage, a tattered remnant of another and happier day. Unconsciously he shoved the glass of Jameson's out of easy reach. "Let's hear the story."

It was a strange tale, even in Billy Goat's, perhaps a strange story especially in Billy Goat's. On her way home from the Andes, Fran Hurley had decided she would have a brief look at the other wonder of South America—the Amazon—and had spent a few days in Manaus, the last of the cities on the Brazilian side of the Amazon Basin. At a cocktail party honoring a visiting Japanese manufacturer, she met a faintly mysterious woman, a very interesting woman who, when she learned that Fran Hurley was returning to the States to spend several months working on a series about midwestern cities, pleaded with her to stop by her house the next day for a drink. At that time, she entrusted Fran with this—Fran removed a manila envelope from her purse—and begged her to deliver it personally to Red Kane in Chicago.

"The woman was under grave stress, Red." Fran's brown eyes were steady and confident. "She told me it was something that deeply troubled her conscience, that she would only be able to sleep at night if she could do something about it. She said you were the one man in Chicago who might be able to help."

Red gallantly thanked the young woman for serving as messenger and promised, somewhat foolishly, that he would do whatever he could. He slid the envelope into the inside pocket of his jacket and chatted pleasantly for a quarter of an hour with Fran Hurley about her series on midwestern cities, a series that he suggested could prove a good deal more hazardous than scaling the heights of the Andes.

After she left, he removed the envelope from his pocket, unfolded it, and pried open the tightly sealed flap. A letter, a couple of papers, and a photo. He eased the photo out—a color Polaroid print of two naked human beings, one of them Harvard Gunther and the other a young girl. Gunther, his face shining with pleasure, was doing unspeakably perverse things to the child.

Red stuffed the photo back into the envelope, jammed the envelope into his pocket, gulped the rest of his third Jameson's, and walked unsteadily across the river back to the city room of the *Herald Gazette.*

It took all the willpower he had not to open the envelope again in the elevator riding up to the fourth floor. There was no one else on the elevator; why not have a peek? *Because someone might get on at two or three, dummy, that's why.*

In the relative privacy of the pastel partition around his desk, Red opened the envelope again and gingerly extracted the letter. "I am putting my life in your hands," the letter began.

Red glanced through it quickly, then read it more carefully. The woman was speaking the truth, all right. She was, indeed, putting her life in his hands.

Her name was Rita Lane. She had been in the business of providing young girls for rich businessmen. One such young woman, Adele Ward, had "accidentally" died while satisfying the needs of Harvard Gunther. She was present at the young woman's death. Gunther had hushed it all up and paid her a huge sum of money. Afraid that Gunther would kill her eventually, she had taken all her savings and fled to Brazil to begin a new life, "free from all the things I had done in the United States."

Only, freedom had not come. The ghost of Adele Ward continued to haunt her, appearing in her dreams at night and, more recently, even when she was wide-awake. "I look out my window at the Rio Negro and see her standing in the middle of it, walking on the water, arms outstretched, pleading with me to give back her life, or to punish the man who had killed her.

"He is a monster, Mr. Kane. Some of the other men are weird and kinky, but none of them were into killing. Gunther loved every second of the girl's death agony. I don't think he intended to kill her. He seems to get his kicks out of sparing their lives at the last minute. This time he went too far. He enjoyed killing this bound and helpless victim so much that I'm sure he will try it again, if he has not done so already."

Rita Lane claimed she possessed evidence, even more damning to Harvard Gunther, that she would entrust only to Kane. Would he please fly to Manaus in Brazil so she could give him the evidence and free herself from the haunting spirit of Adele Ward?

There were two more pictures in the envelope and a copy of a handwritten note to Rita Lane on Regency/Hyatt stationery assuring her that the "material is now food for fishes at the bottom of Lake Michigan."

The handwriting in the unsigned letter was vaguely familiar. Red searched through his correspondence file for a handwritten note from Harv Gunther commenting on one of his columns. No, not the same.

He considered the evidence in the envelope judiciously. Hardly enough for an exposé of Harvard Gunther. He opened the locked compartment of his desk and dropped the material into the Gunther file. Then he relocked the desk and slipped his key ring back into his trouser pocket. "I've never been to Brazil," he remarked thoughtfully to himself.

He was inclined to believe the woman's story. If Gunther wanted to trap him, even kill him, there were less elaborate ways of doing it. Why not make a quick flight to Brazil? He told Steve Leary, the managing editor of the *Herald Gazette*, that he would be out of town for a few days hunting down a story, and politely declined Leary's offer of expense account help. "I have to be away a couple of days," he murmured to Eileen, who was preoccupied with a long and complicated trial involving contractors' political contributions and kickbacks. "Afraid it's a secret. I'll stay in touch."

"Be careful," she replied. "Don't forget a raincoat." Red reflected that his mother had often said the same thing to him, but that on Eileen's lips the words were liberating rather than constraining. Nonetheless, to his regret, he didn't bring a raincoat.

On Wednesday nights, at five-fifteen, Varig Airlines flight #805, an ugly, slightly decrepit DC-10, lumbers out of the Miami airport. Hours later it touches down briefly at Santo Domingo and then lifts off again into the night sky for Caracas, where it lands a little after ten o'clock. Then, once more, flight #805 points its nose into the dark skies and wings its way toward the equator.

"If we crash anywhere between here and Manaus," said

the cheerful American businessman sitting next to him, "we'll be eaten by the natives. There's nothing but jungle down there."

"Natives in the jungle, sharks in the ocean," Red replied, turning away from the businessman and trying to sleep.

Somewhere after midnight he did fall asleep, only to be awakened unceremoniously by the cabin attendant making sure that his seat belt was fastened for their landing at Manaus.

Curious, Red watched out the window as the plane turned into its final approach. The scattered lights were obviously the city—a million inhabitants according to the guidebook he had purchased at the Miami airport. And all around the lights, nothing but black—the darkness of tropical rain forests, although most of the best lumber had already been torn from the immediate vicinity of Manaus, only second-growth jungle, but jungle just the same. Then they crossed a broad band of darkness of velvety texture, different somehow from the blackness of the rain forest. The Amazon River. Crash in the jungle and the Indians eat you, in the river and the piranhas eat you. Red shivered. He regretted the waste of his marriage and considered making an Act of Contrition. Before he could decide on such a drastic step, however, the landing gear of the DC-10 touched down, lightly enough, for a perfectly safe landing. Here I am in the jungles of the Amazon, Red thought ironically, conveyed into the heart of darkness by a DC-10.

Manaus was a duty-free port. The guidebooks said that was the reason why there were so many Japanese electronics factories built around the town, which meant, for reasons Red could not fully understand, that the Brazilian customs officials were more difficult than Red had expected in a Latin American country—and the guidebook said further that Brazilians did not like to be called Latin Americans. They were Brazilians. Or even better, Americans.

Despite the late hour, there were taxis waiting for the flight, the only direct flight from the United States all week—much the way the buckboards used to wait for the stagecoaches in the days of the American West. A taxi, which was certainly no more comfortable than an old buckboard, conveyed him for the ten-minute ride to the Tropical Hotel, on the banks of the Rio Negro a few miles up from Manaus. A distinctively Brazilian exterior, faintly Moorish, with high ceilings and thick beams, and the heavy wood furniture saved it from being an ordinary modern luxury hotel.

Eileen would like it, he thought, homesick already.

He and his wife had never traveled together, afraid perhaps to be with each other for a sustained interlude with no escape hatches available. Yet whenever he left the country on assignment he fantasized that she was with him.

After deep but pleasant dreams in which he and Eileen explored the jungle along the Rio Negro in an outboard-powered canoe, Red awoke in the middle of the morning to the noise of raucous German tourists in the corridor. Peeking out the window, he saw thick mists obscuring everything beyond the driveway of the hotel. He called Rita Lane's number, identified himself, and was invited to lunch about one-thirty. The relief in the woman's voice was palpable.

He drank a cup of coffee for breakfast, hoping it was made from bottled water, ate two pieces of fruit, having carefully peeled off the skins, and set forth on a brief exploration of the city, an old rubber center with an opera house in which Caruso had sung in the beginning of the century, and a wrought-iron fish market designed by the man who had created the Eiffel Tower. It was late autumn in Brazil, and the mighty Amazon, shrouded in mists that Red thought were menacing, was low. He decided that he did not want to take a cruise on the Amazon and that the quicker he could get back to Webster Avenue in Chicago, the better he would like it.

Manaus was part elegant crone and part unfaithful bride. Almost a million people lived in the city, many of them in grim poverty. Yet the streets and graceful squares were lined with skyscrapers and shops filled with expensive clothes and electronic marvels. The stately houses of the rubber barons, most of them needing a coat of paint, suggested a certain dignified if run-down elegance. It was in one such house that Rita Lane lived.

A pretty black girl opened the door, smiled respectfully,

and led him to the back of the house, onto which an American-style swimming pool and patio had been appended. It was a bizarre mixture of the late nineteenth and late twentieth centuries.

Rita Lane was a lean, hard, attractive woman in her late thirties, mildly sexy until you realized how cold were her unblinking brown eyes. She was not, in any case, Red's kind of woman.

She wore a thin caftan of some sort of bleached muslin material, and she arose eagerly to shake Red's hand as soon as he was ushered onto the patio.

"Do come and sit down, Mr. Kane," she murmured, sounding a bit like a memsahib in British India, doubtless the mask she was wearing. "It is such a relief to be able to talk to you."

The patio was surrounded by a high brick wall, lined with carefully cultivated flowers, and protected from the sun by neatly trimmed trees. Several servants, all black women, hovered anxiously in the background. Red caught a glimpse once of a handsome, muscular, light-skinned man standing in a doorway. Rita Lane was enjoying the good life for herself, despite the terror that lurked just beneath the surface of her cold eyes.

"You need not be afraid to eat and drink anything, Mr. Kane," she said smoothly. "We are very careful to avoid all the local germs and parasites. Here." She offered him a glass. "It's a Brazilian drink. I'm sure you'll enjoy it."

It was sweet but not sticky, and smooth. Rum and vodka, maybe, with a terrific delayed-action punch. He didn't mind. If he was going to fly back to Chicago tonight via Mexico City, he would want an afternoon nap in the hotel away from the heat, the mists, and the sand flies and other beasties.

He might have imagined it, but as soon as he sipped the drink, he heard samba drums pounding in the distance.

Rita Lane offered no apologies for her past. If she had her life to live over, she told him, she would have done it differently. But the past was the past. She had a number of investments in both the United States and Brazil and some "interests" in Manaus. "All of them quite legal and legitimate," she said with a mirthless smile. The "incident" in

Harvard Gunther's Gold Coast apartment had forced her to retire before she had planned to and to leave the United States, which she had been reluctant to do. "But living here has worked out quite well." Again the mirthless smile. "If only... if only it hadn't happened."

She recited a self-serving story about how she had taken care of her "girls" and ensured that no permanent harm was done to them. Most of them finished school eventually; some even went on to college. They considered their trade to be more of a game than anything else.

The typical line for a madam, Red thought. Justifying herself with the heart-of-gold argument. She had a heart of gold, all right. Pure gold bullion and every bit as hard.

"We had provided girls for Mr. Gunther before." She signaled the young black woman to begin serving lunch. "His needs were unusual, perhaps, but not excessive. I was somewhat concerned once when a transformation appeared to come over him, as though there were a..." She hesitated over the word. "...a demon inside him. He recovered quickly, however, and was his usual charming, gracious self."

"I bet." Red dipped into the fish stew and was surprised to find it quite tasty.

"I had some reservations before this final incident, but, candidly, they were not serious. You must understand that my associate and I are not in the room with the client during the actual encounter."

"Someone was taking those Polaroid pictures."

"We had a special time release camera for the clients who... ah... required such pictures as part of the transaction. Mr. Gunther was one of those clients."

"I see." The fish stew was no longer all that tasty.

"Mr. Kane, I am absolutely certain that the ghost of Adele Ward is here with us now. I see her in my dreams almost every night, I encounter her at the fish market, or on the river, or even at cocktail parties for the visiting Japanese. She appears briefly, her eyes filled with tears, pleading with me to avenge her death. She was not a very intelligent young woman, Mr. Kane, but she was sweet and fragile. I did not anticipate what would happen, but I still feel responsible."

"I see," Red said guardedly.

"As you doubtless know, the Macumba religion is very powerful in Brazil. I have become very close to a 'mother of a saint' here in Manaus. Adele speaks to me through that woman and begs me to release her so she can join her little brother in the happiness of heaven. She is fated to roam the earth until Harvard Gunther is punished for her death."

Despite the tropical heat and the dense humidity, Red felt his flesh crawl. A voodoo curse on Harvard Gunther, a nice touch.

"No one"—Red scratched his chin—"has been able to cast a spell—or whatever you call it—to free Adele so she can go to heaven?"

"Please, Mr. Kane, this is not voodoo superstition. Spells do not release souls from purgatory, only justice."

A retired madam on the lamb in the jungles of the Amazon, obsessed by voodoo rituals, demanding justice for a murdered girl in order to release her from purgatory. And Redmond Peter Kane was supposed to be the hammer of God.

"I'll do what I can, Mrs. Lane."

"It might be very dangerous." She leaned forward and placed her ice-cold hand on his.

"Living in the same city with Harvard Gunther is dangerous." He carefully salvaged his hand. "You better tell me all you know about Adele Ward's death."

Rita Lane and her "associate" had heard the girl's screams change from pain, which was to be expected, to desperate terror. They broke through the door in time to witness the last seconds of Gunther's insane cruelty.

"The girl was dying, Mr. Kane, and he was laughing like a little boy at a Halloween party."

They tried to revive Adele. Several of Mr. Gunther's "associates" calmed him down. He became frightened just as the girl died. "He promised he would take care of everything. He gave us a large sum of money in cash and pleaded with us to leave the house and to leave Chicago at once. He was, somehow, a broken man, terrified, not thinking clearly, not in control of his own emotions."

"So confused," Red observed thoughtfully, "that you were able to leave with your special Polaroid camera?"

"That's not true, Mr. Kane." Her cold brown Levantine eyes did not waver. "We had just the pictures. We would not have dared to try to take the camera with us. Mr. Gunther's associates had not at all lost their self-possession."

"But you did manage to take the photographs themselves with you."

"We obtained those before his associates came into the bedroom." The granite expression on her face did not change in the slightest.

"Quick thinking," Red said.

"One needed insurance." She shrugged her shoulders lightly. "Do drink some of this wine, Mr. Kane. Our country—Brazil, I mean—produces excellent wine.... We needed some protection from Mr. Gunther. I was very much afraid that when he became himself again he would ... wish to eliminate my associate and myself."

"So you dropped him a note about the photographs and told him you didn't want any more money, warned him not to pursue you, and vanished from the United States?"

The drums were louder now. And closer.

"Precisely." She filled her own wineglass. "I'm sure he has tried to pursue me, Mr. Kane. He has not been successful, yet. And I am not without protection here. Mr. Gunther is an old man, erratic and unpredictable. I am inclined to think that he will leave well enough alone in this matter. Alas, I cannot afford that luxury. Adele's troubled spirit will not permit it." She glanced around nervously, as though expecting the murdered girl to walk through the garden and onto the patio.

His brain dulled by weariness, alcohol, the pounding drums, and the Amazon mists, Red would not have been surprised either to see a ghost.

"You want me to take your doomsday machine, then—affidavits, pictures, the whole business?" He put his hand over the wineglass to prevent her from refilling it.

"Not as an insurance for my life, Mr. Kane. I wish to transfer to you the responsibility for Adele Ward's spirit, if you will accept that responsibility. I don't care how you use the pictures or the affidavits. Her soul will be in your custody if you will accept this envelope."

She produced from underneath the table a thick envelope, sealed with transparent tape. Red slipped his finger under the flap and pried it open.

He glanced briefly through the contents—enough to embarrass Harvard Princeton Gunther permanently.

Did he want to become involved? Her empty brown eyes hinted that Rita Lane was probably a bit of a sociopath, devoid of the conscience and innocent of the emotions that restrained most human beings. Unfortunately for her, she was not immune from superstition, especially that powerful mixture of Portuguese Catholicism and even more superstitious African paganism that was the matrix of Brazilian culture. Macumba or Condumble or whatever it was called up here had broken through her hard shell. Perhaps she had begun to dabble in African cults as an amusement. Then the faint feelings of pity she felt for Adele Ward had become an obsession. Handing the materials over to Red Kane was a magic ritual, one in which she expected him to cooperate because of his long public crusade against Gunther. Engaging in the ritual would expiate her own guilt and put to rest the soul of Adele Ward.

Why not?

Red replaced the material from the envelope and sealed it again with the weakened tape and said, "It's my responsibility now, Mrs. Lane."

Her shoulders sagged in weary gratitude. "I'll never be able to thank you enough." There was a touch of invitation in her gratitude.

No, thanks, Red decided quickly. Better a piranha than a Rita Lane.

He retreated from the sound of the drums and the humid, misty streets of Manaus to his room at the Tropical and fantasies of Eileen with him on a vacation in Brazil. The tropics would really turn her on, he thought with regret as he fell asleep. Someday they would do it, he told himself, knowing that it was a lie.

Early in the morning two days later, the ghost of Adele Ward, a pale, washed-out little blond with huge eyes, was crammed into his Varig flight bag, and Red left the so-called green hell of the Amazon for Mexico City and that afternoon returned to Chicago, a city, God knows, with its own problems but not notably haunted by the spirits of slain teenage prostitutes.

Rita Lane's material was damning indeed, but not quite strong enough to do in an established civic leader like Harvard Gunther—not without more evidence.

It took Red a few days to recover from the fatigue of so much travel. Then, the Monday after his trip, on the inside front page of the *Herald Gazette* was a headline that announced, "Civic Leader Gunther Stricken." Harvard Gunther was in Northwestern University Hospital with a severe heart attack. His condition was described as "guarded."

Red's catholic sympathies included not only the poor and the oppressed but also the sick and the old. Harvard Gunther's life was winding down. It would be a long time, if ever, before he would be capable of ordinary sex, not to say, S and M sex. Why go after a sick old man?

Rita Lane's materials were deposited in the Gunther file in his locked cabinet and left there. A few weeks later he was involved in a public fracas with the Mayor, and Wilson Allen fired him. In the frantic publicity of that conflict, he more or less forgot about Rita Lane and Adele Ward.

Except in his dreams.

4

On the day of his Saint Paul act on Wacker Drive, the Gunther case now definitely open again, Red tapped the Lane file against his word processor. In his imagination he could see the dark waters of the Rio Negro, feel the clammy tropical mists, and hear the manic, insistent beat of the samba drums. He even pictured himself and Eileen, exhausted and satisfied, in a sweaty tropical bed, covered perhaps by a mosquito net.

Two columns, one on the demolition scandal and one on the young prostitute, would finish Harv Gunther, blast him off the boards of the Opera and the Art Institute and the Chicago Symphony and the Community Chest, and force him into a courtroom. Moreover, public outrage would be so great that bribes and murders would do no good and Harv would know that.

Red's plan was to question him relentlessly about the Pulaski demolition case and then throw in a sudden question about the murder of Adele Ward. Any comment at all would make the story publishable.

There was no reason why Gunther should talk to him about anything. He could find out how much Red knew about the Pulaski business without having to listen to his questions. But the old man was vain. He loved to see his name in the papers and he prided himself on his ability to outsmart reporters, not without reason.

Red was getting old.

He had told himself that he had no right to risk harm to Eileen and the kids. But the risk was small, and there was not the slightest doubt what Eileen would say if he told her about the murder of a teenage prostitute.

He held back because he was sick of shrill, righteous, and incompetent "investigative reporters" and the sleek young editors that published their stuff and won prizes off their shoddy work. He was no fan of Ben Bradlee and had only a slightly higher opinion of Woodward and Bernstein. But at least they'd done their work well and revealed something that was indeed crucial to the national interest. Their imitators felt that every person in public life had forfeited the right to a reputation and that the public's right to know implied the right to know everything, no matter how irrelevant. The "investigative" types in Chicago either set up cameras behind one-way windows to catch pathetic little building inspectors, or cadged leaks from government attorneys who were pleased to be seen with famous media types in bars.

Red had worked for his Pulitzers. The arrogant sixties-generation reporters didn't know what the word meant.

And the editors who turned them into media heroes were like Wilson Allen, who came up with such great headlines as "Pol Does Favor for Friend" or "Three More Pols Indicted" or "Public Officials Seek Votes."

Red didn't want to be associated with such trash.

And he did find out about the Pulaski scam in a bar.

I went to Brazil at my own expense to interview her and collect the names and the pictures, he defended himself.

Shit, replied the critic in the back of his head. *It's all shit.*

She would have died anyway, probably of heroin addiction. As long as there were rich men with kinky sexual needs, there would be pimps and madams to find the lonely runaway kids who would do anything for a few bucks or a fix. He wasn't going to stop it.

But Harvard Gunther won't send any more of them to heaven before their time!

He looked at his watch. Three-thirty. Harv would not want to appear to be under pressure. No return call till tomorrow. Gunther was not as important as the fire that was burning inside him for Eileen. Had there actually been a time a few hours ago that he had vetoed a plan to fall in love with her again? Absurd.

No way.

Yet it was too early to go home. Eileen wouldn't be there yet.

He reached for a cigarette, the first one since the cosmic baseball bat had pounded into his head. He desperately wanted one. And a drink too.

He tossed the pack into the wastebasket. *Who needs them?*

He retrieved the package, uncrumpled it, and considered. *I need them, that's who needs them. And I need a drink too.*

He threw the pack back into the basket.

He needed Eileen. That was a legitimate need, wasn't it? Of course. The dull ache for her in his brain had become an imperious demand. *Dummy. You've been impotent with her for six months and now you can't wait to get your hands on her.*

You're like a young man who has just fallen in love.

He thought briefly of her lying in a hospital bed, both legs in traction as a result of a Harv Gunther–engineered accident. He vowed that he would not permit it to happen.

He opened the file in his word processor memory that contained the first draft of his novel, a file that was not supposed to be locked in the *HG* computer but that no one else would ever find out about. He had not finished it because he could not think of an ending. Now it was perfectly clear how it had to end. His hero was not the tragic figure he'd tried to make him. Behind his comic persona, there was more comedy. His self-image as tragic was the highest comedy. Laugh at him; make him laugh at himself. Finish it up, go through and disguise the stuff that's too autobiographical, and send it off to Paramount.

As he slashed away at the text with his "delete" utility, he whistled "You're Irish and You're Beautiful" from Victor Herbert's *Eileen*.

He stopped for a moment, trying to understand what had happened to him. It or He or She or Whatever had zapped him. Now he had quit smoking, started to work again on an important story, found the way out of his novel, and fallen in love with his wife. Moreover, it was three-thirty and he didn't need a drink.

He reached into his drawer and opened his own private file, articles about him, wedding pictures, clips of his best columns, personal letters, notes for a second novel. He glanced at the letter he wrote John a month or so ago about his days in Korea. Those days suddenly seemed only yesterday. *I told Johnny to treasure his youth, knowing it was dumb advice. Now I have to treasure my renewed youth.*

He leafed through the pictures and clippings in the Kane and O'Meara and Gunther files. His life raced by him like a troop of horses nearing the finish line—Korea, his youthful journalistic idealism, the enthusiasm of the Kennedy years, disillusion, 1968, the Conrad Hilton riots, his retreat behind the mask of cynical and dissolute wit in his column, the waxing and waning of his marriage.

I've made a mess out of things, he thought sadly.

I don't know who You are, he told the wielder of the cosmic baseball bat as he drifted deeper into a reverie, *but thanks anyway for making me young again and giving me another chance.*

Later, the daydreams over, he went back to the "delete" utility and to whistling "You're Irish and You're Beautiful."

Eileen, God bless her, would be in for one hell of a surprise.

5

Feature article from *Chicago Sun-Times*, June 9, 1983

Women Must Try Harder, Lawyer Says

Eileen Kane thoughtfully touches her lip with the frame of her reading glasses. "Both laws and litigation to protect the rights of women," she says, releasing the glasses that hang around her neck on a brown ribbon that matches her suit. "In the long run, however, we will have to win by imitating Jesse Owens in the 1936 Olympics."

What does she mean? The reporter was a long way from being born in 1936.

"So was I." Kane smiles, a surprisingly warm, almost mischievous smile, and her piercing green eyes dance momentarily. "My husband told me about it. He even claims they didn't have TV in those days.... The German track judges called faults repeatedly on Owens in the broad jump. Finally, with Hitler watching, he took off a foot before the starting line and still made a world record. Thus it must be with us. No matter how many decisions we may win, we will only be fully accepted in the professional world when we prove that we are much better than men at the same jobs. 'As good as' is not good enough."

That does not seem fair.

Kane shrugs slightly. "So?"

Eileen Anne Ryan Kane is a strikingly handsome woman. In her brown suit with gold buttons, white belt, and pleated skirt, and a white-on-white blouse with a beige scarf, she manages to look both professionally competent and discreetly feminine. Some jurors have said that she reminds them of a nun when she addresses a courtroom. "Not an ordinary nun," one juror remarked. "More like a modern nun who is a college president—all the old discipline combined with modern flair."

It is a fair description of Kane, who is now hailed as one of the best trial lawyers in the city.

Yet she has been severely criticized by activist women lawyers for not being more involved in feminist protest against the chauvinism that, Kane candidly admits, permeates the legal profession.

If the criticism, which often has been stinging, bothers Kane, she does not show it. Nothing seems to shake this gifted woman's cool self-possession.

"I cannot understand why women are not willing to let other women pursue their own agendas." She touches her tightly bound black hair, lightly tinged with gray, as if making sure that every strand is in place. "Why must everyone fit in the same mold? There is only a limited time available in a day, a week, a year, a lifetime. My instincts tell me that I do more for the cause by handling *pro bono* cases for women victims of discrimination than I would by attending meetings or marching on picket lines. Why should I not follow my instincts?"

One senses that this woman has every intention of following her own instincts. And one would be willing to yield to her self-image of the coolly rational professional if it were not for those smoldering green eyes that disclose smoldering fires of who knows what passions. That women are mysterious is usually a cliché of male chauvinism. Most women are no more a mystery than most men. But this woman, for all her poised rationality, is unfathomable.

How can she justify the defense of men who are criminals? she is asked. The smoldering fires blaze momentarily.

"In our legal system, a person has the right to be presumed innocent until he or she is proven guilty. Judgments made in the city rooms of newspapers ought not anticipate the judgments made by a jury of the accused's peers. If one person, no matter how evil, is unfairly convicted in the press, before the evidence is heard, then all of us lose a little of our freedom. The defense attorney, insisting that the burden of proof beyond a reasonable doubt is on the prosecution, is defending the freedom of all of us."

A standard argument for adversary justice, isn't it?

"Perhaps." She is not interested in pushing the debate. "That does not make it a poor argument, however."

Would she defend any criminal who came to her seeking help?

"Not necessarily," she replies crisply. "I judge each case on its merits."

What about a member of organized crime or a rapist?

A twitch of dissatisfaction on her carefully defined lip. "I cannot cope with such categorization of people. An allegation is not a conviction. Normally I would not take such cases, but I certainly would not exclude the possibility, depending on the circumstances."

She pauses, fusses with the gold cuff links of her shirt, and continues. "Nor can I understand why women are not more concerned about the rights of the accused. I think the rape laws ought to be stricter and more strictly enforced. But cannot women understand that when even a rapist is presumed guilty before a trial, they suffer too?"

What does she mean?

"Women are a victim group in society. When those in power begin taking rights away from some group, the victim groups are always next. Do you think women will not suffer inevitably if the federal government is permitted to continue the practice of inducing suspects to commit crimes? Abscam, Greylord, the DeLorean case—in all of them the FBI has gone into business of committing crimes to convict those who are suspected to be criminals, often with flimsy evidence. I can't understand why the so-called defenders of the rights of women don't realize that we are the next victims. Nor do I comprehend why you journalists don't realize that, after they put the judges in jail, you're the next targets."

It's all very calm, matter-of-fact, reasonable. She hardly raises her voice. Only her eyes reveal the intensity of emotion lurking behind those words. Is she not a little less cool and self-controlled than she appears to be?

"My sisters will tell you I had the worst temper in the family."

What happened to it?

She shrugs lightly, dismissing her anger. "I learned that it accomplishes nothing."

Does she regret not pursuing the musical-comedy career she might have had?

"I'm afraid that's mostly legend." Her eyes narrow in minor impatience. "I wasn't that good."

Her performance as Mayor Byrne at the last Bar Association dinner was reputed to be sensational.

She colors slightly, not displeased at the praise. "I'm afraid the competition for light soprano roles is not very intense in that illustrious organization."

Is it difficult to be a wife and mother and practice law full time, as she has done since her marriage?

Again the slight, almost indifferent shrug of her shoulder. "I think the opposite might be even more difficult."

Does her husband, *Herald Gazette* columnist Red Kane, approve of her career? Did he object to her continuing it after they were married?

"The question simply didn't arise," she says, as though she is baffled that anyone might think it would.

Is it difficult being married to a man whose column appears every day?

"The children and I take the position that we don't read Mr. Kane's columns. That deflates the hasslers after their first attack."

Is there a lot of hassling?

"More of the children. Particularly priests and nuns. Something about serving the Church seems to give many such people a special enjoyment in making life difficult for the children of the moderately famous."

Would the children be happier if Mr. Kane were not in the limelight?

"Of course not." She rearranges her letter opener. "We are proud of his awards. Mr. Kane is a very distinguished journalist. We may have to cope with a certain amount of harassment. We are perfectly prepared to do that and consider ourselves fortunate in the bargain."

What about the repeated rumors of divorce?

Kane laughs, a much richer laugh than one would have anticipated.

"Was it Alfred Lunt or Lynn Fontanne—I can never remember which, but let's say it was Lunt—who said, 'Murder, oh yes; but divorce, never!'"

And who would have the better grounds for murder?

"Mr. Kane, of course." The answer is swift and unhesitating. "A kid fresh out of law school could win an acquittal in a half hour."

6

"There are"—Lee Malley, editor of the *Sunday Magazine*, leaned on the edge of Red's desk the day of Red's mind-blowing experience on Wacker Drive--"three theories going around, one of them original with me."

Lee, a lean man with a thick black beard and pirate's black eyes, was, as usual, a picture of funky chic—designer jeans, a tailor-made denim shirt, and hand-tooled western boots. An Irish Sammy Glick, Red had said once in an unfair mood, in radical clothing.

Red looked up from his novel, at which he'd been working furiously after he had paged through the Kane, O'Meara, and Gunther files. "Huh?"

"Red Kane comes into the city room; after saying a kind word to Wilson Allen he whistles a merry tune, jokes with the help, and sits at his computer grinding out copy all afternoon, humming Victor Herbert, all phenomena which demand explanation."

"Really?" Red grinned like an idiot.

"One theory is that the Drink has finally dulled his brain cells beyond repair."

"Feasible."

"Not necessarily. The effect is too sudden. The second explanation is that, this being the Feast of All Hallows, Redmond Peter Kane has had a powerful religious experience, one that has transformed his character."

"Unlikely."

"Decidedly. That brings us to another possibility. Aforementioned Kane is getting action with someone more passionate than the lissome Melissa. Noting the warm glow on his face, we conclude that our hero had himself an excellent screw this afternoon. Comment?"

"As always, Lee"—Red leaned back in his chair—"you are both cultivated and ingenious. Who else in this bastion of obscurantism would recognize Victor Herbert? But don't you know the name of the play whose songs I have been humming?"

"You win, as always, Red. What is the play?"

"*Eileen*."

"Touché! You glow at the thought of returning home to your lovely wife who even now is dauntlessly battling for the freedom of that admirable athlete Hurricane Houston." Lee's narrow, comic face became serious. "That shows good taste."

None of his friends or colleagues could understand why Eileen wasn't enough, indeed more than enough, for Red. Neither could he, for that matter.

"I always thought so." Red tried to smile enigmatically and turned to his CRT.

"Give her my love." Lee turned to leave. "And tell her that I'm all for her against the beastly Roscoe."

Donald Bane Roscoe was an incompetent and ambitious young United States Attorney who figured that if Jim Thompson could become Governor on a record of convicting celebrities, there was no reason why he couldn't do it too. Having run out of politicians, Roscoe was in hot pursuit of sports figures. His current target was a naïf named Leroy "Hurricane" Houston who had once dunked for the Chicago Bulls. He had signed a few documents at the behest of the creditor vultures who had taken his money, and had by so doing apparently violated the law of the United States of America and threatened its peace and prosperity.

Eileen Ryan Kane had been chosen by Minor, Grey, and Blatt, her prestigious law firm, to fend off Donald Bane "The Big Bane" Roscoe and salvage some shreds of Hurricane's life. Red would not have bet against her. Neither would anyone else.

After Lee had strolled away, Red pondered his words. That which Red had encountered on Wacker Drive was certainly an invader, an overwhelming force that had moved in and taken over.

Yet it was womanly in its affection and tenderness.

Later, if his psychiatrist had asked who was most like the invader, Eileen or Melissa, he would have replied unhesitatingly that It, She, He was very like Eileen. But that wasn't the way the question was put and Red was afraid to venture the response.

He instructed the machine to produce his dedication page.

"For Eileen," it said, rather unimaginatively.

He pondered it and then, in a burst of genius for which he congratulated himself, added the title of the Victor Herbert song, "You're Irish and You're Beautiful."

He replaced the Kane, Gunther, and O'Meara files in the locked drawer. A lot of one man's life in those three folders; the images that raced through his head before he turned to his novel were as powerful as a week-long Jesuit retreat. And now he had new opportunities to rearrange the trajectory of those images.

A second chance for everything that mattered in his life.

From the window in the far corner of the city room he saw a small slice of the green glass skyscraper that had started it all.

Warm breast and ah! bright wings.

Who the hell are you, he asked the presence that had lain in wait for him behind the building, *anyway*?

And what do you want from me?

7

It was typical of the Chicago transportation system, Red told himself considering a theme for a column and discarding it as trite, that when you are reluctant to arrive home and face your wife, it delivers you with speed and efficiency. On the other hand, when you can hardly wait to take her in your arms and overwhelm her with the love that is pounding in your heart, the bus driver slows down because he's ahead of schedule.

He sighed and removed Richard Wilbur's collected poems from his jacket pocket. Someday he would catch up on his failure to finish college.

"Never heard of Richard Wilbur," he had said brusquely to John when he was given the book at the end of the summer.

"Really?" the adolescent word that can mean everything and nothing. John was a big kid, taller than Red, with his mother's black-Irish good looks and a lock of curly blond hair hanging over his forehead, a gentle giant like in the Merlin Olsen flower ads on TV, serious, often humorless, and almost always intimidated by his father.

How could I intimidate anyone? Red often wondered.

"Is he like Wallace Stevens or John Berryman?" Red rose to the defense of his own erratic pursuit of the poetic greats.

His massive and graceful son considered the question as if it were worth half the score on his SAT. "More like Theodore Roethke, I think."

What kind of a nineteen-year-old reads Theodore Roethke? Red wondered.

"Maybe you'd better give me Roethke for Christmas," Red murmured.

"Really," his son muttered enigmatically.

Blew it again. Joking about something about which John is very serious. Why doesn't he laugh when I say something funny? Everyone else does.

"He wants to be a journalist like you," Eileen had whispered later in response to that question, "and doesn't think he's good enough. He worships you."

Red had argued that no one became a "journalist" and that no one worshiped him. Eileen had sighed in exasperation and the discussion ended.

Wilbur, he had found, was a man unique unto himself. Small wonder that John was shocked by his father's ignorance.

He opened to the poem he had started in the morning, "Objects." The poet had discovered wonder in ordinary objects, the weave of a sleeve, brick walls, sunlight. How was he going to end it?

> ...oh maculate, cracked, askew,
> Gay-pocked and potsherd world
> I voyage, where in every tangible tree
> I see afloat among the leaves, all calm and curled,
> The Cheshire smile—which sets me fearfully free.

Fingers trembling, Red shoved the book back into his pocket. He sensed that logjams were breaking apart inside him, underbrush was being torn up, the concrete wall was at last yielding to the bulldozer. The self who had been buried so long was shoving its way out of the tomb—fearfully free.

Later the psychiatrist would see this experience as the second major sign, and indeed definitive proof, of incipient schizophrenia. "A long rest," she would say imperiously. She was quite uninterested in Wilbur's poem, which she waved aside impatiently. "The poem is not important to me; what is important is your reaction. At that time you had already begun to dissociate yourself into two persons, one good if hitherto unrevealed and the other bad and well known. You had made the initial and damning steps away from reality."

Red tried to explain that there were not two different Red Kanes, only one. He was using the half-facetious metaphor of the "old" Red and the "new" Red in imitation of Art Buchwald's "Old Nixon" and "New Nixon." What had been set fearfully free by the sparkling green glass skyscraper was not another person, but rather his own best instincts, of which he had been afraid for forty years. He knew now that it was all right to risk those instincts. The metaphor was mostly ironic.

The shrink would have none of his irony. "You were already dissociating. Admit the truth. You were terrified even then as your hold on reality grew weaker."

Maybe the first twitchings of a fear that he would not be able to make the most of the new life that had been given him earlier in the afternoon. Yet love, now mixed inextricably with imperious desire, was so strong inside him that such a fear did not seem to be very important. Of course, his life would be different from now on.

"You see?" She jabbed her stubby finger at him triumphantly. "The schizophrenic illusion of being born again, a neonate still clinging to the umbilical cord."

Red decided not to tell her about his walk down Webster from Lincoln Park after he had climbed off the 151 bus at Webster and Stockton. He remembered how astonished he'd been by the film *My Bodyguard* to which John had dragged his protesting parents. For twenty years both of them had passed through Lincoln Park almost every day without noticing it. The movie made them see it for the first time as the lovely blend of trees and meadow and water that it was.

Now, although it was dark and he was in a hurry to go home to his wife, he saw the park and the zoo again, places of wonder and mystery in a wonderful and mysterious city.

He drifted out of the park and toward Clark Street in a blissful trance, feeling that all the world was a show staged for his entertainment. The streetlights cast their glow for him. The high-rises on the edge of the park pointed to the sky for him. Clark Street spun its web of glittering fascination in either direction for him. The homes on Webster, lurking in the shadows behind the trees, invited him to share their promise of warmth. The lines of closely packed cars on either side of the street hinted at stories of life and love, struggles against the powers of darkness that would, in the long run, end in victory.

Then his own home, a house he had never liked, but that now seemed the sacred center of the universe. It was an old three-story, built after the Fire—the second of the four stars in the Chicago flag—when gracious living meant many small rooms, fourteen in this case, instead of a few large ones.

They had purchased it shortly after Eileen started at Minor, Grey. She had insisted that property values in Lincoln Park would soon go through the sky. "And, Red, it has a stoop and even a front porch!"

He was quite unprepared to face such a hunger for urban life in his mate. Asked before the fact whether Eileen would like front porches, he would have dismissed the question as absurd. She would not even notice whether a house had a front porch. He did not want to live near the "Lincoln Park Limousine Liberals," as he called them in his column, and would have much rather escaped from the city completely, even if that meant joining the ranks of the "Sophisticated Suburban Parasites," as he described such escapees in the column. Moreover, he was irked by the impossibility of finding a parking place for their always-aging pair of cars—one inevitably a VW, the other inevitably a Volvo—on the Near North Side of the city.

He also worried about the Near North drug culture as the kids grew up.

But, hell, if it was what Eileen wanted, what difference did it make? St. Clement's was a reasonably safe school when the kids were younger, and St. Ignatius's and the Convent of the Sacred Heart when they reached high school age.

For most of the last ten years the house had been in a state of constant rehabilitation, an apparently endless supply of workmen arriving each morning to tear down one wall and put up another. Eileen enjoyed it, so Red avoided the mess as best he could and brushed the sawdust away as unobtrusively as possible.

Finally, last year the rehabilitation was begun again, this time systematic and total, under the direction of his son, of all people. The result was undeniably attractive. The fourteen rooms were combined into eight—or seven if, like Red, you counted the first floor with its kitchen/living room/dining room expanse as one. The result was an open and airy "domestic habitat"—to use John's term—with throw rugs on polished hardwood floors and rescued moldings that Eileen's friends pronounced to be treasures, skylights, and a tree-covered patio deck in the back for outdoor eating in the summer. A classic "lofting" of an old house. The furniture was mostly beige cushions and brightly colored pillows. The walls were decorated with posters from Chicago and Paris and brightly colored sunbursts painted by Cathy Curran, a Ryan cousin and the wife of Nick Curran, Eileen's law partner. (Red would have much preferred walls covered with Cathy's misty nudes, but they owned only one and that was relegated to the kitchen lest it shock the children's friends.)

A scout from *Architectural Digest* has photographed the house, though nothing came of the possibility of a feature. Johnny was too young anyway, Eileen had said crisply.

If *AD* was even interested, Red supposed that the remodeling must have been ingenious. So he kept to himself the reaction that their house might make a nice funeral home for Martians.

Red kept to himself his opinion that the original architects and owners would have been horrified by the desecration. His son was too happy over the plaudits from Eileen's friends for Red even to hint that he thought the place a little weird.

My son the photographer and interior decorator. And my daughter the actress. And my other daughter the delinquent.

John was even bigger than Red, a handsome blond giant who had displayed on the floor of the St. Ignatius gym more grace and coordination than Red would have believed possible in a big kid his age. His mother's genes, no doubt. He was on the second string of St. John's basketball team, although he was only a freshman.

Why Minnesota? Red had asked irritably when his nervous son told him where he wanted to go to college.

Because he wanted to experience the rhythms of prayer and work and nature in a Benedictine environment. Do you mind, Dad?

Red was scarcely aware that there *was* a Benedictine environment. No, he didn't mind, not as much as he minded that the anxious young man was afraid of him.

You like girls, you date. I don't really mind if you want to be an artist of a sort. It runs in your mother's genes. But why do I scare you?

He did not scare seventeen-year-old Patty, a black-haired, full-bodied carbon copy of her mother—they fought over the same dresses. Patty wanted to be an actress, perhaps a reflection of her mother's abandoned musical-comedy career. Red often tried to convince himself that Patty practiced her roles on him—currently the angry elder daughter who hated her father.

"I'm sure," she'd shouted at him with the angry adolescent's contemptuous opening line, "that eighteen-year-old girls have to tell their father the life history of their date's family."

"I just wanted to know more about Jeff," he had replied mildly.

"Look them up in *Who's Who*," she had thundered in response.

"Good line," Red conceded genially.

"MoTHER, he never leaves me alone," Patty wailed, and stormed out of the room.

"His father is a lead violin in the Chicago Symphony." A thundercloud appeared in Eileen's green eyes. "Very distinguished. Jeff goes to Loyola."

"I was only asking." Red raised his hands in innocent appeal.

"You and Torquemada."

"Another good line."

Patty at least would fight with him. Fifteen-year-old Kate, a slender and willowy blond like her grandmother and namesake Kate Collins Ryan, replied to his questions only with sullen grunts.

"You were smoking pot, weren't you, Kate?"

"No."

"I know the smell of pot."

"I wasn't smoking it."

"Your mother has told you about what could happen if the police should catch you?"

"I wasn't smoking pot."

"You're not telling the truth, Kate."

"I am too."

And so it went. "She's your child," Eileen had said. "A Kane in every way."

"She looks like your mother."

"She acts like you and your mother."

"You never met my mother."

"You told me enough about her. She's a Kane."

"And you hate Kanes?"

"If you think that, you've had more to drink than I thought."

"Good line," Red admitted again, thinking that if he were a normal man he would take her in his arms and reward her properly for loving Kanes despite excellent reasons not to.

Red did not worry about Patty. She'd grow out of her stormy late teens and be as fine and self-possessed a woman as her mother. Poor Kate, however, was indeed a Kane, with all the Kane potential for self-destruction. She had been in trouble since she started to walk, and did everything she could to hide her loveliness—ugly clothes, grotesque hair-dos, thick and unnecessary makeup. *Why won't she talk to me about what's eating her?*

He paused for a moment, considering the invitation in the lighted windows of his home, the Parisian posters with which John had decorated the living room "area" creating a kind of Christmas-tree color (though Red thought privately that by now French posters were a cliché) and hinting at special warmth and affection.

Most of the time he was part of the furniture in the house, much like Luciano, the affectionate and stupid family Labrador. Objects and people were moved around him so as to minimize inconvenience and delay. Occasionally, someone patted him on the head as they would pat Luciano. A nuisance, but on the whole a lovable nuisance except when he lost his temper at the children and risked the stern reproof in his wife's eye, a reproof that said, "Leave them to me, you dolt. You lost all power over them long ago."

There are serious problems in that home, he thought to himself. *Most of them are your doing. It isn't too late to reverse any of them. And thank God you're being given another chance.*

Again he had the sense of ice floes coming apart inside him and felt fear. Long before the shrink would press the point, he wondered if perhaps he was coming unhinged.

So what if I am? he decided, and walked up the steps of

Eileen's beloved door stoop—on which she often sat on spring and summer evenings when they were not at the lake, gossiping with their neighbors as his mother had done in South Chicago when he was a very little boy.

He would go into his home, in a certain sense for the first time, and share the love that had possessed him at Wacker and Wacker with the fascinating woman who had appeared in the *Sun-Times* feature pages last June. Not by telling her about it, for he did not know what she might say if he claimed an ecstatic experience, even if she had somehow occasioned it.

But by loving her.

8

Red drew his breath sharply. Eileen was at her vanity bench, working on her face with customary precision. On the bed lay her new black cocktail dress. So her lingerie was black lace, not quite what one might buy at the expensive erotic lingerie shops that one could find even in the fashionable malls like Water Tower Place, but still devastating enough to make any man gasp with desire.

Especially a husband whose soul was filled with love, love that was now focusing on his mysterious and wonderful wife.

Red, whose reading habits were completely eclectic and whose memory was virtually unlimited for quotes and weak to nonexistent for sources, thought of a line he'd read somewhere recently about a naked breast in Delacroix's painting *Liberty*, "the exposure itself, built into the costume, is an original part of her essence—at once holy, desirable, and fierce."

Right.

"Home early, Red," she said, not looking away from the mirror. "The kids are driving down to the Cathedral from school. Patty has play practice. Was Luciano hanging around outside? He ran away again."

"I let him in."

He told her long ago that she was the perfect woman for him. That was surely true. Red had suffered weak women for much of his early life—his mother and her sisters especially, women whose tears and complaints and nagging recriminations completely paralyzed him. Eileen was the exact opposite. She cried occasionally at movies and at rites of passage like children's graduations, but her tears were emotional releases, not tools for manipulating others. She should surely shed a few tears of pride tonight at her brother's "empurpling" party.

"Did you remember to pick up your clean suit?"

"No."

"You did call Katie's algebra teacher?"

"No."

"The quarterly tax form?"

"Uh-uh."

The usual litany of gentle reprimands for irresponsibility. He was an amusing little boy who tried your patience, charming but not very bright—like Luciano. Such was the final state of her fabled temper, about which Kate Ryan had warned him in 1956. A green-eyed witch growing old.

Well, not very old. And certainly not unattractive. She was, as far as Red was concerned, physical perfection. Before he met her, he'd had more than enough experiences with slender, pretty, insubstantial women. Even when she was a girl, Eileen's round, milk white Irish face could not be called pretty, much less beautiful. Her eyes were a bit too far from each other, her chin a too sudden break in symmetry, her nose not quite long enough.

Yet at her mother's wake, when she was still a teen, Red had thought it an interesting and indeed striking face. Time had been good to it. The soft lines of the years, working with the smoldering magic of her witch's eyes, made Eileen's face strikingly handsome, the kind of face that, if she walked by you in a restaurant, you would turn to look at, confident that you would not be embarrassed because everyone else in the room was doing the same thing.

And her body was exactly what Red's fantasies demanded of a woman. He told her once, long ago, that when she took her clothes off she was a Goya nude with muscles, sending Eileen into one of her rare fits of giggling. Yet it was an honest description—broad shouldered, deep breasted, slim hipped, Eileen had the solid arm and leg muscles of a woman athlete. Before she gave up golf as too time-consuming, she had been better than Red, no great feat, and was so good at tennis that he refused to consider playing with her much less against her.

There wasn't much time now for golf or tennis, but the swimming pool and the exercise room kept her as firm as she was the first time they made love. She could still wear the clothes that she had packed for her unexpected honeymoon and did so on occasion for morale purposes, and to impress Patty, the two of them thick as two women pickpockets, stealing each other's clothes and bickering as if they were two sisters instead of mother and daughter.

Not everyone's armful exactly, but Red could not have designed for himself a better bed partner. Neglecting her was like wasting a natural resource. Life was slipping through his fingers. Not all that many years left. The waste must not continue.

As he watched her, admiring lace-covered leg and thigh and breast, his love for her made him light-headed. Too much time had been foolishly wasted. Whatever the explanation for his past lack of desire, he was confident that he would never be impotent in this woman's presence again.

"Something wrong, Red?" She continued to dab around her eye.

"I brought an ... uh ... present." He sat next to her on the bench.

"Why, Red, roses! How sweet!" She smiled as she would have if Luciano had learned a new trick. "Any reason?"

"Your brother has been made a Monsignor. I thought that was enough reason."

She didn't say that he pretended not to like her brother.

"Wonderful. I'll find a vase before we leave."

"Actually I brought two dozen." He offered her the second bundle.

"How nice." She was mildly distracted, wondering perhaps if Red was drunk. "One for home and one for the office?"

"One for today"—he took her hand gently—"and one for the first day long ago I thought of giving you flowers and didn't do it. I figure if I turn up with two bundles once a week for the rest of my life, I may catch up."

"Red..." Her voice trailed off.

Delicately he kissed her lips, barely brushing against them. She sighed deeply, her breasts moving up and down. With light fingers he touched one of the breasts, probing gently beneath the lace. He moved a fingernail toward her nipple.

"No!" She twisted away from him, her mouth a thin, angry line. "We'll be late for the party."

He had not quite expected her to be angry. It certainly made her more attractive.

"I love you, Eileen." He tried to recapture her hand.

"You ignore me in bed for six months," she stormed, hands on barely covered hips, witch's eyes blazing, "and then you sneak into my bedroom with calf eyes while I'm dressing for a party and expect me to fall in your arms! Think again, lover boy!"

Ah, the woman would need courting. So much the better. God knows, she's entitled to it.

"I did bring roses," he pleaded, trying to control a grin of pleasure and anticipation.

"Stop grinning at me!" she raged. "You have no right to ogle me like a horny teenager!"

"If you only knew how gorgeous you look, you'd grin too. Much better than Joan Collins in *Playboy*."

"I'm younger than she is." Eileen, never able to resist his grin, began to smile.

"Much prettier tits," he added tentatively, making her blush. *Aha, progress.*

"I'll put the flowers in a vase." She averted her face from him, still blushing. "They really are very lovely. Two vases."

"As red as you when I praise your tits."

"Red...you're shameless."

"I'm sorry, I'll withdraw the compliment."

"Don't you dare." She strode out of their bedroom, still

upset but now conscious of the effect she was having on him and pleased with herself.

The girls must not have been home, Red realized, or Eileen would not appear outside the door in bra and panties. At least not when he was around.

He considered the situation with diminishing confidence. What if he had lost his skills at courting her? It had been such a long time.

"They look very nice," she said as she returned, a vase in either hand. "Thank you." She rearranged the flowers with impatient fingers, avoiding his eyes.

"So do you. Red and black. A lingerie ad for *Chicago* magazine."

She considered him speculatively. "Well, at least that's better than a J. C. Penney ad." Then with a canny grin, "Actually, I think the best I could do would be a *McCall's* ad. Maidenform woman arranges roses. Not that I'd complain."

"Without prejudice to later events, might I at least have a kiss?"

She bit her lip, striving to control resurgent anger. "I suppose."

Red took her in his arms, his heart beating insanely. The stiffness of her body said reluctant submission to an obligation. The kiss must be carefully gauged. Enough to be arousing, but not enough to touch the hair trigger on her temper, to which she was also entitled. Warm, even mildly hot, but not steamy.

He pushed his lips against hers, not invading her soul yet, but knocking at the door.

The stiffness went out of her. She sagged in his arms, submissive as the witch girl always was when she surfaced. Red took an unapproved second kiss.

"I didn't say two," she murmured, her eyes rounding, her mouth falling open, her nipples visibly hardening against the thin fabric of her bra.

Ready, Red decided, but not quite ready.

"Come on, woman." He released her and, for good measure, patted her ass appreciatively. "Gorgeous rear end too. Put your clothes on. We have a party to attend. In honor of a Monsignor."

Baffled by the stranger who had crept into her boudoir, Eileen slipped the frock over her head and let it fall on her shoulders. She tried with clumsy fingers to arrange it. Red pushed her hands away, straightened out the dress, and zipped it up. She accepted his assistance in passive silence.

He shoved a purse in her hand and dragged her toward the door. "We're late already. You spent too much time with those roses."

"Red..." She considered him with a worried frown.

"Yes?" He was still uncertain, but he had to act like the grinning and triumphant lover or he'd lose his nerve completely.

"Is...is there anything wrong?"

9

"Is there a shortage of John Jameson's that has not been brought to my attention?" Monsignor John Blackwood Ryan, rector of Holy Name Cathedral, domestic prelate to His Holiness Pope John Paul II ("Papal broom pusher," sniffed his sister Nancy O'Connor, the science-fiction writer), student of Alfred North Whitehead and William James, and reputed gray eminence to Chicago's Sean Cardinal Cronin, considered his tumbler carefully, comparing it with the glass of Perrier in his brother-in-law's hand.

When Red and Eileen had entered the Cardinal's suite, where the party was in progress, Eileen had predictably embraced her brother and wept happily. "I'm so proud, Punk, my little brother a Monsignor."

"It doesn't mean what it used to mean," the little priest accepted her affection with the contentment of a well-cared-for Irish wolf-hound. "No higher discount on cars."

"What would you trade it for?" Red extended his hand.

"Ah, Redmond. You seem especially genial tonight. A scoop in the wind? What would I trade it for?" He lowered his voice to a conspiratorial whisper. "Another touchdown for the Bears on Sunday?"

"You're both impossible," Eileen said.

"The age-old lament of Irish women," Blackie sighed. "Don't worry, Redmond. Translated it means 'I wouldn't trade you for anyone, at least not for anyone I've met yet.'"

After that exchange Red had been trying to corner the new Monsignor all night—when he was not preoccupied by his new obsession with his wife—but a gaggle of young women, including his two daughters, surrounded Caitlin Murphy next to the cleric, making any conversation that was carried on in less than a bellow impossible. Finally Red managed to ease the young women out of the way and stir up Blackie's curiosity about his Perrier glass.

"I read my own columns about drinking and gave it up." Red sipped his mineral water. "I'd like to ask you something before the night is over. Doing a little research."

"Fine." The priest peered through his thick rimless glasses at Red's Perrier glass. "One more turn around the room. When the Cardinal comes in and all the young women flock to him, we will slip off to the side.... I am delighted, of course, that you have forsaken the Creature. Thus the supply of Jameson's will perdure for several more years, even if the Republic of Ireland should unaccountably embargo it."

"A decade maybe." Red lifted his tumbler in a respectful toast.

Later his shrink would make much of the kissing before the party.

"Have you stopped to consider the impact on your wife? No, of course you haven't. You virtually rape her and then you force her to attend a family party. Can you not imagine how humiliating it was for her? You were already well into your schizophrenic withdrawal from reality."

If she didn't believe that Eileen was happy during that part of the evening, she could ask their daughters, whose suspicious glares at their late-arriving parents vanished as soon as they saw their mother's mysterious smile. Or ask Caitlin Murphy, the reigning blond goddess of the third generation, a gorgeous mischief-maker, who suggestively rolled her eyes, her grandmother Ryan's teasing eyes. "UNcle RED-mond, who's the beautiful WOman?"

Caitlin was a slightly more curvaceous and infinitely more mature version of their Kate, who followed her around with mute worship. Red hoped that there might be some imitation as a result of the adoration.

He also wondered whether coming to the party might not have been a mistake. He was not ashamed of his obsession with Eileen. But it was still a very intimate and private obsession that he did not want to share with his noisy in-laws. Did their compliments to Eileen hint that they sniffed reawakened sexual interest in her husband's soul?

With the Clan Ryan you could never be sure, but it was wise to expect the worst.

"Diana and Juno," Joe Murphy, looking like the Jungian therapist he was in a three-piece charcoal-gray suit, rimless glasses, thick black eyebrows, and a short silver beard, murmured next to Red. They were both watching their wives in a lively conversation across the room.

"Which is which?"

Hands in pockets, Joe lifted his thin shoulders slightly. "Take your choice. Ever wonder what they say about us in those incisive tête-à-têtes?"

Mary Kate was taller, fuller, and more volatile than Eileen, fair skinned like her mother, with blue eyes and gold-and-silver hair. Red imagined them both as naked Greek goddesses and found the fantasy appealing.

"I have a hunch, Joe, that when they put those two lovely heads together that way and their eyes cavort like the Hubbard Street Dancers, we are not even on the agenda."

Joe chuckled, a quiet laugh appropriate for a consulting room in Geneva. "In the almost quarter century since I proposed to Mary Kathleen, as I had the temerity to call her then, and was accepted before I could change my mind, I have learned that Ryan women expect that they be simultaneously adored, cherished, protected, restrained, and enjoyed." He paused thoughtfully. "Especially the last."

I fail on the last four, Red thought. *And get a "D" at best on adoration.*

"The last is the hardest," Joe continued. "Because it requires that we acknowledge our own anima, the womanly aspect of the self."

"You can only enjoy a woman"—Red could not detach his gaze from the two matron/goddesses—"when you're at peace with the woman part of you?"

"Life-giving, pleasure-absorbing dimension of the self." Joe nodded in approval. "We'll make a good Jungian out of you yet, Red." Joe patted his arm and drifted into the crowd, gently as he did all things.

Both Red's daughters assured him that Uncle Joe was, like, totally sexy.

Enjoy Ryan women? Red wanted to enjoy Eileen as badly as he had wanted anything or anyone in his life. His palms were clammy, his nerves raw, his teeth locked. He could not take his eyes off her nor banish from his imagination lascivious images of what they would do with each other before the night was over. His need for her was dissonant background music to the party. It threatened to drown out the conversation, to seduce him into whiskey-tenor songs, even to trick his feet into the reckless steps of a Kerry reel.

He wanted to shout, to run, to fly.

Above all he wanted her, as if she were a mysterious woman he had never met before.

Perhaps that is the secret of it all, he made a mental note for a future column; *you become obsessed with your own woman when you realize that for all the years you have known her she is still a mystery.*

He decided that such a hormone-generating thought was not appropriate for a Ryan party.

Like all Ryan parties, it was loud, lively, and laughter drenched. There were no outsiders; in-laws were, by definition, part of the family and on a totally equal plane with the others. Except for Red, who felt patronized and suspected that he had never been forgiven for seducing the family's little green-eyed witch.

Old Ned Ryan, blue eyes glowing, silver hair neatly combed, arm in arm with his younger second wife, watched it all with the expression of a bemused patriarch, not quite prepared to believe that he could possibly be responsible for all these tall, loud, space-consuming people.

The Ryans lived and thought like Chicago Irish upper-middle-class professionals, more cultivated perhaps, but bourgeois to the core. Two lawyers, a writer, a priest, a psychiatrist—married to a journalist, a broker, a professor, and another psychiatrist. There was probably enough money in the family to justify a move to Lake Forest, the Ultima Thule of Irish upward mobility. But Ryan culture did not permit a consideration of such a change. Lake Forest was for the "aristocracy," as Eileen had muttered disdainfully at an Ireland Fund dinner. "We don't belong there."

It was not a compliment to Lake Forest.

More cultivated than many of the South Side Irish—"We actually know there is an Orchestra Hall," Packy Ryan, Eileen's brother, had laughed, "and find ourselves inside of it on occasion though we usually fall asleep during the second movement"—the Ryan clan could not imagine living anywhere but in the city of Chicago. A suburb was in the same category of unacceptable places as Ulan Bator.

"It's a little hard," Joe Murphy, an exile from Boston and Mary Kate's Jungian husband, had remarked, "to vote in a Chicago election, hard, but of course not impossible."

Yet Ned Ryan had been raised in Lake Forest and was surely part of the young aristocracy of his time, two facts that Red had decided long ago were not appropriate matters for discussion with his wife—a wife who was now watching him with a blend of unease and fascination.

"You certainly seem to be enjoying yourself, Red." Eileen considered him cautiously, her eyes flicking to his Perrier glass. "Charming all the lovely Ryan granddaughters."

"The Monsignor said I was to do that until Cardinal Cronin came." He rubbed the tip of her snub nose with the glass.

Her dubious smile hinted at fear and fascination and bafflement in equal parts. "Please don't look at me that way in public, Red."

"I can't help myself." Teasingly, he brushed the glass against her bare shoulder. She shivered and quickly turned away. Then she turned back. "Are you sure nothing's wrong?"

"Absolutely nothing."

She didn't seem persuaded—like the woman who had heard a convincing argument that the world was flat.

Red had always felt that Eileen and he were being carefully evaluated at these family gatherings so that the clan could have a secret summit meeting to discuss what they could "do" about him and the torment he was inflicting on "poor, little Eileen."

In his newfound joy, he realized that that fantasy was absurd. The more characteristic Ryan reaction was that of Caitlin, who would sit next to him on the sands at Grand Beach and taunt him about the split infinitives in his column. As did most of the rest of the world, he amused the Ryans.

Momentarily he thought about the limo that had started the day's adventures. Was it a message from Harvard Princeton Gunther or just an accident? Why would Harv be so upset about the Pulaski case? Unless he saw a connection with Rita Lane? Had he perhaps found Rita and disposed of her?

Uneasy, Red made a mental note to call Brazil the next morning.

"Note that the Lord Cardinal has appeared." Monsignor Ryan had quietly glided up behind him. "And that, as predicted, the adolescent women—including, I remark, your wife—have swarmed around him as if he were the newly ordained curate at a suburban parish." He sighed noisily. "The Lord Cardinal was, as you doubtless know, never a newly ordained curate. He remains emotionally fixated at that stage of development."

Blackie Ryan, four years younger than Eileen, was her "favorite sibling." Indeed he was the favorite of all his brothers and sisters, the only member of the clan who was not strikingly good-looking. He was short, with a tendency to be pudgy, and his kinky hair was thin above a high quizzical forehead. His father's shrewd, kindly eyes hid behind thick glasses, making him look like an inoffensive, superannuated acolyte, one that you would hardly notice in the sacristy because he was almost indistinguishable from the furniture.

He was also perhaps the shrewdest politician in Chicago,

Sean Cronin's top adviser, a man of powerful intelligence and unerring instincts. He hid behind the mask of helpless ineffectuality because God had given him the mask.

"You guys get a lot of this Pentecostal stuff?" Red asked, accepting the new glass of Perrier that seemed to materialize in the Monsignor's small fist.

"Ah, that's the matter with which you are preoccupied? It is perhaps a fading phenomenon, a punishment on us for excluding emotion from religion for too long a time. In the lives of some people, it seems to be a useful religious phase. For others I fear it represents a craving for novelty."

"A lot of them freak out?"

"There's a baptism of the Holy Spirit, so called, in which people collapse on the floor." Blackie's eyes were blinking as he tried to judge the drift of the conversation. "It seems relatively harmless. Of greater interest to me is the common-enough though infrequently discussed ecstatic experience with which you are doubtless familiar from William James's *Varieties*?"

"Doubtless." Red made a mental note.

"There is good research data"—Blackie swirled his Jameson's, content now that he had found the right subject—"to suggest that perhaps a third of the population have such experiences once, five percent frequently. You will recall the descriptions: time stands still, the world rushes in, the person is filled with peace and joy and fire and light and laughter, there is an absolute certainty of goodness.... That sort of thing. Your man Carl Gustav Jung—or should I say, in the circumstances, Joe Murphy's man—apparently had some such experiences, as I'm sure you know."

"Of course." Red hoped that the priest could not hear his pounding heart. "Are they sane?"

"Paragons, according to the sociological literature." He considered his mostly empty Jameson's glass as if he suspected someone had stolen some of it. "On the whole they are healthy and active people whose lives become even more healthy and active as a result. Often such experiences are a turning point, particularly in the young. Some scholars think that the Transfiguration story in the Gospel represents, with theological overlays, of course, a memory of a religious experience in the career of Jesus, after which he knew that it was his destiny to go up to Jerusalem and die."

Red caught sight of Eileen's profile across the room. How could you lust for a woman as much as he did and still have a religious experience?

"Mostly for religious, priests and nuns and the like?"

"They've done the writing about it, of course. For most of our history they were the only ones who could write. It does seem, however, that married people are by no means excluded. In fact, the research shows that sexual love often occasions it."

"God kind of slides into bed with you?" He had caught Eileen's eye over the Cardinal's shoulder and winked. She blushed and turned away.

"I see no reason to doubt"—Blackie reflected on the remnants of his drink and sighed heavily—"that they are of God, special graces, special gifts, but I don't believe they're miraculous. For one reason or another, the veils slip away and one sees the deep processes of the cosmos more clearly than one sees them at ordinary times and comprehends that they are processes of enormous love."

"I gather that we don't know much about them scientifically." Now all he could see in the crowd of men and women talking to the Cardinal was a curve of part of Eileen's delightful rear end. Lust, love, affection, tenderness, guilt, desire, need, adoration—how did you separate them? The presence in the green glass tower, the Cheshire smile, the complacent woman soon to be enjoyed on his bed, how did you unmix them? God and Eileen, how untangle them?

"The misfortune is that most people think they are of God and probably religious, but have nothing to do with the Church. Sometimes there's a temporarily unhinging aftereffect and the person is carted off to a shrink who, unlike your beauteous sister-in-law Mary Kate Murphy, does not believe in God or ecstasy and proclaims the person a victim of schizophrenia. It can be very disturbing."

"That sort of experience can unhinge a person?"

"Oh yes, most decidedly. Come, let us slip away to my room. I have a couple of books which you might find interesting. . . . Indeed, these interludes are so powerful that many of those who experience them do not want them again for all their pleasurableness. Love is not an easy emotion, Redmond."

"What is love?"

Blackie turned to stare at him as though he had asked a profoundly original question, one to which the species had never addressed itself before.

"I suppose it is a judicious blend of affection and passion. Like a martini, it is the blend that is important."

They walked down the dark, dingy corridor of the Cathedral rectory and into the rector's suite, in which almost every available flat surface was piled with several stacks of paper or books. On the wall were pasted with barely adequate transparent tape three aging posters of Pope John, President Kennedy, and football quarterback John Unitas of the Baltimore Colts.

"The three Johns of my adolescence," Blackie would remark apologetically.

"Unitas was the best quarterback ever," Red observed.

"Only those of our generation"—Blackie was fifteen years younger—"remember him."

"Nice Madonna, saucy Norman teenager."

"The old fella gave it to me at ordination." Blackie inspected the empty votive-light glass in front of the medieval carving, apparently baffled as to how the candle had burned itself out. "He said it looked like my mother."

"It does."

The priest cleared a chair, shoved it against a file cabinet, and climbed from the chair to the top of the cabinet. He reached into a section of bookshelf behind the cabinet, probed around for a bit, and emerged with two volumes from which he blew large quantities of dust.

Red noted on his crowded rolltop desk a page with the typewritten legend "Chapter One: Saving Professor Whitehead from the Protestants." Beneath the title was a handwritten scrawl. "Difficult. He WAS a Protestant."

"Aha!" Blackie waved the books triumphantly. "I knew they were here. This one"—still on top of the cabinet he passed it down to Red, like a wizard dispensing gifts from his magic carpet—"has some rather interesting quotes. And this one is an English medieval mystic, who is the only one of that crowd I can understand. Name of Richard Rolle."

He dropped the first on the floor as he reached for the second.

"Murphy's Law," he murmured. "The obverse of Anselm's ontological argument. Do you know it, Redmond?"

"If God is possible, he is?"

"Precisely. And our fellow ethnic, Murphy, has a parallel insight. If disorder is possible, it is. Should I ever finish my tract on William James, I may endeavor to revolutionize philosophy by demonstrating the link between Murphy and Anselm."

Red helped the priest scramble down from the cabinet. "I'm not sure that it will make much of a column," he said lamely, fearing that he had told his brother-in-law too much.

"There's an article somewhere." Blackie stood in the middle of his study, one foot still on the ottoman that was his base camp on the descent from the cabinet. "Let me see...."

He reached behind his desk, produced a key from the windowsill, tried it unsuccessfully in a number of desk drawers, and finally opened one of them.

"Aha, an article from what Jimmy Breslin is pleased to call *The New York Times Newspaper.* So it must be not only true but officially true. Also a package of English shortbreads, remarkably fresh considering. Have an article, Redmond. Have a shortbread too."

Red accepted the tattered article and declined the shortbread. "Maybe it will make a column after all."

"It might." Blackie munched blissfully on his shortbread. "Consider that perhaps ten percent of the people in the country have had or are having, more or less routinely, experiences which, if one is to believe them, make sexual intercourse look dull. Consider also that most of them are afraid to talk about such experiences even to their spouses, to say nothing of their doctors and their priests."

Back in the party, the music had begun and the various generations of Ryans, incorrigible dancers, were moving about the room in graceful patterns, like an improvised *Swan*

Lake. All but Blackie, who contended, with considerable reason, that he was utterly innocent of gracefulness.

Red took his wife's arm firmly and moved her against his chest.

"Red... you're dancing!"

"Naturally." Through the bare flesh of her back he felt her heart pounding against her ribs. She was frightened of him. Well she might be. He loved her all the more for her terror.

"Something HAS happened." She looked up at him anxiously.

"Just because I dance with my wife?"

"Because you dance with me THIS way."

He drew her even closer. Something was indeed happening to both of them, something more than merely a periodic resurgence of passion.

"Any man who wouldn't hold you as close as he could would be an idiot."

She backed away a fraction of an inch and he reclaimed her, his whole self melting with affection for her. *A simple evolutionary adaptation to keep the male and female together so the children should survive. Nothing more. Nothing special. I'm not the only man who feels this way about his wife.* He moved his fingers a suggestive fraction of an inch against her ribs.

"Red..." She swallowed hard and put on her stern legal face.

"Yes?"

"Nothing."

Then she tried again. "Red..."

"Uh-huh?"

Her expression changed as her thought must have changed too: the legal face replaced by the wanton bedroom face. "Nothing. Only that I love you. No matter what happens."

"Nothing bad is going to happen."

Before she could reply, Caitlin and her crowd had surrounded them and were singing, "They have the time, the time of their life, I saw a man he danced with his wife, in Chicago, Chicago, my home town!"

Eileen turned flaming crimson but did not seem unhappy at the attention. Quite the contrary, she joined in the chorus.

In the distance the new Monsignor beamed like an Irish Buddha. How much had he guessed?

Much later, when his back was against the wall and they were trying to lock him up, Red would consider turning to Blackie again, knowing that there was at least one person who did not think he was a quasi schizophrenic.

But then it was too late.

10

They had a nasty, dignity-scorching fight in the Cathedral parking lot, two anxious animals who needed each other desperately trying to pretend that they were above it all.

Patty wanted to drive Kate home in the Bug. Eileen insisted that she would drive them both home in the Volvo and "your father" would follow in the VW.

"MOther, I'm SURE I can drive home. After all, I'm EIGHTEEN."

Patricia Anne Kane was the shorter of Red's two daughters—curvaceous, dramatic, outspoken, every inch a Ryan woman, stamped out of the same press that had produced her mother and her aunts. Round face, luxuriously budding young body, rapidly changing blue eyes, nervously gesturing hands, Patty could change from hoyden to revolutionary to archduchess in less than thirty seconds. No opinion was ever muted, no outrage ever overlooked, no alleged parental injustice ever unprotested. She had once been "Daddy's little girl" and now apparently despised him, with good reason, Red assumed, though he was never quite sure what the reason was.

"You're not eighteen till next summer, young woman."

"REALLY," their daughter exploded in hurt and offended anger, an innocent victim of parental naïveté. "It's time you started to grow up."

Kathleen Elizabeth Kane, an ethereal, slightly stooped, blond waif, stood quietly next to her sister, seemingly unaware of the conversation, the car, her parents, the Cathedral parking lot, and, quite possibly, the present cosmos. A radiantly lovely potential model, Kate had blue eyes that were usually dull with indifference or boredom or possibly drugs. Patricia and John would grow up to be reasonably mature adults no matter how badly Red had failed them. Katie? Red had seen those eyes too often on runaway girls turned prostitute.

"Red?" Eileen deferred to him, an unusual event.

"If she's old enough to go away to college next summer, she's probably old enough to navigate a VW down Clark Street." He pushed his finger against the girl's snub nose, so like her mother's. "If she piles it up, I know a good lawyer."

"Really," Patty murmured softly, astonished that her father was suddenly on her side.

"Volvo, not VW," Eileen said, in the tone of a pol settling for the best compromise she can get.

But as soon as she and Red were inside the Bug, into which Red's long legs never wanted to fit, Eileen exploded. "I wish to hell that you'd give me some support in rearing your children," she shouted. "I can't be mother and father both to them all the time!"

"You asked me what I thought," he pleaded, easing the car out of the parking lot.

"I expected you to back me up." Her voice was tight with outrage. "Why else would I have asked you?"

"I thought you really wanted my opinion."

"Your opinion on child rearing is useless."

"I haven't seen the famous Eileen Ryan temper in ages."

"I haven't seen the famous Red Kane lover-boy act in ages, either."

I think I am in real trouble now. What do I say?

"Red...please watch the stop lights!"

I had better say nothing at all.

They had crossed North Avenue before Eileen renewed the conversation.

"What is that tune you're whistling?"

"Was I whistling?"

"Of course you were. It sounds like something from Victor Herbert."

Red whistled the tune again, though he knew damn well what it was. "'You're Irish and You're Beautiful.'...It's from—"

"I know damn well what it's from."

More silence. Then a new beginning from the namesake of the play.

"Mike Casey the Cop looks happy, doesn't he?"

Casey, a Ryan cousin, was the acting Superintendent of Police who had been forced out of office because he was too competent, too intellectual (he'd written books!) and too white at a time when it was politically wise to have a black as top cop. He had married his childhood sweetheart, who owned an art gallery, and was now turning out "neighborhood" paintings at a furious clip—and acting as an unpaid (on his own insistence) but almost daily consultant to the Superintendent.

"With a wife as glamorous as Annie, he should look happy. I'm glad that I wrote that column when they dumped him. It was a cheap shot. They knew he was about to retire, so they fired him as Deputy Superintendent and demoted him to a watch commander. He'd put too many of the Mayor's thugs in jail during the past twenty years."

"I remember the column."

Didn't she claim never to read the column?

"Were you and Annie sweethearts ever in grammar school?" she asked, as he turned up Lincoln.

"I should have been so lucky."

"You and Blackie were certainly chummy tonight. What are the books he gave you?"

Typical Eileen. Direct and blunt. I'd better do something.

"Some stuff for a column."

That ended the conversation.

What do I do now?

As they stopped in front of their house, parking behind the Volvo, he knew what he would do. To hell with the consequences. He turned off the ignition, turned sideways in the cramped little car, and took her in his arms. There was nothing delicate or gentle about his kiss this time. It was sustained, passionate, demanding, imposing his will and his desire on her. She responded indifferently at first and then with passion of her own, fire racing to fire.

He plunged a hand underneath her skirt, grasping a solid, waiting thigh.

She bowed her head against his chest. They huddled in each other's arms like two lost lovers who were the only man and woman left in the world.

"Red," she breathed deeply, as if surfacing after a high dive, "are you sure there's nothing wrong? Did you see the doctor . . . ?"

"Nothing at all." He kissed her throat. "I've never been better."

Red's other hand became involved in working its way through her trench coat, under her dress and bra, in quest for the nipple it had almost captured before the party. Eileen breathed more deeply, this time with a half-desperate catch in her sigh.

They clung to each other a little longer, drawing the foam off the top of a chocolate soda before digging into the ice cream. Red thought that perhaps heaven was eternal foreplay.

"We should go inside," Eileen whispered. "The kids will wonder what we're doing."

"They'll never guess."

She tore away from him suddenly. "I am not a teenage sex object to be fondled by an adolescent male with repressed masturbatory fantasies. I SAID, we should go inside."

His feelings hurt and his ardor extinguished, Red released her and bounded around to open the door of the car for her and help her out.

Savagely she brushed his hand away and strode toward the steps to their house. Then she halted abruptly, hesitated, and turned toward him, hands plunged in the pockets of her trench coat, head tilted apologetically like that of a young lawyer who has committed an unintentional gaffe that insulted a wise old judge.

"Sorry, Red. I guess I'm scared. You can feel me up anytime you want. That was wonderful. Like a whirlpool filled with pink circus candy."

"All Ryan metaphors are about sweets."

"We all have sweet teeth. Am I forgiven?"

"It wasn't teenage fondling?" He was not quite ready to grant absolution.

"Oh, sure it was. But I've had a teenage crush on you since my mother's wake. I'll never get over it. I'm as bad as Patty with Jeff or Kate with Mark...." She dug her head lower in the still night air. "When things are good between us I become aroused just thinking about you."

"Oh." Red gulped, wondering how you respond to such a statement. He took her arm to guide her toward their house. "That long ago?"

"Mm-hmm." She leaned against him. "You were so compassionate. You understood our pain better than anyone else."

Red felt giddy as they ascended the stoop. Not only had she capitulated for the night, she had engaged in more self-revelation in one paragraph than in the previous twenty years of their common life. Icebergs should melt slowly. Women should not wipe away their defenses so quickly—and capture your tenderness so easily.

Compassion? A compassionate adulterer? This was all getting out of hand.

"Thank you," she said softly as Red held the door open for her. Her witch's eyes, glowing in the dark—or was it the reflection of the streetlight—studied him thoughtfully.

"I think I'll take a quick shower," she said inside the house, as she'd peeked into Patty's room to make absolutely sure that no terrible fate had befallen her daughter on the ride home. "It was terribly hot in that rectory."

"I'm in no rush," he laughed. "Take your time."

He had effectively seduced her for the night, no great feat, after all, with a woman with the normal supply of hormones and no sex life for several months. But, despite the invitations she had been issuing for the past several weeks, his renewed courtship would require patience, skill, tenderness, and time. She was puzzled, resentful, frightened. She didn't want to be hurt again. She didn't trust him, and with good reason. Her anger had returned, lurking just beneath the skin of her personality, a good sign perhaps, but it would have to be watched. There was a lot of hard work ahead. Love, unaccountably, always seemed to demand hard work.

I will have a quick drink, he decided, *and ponder the mystery of my wife with the eyes of a witch.*

Oh damn!

Well, I suppose the only alternative is to look at Blackie's books.

As soon as he heard the shower running, he slipped up to the small room on the third floor that doubled as his study and an occasional guest bedroom. *An embalming room in the Martian funeral home,* he thought, as he sunk into the uncomfortable posture chair his son had provided for Red's moments of thought and reflection. The first book Blackie had given him was a collection of descriptions of experiences very like his own.

Eagerly he scanned the pages—"deep calling to deep" ..."wafted upwards, bursting with emotion"..."goodness and power penetrating me altogether"..."presence about me and within me"..."fire, light, heat"..."Sights, scents, and sounds blended into a harmony so perfect that it transcended human expression, even human thought. It was like a glimpse of the peace of eternity."

His hands were wet. *I'm not the only one. I'm not going crazy. It's real. Why me? And where does Eileen fit in, this green-eyed mystery woman I've never known? This odd creature who confesses to a lifelong adolescent crush on me for a virtue which I utterly lack?*

He cocked his ear. The shower water was still rushing through the pipes. Fastidious passion.

He opened the Penguin Classic edition of *The Fire of Love* and thumbed through the pages. A passage caught his eye.

"I cannot tell you how surprised I was the first time I felt my heart begin to warm. It was real warmth too, not imaginary, and it felt as if it were actually on fire. I was astonished at the way the heat surged up, and how this new sensation brought great and unexpected comfort. I had to keep feeling my breast to make sure that there was no physical reason for it.... Once I realized that it was from within, I knew that this fire of love had no cause material or sinful but was the gift of my Maker."

Rolle thought it was God. Hell, so did I.

The Holy Ghost with warm breast and ah! bright wings. A Holy Ghost who seemed, somehow, interchangeable with Eileen. Again he asked a question that would haunt him in the weeks ahead. *Why me? Why should Redmond P. Kane, of all people, get a spectacular kick in the behind from God at that age in life when he had given up on all his dreams?*

That night it didn't matter. If it really was God who had swung the cosmic baseball bat, who was floating with an impish grin in the leaves, then it was God somehow linked to Eileen.

The shower water stopped gurgling in the pipe next to his chair. He tossed the two books on his desk and rushed to the door.

Then he hesitated and returned thoughtfully to the desk. No point in leaving them lying around where someone could pick them up and misunderstand. Eileen?

She would not probe in his study.

She had peeked in the U.S. Attorney's secret files, had she not?

He fumbled through the center drawer, found a key, and hid the two books in the file compartment of the desk, a storage space he had never used before.

Then he hurried to his freshly showered wife.

He would open the compartment six weeks later, hoping that the two books would protect him from the mental institution for which he seemed to be destined. Blackie had been right, such experiences do indeed have the power to unhinge you.

The shrink was totally uninterested. "I don't need your devotional manuals" —she pushed the books to the edge of her desk; they would have fallen to the floor if Red had not caught them— "to know that you're not the first schizophrenic in the history of human self-deception."

"Quasi schizophrenic," Red muttered wearily.

That night, however, he did not worry about his sanity. He would sort things out in the morning. For the moment, it was sufficient to know that the Lord God had entered his life like a barrage of skyrockets exploding over Grant Park on the Fourth of July. The first order of business was to envelop once again his wife in the fire of love that had, in some as-yet-inexplicable way because of her, taken possession of him on the banks of the Chicago River.

As he cautiously entered their bedroom, she came out of the bathroom, glistening and glowing in a white terry robe and smelling of soap and bath oil. Her hands rested uncertainly on the belt of the robe.

His heart was beating so rapidly that he was sure she could hear, perhaps even see the blows against his ribs.

For Red the perfection of sexual pleasure was the fulfillment of his partner's passion. To lead a woman from quiescence and perhaps indifference through interest, then arousal, then body-wrenching need when for a few precious moments she was utterly dependent on him, to manic cries of fulfillment and glowing complacency was a skilled craft; an accomplishment of considerable merit. Sometimes in the delirium of the rare love/lust for his wife the craft became an art, occasionally a high art.

Analogous to writing a prize-winning column.

And when it was finished he felt as let down as when a column was locked into type. Skill with words did not make you a distinguished journalist. Neither did skill in tenderly assaulting and capturing a woman's most intimate and sensitive parts make you a man. Red was ashamed of the experience in which he had learned his skills and dismayed that they promised more manhood than he seemed to possess. In bed he was capable of high art when he created ecstasy for Eileen. Everywhere else he was a dunderhead.

As he considered his doubtful but willing wife on this Night of All the Saints, Red assured himself that this time it would be different. What he promised in lovemaking, he would deliver in love.

Sometimes, he reasoned, you undress a woman slowly and leisurely. Other times you strip her with a few quick, imperious movements, shocking her with your speed and causing her, in a delightful gesture of modesty, to cower temporarily behind crossed arms and extended hands. You make your choice, if you have any sense, based on an instinct for what she wants.

Tonight, beyond any doubt, was for a quick disrobing.

"I'm afraid I don't look all that erotic," she said shyly.

It was the smell of soap, normally innocent of eroticism, that slashed away the remnants of Red's restraint. Fervently he tore open the robe, peeled it off her, tossed it on the floor, and assaulted her with demented caresses. Her lips tasted of mouthwash and, faintly, of old-fashioneds. "Dear God in heaven, how much I love you!"

He removed the hands and arms that had covered her body with momentary instinctive protection, extended her arms, and drank in her beauty.

The moment was both bitter and sweet. Bitter because of his memory of the wasted years, and sweet because of the anticipation of the years to come. Bitter because he would never love her enough, sweet because there would be so much pleasure in trying. Even the marks of time, the lines and creases, the folds and softness that resisted Eileen's stern self-discipline made her more attractive.

"You're disconcerting my modesty, Red," she said, not altogether displeased.

"That's what husbands of women as beautiful as you are supposed to do."

"There's that." She bowed her head, pleased and flattered. "Disconcert as much as you want."

"I intend to."

"Red." She pulled lightly against his hands as if to escape for a moment or two.

"Yes?" He paused.

She tried to say something and then gave it up.

"What is it, Eileen?" he demanded firmly. Restrain, that was what Joe Murphy had said.

"We're falling in love again, aren't we, Red?"

It was not what she had wanted to say, but it would do.

"It's your fault, woman. You've been trying to seduce me for the last three weeks."

"Five, actually."

"It's going to be different this time." He kissed her confidently, feeling in the words their own truth.

"It already is.... Redmond Peter Kane, you are absorbing me like I'm an old-fashioned double chocolate malt with real malt. Now I AM embarrassed."

"With two scoops of whipped cream," he eased her back gently to their bed and began to unbutton his shirt. Eileen waited submissively, willing herself to be a complete gift, the way she always did when the lovemaking had begun in earnest. Her lips parted, her jaw sagged, her eyes rounded in total adoration.

That adoration usually scared Red, sometimes even into impotency. He did not deserve it. Yet often in love and occasionally even when they were eating lunch or watching the TV, he would catch the worshipful green eyes devouring him. Tonight, for a change, he thought he might deserve to be devoured.

The Cheshire smile seemed to whisper a warning in his ear. *Not that way, you clumsy dolt. You know better than that.*

"Why are you staring at me that way?" Eileen drew her knee upward in protection of her loins and lowered her eyes. "You're really embarrassing me. I'm not a prize you won at a raffle or something like that."

"I'm admiring the mystery woman"—he removed his trousers—"that has somehow found her way into my bed."

"Red," she laughed affectionately, and opened her eyes, "I'm not a mystery woman. I'm your wife."

"That's irrelevant." He discarded his shorts. "As to what I'm doing, I am lusting in my heart after you."

"That's what Democrats tend to do."

"You read the Bible lately, Ei?" he asked casually, folding his arms and standing, naked and powerful lord of the manor, above her.

"Good Lord, Red," she laughed, "you're quite mad."

"I came across a poem from the Song of Solomon in a

book the other day. The girl says to her guy that until the sun goes down, he should roam her body like a gazelle or a young stag roams the mountain."

"Dirty book," she murmured, now soft and alight with desire.

"Interesting place to find a love manual." He sat next to her, as though he were going to begin an advanced seminar on Old Testament studies.

"Please, Red," she begged.

With his index fingers he traced designs on her body, from her shoulders to her loins and back. She squirmed beneath his hands, on fire with need. "Does that feel like a gazelle? Or a young stag?"

His caress turned into a tickle and she squealed with pleasure. "Please, Red, oh, stop it, PLEASE."

She grabbed one of his hands and pretended to try to fend it off. He retaliated by locking both of her hands in his right hand and holding them above her head. He continued to probe and torment the familiar yet always mysterious contours of her flesh.

"You do this to all your slave girls here in Jerusalem, fella?"

"Jerusalem?" Red suspended his explorations temporarily.

"The geek in that book, Solomon or whatever, calls his woman Daughter of Jerusalem. Hey, Redmond Peter Kane, stop that!"

"When I'm ready." He brushed her lips with his own. "And tonight that won't be for a long time. Understand?"

"Yes, master." She tried to wiggle away, deliberately provoking him. He pinned her firmly to the bed with his free hand and kissed her tenderly, lingering against her lips, and traced his magic designs, more demandingly this time. "That's what we do to the good slave girls here in Jerusalem ... only trouble is then they expect it all the time. They turn Irish on you."

"The Daughter of Jerusalem turns into a Mother from Sligo." She groaned and through clenched teeth murmured, "Did you say till sunset? You can let go of me, darling. I'm not going to run away and it's a shame to immobilize your hands when you can do other and more constructive"—wild laughter—"things with them."

"Okay, but you asked for it."

Lovingly, with both hands, he cupped one of her magic breasts and ever so lightly fondled it, his fingers skillfully playing with its warm fullness. Ah! bright wing. Then he bent over her and teased the already firm and eager nipple to full rigidity.

Frantically Eileen clutched the headboard of their bed. "You're killing me, Red," she pleaded abjectly.

So easy to arouse. A passionate woman who had been deprived of sex for much too long a time. Regret filled his soul as a melting river at the end of a hard winter fills its flood plain. Regret made him love her all the more. He would spend the rest of their life making up for his past failures. Still holding the captive breast with one hand, he shifted his attention to the other. "Don't stop." She threw her head backward in a burst of wild ecstasy. "Never stop. Do it to me forever."

"Ah, the woman sings a different tune." He bowed over her, hesitated for a second while she tensed with the knowledge of what was coming next and began to nibble on her flesh with delicate touches of his teeth. A surefire curtain raiser.

"Good God!" Eileen tried to stifle a scream as her body arched up from the bed.

Maybe, Red thought. *Maybe*.

At least someone very much like Him.

With his hands and his lips, he took away his wife's sanity, her separateness as a person, her boundaries of self-protection. He turned her into a wet, twisting mass of desperately aroused womanly need, completely dependent on him for satisfaction. He caressed her and played with her and made her play in response. He made her laugh, he made her cry out with pleasure, he overwhelmed her with affection and flattery, some of the latter in comic pseudo French which sent her into paroxysms of giggling.

What does she see in me? he wondered in a remote part

of his brain that was not preoccupied with the activities of the moment. *This woman has too much depth to be bowled over by someone who looks like an aging and slightly dissolute baby-blue-eyed ex-linebacker. Why me?*—a question he would later address to Blackie Ryan.

"When is sunset?" she begged as in desperation she dragged him down on herself like a drowning woman clinging to a lifeguard. "Red, I'm not joking, I really can't stand it anymore, oh, please, please. I'm not a teenager...."

"If that woman from the *Sun-Times* could see you now, she'd think you were; and it's sunset when your husband decides it's sunset...understand?"

"Right!" She laughed hysterically. "Except don't those gazelles of yours ever wear out? Don't they ever"—another burst of giggles—"ever need to sleep?"

As he held her poised precariously above the abyss of rapture, another monumental wave of love for Eileen washed through Red's spirit as healing grace. *Perhaps*—the thought rushed through his head—*that's the way the One with the baseball bat feels about me.* His lips returned to her face with infinitely delicate kisses. All right, he had failed all his other responsibilities to her. He'd only been a good husband on the rare occasions when his body was driven by lust to seek entry into hers. Nonetheless, that was better than nothing. Only a coward would deprive a splendid woman of this joy which was so easily given. Only a fool would not take the risk that joyous passion might transform the rest of their relationship.

Slowly he increased the intensity of his kisses until they became darts of fire burning at her eyes and lips, throat and cheeks, chin and forehead. She tried weakly to turn away from the scorching demands of his lips. Furiously he kissed her into submission. "I love you, Eileen," he murmured, stroking her cheek. "I'll always love you."

"I know, Red." She smiled weakly, content to prolong this moment of suspended passion forever. Deftly she moved his lips back to her breasts. He tasted the sweetness of each nipple while his fingers, still gentle but now demanding, sought once more her helplessly waiting loins.

Stretching luxuriously, Eileen slipped away from him and jabbed at his ribs. "The thing is, King Solomon, that your Daughters of Jerusalem tend to have their own herds of gazelles or, to quote your text"—she wiggled on top of him—"their own little foxes."

"Hey, cut that out," he protested. "Get off me. I'm the master."

"Not in this bed." It was her turn to make sport of him, to tickle him into delirium, to work her own designs with her fingers and her lips—the little foxes of her amusements.

"Darn it, Redmond Peter Kane, hold still," she ordered. "You started these fun and games and I have some new tricks I want to try."

As the narrator in Red's novel remarked, when a woman decides that it is time for sexual sport, she engages in it with a single-minded skill and cunning that makes even the most experienced male seem like a callow neophyte. Eileen dragged him down into a primal swamp of not-quite-fulfilled desire, a swamp that smelled of lavender liquid soap, sweat, aroused woman, and Scope mouthwash and was inhabited by demanding kisses and gentle but persistent fingers and darting electrical impulses that exorcised his guilts and his regrets, his convictions of failure and worthlessness, his self-hatred and self-contempt. He sank into the sweet, savory, and tenaciously strong warmth of mother earth.

A swamp like Wacker and Wacker? Nothing could be like that. Yet Eileen's soft green-eyed electrical swamp was not unlike it, either. As he would try later to explain, unsuccessfully of course, to his therapist, Eileen was like God and not like God; God was like Eileen and not like Eileen.

Such, Blackie Ryan would insist, is the precise theological nature of sacraments.

"It's about time, I think; I mean, I can definitely see the sun going down over the lake." He pushed her away for a moment's breath.

She rested the side of her face against his belly. "Can you now? It seems like three o'clock in the afternoon to me."

"Ah sure, you're a terrible green-eyed witch woman." He patted her rump. "You'd try the patience of a saint."

"Saint Red of Lincoln Park," she gasped as he made his final preparations to enter her. "A whole herd of gazelles..."

Then, with giddy laughter Red Kane and his woman

gave themselves over to the completion of their delightful work. Their love became an unrestrained eruption of two fire storms compelled to merge forever. They twisted and turned and tumbled, clawing and moaning, groaning and scratching, shoving and pushing in a violent wrestling match of love, both of them acting without thought or plan but in the full grip of hungry instinct. Finally there was satiation and peace. The naked female animal who had raced wildly down the mountainside with him was now a peaceful little girl, asleep in his arms. He drew the comforter and sheet protectively over her and turned out the lights.

All he had to do the next day was write a seven-hundred-word column. She had to appear in court and fight Don Roscoe for the freedom of Hurricane Houston.

"I like it here in Jerusalem," she purred as she snuggled cozily against him.

"Huh?"

"Forgot the Song of Solomon already?"

Poor woman. He kissed her forehead lightly, brushed her breasts in a farewell promise, and drew her closer.

Did you like that?

The question was addressed to God. Since there was no answer, he continued the dialogue.

I don't know what the hell You're getting me into, besides my wife. So far I like it. Keep it up. This being a mystic is fun.

The dialogue was cut short by deep, serene, and self-satisfied sleep.

Then from far away, in a harem peopled by hundreds of houris who looked like Eileen, he heard someone crying.

He struggled out of the dark paradiselike cave in which he had been drifting. *Something wrong with one of the girls. Need my help. Must wake up and help them.*

The weeping was not down the hallway, however. It was in his own room. Eileen, who almost never cried, was sobbing.

She's freaked out, he thought, struggling through the shades of confusion for consciousness. *Is she having a heart attack? Did I hurt her? My God, what have I done?*

Then he was fully awake. Eileen's weeping was hysterical, deep body-wracking gulps of grief that shook her like an influenza chill and shook him as he tried to hold her close.

"It's all right, kid. It's all right. Just a terrible nightmare. I'm here to take care of you."

He turned on the dim night-light on their bedstand. Eileen was wide-awake. "What happened?" He held her as closely as he could and began to stroke her back. "A nightmare?"

She shook her head negatively.

He continued to caress and kiss her, gently reassuring her. Slowly his therapy took effect.

"Better?"

She nodded her head and reached for the tissue box on the bedstand.

"I'm sorry, Red," her voice choked. "So sorry."

Then, broken and exhausted, she was asleep again in his arms. A little girl from whom Santa Claus had been taken cruelly and unnecessarily.

Red turned off the light, more troubled than he had been since he turned the corner at Wacker and Wacker.

What could do that to Eileen? The woman to whom he thought he was married was quite incapable of anything that would occasion that kind of grief.

What had she done? Or what did she think she had done?

This is not supposed to be part of the act, he protested to his unresponsive dialogue partner. *If Eileen is going to be hurt, we call the game right now, understand?*

The other had no response, apparently uninterested in Redmond Peter Kane's rules. As he struggled to recapture sleep, he remembered vividly the four important lovers of his life—Jane, with whom he experienced love for the first time; Helga, who taught him sex when he was far too young to cope with it; Marian, the first woman with whom he fell in love; and Eileen, the teenage witch girl that he finally married, almost despite himself.

Book TWO

I was at Mary's, and happening to say something of the presence of spirits (of whom, I said, I was often dimly aware). Mr. Putnam entered into an argument with me on spiritual matters. As I was speaking, the whole system rose up before me like a vague destiny from the Abyss. I never before so clearly felt the Spirit of God in me and around me. The whole room seemed to me to be full of God. The air seemed to waver to and fro with the presence of Something, I knew not what. I spoke with the calmness and clearness of a prophet.

—James Russell Lowell

II

From the Kane File

Time, July 18, 1983

KANE KILLED

The self-styled "last of the Irish reporters" in Chicago was summarily fired last week. The *Chicago Herald Gazette* unceremoniously dumped two-time Pulitzer Prize winner Redmond "Red" Kane. *HG* editor Wilson Allen charged that "Red Kane is nothing but a loudmouthed Irish Catholic racist and a solitary drunk."

Kane, 53, a tall and wanly handsome man with mischievous blue eyes, has been entertaining Chicagoans for the last 15 years as must breakfast table reading along with his more famous rival, Mike Royko.

His attacks angered Allen, brought in last year to boost the paper's sagging circulation, when they turned against the paper's own editorial policy and against Chicago's new Mayor. Kane charged that "There is a massive conspiracy of silence among my fellow journalists to hide that several times a week the Mayor does not show up to work. If Dick Daley failed to appear even once in the old days, we would have been all over his staff. Our new Mayor may be home reading German novels, for all I know or care, but why don't City Hall reporters ask where the hell he is? I'll tell you why not. The press has a double standard. It doesn't ask the embarrassing questions about a black or woman Mayor that it would about a white male Mayor."

The Mayor replied with a blistering press conference attack, accusing Kane of being "a shanty Irish racist who works on his column a half hour a day. He is not interested in understanding black cultural differences or values."

In his next column Kane responded that it would be fine with him if the Mayor worked only 15 minutes a day. "The point is not how long the Mayor works; maybe we'd be better off if all public officials spent a couple of days a week home reading German novels. The point is that my fellow journalists don't ask why he's not around City Hall. As for being 'shanty Irish,' I guess I have to admit it's true. When I was a kid we lived in something pretty much like a shanty, because we were poor back in the 1930's. Alas, my father was a steel worker, not Congressman Bill Dawson's bagman."

This was the last straw for editor Allen, already impatient with Kane's jabs at him as "a carpetbagger who gets lost west of Canal Street and south of Van Buren."

Kane was abruptly ordered to clean out his desk and leave the city room in two hours. Syndication of his column "Kane's Korner" was canceled "effective immediately." Furthermore, Kane was told to "see your lawyer" about payment on his long-term contract with the *HG*.

One Kane loyalist said that Kane had been the inside choice to edit the *Herald* last year. "Red didn't want to campaign. He wanted to be anointed. There were hard feelings between him and Allen since day one."

Another reporter insisted that Kane is an anachronism. "He has no philosophy, no perspective, no social concern; he belongs in the 1950's. He was once a great reporter, but he sold out to the Establishment and his masters finally did him in. The famous Kane wit is nothing more than a defense for his monumental ego."

Kane found support from an unexpected source, frequent target Sean Cardinal Cronin. "The suggestion that the Irish are more racist than other groups in society," Cronin snapped, "is in itself racism."

At Ricardo's, the hangout of Chicago's best reporters, there was agreement that Kane was finally finished. "It's an end of an era," one said sadly. "But all eras must come to an end sometime."

Allen agreed. "Chicagoans may have enjoyed his irresponsible attacks at one time," he said. "Not anymore. Chicago has grown up and Red Kane hasn't."

Kane himself took his dismissal with characteristic nonchalance. He would settle down to being a house husband, he told a TV interviewer (his wife is a successful trial lawyer). "And maybe finish my novel. It's about an editor who knows what the people of Chicago want because he eats lunch in the executive dining room and goes to two lakefront dinners and one suburban cocktail party every week."

Chicagoans were betting that, house husband or not, they had not heard the last of Redmond Kane.

The New York Times, July 28, 1983

CONTROVERSIAL CHICAGO COLUMNIST REHIRED

CHICAGO, July 27—Bradford Winston, president of the Herald Company and publisher of the *Chicago Herald Gazette*, announced today that the controversial column of Redmond Kane would continue to appear in the *Herald Gazette* and subscribing papers.

"We hope to carry 'Kane's Korner' as long as Red wants to write it," Winston told a press conference. "There were just some hot tempers and a few misunderstandings."

Mr. Winston would not comment on the question of whether the reinstatement of Mr. Kane, fired last week by *Herald Gazette* editor Wilson Allen, was a victory for the veteran columnist in his running battle with Mr. Allen. However, sources close to the Herald Company reported that the company had been inundated with letters demanding Mr. Kane's return and attacking Mr. Allen's remark that Kane was "shanty Irish" and a "solitary drunk."

A spokesman for the Mayor said that he was delighted by Kane's return. Last week the Mayor had bitterly attacked Kane as a "racist." However, yesterday he told reporters that Kane was a Chicago institution. "Breakfast without Red would be like autumn without the Bears. Who will we have to kick around every morning?"

Mr. Kane informed reporters that they would find his reaction in tomorrow's "Kane's Korner." Mr. Allen was unavailable for comment.

July 28, 1983

Kane's Korner

RETURN OF THE NATIVE

by Redmond Peter Kane

How come I'm back here mouthing off as usual?

I'll tell you how come: all the solitary Irish drunks in town rose up to support me. Anyone who knows anything about the city west of Halsted and south of Harrison knows that we solitary Irish drunks stand together when anyone hints that our love for a few jars each night makes us incapable of doing our jobs.

So my plans to be a house husband have been frustrated.

I don't think I would have been much good at it. I never have been able to work those disposal things they have in sinks nowadays.

I must, however, say a word in defense of drunken Irish reporters. It should be confessed that we Chicago Irish who turn to the journalism racket have a weakness for the "Creature." Most of us end up as fall-down drunks before we're forty-five—and even on the barroom floor we can still outwrite your "socially concerned" WASP and Jewish 1960's punks from New York.

There's only a handful of us still around. The younger generation has turned to scholarship and law, finding them even easier, if not more honest, ways to earn a living.

Our womenfolk, all paragons of sobriety, are replacing us in the trade. When they have taken over the newspaper world in about five years, the rest of you will wish you had us male Irish drunks back.

Anyway, I'm not really in the tradition of the best Chicago Irish reporters. I'm not a fall-down drunk and probably never will be. If I were going down that path, I would have done it, with ample reason, long ago. Like maybe the day Nixon was inaugurated.

I don't drive when I've had more than one drink. I've

never been thrown out of a bar, I've never been charged with disorderly conduct (which some of the 1960's punks can't say), and I've given up drinking a couple of times for Lent.

I probably drink too much. Maybe I ought to give the jars up altogether, like my kids periodically make me give up smoking, unaccountably wanting me around a little longer. Maybe I should prove, as the nuns used to say, that I'm the master and not the slave of the Drink—that was in the days when nuns were into religion and not social protest.

Sad to say, I've let the tradition down: the Creature has never put me in the hospital, not even with a mildly broken wrist.

Why do Irish reporters drink? Because we're a primitive people? Because our mothers didn't love us enough? Because our sex lives are poor? Because we're superstitious papists?

Well, maybe. But I have another theory. I think we see things too clearly. We know that all reporters are whores or they wouldn't be in the business. That's not so bad. Any good journalist knows it in his heart.

We also see that the pimps for whom we work no longer know how to run a good whorehouse.

And that's enough to drive a man to drink.

12

A letter written in September of 1983 from Redmond Peter Kane to his son John Patrick Kane, at St. John's University, Collegeville, Minnesota

Dear Johnny,

I'm surprised that your teacher in twentieth-century history is aware that the Korean War, happening as it did before 1960, was part of the twentieth century. I'm even more surprised—though not displeased—that he suggested that the class might collect archives from fathers who had been in that war. I'm probably most surprised that you wonder why I never talk about my war experiences.

Was I a hero? I never thought so, but if your mother says so I guess I must have been. All I can remember is that I was scared stiff much of the time, and spaced out—as you kids would say—the rest of it.

I was most spaced out when I saw the gun turret swinging in my direction. I'll start there with my description of the actual combat. But you won't be able to understand that unless I fill in a bit of why I thought I had to be a priest at that time of my life. It might be an interesting curiosity for your professor.

Maybe even for you.

In May of 1950 the Communists were making plans to invade South Korea and I was making plans to return to the seminary. To prove I meant it—you'll find this hard to believe, John—I gave up drinking. For the first several months in Japan, violating my promise to my mother (whose weekly letters had exhorted me to remain on the paths of virtue by not even leaving the barracks) that I would not drink till I was twenty-one, I began consuming beer at a rate better than the average for our forces in Japan. The average was pretty high in those days when we didn't have heroin or cocaine to kill the pain of feeling bored and sorry for ourselves.

Killing pain was the only kind of killing that the army of occupation had in mind. The war was over. Even some of the career noncoms admitted that there wouldn't be another for a long time.

That was all right with me. I didn't mind the Army, but I had doubts when I thought about it, which wasn't very often, that I'd ever be able to kill anyone. In my dreams at the end of the rare day spent on the rifle range I would see bullets crashing into my father's head.

No, Johnny, I was not the stuff out of which professional killers are made, much less war heroes.

At Christmas I went to Confession and promised that I would give up the booze. The chaplain, a weary man who had stayed in after the end of the Second World War because his Bishop didn't want him back—I never found out why—was not impressed by my commitment. He didn't know my capacity to use sheer raw willpower in the name of conscience, like a bulldozer smashing against a reinforced-concrete wall.

When I was off duty, I would borrow a key from the Protestant chaplain and sneak into the chapel to pray. Jesus wasn't there, because the Blessed Sacrament was locked away safely somewhere else (you could never be sure when the Vikings might arrive with profanation in mind, or the ACLU worrying about separation of Church and State). Still it was a quiet place to reflect and pray. I said more prayers in those few months in Japan than I have in the rest of my life combined. I felt very close to God and imagined that He was very close to me. As Bill Cosby would later say, "It's just you and me, Fella, right?" Some days, hours would pass without my realizing it, hours of peace and contentment I've never known since.

Most of it was self-deception, I suppose. The bulldozer banging away against the wall. Yet to be honest, I feel that beneath the synthetic horseshit of my emotional problems there was probably some authentic faith and piety which I'm sorry I lost. I was convinced that God loved me and I loved God. Excuse me, John, if I sound like I'm preaching, but I'm trying to recall, in case it should be of any interest to you, who I was in those days.

I was horrified by the way the officers and men of our division threw themselves into debauchery with reckless enthusiasm—as though their next assignment would be on a desert island devoid of women and booze.

I liked the Japanese, however, and felt sorry for the young prostitutes, meek, defenseless women, like my mother, it seemed to me. And hence needing my protection. I would come back a missionary and convert them to Christianity. The Columban and Maryknoll missionaries to whom I spoke told me that the old religions of Japan had been wiped out by defeat in the war and that the country was ripe for a new faith. They were wrong, of course, but in those days, I believed that priests were almost never wrong. I was, as one of the curates at St. Ursula's told my mother, a "priest fan" —I hung around priests. I've always hoped that one would tell me what God wanted me to do. Father John Raven said long ago that all God wanted was for me to let Him love me. Somehow that seemed and seems too easy.

I no longer yearned to earn my way back into the Chicago seminary system. (Why I had been thrown out is not part of this story.) If Maryknoll would take me, that's where I belonged. I would dedicate my life to being a modern Saint Francis Xavier. No, better than that, I would succeed where Xavier had failed.

I helped a missionary in Yokohama three nights a week by trying to teach English to about a dozen Japanese sixth-graders. They were too polite to tell me that they didn't have the slightest comprehension of what I was saying. It didn't much matter. I made faces and acted the parts of American film heroes—gunmen, cowboys, Indians, fighter pilots, cops. The kids imitated me and taught me some traditional Japanese hero roles. I can still hiss like a pretty good samurai.

We had a ball those evenings. I've often wondered what has happened to my eager and polite kids. I had more fun with them than I've had with you and the girls, probably because if kids are not yours, you can relax and goof off with them. You don't have to worry that you might let them down the way you were let down.

But that's beyond this story too, isn't it?

Father Sullivan, the young Maryknoller, looked like a vocation ad from a missionary magazine: thick black hair, a pale Irish face that always needed a shave, and intense, zealous blue eyes. He spoke with a rich Brooklyn accent. Ordained during the war and sent out to Japan as soon as the missionaries were permitted back in, his parish was one of the best Brooklyn parishes in all the world. In those days I thought that's what Japan needed.

"We're going to convert this whole country by 1980, Red," he enthused one night over coffee in his book-filled, Pullman compartment study, after my kids had bid us a courteous and opaque good-bye. "The fields are ripe for the harvest. Can't you tell it in the respect they give us? They know we're bringing them the truth."

God help me, I thought that's how the polite little kids thought of me, a bearer of truth as well as an entertaining comedian. Actually, they probably told one another I was a stupid, but very large and mildly diverting, foreign devil.

"What about the immorality?" I said, echoing our chaplain's opinion that the Japanese were the most sexually degenerate people in the world.

"They're hungry for God." Father Sullivan dismissed my fears with a wave of his hand. "Once we give them God, they won't need women so badly."

Maybe, I thought to myself, but it is terribly easy here to buy a woman—like walking down to the corner delicatessen to buy a quart of milk.

Father Sullivan is still in Japan, John. He left the priesthood in 1965 and married a Japanese woman. I visited him a couple of years later when I was coming home from Viet Nam. He was teaching English to Japanese teenagers, living in one of those Japanese houses with the sliding screens, and relishing the adoration of his wife, a stocky Japanese woman from the countryside. He wasn't Japanese yet and probably never would be. But he wasn't American anymore, either.

"These people know how to enjoy life, Red," he said expansively, as we sat on our haunches and ate with chopsticks while his wife bustled around like a happy slave.

"Fatha Sullivan, he dead!" I wrote in my notebook on the way back to the Hilton.

Well, we didn't convert Japan, and it converted a lot of us, just as Shusaku Endo, their great novelist, always told us Japan would. Still my revived vocation kept me out of worse trouble in Japan. A few weeks after that conversation, when I was looking down the gun barrel of a North Korean tank, I was thankful that I had reformed my life. I would stand in moments before God's Judgment seat as a sinner indeed but as a penitent sinner.

Oddly enough, if I had not been ready to die, I suspect my life would have ended right there in the dust outside of Taegu.

On the 25th of June I was writing my letter of application to Maryknoll. I would be discharged in January, I told them, and as soon as I returned home I would enroll in Loyola for the second semester. With some courses in both the first- and second-semester summer sessions, I would have two years of college credit by the following autumn. Would it be possible for me to enter the seminary then?

With any luck I would still beat my brother Parn to the altar.

I had been postponing the application, probably because I was afraid to take the risk of being turned down again. The day before, however, my girlfriend, Betty Louise, had written me she was marrying Johnny Grant. "I hope you'll pray that we have a happy marriage," she said. "We love each other so very much."

It was a bucket of ice water after an all-night binge. Betty Lou's letters were cheerful and affectionate, as unlike my mother's dire warnings as June is unlike December. She was a fallback position if Maryknoll didn't want me or if I fell from grace again. Whose letters would I wait for anxiously every week and worry about if they were a day late?

I wrote her and assured her of my prayers that she and Johnny would be happy. They weren't, incidentally. Johnny is a fall-down drunk, one of their kids was killed in Nam, and another is a gay activist. Poor Betty Lou.

However, her letter called my bluff about Maryknoll. The next day I sat at my desk and painfully began to compose my application, working over it like I was a semiliterate filling out a social security form.

Our platoon sergeant rushed into my quarters. "The Commies have invaded South Korea, sir. We have a real live war on our hands."

Why did he call me "sir"? Well, as odd as it may sound, Johnny, Congress had made me an officer and a gentleman—officer's candidate school at Fort Benning after my basic training. I was as well trained to be an infantry officer as is your sister Kate.

The Sarge was excited, a Regular Army man delighted about a return to the good old days of combat.

"Go tell Captain Landis." I removed my Maryknoll application from the typewriter. "I'm sure all leaves will be canceled shortly."

"Yes, SIR." He saluted briskly and dashed off to recall our company commander from his mistress's apartment, where he went routinely without the formality of permission to leave the barracks.

The Sergeant was a tough man, tough enough to survive two years in a North Korean prison, tougher than Captain Landis, who died after a few months in the camp.

I knew when he left that it was my fate to die in the war. I would die young, just as my father did. I would go right to heaven because, God be praised, I was in the state of grace.

We were utterly unprepared to fight. I overheard our regimental CO discuss the condition of the outfit with the battalion commander.

"Has the United States Army ever been in worse shape, Frank?"

"Occupation armies are generally pretty demoralized, sir." He rubbed his chin thoughtfully. "Too much soft living—cheap booze, easy sex, weak discipline, and make-believe training exercises."

"I wouldn't want to have to lead them in combat for more than five minutes." The CO pounded his hand into his fist.

"Neither would I, sir."

Now they were going to have to lead us in combat. Most of us would die, of that I was certain.

I gathered my notes, folded them inside the half-finished letter, put the packet into a biography of Francis Xavier, and began to assemble my gear for our trip to Korea—and, as I thought, to God's Judgment seat.

Back to the PC, John, and more stories of how your father almost lost the war in Korea. I suspect that this is the longest letter from a father to a son since Lord Chesterfield. At least I'm not sounding too much like Polonius. I hope not, anyway.

If you should observe that I'm probably writing this as much for myself as for you, you'd certainly be right. I don't think often about those days anymore. Maybe I'm writing such a long letter so I can exorcise some of the dreams, especially the one in which the turret points right at me and then belches flame which consumes me.

The North Korean tank commander behind the turret was just a little too slow. The poor guy must have seen O'Day and me. Slowly the turret spun in our direction and the gun lowered toward us, only half a football field away, like a nun's accusing finger. The machine gun in the second tank began to chatter. I had the absurd fantasy that the tanks were toy vehicles and the soldiers huddling behind them were the lead models I used to mold as a kid.

"Steady, O'Day," I muttered sternly as I tried to aim my rocket launcher. The bazooka, I had been taught at the officer candidate's school at Fort Benning, is a highly effective and economical antitank weapon if properly used.

"So long as you have two men who are not afraid to die," whispered one of my classmates.

The weapon was named after a stovepipe musical instrument used by radio comedian Bob Burns, the "Arkansas Traveler" (so long ago when hoboes could be comic figures, indeed when the radio audience knew what a hobo was). It was a primitive rocket launcher. One man held the pipe on his shoulder and aimed it. At the proper moment the other man popped the rocket into the rear end of the tube. The former was exposed to enemy fire much longer than the latter.

The first man on the bazooka team had bugged out, I was not sure when or how. I knew that if I ordered O'Day to fire the launcher he would probably bug out too. "Give me the fucking thing." I grabbed the tube off his shoulder. "Prepare the ordnance."

Thus, Johnny, did your dad, a man no more designed to be a professional soldier like one of his brothers than a priest like the other brother, begin his efforts for Harry Truman's "police action" in Korea, one of the worst foul-ups in a military history that, it turns out today, has been one long string of foul-ups.

I had heard the stories that we'd won the Second World War because the other side made more mistakes than we did, but I was still confident that somewhere there was a CO who was in control. The foul-up during our first two days in Korea was so bad that I was forced to abandon that notion of the Great CO in the Sky who was in charge of everything. The United States Army had no idea how to stop the North Koreans as they swept down the peninsula. We were a handful of pebbles thrown hastily against the tide.

Even then, not knowing about the other blunders from 1775 to 1918, I was dismayed by the mess the Army made of the early weeks in Korea.

A new military term was born—"bug-out." It meant desertion under enemy fire and was technically punishable by death. However, the Army would have had to execute thousands if it tried to enforce its own law. Soft, ill-equipped and unprepared occupation troops discovered that their commanders were incompetent and ran from the enemy. There were probably other bug-outs in our history, but none of us had ever heard of them. The troops and officers who held their ground had to be resistant to contagious panic.

I watched the bug-outs like I was watching a movie about Custer's Last Stand. It was a drama happening in front of me, but I was not involved in it. I was not afraid to die. I knew I was going to die. I was in the state of grace. If I was nervous, it was less because of fear than because of the disturbing realization that there were people out there trying to kill me. Why would they want to do that? I asked myself, quite irrelevantly, as I prepared to kill some of them.

In the back of my skull a voice whispered that it was all too improbable. Of course, I wasn't going to kill anyone.

Baker Company was assigned to a roadblock outside of Taegu to cover a "redeployment" of the regiment in front of us. As we finished digging in, Able Company of that regiment came down the road pell-mell, in jeeps and armored personnel carriers and on foot, like a crowd escaping from a burning theater. Their officers were running as quickly as the men.

"Get the hell out of here," yelled the terrified soldiers, as some of them ducked behind our foxholes to escape artillery bursts across the road. My platoon was on the right side of the block, hunkered down in shallow foxholes on the rim of a low hill, a blistering and dusty saucer edge under the noonday sun.

"Kane, you're in command," Captain Landis shouted at me. "I'm going to find out what the CO wants us to do."

God help me, I believed him. A West Pointer doesn't bug out.

When he didn't come back, I suppose after fifteen minutes, though time meant nothing, some of the men broke and ran down the road. I didn't make any attempt to stop them. No one at Fort Benning had said what you were supposed to do when your troops bugged out.

I learned later that most of the company held on till the North Korean artillery fire became heavy. My platoon probably would have bugged out too, but the enemy apparently didn't know there was anyone in our position. ("Gooks," we called them in those days, though believe me, there was no hint of racial superiority in the term. After all, they were beating us.) Then the artillery quieted down. There was total silence, save for the foolish singing of idiot Korean birds who probably thought that the strange thunderstorm was over.

Then the enemy came over the opposite ridge, the first time we'd seen them, make-believe little soldiers in the distance with three make-believe tanks. Slowly, confidently, the tanks and men drifted across the rice paddies toward us, occasionally disappearing behind the clouds of dust the tanks created on the road.

"Hold your fire," I ordered, as though I knew what we were doing—and as though the Koreans were in range of our one-fifty-caliber machine gun and two Browning automatic rifles. Dimly I realized that the enemy was unaware of us and that we had the tactical advantage of surprise. I would like to be able to say that I told the men not to fire till they saw the whites of their eyes. All I managed was, "O'Day, give me that fucking bazooka."

I had not done very well in marksmanship training in OCS and had fired the antitank rocket exactly one time. We were conserving our short supply of ammo in those days.

The base of the turret was caught in my cross hairs. "Now, O'Day," I said softly, surprised by the Gary Cooper sound of my voice.

My ear exploded, my shoulder buckled as though I had been hit with a cop's club, and I choked on the smell of the exploding rocket. An image of the cop's club on my father's head flashed through my brain. There was a soft rumble in the distance and then a searing blast, like someone had opened the door of a furnace at the South Works.

To my astonishment, the Korean tank had blown up like

a Fourth of July firecracker. Their advancing troops hesitated. "Open fire," I ordered. The small-arms fire around me sounded like the clicking of rosary beads because my ear had not yet recovered from the rocket launching.

"God damn it, O'Day, another rocket," I shouted, wondering why my voice was so far away.

I aimed at the second tank, wildly, fearfully, because its machine gun had discovered us and its bullets were picking their way through the dust in our direction.

As soon as the rocket exploded next to my ear, I shoved O'Day into a foxhole and fell on top of him. The bullets brushed by, just missing.

As from a great distance, waves washing on the beach, I heard my men cheering and felt the heat of another fire. I peered over the edge of the foxhole. The second tank was on fire too. I wondered if the men in either tank had wives or sweethearts somewhere. I had neither. I never would. I was going to be a priest.

The Korean troops took cover in the dried-up paddies and returned our fire with as much accuracy as ours; no one was hitting anything—blind actors in an insane play. They were probably calling in their artillery, I thought. And almost as though I had caused it, I heard the whooshing sound of howitzer ordnance and dull thuds.

This is the end, I thought. I killed those men to save my troops and it didn't do any good.

But the puffs of dirt and dust were on their position, not ours. The remaining tank seemed to hesitate and then abruptly turned around and scurried down the road. I was now so confident of my ability with a rocket launcher that I thought about blasting him to pieces too, and then worried about the families of the men I might kill. We had beaten them. Was that not enough?

There was not much chance of my men hitting anything, but I ordered them to cease fire. "Conserve your ammo," I said. "We'll need it when they come back."

That sobered them up.

"They bug out too, sir?" said Private O'Day, who was maybe six months younger than I was.

I considered that. "They fuck up as much as we do, O'Day," I said wisely. "Well done with those rockets. If we get out of this mess, I'll see you're rewarded."

Big fucking deal, I think now. But we did get out and O'Day did get a silver star and did survive the war. I keep meaning to find out what happened to him after that.

The rest of the day we hunkered down and watched American jets, silver flashes in the cruel blue sky, blast the hell out of the next ridge of hills and listened to the steady thump of American artillery in the distance.

"Sure does look like they want to get us out of here, really bad." I joked to my men—note that they were "mine" now—mostly to cover up the fact that I had not the slightest idea of what to do next other than wait for someone, anyone from the Commander-in-Chief on down, to appear with instructions for me. Only after the sun set and it began to cool off did I realize that I had not said the Act of Contrition when that tank turret was swinging in my direction.

I never saw another live North Korean, except for a few prisoners, and never fired a weapon in Korea again either. That was my combat career, an enemy attack turned back. No American casualties, six enemy dead in the two tanks. I had killed all six of them. I still dream about them. Now they have acquired faces and personalities. They were the enemy, of course, they were trying to kill my men and to impose a communist government on our ROK allies. As bad as ROK is, it's still a lot better than the lunatic asylum north of the 38th parallel. Still, I killed those six men, cut off their lives before they had a chance really to start. I don't exactly feel guilt—or at least not like I feel guilt for my other sins. I feel sad that they are dead. I hope there's a life after death so we can have a beer or two to straighten it out.

Even now I can't quite believe what I did that morning. "You have a streak of heroism beneath all the talk," your mother said to me one night when I awoke from a dream in which those six men were pursuing me, demanding their lives back. "Why did you shoot at the second tank?"

Like a lot of her other comments, I was not sure whether my wife was speaking in admiration or exasperation.

I said, "More like a streak of insanity. Don't worry about it. I'm cured."

I wasn't cured. I did much the same damn fool thing fifteen years later in Nam during Tet. (I didn't say the Act of Contrition then, either.)

Anyway, about midnight on that Korean hill, we heard the sound of trucks and personnel carriers coming down the road. I darted out, at considerable risk of being shot.

"Fourth platoon, Baker Company, Second Battalion, Twenty-ninth Infantry Regiment," I yelled, hoping they didn't think I was a Gook.

"What are you doing here, son?" demanded a lean, silver-haired Brigadier General.

"We were ordered to hold this ridge, sir."

"Just a platoon?" He peered at my face in the darkness.

"The whole company, sir."

"Where are the others?"

"I don't know, sir."

"Bug out?"

"I don't know, sir."

The General grunted. "Anything ahead?"

"Two burned-out tanks, sir."

"Ours?"

"Theirs, sir."

"Your action?"

"Antitank rocket, sir."

He grunted again, and I thought I saw a flicker of something in his eyes under the starlight. "Tell your men to fall in. We're redeploying."

"In the direction of the enemy, sir?" I hesitated, not sure my men could take another firefight.

"Toward Pusan, son. You've been facing south all day."

Your father, great tactical genius that he was, had not noticed the sun moving from left to right across the sky.

There was a brief note about us in the official Army history of the war. The enemy had thrown an encircling arm around the south fringes of Taegu, attempting to surround the remnants of the Twenty-fourth Division. American artillery fire, bomber attacks, and effective rear-guard action defeated the tactic, and most of what was left of the Twenty-fourth escaped to Pusan. Major General Dean, our divisional commander, was captured resisting enemy tanks with a bazooka.

We were that effective rear guard. I kind of wished that the military historian had given us credit for pure dumb luck and nothing else.

When we passed the second tank, I saw a corpse in moonlight, hanging outside the hatch. Probably it was the man who had been firing the machine gun at O'Day and me. The picture of his limp body is scorched on my memory so that I will never forget it.

The next morning the General told me I was acting CO of the company and would be recommended for the Distinguished Service Cross.

"Private O'Day should be decorated too, sir."

The General, who later became Army Chief of Staff, grinned. "I'll take care of it, son. You're a good officer."

Maybe I would have been, but my combat career was over. During my brief term as CO of Baker Company, we suffered only one casualty—me.

Hero as goat, Johnny. I suppose in your rhetoric class they've told you about irony?

Anyway, in a few days the Pusan beachhead was swarming with troops and equipment. The Army was preparing to fight the war the way it liked to fight, with an overwhelming superiority of men and matériel. There were rumors that the Marines were going to land somewhere up north to surround the whole North Korean Army the way they tried to surround us at Taegu.

My outfit, including some of the shamefaced bug-outs we found in Pusan, men who had been fortunate enough to bug out in the right direction, was built back up to full strength by replacements they had found in Hawaii. "Green replacements," I had the arrogance to call them. We were rushed from place to place along the Pusan perimeter to resist enemy probes, but never quite made it in time for combat. I was convinced of my invulnerability. So were the men in the company, who had turned my fumbling with the bazooka into a legend.

The night before the breakout from the beachhead the air was shattered by a titanic artillery duel, nothing like Stalingrad, I'm sure, but a big deal for us, Jove and his friends playing with bowling balls in the sky. Gradually, the guns on the other side fell silent, wiped out by superior American power.

"It'll be a piece of cake tomorrow," I told my men.

At that moment a stray enemy shell, one of the last they fired, I suppose, banged into our line of foxholes, more or less as an afterthought, it seemed—far enough in front of us, I judged, so that we would not take losses.

The cop's club again, this time as big as a skyscraper, slamming into my chest and shoulder. Incredible pain, an iron of fire pressed against my body, then sleepy dullness—life slipping away.

"Good God, the Old Man has bought it," O'Day was sobbing above me.

This time I did say the Act of Perfect Contrition. Or at least I tried to. In the States when the war was over, O'Day, who was not much of a wit, insisted that what came out was the grace before meals.

Great Joker, Red Kane.

I also think I told God I loved Him, but I cannot remember with any certainty.

After that, wild dreams and intense pain alternating with drugged sleepiness. Someone in white said, "No problem here." Then darkness, a bumpy ride in a truck during which my chest felt like it was in a volcano. Then motion sickness in an airplane picking its way through a storm.

Finally, a white and comfortable room in a hospital. And a pretty face with a halo of blond hair above.

"Hey, we got ourselves a sure-enough hero here." Pure mountain red-neck accent. "And he's kind of cute, too."

And that, Johnny, was the end of my "suffering" in the Korean War. As I reread this letter, I wonder if you will feel that the naïve, troubled, and badly frightened young man could not possibly be the same person as your father.

Probably you will not be able to believe it.

Neither, anymore, do I believe it. Yet I wish I could go

back to that hospital room and live my life again. Which is a paternal Polonius saying, "Don't waste your youth because you have it only once."

Big deal.

13

When Red Kane came back from Korea he became a journalist instead of a priest, but a journalist with a missionary's zeal, much to the dismay of his colleagues and especially of his mentor, Paul O'Meara.

"Look, kid," said Paul one day in 1953, tossing aside the commodity pages of the *Chicago Journal of Commerce*, "why don't you leave some corruption for the next generation to fight? You don't have to clean up Chicago all by yourself."

Red felt his face grow warm. Paul was his hero, his ideal, his substitute father. Hence, Paul's occasional ridicule of Red's zeal struck at the heart of his new mission in life.

"All I'm asking is why we don't tell the truth about what is happening," Red said, feeling like an altar boy who had just been reprimanded by Monsignor.

They were sitting in a bar on Wells Street where the pols hung out. It was only ten-thirty in the morning and too early for even the thirstiest pol to be gulping his first scotch and water. Not, however, too early for Paul, who was reputed to have a drink with breakfast.

"We all know," he replied, caressing his drink lovingly, like part of a woman's body, "that Senator Joseph McCarthy is a drunken phony, but we don't say it. We all know that Martin Kennelly, whom we praise as an honest Mayor, is totally incompetent, but we don't say it. We all know that your friend Harv Gunther is a crook, but we pretend that he's a civic leader. Don't you get the point? What we know isn't always news. What is true is not always what we print. We're in the news business, not the truth business."

Paul was thirty-five years old, though his disorderly white hair, long by the style of the time, made him look older. He was handsome in the red-faced, pudgy style of an Irish bartender or undertaker, perhaps fifteen pounds overweight, already an alcoholic, it was whispered, because his bitchy wife and six noisy kids had driven him to it. He spoke as he wrote, smoothly and elegantly, putting graceful sentences together effortlessly and delivering them in a flowing, whiskey-baritone voice that suggested he might have been an actor instead of a reporter if he had so chosen. He was political editor of the *Herald Gazette* and was supposed to be in line to succeed Mike Kelly as editor when that giant, about whose alcohol addiction there was no debate, finally did himself in. Paul was also, by universal agreement, the best goddamn reporter in town.

He took Red under his wing, taught him how to write a lead, how to end a story, how to limit truth to 750 words, how to conduct an interview, how to spell, how to punctuate, how to fight rewrite men, how to keep editors happy—the rote technical skills that he had to learn before he could fulfill his dream of becoming a great journalistic crusader.

"We go after an occasional crooked cop, or even a crooked police captain like Tubbo Dan Gilbert when he runs for State's Attorney, but we ignore the corruption that pervades every aspect of city government life," Red said hotly.

"Better say 'every aspect of life,'" Paul sighed. "Don't think that the boys over at the Continental Illinois or up at the Chancery office are any more honest...and you noted that the paper which did Tubbo in—and a lot of good men like Senator Scott Lucas, too—published a feature series on him not long before in which he was not Tubbo Dan but the Fabulous Dan Gilbert."

"Why?" Red demanded. "Which time were they deliberately lying?"

"Easy, lad, easy." He gestured soothingly at Red with his glass and sipped gently from it. "The first piece was probably written because someone over there owed Tubbo a favor and the second because the editor or the publisher or somebody decided they needed an exposé and maybe another Pulitzer, which they got, incidentally. I don't blame them, though

Lucas was a good majority leader in the United States Senate. Too bad."

It was the autumn of 1953, the war in Korea was over, Stalin had died, a frightened young Elizabeth II had been crowned Queen of England, Eisenhower was destroying the English language at his press conferences, the Rosenbergs had been executed, Leon Uris's *Battle Cry* was on the top of the best-seller lists, *Roman Holiday* with the wondrous Audrey Hepburn was everyone's favorite film, and Marian and Red sang "I Love Paris" in her car on their dates. Red told her they would go to Paris on their honeymoon after she graduated and he won his first Pulitzer.

He was home from the wars, with some interesting scars and an occasional twinge in his arm and chest to remind him of the shrapnel that had saved him from fighting the rest of the Korean War. Weeks after he was wounded he learned the details of the great military victory of the Inchon landing which had boxed up the whole North Korean Army. It would be the last victory for the American military in this century. Thirty-three years without winning anything, not bad for the most powerful nation in the world with the biggest defense budget in the world.

Douglas MacArthur blew Inchon by letting the Chinese mousetrap him up at the Yalu River.

Red had fallen from grace in Japan. The missionary position and a lot of other positions, too, replaced his missionary vocation. He never did find the letter of application he had been working on the day of the Korean invasion, nor the biography of Saint Francis Xavier into which he had folded it. He was now a reporter for the *Herald Gazette*, a frequently bored night-school student at Loyola, and a hopelessly bemused suitor of Marian Tracey, whom he hoped to marry as soon as she graduated from Barat College of the Sacred Heart in Lake Forest.

Red became a reporter by accident, more or less. Mike Kelly's son had been in his company and credited Red with saving his life that hot noontime outside of Taegu. The old man took him out to lunch after he returned from Japan and offered him a job. "I don't know whether you want to be a newspaperman or whether you'd be any good at it," he boomed at Red—Mike had two voices, loud and louder—"but if you want a shot at it, you'd be welcome at the *Herald*."

Red's teachers in high school had said he could be a good writer if he learned to spell, but it hadn't made much of an impression on him. What need did a priest have to be a writer?

When it turned out that he wasn't good enough to be a priest, he had to be something. Why not a journalist? It was no worse than anything else if you can't be a priest. So Red took the job, served as a copyboy for six months, and then was promoted to the police beat. That was the way young men learned the trade in those days (unless they served as slaves in the City News Bureau, a job that for many Chicago journalists was the first step to chronic alcoholism). No one started out as an investigative reporter, not even on the *Washington Post*.

Red was confident that he had found his vocations—journalism and Marian. His mother objected to both, Marian because her family was too "hoity-toity" and journalism because "You'll meet the wrong kind of men." She was right on both counts, to tell the truth. Her real objection, however, was that the *Herald* and Marian were obstacles to his return to the seminary. Having lost both her husbands, Red's mother wanted to share her sons only with God. She watched over what she thought was Red's vocation with the vigilance of an Irish warrior queen protecting her domain from Danish pirates and Norman invaders.

Lindy, the blond nurse at the hospital in Yokohama, was his downfall, and God knows he was ready for a downfall. Korea had wiped God and sin temporarily out of his mind. Lindy was there to replace them. A sleek and slender little mountain creature from the hollows of West Virginia, with no sense of sexual morality at all. "I had my first boy in sixth grade," she laughed one night. "It was lots of fun."

She was a competent nurse and responsible in her care of patients and hospital supplies—at a time when a lot of safe money could be made by snitching drugs for the black market. She was also a devout churchgoing Baptist. But as she put it, "Ah'm sure God doesn't object much to screwing. Otherwise why did He make it so much fun?"

A position with which Red had come to have some intellectual sympathy through the years.

They didn't make love in the hospital. Lindy didn't think that would be "ethical." She did, however, tease Red so openly that he was delirious with desire for her by the time he was finally released. That night, ignoring his mother's warnings about the dangers to his virtue and his vocation that he might encounter from nurses, he made love to Lindy.

She was astonished at his skills. "Where did a sure-enough Irish Catholic boy from Chicago learn so much so young?" she demanded dreamily as she stroked his back. Lindy was his most sensuous sexual partner before Eileen and a more comic and fun-loving bedmate than Eileen.

Red couldn't have enough of her. When they were not together he could think of nothing else. He was obsessed, he later decided, and thought he was in love, neither the first nor the last time he made that mistake.

He was also convinced that he would be sent back to Korea. The last time he had wanted to face the end in the state of grace. This time he wanted to face it with as much experience of pleasure as possible. When he found out that he was being redeployed to the United States, he told Lindy that they were going to be married. Life without her would be impossible. They loved one another. Why not marriage?

"You don't give me orders, Irish," she said, serious for a moment. "I don't care whether you're a captain and a hero; you ask."

Red asked.

"We're great in bed," she said slowly in the same tone of voice she used for explaining Scripture quotes, "and I like you a lot, but it wouldn't work.... I know you're going to try to persuade me that it would, and you're clever with words, but in a couple of years you'll thank me for saying no."

Red begged, he pleaded, he raged, he sulked. He even made a little progress. But Lindy finally stuck to her guns and they parted coolly, with Red playing the hurt-and-rejected-lover role.

He remembered God on the MAT DC-6 flying to San

Francisco. With that memory came the terror that they would crash and his Act of Perfect Contrition wouldn't be perfect enough to satisfy God. He found a priest in a parish church near the Presidio and poured out his sins, prepared to take his bawling-out like a man.

"If that plane had crashed and you were not able to make an Act of Perfect Contrition you would have gone to hell for all eternity. Do you realize that?"

"Yes, Father."

"The woman carries the burden of mortal sin on her soul. You are damning her to hell, too, unless she confesses it."

"She's not Catholic, Father."

The priest hit the ceiling. "Then she is almost certainly damned. She does not have the grace of Confession. Most Protestants do not know the Act of Perfect Contrition. You must do penance for the rest of your life to storm heaven to win forgiveness for her. Do you understand?"

"Yes, Father."

Red knew even then that the priest was wrong about Lindy. Maybe he would have gone to hell for their sins. But God would not have damned Lindy. First of all, she didn't think it was a mortal sin. And second, God had to love Lindy as much as he did. How could anyone help but love her?

Lindy freed him of his vocation to the priesthood. The intense young Jesuit who presided over the Young Christian Students group at Loyola, to whose meetings Marian dragged Red, gave him a new vocation. The Catholic layman, Red learned, had a vocation too, to the "temporal order" in which he bore witness to the Church and to Christ by exercising the "witness of professional competence." "You don't become a butcher," the priest enthused, "to make converts in your butcher shop. You become a butcher to serve people by providing them with meat and by doing so in the most professionally excellent manner."

So Red joined the staff of the *Herald* with a deep conviction, which his mother could not comprehend no matter how often he tried to explain it to her, that this was as much a vocation as his previous commitment to Christianize Japan.

Red couldn't explain it to Paul, either. But Paul never

ridiculed his religious motivation, except by pointing out that the young secretaries at the *Herald* found Red more attractive when he was playing his comedian role.

"How are we ever going to end the corruption?" Red demanded that morning in 1953. "Will we ever elect a reform government?"

Paul sighed. "That will change the actors but not the play. Take the traffic court in which you're so interested. Every traffic court in the country is crooked because you have an elaborate set of laws which must be arbitrarily enforced and which can cause some people to lose their right to drive, a right on which they think their lives or their livelihoods depend. Corruption is inevitable."

"We have to change that," Red insisted grimly.

"Clean out the present mess," Paul predicted, "and you'll have a worse one. Let me tell you my favorite reformer story. Frank Knox, him that was Secretary of the Navy during the war and not a bad one at that, decided after he and Alf Landon were buried in the 1936 presidential election that the time had come for him to have some political power locally. So the *Daily News*, which was his paper, decided to run Tom Courtny, the State's Attorney, against Ed Kelly, the stumblebum who was Mayor. The *News* was immediately filled with pictures of Tom smashing gambling machines with an ax as he personally led raids against what we didn't call the crime syndicate in those days. The other papers dutifully reported the raids but without so much enthusiasm. We didn't say that the joints were open two days later. Nor did we tell the people of Chicago that all the time Tom was running as a 'reform' Democrat, and indeed a gambling-table-smashing Democrat, he and the brother of the local pastor were running the biggest book in the city, four blocks from the parish rectory."

"Why not?" Red demanded fiercely.

Paul sighed again. "You haven't been listening, son. First of all, it was truth not news. Secondly, we knew Ed Kelly and the machine would bury him anyway."

"It's gotta stop somewhere, Paul," he replied fervently. "I'm going to do all I can to stop it."

"Lots of luck, kid. I thought that way too when I was your age. Davie, this glass seems to have been affected by rapid evaporation. Could you wet it again, ever so slightly?"

From the Kane File

Time, March 22, 1956

"A reporter has a vocation as much as a priest," says the youngest of this year's Pulitzer Prize winners. "The priesthood is more important, maybe, but that does not mean that the other vocations are any less Catholic or Christian. The new generation of Catholic laity understands that just as the priest's mission is to the Church, our mission is to the world."

Twenty-six-year-old Redmond Peter Kane, tall, broad shouldered and movie-star handsome, once studied for the Roman Catholic priesthood and then earned the Distinguished Service Cross for valor in Korea. All he would need to look like a priest is a Roman collar beneath his curly brown hair and serious blue eyes.

"Dedication isn't enough," Kane insists. "We have to be good at what we do." While some fellow reporters think there is a touch of the fanatic in Kane's zeal and his monastic life—he lives with his mother and dates rarely—they do not question that he is good at what he does. His investigation of the connection between organized crime and corrupt traffic court judges receives the plaudits of all his colleagues.

"It's the kind of mature work we'd expect from a man ten years older," says *Herald Gazette* editor Mike Kelly, who describes himself as "absolutely delighted over the prize."

Kane seems less delighted. "The Kefauver committee can roam around the country attracting attention to organized crime and itself," he says sternly. "Unless local authorities take a hard look at what's going on in their cities, nothing will happen. In a few months or a few years the Cook County Traffic Court will be as bad as ever."

Kane's solution? "We need to restructure institutions, a whole new approach to traffic regulation, for example. We also need a reform of morals, motorists, judges, lawyers, police; everyone involved must realize how much harm they are doing to the social order." He smiles slightly, hinting at the famed Kane impish wit. "We reporters must realize that even more important than winning prizes is telling the truth."

"Red Kane still has to grow up," says one disgruntled Chicago veteran, who thinks Kane was "too young" for the prize. "Give him ten years and maybe he'll be a pretty good reporter."

Editor Kelly disagrees. "We could use twenty more like Red."

Herald Gazette, October 15, 1956

STEVENSON WOMAN SAYS "THE VICTORY DOES NOT MATTER"

by Redmond P. Kane

Kate Collins Ryan's lively blue eyes sparkle with amusement. You feel that she sees through you and still finds you entertaining.

"So you think that one should only work for a candidate who is likely to win?" she asks.

You squirm uncomfortably. You're the reporter, after all. You should be asking the questions.

No. You merely wondered about how it feels to coordinate Women for Stevenson in Illinois when the poll shows your candidate far behind the enormously popular President Ike—despite the President's health problems.

Mrs. Ryan, a stylish and extremely attractive woman in her early forties, slender, pale, and elegant, has a knack of not answering your questions. "You're like my kids. A new generation of cool, dispassionate professionals. Never would do a darn fool thing like joining the Communist party when they were young."

Mrs. Ryan has steered the conversation to a delicate subject, her onetime membership in the Communist party. Does she feel that it is an obstacle to her political involvement now?

Again no direct answer. "Sometimes I wish that kids these days would just once do something stupid so they could learn from the mistakes of youthful enthusiasm. How many youthful mistakes have you made, Mr. Kane?"

You stir uneasily. She's too pretty to be a mother superior and too humorous to be a policewoman, but you have to watch your step with Kate Collins Ryan.

She continues to fuss with the reluctant mimeograph as the interview goes on.

Plenty, you say fervently.

She seems surprised. "Really? Now, my kids would never admit that. Anyway, I suppose that each generation needs its own style. You cool professional types are likely to be replaced by raving maniacs who will make me look sober and responsible. The thing is to learn to stick by your convictions whether or not you think you're going to win. Isn't it?"

Finally an answer to your first question. Before you can note it down, you find yourself pressed into service to repair the mimeo. It is necessary, you note gently, that the stencil be put on right side up.

How does Mr. Ryan feel about Mrs. Ryan's political and social involvement? Of course there is no straight or immediate answer. You discuss her daughter's medical school training and her boyfriend, who is a psychiatrist. You discuss her son, who wants to be a priest as your brother does—how she knows that you do not ask. You hear about a teenage daughter with green eyes that is the only quiet one in the family, except when she loses her temper. Then she's really beautiful. She may be a witch, you are told, but a beautiful witch. You'd like her. You are the type that goes for beautiful witches with flaming tempers.

You suggest in self-defense that perhaps the daughter who wants to be a psychiatrist like her boyfriend comes by it naturally. Maybe so too does the green-eyed witch.

"I don't know how Ned puts up with us," she says of her husband, a distinguished Chicago attorney and retired Navy Admiral. "I guess he must enjoy the act."

You realize belatedly that another one of your questions has been answered. The mimeo is working again. You thank Kate Ryan for the interview and slip away quietly before you are inveigled into meeting the green-eyed witch. Life has enough problems as it is. You tell yourself as you ride down the elevator that if the teenage girl grows up to be like her mother, she won't need witchlike powers to be an amazing woman.

14

The last time he saw Paul was on a wintry night in January of 1963, a couple of months after the Cuban missile crisis. Paul had remained profoundly skeptical about the Kennedys until the crisis. He teased Red with stories of the President's marital infidelities, gossip that if anything understated the President's obsession with sex. Red didn't believe the stories in those days, not really. On the other hand, he was in no position to be critical. His own confusing and unsatisfying love affairs were always with beautiful women of the sort the President was alleged to be pursuing. Nor was it clear to Red that if he ever did marry—and that seemed unlikely—he would be able to remain faithful to one woman.

The missile crisis, however, made a believer even of Paul. Revisionists like that silly Kennedy hater Professor Gary Wills, Paul had argued, might rewrite the story of those tumultuous October days to deceive the young who were not alive or couldn't remember them. The revisionists could only do so by blocking out their own memories of the events.

Paul and Red had eaten supper at Ricardo's, the official hangout of the press, and both of them had drunk too much. They walked back to the paper in the snow, to plan a series they were going to do on the civil rights problem. They both felt that the race issue was bound to explode soon and that the Kennedys would have to abandon their caution after the 1964 presidential election.

"Ten years, is it?" Paul asked, pouring both of them a strong drink from the J & B bottle that was always stashed in a locked drawer of his desk.

"More like eleven." Red sipped his whiskey uneasily. Time

was slipping away. He was thirty-two years old now, a prize-winning reporter who already drank too much, a frequent TV guest, and an accomplished if unhappy bachelor-about-town. Yet he still felt like a dumb kid in Paul's presence.

"God knows you've done well." Paul gulped half of his glass of scotch. "I bet you win another Pulitzer in this decade."

"It doesn't make any difference," he said. "The important thing is to do the job well."

Red was at the height of his Kennedy idealism—competence, intelligence, service, vision. There were some problems left, but the cool, pragmatic rationalists like Red would solve them all. Resist communism all over the world and conquer injustice at home—probably before the 1968 presidential election.

He still went to church on Sunday, but his sex life kept him away from Communion. He told himself occasionally that he was exercising his lay vocation and that eventually he would straighten out his relationship with God. However, the pleasures of the job were so great that he no longer needed a sense of vocation.

"Are you on to something, Paul?" Red asked cautiously. Red's friend had seemed especially preoccupied in the last couple of weeks since Red and Gayle, his blond model, had returned from a week in Acapulco.

"Nothing special," he murmured, filling both glasses again with a faintly unsteady hand.

"The fun's gone out of it for you, hasn't it?"

Paul shrugged and downed most of his glass. "What's fun?" he asked, the way Pontius Pilate might have asked, What is truth?

"Anything interesting from your friend Harvard this afternoon?" Red sipped at his drink much more cautiously.

Red was still living at home. Dav, already a Captain in the Army, was at the embassy in London; Parn was doing graduate work in canon law in Rome. Red felt that he couldn't leave his mother alone. She didn't like his late hours and certainly suspected that he wasn't a celibate. But they had a kind of unspoken agreement that he would live at home and she would not ask any questions. The nights Red was home, he read until he fell asleep—fiction, history, psychology. Catching up on the college education he had not had time to finish.

His mother kept after him about "finding some nice girl." Yet any nice girl he might find would be instantly rejected as a threat to his mother's power over Red. Sure enough, when Red finally did find a nice girl, or maybe was found by one, his mother hated her on sight. So Red defended his Irish bachelor state—a stereotype to the point of caricature—with the excuse that he had to take care of his mother. It was commonly said among his friends that Red Kane would not marry while his mother was still alive. Since she was in her early fifties, it looked like a long-term sentence to bachelorhood.

"Don't pry, kid," Paul snapped. Then he added quickly, rubbing his hand over his eyes, "Sorry, Red, feeling a little tired, I guess. You understand how it is with me and Harv. He knows I want to put him behind bars and he enjoys the game."

"Like playing poker with a hungry tiger."

"Something like that. Walk me over to the bridge, will you? I have to meet a person from the opposition on the other side. You ought not to keep Gayle waiting."

At the mention of her name, he felt his lips moisten. She was a luscious dish, uncomplaining about his demands, even if she was, like so many beautiful women, devoid of intense sexual feelings and needs. On a cold winter night a reasonably warm blond is just what a lonely Irish Catholic reporter needs.

Red had no premonition when he shook hands with Paul in the blinding blizzard. It was a quick handshake because Red wanted to get to the State Street subway station and out of the snow.

Paul was never seen again.

The night with Gayle was like the others, maybe a little better because of the contrast between body heat and winter storm. Red could survive for months, even years, without a woman. Then the fantasy would begin again and the obsession follow shortly thereafter.

The fantasy was to pursue and capture a woman and

then to make her deliriously happy. The first two phases were easy. On the third he always failed. Routinely he would choose women who had no interest in his special sexual skills. After sex was over, he had no idea of how one would go about making a woman happy.

Red told himself that if he ever discovered a woman who really wanted an accomplished lover his problems would be solved. Then he did discover one such woman—or perhaps it was the other way around—and he learned that such entertainments suffice for no more than a couple of months.

The next morning, about ten-thirty, Joe Crawford from the *Sun-Times* was on the phone.

"Did you see Paul last night?"

"I ate supper with him and walked him over to the bridge. Were you the one he was meeting? He was kind of obscure about why."

"Called me late in the afternoon, said he had to see me at nine-thirty. Mysterious. I thought I saw the two of you on the other side of the bridge, then the snow blocked my vision. When it cleared a little I didn't see either of you."

"Notice the time?" Red stood up from his desk uneasily.

"Nine twenty-five."

"You saw us all right. He walked across the bridge into the snow."

Red motioned for Mike Kelly, who was drifting through the newsroom on one of his periodic reconnaissance trips in which he seemed to observe nothing and actually saw everything.

"And didn't emerge on the other side." Joe sounded nervous. "After a half hour I crossed over to your side and there was no one there. Called him at his apartment last night and this morning. No answer."

"Any cars cross after you saw him and before you crossed?"

"Good God, Red, no! You don't think..."

"Hang on, Joe, I'd better tell Mike...."

That was it. There were many ways Joe could have been deceived. Paul might have crouched behind a pillar of the bridge and remained unseen in the darkness and the snow. Then when Joe strolled to their side, Paul might have walked in the opposite direction, caught a cab, and slipped away.

Or he could have jumped into the river, which did not freeze over till morning.

Or he could have been pushed. But by whom?

His family was well provided for. Paul had made a lot of money in the stock market boom during and after the war and invested it well. It was in a joint account with his wife so that she could use the money immediately. There was also a million-dollar life insurance policy for which she would have to wait either seven years or until a court pronounced him dead. Both the policy and the investment portfolio, about which Paul had never spoken to anyone as far as the cops could learn, dated back twenty years. There were no signs of any immediate preparations for departure or disappearance.

"All that money and he still put the bite on us for ten dollars here, twenty-five dollars there." Mike chewed meditatively on his cigar.

"The money was for his family," Red replied defensively.

"You were the softest touch of all." Mike considered the end of his cigar, debating whether to relight it. "But then, you're a soft touch for everyone in the city room, Red."

Mike warned Red at least once a month about saving his money.

"It won't do me any good when I end up in the Chicago River." Red turned on his heel and strode out of Mike's office.

The word went around the *Herald Gazette* quickly: Leave Red alone for a couple of weeks.

Red was able to tell the police only that Paul had seemed tired and preoccupied. He added that Paul often seemed that way.

"There was nothing unusual about his mood, Officer. He was a melancholy man as long as I've known him."

He had never snapped at Red before. But Red thought the cops were too dumb to take that seriously.

Harv Gunther informed the police that Paul was in fine spirits and had spoken of a vacation in Arizona during which he could watch the Sox in spring. "He was convinced that they would be red hot this season, really excited about their prospects."

That comment made Red suspicious. Paul was certainly a Sox fan. He'd gone on spring training trips before. But he had said nothing to Red about such a trip.

"Doesn't prove a thing," Mike Kelly boomed, tossing a pile of papers on his desk. "And everyone knows that you hate Gunther. It won't stand up."

"I know that." He was looking out the window of Mike's office, staring at the Wabash Avenue Bridge. "Still, Gunther is lying. And I wonder why."

"Because it is in his nature to lie."

So the investigation faded away like the end of autumn. Three years later the courts decided that Paul Thomas O'Meara was officially dead.

If he was still unofficially alive in 1983, he was not an old man, only in his early sixties. Probably he was murdered that night by hired guns of Harvard Princeton Gunther. Yet Red was never completely convinced. Next to the thick Gunther file in his locked cabinet was a thin file on the disappearance of Paul O'Meara.

Before he was swatted with the cosmic baseball bat, Red occasionally removed both files and stared at them, kicking himself for leaving Gunther free on the streets of Chicago and for failing to avenge Paul.

Two more failures about which to feel guilty.

from the Opinion Section of the Sunday *Herald Gazette*, September 1, 1963

WHAT NEXT FOR CIVIL RIGHTS MOVEMENT

by Redmond Peter Kane

WASHINGTON, D.C., August 28—It was by anyone's standards quite a speech—or should I say sermon? Martin Luther King is a preacher by profession, a religious leader. What we heard from him today was as much religion as it was politics. No one will ever deny that the "I have a dream" sermon is one of the most masterful sermons ever preached.

There is a festive air among the army of reporters who covered the March on Washington. Two hundred thousand Americans of both races came to the nation's capital to demand an end to racial injustice. It is a turning point, his colleagues tell me; American society will never be the same again.

Yet this reporter, acknowledging the justice of Reverend King's cause and the brilliance of his sermon, must also set down for the record some reservations about his strategy.

Passive resistance has been an extremely effective tactic for the civil rights movement. I sensed today that it was becoming a strategy. "We Shall Overcome" is a deeply moving spiritual. I sensed today that it has become a substitute for a program.

One can endorse the demand for immediate justice and still realize that justice cannot be achieved at once. Yet any other alternative than the immediate end of all the effects of racism is now denounced as "gradualism."

I don't see how an intelligent person can reasonably expect change in a society to be anything but gradual. Some of my colleagues here tell me that Gandhi brought the British Empire to its knees with passive resistance. They forget two things—Hindus are a majority in India while blacks are not a majority in the United States. And the bloody war between Hindus and Moslems at the time of partition and independence left several million dead.

Passive resistance as a strategy has historically opened the way to violence, murder, even genocide. It may be necessary to sweep away respect for law to overcome injustice, but if one does so, one should be aware that one may eventually have to reap the whirlwind. Minorities who systematically violate the law for their own just causes may come to learn that they need the protection of the law more than anyone else.

Moreover, the shift from the ordinary political process of negotiation and compromise to the politics of festival and demonstrations runs one enormous risk: The other side can demonstrate too. And the other side might be bigger.

I suspect that the Reverend Dr. King is still a man of negotiation and compromise as he has always been. Certainly most of the other leaders of the March on Washington are committed to gradualism, though they shy away now from the word.

Yet I am afraid. Today American politics went into the streets. Even a slight knowledge of history would make one wary of what happens after politics takes that turn.

The Kennedy administration clearly did not like the idea of the march. It is not their sort of pragmatic practical politics. However, they quickly moved to make it their own, on the whole successfully. Politics on the streets will simply be one more variable to take into account in their skilled and sophisticated calculus. Hence there is no reason to believe that mass meetings and demonstrations will tear apart the social fabric of America and set group against group. There is only a slight chance that such politics might in the long run do more harm to a good cause than good.

Nonetheless, that possibility is a cloud on the horizon, no bigger than a man's hand, as the Bible says, which is enough to make this reporter, who has covered every civil rights conflict since Little Rock and is in his personal convictions solidly on Reverend Dr. King's side, uneasy and uncertain.

from the *Chicago Herald Gazette,* March 1, 1964

Kane New Political Editor

Michael Kelly, editor-in-chief of the *Herald Gazette,* announced today that Redmond P. Kane, roving reporter for the *Herald Gazette,* will become acting political editor, replacing Paul O'Meara, who mysteriously disappeared last year.

"We hope that Paul will turn up healthy and happy. I'm sure no one will be more pleased than Red Kane when that happens. However, until then the *Herald Gazette* needs a full-time political editor. We are confident that Red, who learned the trade from Paul, will do a fine job."

Kane, 32, won the Pulitzer Prize in 1956 for an exposé of scandals in the Cook County Traffic Court. He was recently married to Eileen Ryan, daughter of attorney Edward Ryan and the late Kate Collins Ryan.

15

From the Kane File

from the Opinion Section of the Sunday
Herald Gazette, August 25, 1968—excerpt

CONGRATULATIONS TO ALL AND TO ALL A GOOD NIGHT

by Redmond Peter Kane

I want to congratulate everyone concerned before I bow out of the 1968 presidential campaign—congratulations first of all to Abbie Hoffman, David Dellinger and Jerry Rubin for seducing the Chicago police force into violence. Congratulations to the police superintendent and his subordinates for letting their men run out of control and do exactly what the hippy/Yippie/sicky invaders wanted them to do. Congratulations to the national media for distorting what happened beyond recognition; congratulations especially to Walter Cronkite, that pious phony, for letting Da Mare make a damn fool out of him. Congratulations to Gene McCarthy for sulking around like a spoiled brat. Congratulations to Da Mare for playing into the hands of his enemies. Congratulations to my fellow Chicago journalists for abasing themselves to the juvenile delinquents from New York and not telling the truth about the sloppy journalism of the drunks, dope addicts, sex freaks, and Chicago haters who came to town with press credentials in their grubby paws this week.

Why did we hear nothing on local TV, for example, about the network team that staged its own mock violence when it couldn't find any real violence for the six o'clock news?

Why didn't some Chicago reporter challenge the argument that "advocacy journalism" must make the news when there is no news to fit your message?

Oh yes, congratulations to everyone, because, you know what you've done, you damn fools? You've elected Tricky

Dicky Nixon, that's what you've done. That's how history is going to judge these last few crazy weeks. Brilliant, just brilliant. Don't tell me that there is no difference between Nixon and Humphrey. If you think that, you have no memories and no sense. Will Humphrey end the war quicker than Tricky Dicky? Is the Pope Catholic? Mark my words, four years from now this damn fool war will still be going on. And it will be your fault. I hope you're all proud of yourselves.

Early in the morning after the riots in front of the Conrad Hilton in August of 1968, Red Kane dashed into the dimly lit corridor of St. Luke's Hospital and raced in what he thought was the direction of the emergency room. At the end of the corridor he encountered a security guard who demanded to know who he thought he was. Red threatened to break his fat stupid neck unless he let him into the emergency room. Thoroughly frightened, the guard pointed in the opposite direction. Red turned and raced that way.

At three o'clock in the morning Red had finally entered the door of their apartment on Belmont Avenue, near Wrigley Field. Johnny and Patty were sound asleep, as was the housekeeper. Eileen wasn't home yet. No surprise. The U.S. Attorney's office would have a busy night, trying to reimpose a thin pattern of law and order on the chaos of Chicago. The unrest would only last another day or two. When the TV cameras left the city, so would the rabble. Both would leave behind anger, frustration, disillusionment, and indictments for which there would be no convictions.

A tidal wave of absurdity on which Richard Milhous Nixon would ride into the White House.

Red poured himself an extra-strong shot of Jameson's. Now was the time to get completely drunk, if there were ever such a time.

He wished Eileen were home. She was three months pregnant, the result of a baby they'd made in a furious outburst of passion when he came back from Asia. Red was worried about what might happen to a pregnant woman anywhere near the rabble. Yet it was too late now to draw the line on Eileen. Indeed, it was too late at the very beginning to try to draw such a line.

He had looked for her in the melee in front of the Conrad Hilton, but he hadn't deliberately searched her out. It would have been a violation of their unspoken agreement—Red and Eileen were great ones for unspoken agreements—that neither would ever interfere in the other's work.

The phone rang.

"Red, Jim Craig." He sounded as if he were trying to reassure before bad news. "I'm over at St. Luke's with Eileen. She got a whiff of tear gas last night. She's okay. We've been trying to get through to you for the last two hours...."

"I'll be right over." Red hung up the phone, emptied the Jameson's in the sink, and rushed through the hot summer night to his VW Bug. As he drove recklessly down a mostly empty Lake Shore Drive, he thanked God that he had not drunk the Jameson's. Eileen would not think that he was unavailable for Craig's phone call because he was drunk somewhere.

Eileen's temper, about which her mother had warned him, had faded away with the years, as had their sexual passion for each other, save for an occasional explosive interlude. She had given up trying to reform him with anger. That was a loss for both of them, because her most spectacular outbursts were often followed by equally spectacular sex. The day he came home from Viet Nam, a hero reporter who had risked his life to save Vietnamese civilians in the U.S. embassy, she had raged at him for the better part of an hour, not because he had taken risks, but because he had not kept in touch with her—a perfectly valid reason for anger. In the wild coupling that followed, the best sex they'd ever had together, poor troubled Katie came into existence.

Dear God, he prayed on the way to the hospital, *spare her for me. Give me another chance. I love her. I love You. Help me to be better.*

He was granted the new chance, not that he made anything of it.

Eileen and Jim were sitting on a hard bench in the hallway outside emergency. Her face was stained from weeping, her eyes red and sore, her hair tangled, her white summer suit torn and dirty, her stockings ripped. She was wearing only one shoe. A countess who had barely escaped from a mob.

"I'm all right, Red." She threw herself into his arms. "I'm all right, so's the kid. Don't worry, darling. Don't worry. It's all right."

"Damn it, woman." He held her tightly. "Stop fretting about me and let me fret about you for a change."

All of them laughed and relaxed a bit.

"The doctors want to keep an eye on me for another hour or two, just to make sure that nothing's going to happen."

"Purely precautionary," said Craig lightly.

Red's mind began to operate again. Tear gas could cause a messy face and red eyes. It would not account for the rest of her disarray.

"The rabble push you around?" His hands tightened on her arms.

"Cops," said Craig bluntly. "They thought she was a Yippie."

"In a white suit with nylons and heels?" He turned away and pounded the wall viciously.

"They've gone mad over there, Red. You know that." She dabbed her eyes with a tissue and kissed him again.

"They had her on the ground," Craig said grimly. "Thank God Nick Curran and I saw them before they began to use their clubs."

I should have been there protecting her, Red thought, and then realized that it was a reaction Eileen would not appreciate. So he kissed her instead and muttered, "Bastards! Do you know who they are?"

"They've all torn off their badges," she said soothingly. "We'll try to identify them tomorrow. One cop looks pretty much like any other with those blue helmets on.... Don't blame them, Red. They've been under enormous pressure. Come, sit down next to me... and don't let go, idjit."

All calculated and planned to soothe the angry male and minimize his guilt. Doubtless planned while the doctors were examining her to make sure that the kid—Kate that was to be—was not planning on a too-early appearance.

"They're paid to resist pressure." Red kept his arms around her and prayed again to God that he would not lose her. "Why would they go after a United States Attorney?" he asked Craig.

"Because she's young enough and pretty enough to be a college student. This week all college students are enemies."

Red sighed deeply, letting go as much of his cop-hating fury as he could. *Psychopathic morons.*

"The ultimate violation of your rational pragmatism, isn't it, Red?" She rested her head on his shoulder.

"I think they call it Pelagianism"—he caressed her matted hair—"the heretical illusion that there is no evil in the world other than ignorance. It discounts the possibility of malice. And it doesn't recognize the human potential for demonic behavior. Pelagius"—he untangled some strands of hair—"was an Irish monk."

"Poor man." She snuggled closer.

"I suppose he thought he was going to make the world a better place all by himself. He wouldn't have been able to believe that in the name of peace, a crowd of imbeciles would give the election to Richard Nixon."

"Is he going to win?" She was falling asleep, as she did after they made love.

"Hell yes."

"We'll survive."

Something important within Red Kane's soul would not survive. It had already died.

16

From the Kane File

from the *Herald Gazette*, March 25, 1969

KANE WINS SECOND AWARD, NAMED COLUMNIST

Redmond Kane, political editor of the *Herald Gazette*, won his second Pulitzer last night at the annual awards dinner in New York. After the award to Kane was announced, John

Stanton, editor-in-chief of the *Herald Gazette*, said that Kane would become a regular daily columnist for the paper.

"Red has demonstrated remarkable journalistic versatility," Stanton said. "His first Pulitzer, thirteen years ago, was for a series of stories on corruption in the Cook County courts. This one was for his coverage of the human impact of the Tet Offensive in Viet Nam. The new column which he will write is a recognition that his talent should be given as much flexibility as possible."

"I'm grateful for both the award and the new column," Kane said in New York. "I wish the war was over and I wish my brother had not been killed in Viet Nam last year. The prize is small in comparison with both tragedies."

Kane's brother, Colonel Davitt Jude Kane, was killed in November while driving Vietnamese orphans to a U.S. hospital.

Kane is married to the former Eileen Ryan. They have three children, John, 5, Patricia, 3, and Kathleen, 2 months.

17

In 1972 Red learned from an unlikely source that his suspicions about Paul O'Meara's disappearance were accurate. But he was so shocked by what he had learned, that he couldn't do anything with it.

Nineteen seventy-two was a year of madness. The Republicans broke into the Watergate complex as part of an obscure plot to discredit Democratic chairman Larry O'Brien and instead discredited themselves. The Democrats staged a convention that they claimed was the most representative in history—women, blacks, young people, gays—excluding only labor and big-city ethnics; much to their surprise they were buried in the subsequent election. George McGovern asserted that he was a thousand percent behind his vice presidential nominee and then dumped him. The Palestinians celebrated the cause of justice and freedom by murdering athletes at the Olympics. Angela Davis was acquitted of a murder charge. The baseball players struck at the beginning of the season. The Senate cut off aid to Cambodia, thus opening the way for genocide. A nut hacked up Michelangelo's *Pietà. The Godfather* made heroes of the Mafia. Paul McCartney's "Give Ireland Back to the Irish" was banned by British radio and John Lennon's "Woman Is the Nigger of the World" was banned by American radio. The miniskirt disappeared, which if your woman had legs like Eileen was a terrible tragedy.

In Red's personal world the madness included his wife's poking into confidential government files for him. Unasked.

On the Feast of Saint Nicholas, Kate finally quiet in bed but only because she had been overcome by exhaustion, Red and Eileen were watching TV in their apartment on Belmont, in Wrigleyville as it later came to be called because of the proximity of the ballpark where the Cubs blow their spring lead every year. The apartment was too small now with Kate a contentious three-year-old. Yet that time was one of those interludes when their intimacy was better than it was at other times, not that they ever, even at the best of times, talked about their marriage. They had their own careers and friendships, they made few demands on one another, they had the kids and their bed in common, and the interludes of passion, infrequent as they were, continued to be spectacular. Red's admiration for Eileen increased with each passing year, although he had no idea of what she thought of him. She never ventured an opinion on the subject. Patient nagging had completely replaced anger in their relationship. "I'm thinking of leaving the government," she said at the end of Bill Kurtis on the ten o'clock news.

Red was never able to respond to such statements from his wife because he was not sure whether she was informing him on a right-to-know basis or whether she was asking for his advice and consent. So he usually came up with something ingenious like "Oh?"

"We're indicting men for the sake of indictments. There's no one in Chicago we couldn't indict if we wanted to. We pick the victims who will get us the most headlines." She rose from her chair and turned off the TV. "It isn't even important that we send them to jail. If they plead guilty and we have another conviction for our record, it's enough."

"Are they guilty?" He put aside his book of John Berryman's poetry, wondering what he was supposed to say. For Eileen it was a speech.

She waved her hand impatiently. "Technically, I suppose. Technically everyone's guilty. The daughter of one of the bankers we dragged up before the grand jury the other day attempted suicide because the girls at school tormented her after the *Sun-Times* headlines. Our boss is racing to the Governor's mansion over the bodies of innocent children."

Such hyperbole from a woman like Eileen calls for a husband's arm around her shoulders. Dumb Red didn't think of that till later. Instead he murmured, "You've been under a lot of strain."

"I've had an offer from Minor, Grey, and Blatt."

"Great firm. Top dollar. I can retire and become a house husband."

"Red, you're wonderful." She embraced him and sat beside him on the couch. Eileen's smile always surprised him. From such a strong, businesslike woman, you'd expect a quick movement of lips, a brief show of teeth, and then the next item on the agenda. Instead of punctuating a paragraph, however, an Eileen smile was an invitation to begin a new chapter—warm, soft, inviting.

"What is important is that you'll be happy," he said, sounding like a parish priest instead of a husband.

"I'll be doing trial work . . . Red," snuggling closer to him. They rested peacefully in each other's arms for a few happy minutes. Then she dropped her bomb. "By the way, your hunches about Gunther's involvement in Paul O'Meara's disappearance are well founded."

"Oh?" Red sat up straight, his arms still around her.

"I was in the secret files the other day and stumbled on the records from the investigation our office did when he vanished. I . . . wasn't looking for them exactly." She rested her head against his chest. "I just found them. The FBI was convinced Gunther knew much more about what happened to Paul than he was admitting. There were orders from higher up to abandon the investigation."

"Uh-huh." Every muscle in Red's body strained like a rubber band pulled to the breaking point. Eileen knew more and she knew that he wouldn't like it.

"He was in Gunther's pay, Red."

"God damn it!" He erupted from the couch and strode across the room. Snow flurries were dusting the street beneath their third-floor apartment.

"I hope you're not mad at me." Red turned around. His wife, astonishingly, looked like the principal mourner at a wake. Grieving for her husband's lost idols, he supposed. "I felt I had to tell you."

"Why?" he snapped.

"You would have found out eventually." Her sorrowful green eyes pleaded with him to understand. "Apparently some others know. I thought it was better that you learn about it at a time when there are no other pressures."

"Of course I'm not mad at you, Eileen." He sat next to her and took her hand. "I'm mad at myself for not having guessed the obvious."

A man with any claim to being a decent husband would have made love with her that night. Red wanted to, but could not. The ghost of Paul O'Meara hovered over their marriage bed, exorcising all possibility of passion.

18

From the Kane File

from *Time*, July 14, 1976

POOR MAN'S ROYKO COMES EAST

"It's not fair to say that I'm a poor man's Mike Royko," says Chicago columnist Red Kane with an impish wink. "Not fair to Mike. He works a lot harder than I do. At best I'm a pauper's Mike Royko."

It is an ambiguous response from an ambiguous man. Two-time Pulitzer Prize winner Kane's daily column, "Kane's Korner," will begin appearing this week in the ailing *Washington Star*. "A little bicentennial gift for the national capital," Kane comments, "some of whose citizens have actually heard about Chicago."

Kane, 45, is by universal agreement a clever and witty writer. Some Chicago reporters feel that his column lacks a positive perspective. "Red is a disillusioned Kennedy liberal," says one younger reporter. "His columns are mostly attacks on others because he no longer believes in anything himself."

But a Kane supporter defended the columnist's "countercyclical" approach. "Anyone can expose a traffic court scandal. Lots of us could win a Pulitzer if we happened to arrive in Saigon the day before Tet. It takes real talent, though, to dissent from the conventional wisdom five mornings a week. Take his column when Nixon resigned. It was fashionable to say that the constitutional system worked because a President who violated the laws was forced out of office. Red was the only one who saw the hole in that argument."

"Don't tell me the resignation of our crooked President proves the system works," Kane harrumphed in that famous column. "Why didn't it work six years before, in 1968? We remembered the Checkers speech; we remembered his concession to Pat Brown in which he revealed what a nut he was. Was there any difference between his demented resignation and those two pathetic performances? How the hell did he get elected in the first place?"

In an interview this week, Kane commented that the answer to the question is that the Democratic party gave Nixon the election in 1968 because of the convention disorders in Chicago, and in 1972 by "nominating the weakest candidate since James Buchanan. Now it's forcing us to celebrate our bicentennial by choosing between a peanut farmer who's never held national office and a hack politician who was at best a second-rate minority leader."

Kane was not always so cynical. In his early years as a reporter, he described journalism as a vocation not unlike the priesthood. "The dreams all died between November 22, 1963, when Kennedy was shot, and January 20, 1969, when Nixon was inaugurated. My generation learned how much evil there was in the world and how puny were human goodwill and rationality in conflict with the evil. Now the only hope is to survive and leave our kids a world that is no worse than the one that was passed on to us."

The serious mood passes quickly. "That's pretty heavy for a guy who is going to be read in Washington every day," he says with another wink, "after Sally Quinn and the women's page of the *Washington Post*, of course."

December 3, 1977

Kane's Korner

AN OBIT NOT FIT TO PRINT

by Redmond P. Kane

No one can object if our local folk hero Studs Terkel wants to perform scatological actions on Richard J. Daley's grave. Those who survive a little longer than their enemies have always had that privilege. Nor is it unexpected that Studs would stay up all night working on his scatology so that it would appear even before the late Mayor's body was in the ground. If Studs wants to celebrate the fact that death did to Daley what he and his reformer buddies were unable to do before the poor man is even cold, that's a matter of taste.

Studs, as we all know, has always been a paragon of good taste.

I wonder, however, why the *New York Times*, with its commitment to what is fit to print, would publish Studs's scatology on its editorial page. That's like asking Chief Crazy Horse to write a commentary on the death of General George Armstrong Custer.

I called the *Times* and asked them whether anyone there had had the common decency to ask someone from the other side to venture an opinion. They said sure, they had asked Eddie Hanrahan to do a piece for them.

I suppose they think that because the man whom the Mayor often called "that nut Eddie" went to Harvard he can read and write.

You do two pieces on a man who has been Mayor of the second-largest city in the nation, one by a bitter enemy who rejoices in his death as a political victory for his own side and the other by a man whom the Mayor dumped from his ticket because he couldn't keep the uniformed thugs who were working for him from gunning down a bunch of Black Panthers on a tip that they might have a lot of guns stashed away.

I guess that's what passes for objectivity in the Big Apple.

19

Love was like a jigsaw puzzle when Red was a kid: there were lots of pieces that he knew fit together somehow, but you didn't understand what the pieces were and how they were supposed to be assembled. Indeed, it only gradually dawned on him that they were all part of the same puzzle.

First of all, there was sin—the terrible sin of impurity, which could damn the soul for all eternity. One act of impurity, after a life of stellar virtue, committed the last day of your life, could wipe out all the good things you'd done before that "single, unspeakable act."

The trouble was that the "terrible sin, the unspeakable act," was so unspeakable that you couldn't guess from the nuns' denunciation of it how you went about performing it. Red was not about to commit the sin, mind you. He did not want to go to hell. He merely wanted to know what it was.

He prayed fervently every day that his father was not in hell, that God somehow had given him a chance to make an Act of Perfect Contrition before the cop's bullet ripped into his back. If God had not given him that grace in the last second of life, he would certainly be in hell because he had failed to make his Easter Duty (Confession and Communion) that year. So Red prayed extra hard.

There was not much point in praying for his stepfather. Suicides, Sister Agnes Martha said, went straight to hell for all eternity, unless they were excused by reason of insanity. Red did not like his stepfather much, but he wasn't insane. Nonetheless, he prayed for him too. Sister Agnes Martha told him that "We have no right to judge what grace God might have given the poor man between the time he pulled the trigger and the time that the bullet tore through his brain."

God, he figured, would have to move pretty quickly to pull that off.

With such a fear of hellfire, an evil worse than being sent to Sister Superior's office, even worse than being sent to Monsignor's office, there wasn't much chance of his deliberately committing the "unspeakable act of impurity." Red assumed that he would recognize such a temptation when it appeared. Still he wished that the sisters would be more explicit about it so that he might not trip into it without realizing what he was doing.

Then there was love, which happened between men and women in the movies and at which the boys hooted, even though they wondered what it would be like to kiss a woman the way Clark Gable kissed Carole Lombard or Spencer Tracy kissed Myrna Loy. Love included romances with the girls in your grade, romances that were carried on at great distances and did not necessitate your talking to them. You used the word "like" as a substitute for "love" because...well, Red didn't know why.

His friend Mike Casey was dizzy over Anne Marie O'Brien and vice versa. You and the girl you liked displayed your affection by fighting one another at every opportunity. In seventh and eighth grades, when you began to play kissing games like spin the bottle and post office, Red had the feeling that this was terribly exciting and perhaps slightly wicked, but hardly an unspeakable act.

How could anything with a sweet little girl like Emily Regan be unspeakable? He was less sure about his summer kisses with Jane Heenan. They did strange things to him, but they would not happen again. Anyway, when he confessed, with trembling voice, that he had kissed a girl on the beach, the priest did not seemed unduly worried. He merely warned Red to be "prudent."

There was also what he would now call reproduction. Red had only the vaguest notion of how babies appeared on the scene. That they appeared first of all inside their mothers' bodies was an empirical observation that surprised him when he first made it. He didn't have a clue even at the age of thirteen as to how they got there, except that it was somehow connected to "dirty" conversations that went on in the prairies, where he played baseball, and in the alleys. As a serious and sincere Catholic boy, destined for the priesthood, Red avoided such conversations. "Dirty" applied especially to words and covered a wide variety of language, of which "damn" was the least bad and "fuck" the worst, an almost certain mortal sin. Red did not understand how the making of babies fit with such words or sniggering conversations about toilet activities. He told himself that he did not want to know.

Other "dirty" activities were more troubling—passing around pictures of naked women. He realized that this was horrible, but it did not occur to him that it might constitute the "unspeakable sin of impurity." He turned away in disgust from the pictures, but not before he'd had a glimpse of them and a brief enjoyment of their paralyzing sweetness.

The mystery deepened because on the one hand he would have been horrified at the suggestion that he take off Jane's or Emily's clothes and gaze at them nude and on the other he felt an obsessive curiosity about how girls looked without any clothes. The final piece of the puzzle was his increasing fascination with women's bodies, not only those of his ripening classmates like Emily and the tempestuous Anne Marie O'Brien, but women in films, in magazine ads, on streetcars, on the beach at Twin Lakes in the summer. His own body was growing and changing and doing odd things for which he had no explanation. Somehow there was a connection between this change and his insatiable curiosity about the bodies of women, including women almost his mother's age like her good friend Helga.

Whenever Helga visited, he could not take his eyes off her. His mother didn't seem to notice.

So those were the pieces—sin, love, reproduction, dirtiness, maturation, hunger for women. Even in naming the parts of the puzzle later on in life, Red would use words from the perspective of those years and make his bafflement more organized and systematic than it had been when he was caught in the chaos of early adolescence. Because he did not even have a vocabulary for what was happening to him at puberty, he was not only confused, he didn't know enough to know that he was confused. He and his classmates were about to be swept up in the typhoon of adolescent desire, and the rafts on which they would float were fragile crafts compounded of innocence and ignorance.

First there was Jane Heenan.

"Do you want to skinny-dip, Redmond?" she asked him.

It seemed like a wonderful idea, wild, reckless, and fun—exactly the sort of thing Jane would suggest.

"Why not?" He reached for the strap of her suit.

"I'll take off my own suit." She tugged away, a little frightened by the enthusiasm of his response.

They dashed into the lukewarm water and frolicked in it, pretending that it was all just a summer game and that they were not unbearably aware of their darkness-protected nudity.

It was the summer of 1943. Despite his stepfather's death

the previous winter they were were still spending their precious two weeks at Helga's small cottage at Twin Lakes. Helga would have been happy to entertain them all summer, but his mother refused to "impose." Indeed, that summer their decision to visit Helga had been a last-minute matter, as were most decisions in their family. His mother did not think that it was proper for a grieving widow to have a summer vacation. Clever Helga argued that for the good of the children she must "get away from the house for a few days."

So during the hottest two weeks of August in that incredibly hot summer he ogled Helga and ran on the beach with Jane. The war was a long way off, no TV in those days to bring Stalingrad or the Warsaw ghetto or Bizerte or the Bismarck Sea to their dinner tables. Headlines about the antics of General George S. Patton, Jr., in Sicily were from a storybook world that did not seem to exist on the same planet with Helga's gorgeous legs or Jane's blossoming body or his confused and frantic longings for them.

Jane was from Milwaukee, a tall, athletic brunette with flashing brown eyes, short curly hair, an infectious laugh, and boundless energy—a speeding comet of young womanly enthusiasm with a blazing trail of pranks.

They held hands the first night he was at the lake while they watched *Casablanca*—"round up the usual suspects," what a wonderful line! They sang "Coming In on a Wing and a Prayer" while they ran down the beach after the movie (Jane never walked) and kissed in front of her family's cottage.

His mother was so preoccupied with her own grief that she paid no attention to any of her sons. Parn and Dav—nasty little brats in his mature estimation at the time—ran wild. He could have stayed out all night and she would not have noticed. Jane's family didn't much believe in rules. So they were free to run wherever and whenever they wanted—up and down the hills, along the shore of the lake, through the woods.

They played basketball every morning, Jane beating him at horse and twenty-one despite his height and strength.

She was his first romance, his first love, a dynamic young animal who swept away his defenses of shyness and caution with a single sweep of her arm and a single touch of her lips. When he was with Jane—almost eighteen hours every day—nothing else mattered.

Red was going to be a priest, of course. After he graduated from grammar school he would board the Chicago Avenue streetcar and ride to Quigley, the daytime preparatory seminary near the Cathedral. So would his two brothers. That had been settled long ago. But the priesthood existed in the distant and improbable future and Jane Heenan was now.

The moon had vanished from the sky when they plunged into the water and reveled in its soothing, bathtub warmth. The stars were close enough to touch, the state park next to Jane's house was as quiet as the primal forest, the distant highway silent as a cemetery. Only the trees and the stars witnessed their diving and swimming and then cautious dunking of one another as naked young body brushed against naked young body.

Jane was a strong young woman, and much quicker than he was. So he was the loser in their water fights until he took her in his arms and held her motionless. Somehow her arms found their way around him. They clung to each other, wordless in the darkness, as though they were the only two people in the world. Red wanted those precious moments to go on forever. *Dear God,* he thought, *don't let this ever end.*

She was both soft and strong in his arms, both warm and coolly reassuring. He wanted to touch her new-but-already-swelling breasts and kiss them. He would have if there had been more time. As it was, the pressure against his chest was both torment and delight, the happiest moment of his young life.

Jane's instinct of caution, a silken thread linking them to the real world, asserted itself and she slipped away. Red let her go because he did whatever Jane wanted.

They struggled back into their swimsuits on the beach and lay next to one another, holding hands.

"Great fun," she murmured peacefully. "But we better not do it tomorrow night."

Red agreed, thinking for the first time that it was something he would have to confess.

But he didn't confess it till they went home from the lake because there was always a possibility that he and Jane might do it again, which he did not want to lose. Jane wept copiously when they kissed good-bye his last night, and they both swore they would write every week and keep their love alive forever, which meant until the next summer.

"What's the matter with you?" the priest screamed at him in the confessional in St. Ursula's. "Are you a sex fiend?"

"No, Father."

"How many times did you do it?"

"Only one night."

"And you touched her impurely?"

He wasn't sure what that meant. He had held a naked girl in his arms. He knew it was something he shouldn't do, but it didn't seem to be a sin of impurity.

"No, Father, I only hugged her."

"Did you have sexual intercourse?" A horrified whisper.

It was the first time he had heard the words.

"No, Father."

"Yet you did swim naked?"

"Yes, Father, but it was dark."

"That doesn't make one bit of difference. How old are you?"

"Thirteen," he said. Well, almost.

"Oh, my God, what kind of perversions will you do when you get older!" the priest exclaimed in alarm. "You're bound for hell, young man."

"Yes, Father."

"You want to go to hell?"

"No, Father."

"Then you must stop these terrible mortal sins."

It was the first hint that what Jane and he had done was a mortal sin. Red would later worry about that, fearful that Jane might go to hell because of him.

"I will, Father."

"And you must promise me that you will stay away from that young woman. She is Satan's instrument of temptation; she wants to drag your soul down into hell."

"Yes, Father." At that moment he would have promised anything. Yet he knew, deep down, that Jane was no such thing. It did not seem to be the time to argue. He never had a chance to break the promise.

Red would later contend, vigorously if he had enough of the Drink taken, that he had bad luck. Even in those days another priest would have asked a few questions and guided him through a preliminary of sex education, telling him the truth—that what Jane and he felt for one another was good and wonderful, but dangerously premature.

Jane's father, an M.D., was called up during the winter, and Jane and her mother, they learned the following August, were with him in San Diego. They didn't write. If she returned to Twin Lakes after the war, he did not. Deathless love dies very quickly when you're young.

Shallow, crazy young emotions. Except young people caught up in such loves don't realize that they will shortly pass away, leaving only faintly bittersweet nostalgia. In any list of the loves of his life Jane would be near the top, along with Marian Tracey.

Or so it seemed to him when Red recalled the summer of 1943. He used to tell himself that a romantic glow had covered over what was in fact a rather petty and even tawdry relationship between two ignorant and horny young people.

Five years ago, before Red's most recent love affair with Eileen, they were invited to Milwaukee for her son's first Mass. "Somehow, I wanted you to know," she wrote on the invitation.

Eileen insisted they go. "I want to get a good look at this adolescent sweetheart," she said firmly.

Jane was a disturbingly handsome woman, married to an M.D. on the faculty of the Medical College of Wisconsin, and herself a full professor of English at the University of Wisconsin in Milwaukee. The comet was still moving at top speed.

"Do you have happy memories of those days?" she asked with a directness that had not changed.

"Wonderful memories." Red kissed her lightly. "And you?"

"Definitely."

Her son, an intense, bearded young man, preached a fine homily about the priesthood as an institution of love. Jane seemed to have lucked out. "Jealous of the early rival?" Red asked Eileen as they drove home in the early-spring moonlight.

"Insanely...and impressed by your youthful taste. How did you ever let her get away?"

A fair question and one to which there was no answer. Maybe God was protecting Jane from him.

20

All Souls' Day sunlight was streaming through the skylight, which Johnny, for reasons of his own perhaps, had installed above his parents' bed. Red remembered the feast and remembered that when he was a boy the priest was expected to say three Masses on this day and the pious laity to attend three Masses. Moreover you were to duck in and out of church, saying six Our Fathers and Hail Marys each time, to free with each "visit" to church one soul in purgatory.

Then he remembered he was to have lunch with Melissa at the Arts Club the next day. Why was he looking forward to the meal with some unease despite the astonishing sense of well-being that pervaded his body?

And whence the well-being?

He reached for a cigarette. None on the bed stand. He quit smoking yesterday. Why had he done that?

Then it all came back.

He sat up in bed and rubbed his eyes. Next to him was a thermos of coffee, a large glass of grapefruit juice, two buttered English muffins, and a tissue with "I love you!" scrawled on it in lipstick.

Eileen did not leave love notes lying around. But then, Eileen did not replace herself with breakfast in their marriage bed. She must be in love with him as he was with her. A teenage crush, she'd called it last night. How had the poor, dear, wonderful, passionate woman put up with him for so long?

He decided to defer the question for the moment while he examined his own mental state.

Red removed the plastic wrap from the top of the grapefruit juice and, while he savored its tart taste, gingerly tested his psyche.

Yep, still in good shape. The enthusiasm of the previous day was undiminished. He permitted himself to consider the romps with Eileen. Oh yes, very satisfactory, as Nero Wolfe would have said to Archie Goodwin. No, he didn't have to light a cigarette. No, he wasn't looking forward to the first drink of the day. Yes, he would, as gently as possible, end his off-and-on affair with Melissa. No, he was not afraid to return to his novel. Yes, he would call Harv Gunther. Yes, he would surely make love to his delectable wife again tonight. No, he didn't know how he was going to cut his way through the jungle that separated him from his children, but he was going to try.

He set aside the grapefruit juice, hand squeezed, and opened the coffee thermos, freshly ground coffee beans, judging by the smell. As always, when Eileen did something, she did it well.

Poor woman, she had to work for a living. He blew on the coffee cup to cool the surface of the rich brew. He had merely to write a column, a half hour's work according to the Mayor's generous estimate.

What should I write the column about today? He grinned. *Wonderful idea. Shouldn't take more than fifteen minutes.*

The world today was like Eileen's coffee, thick, strong, and tasty. He savored the warm waters of his shower, the lazy glow of sunlight on the park's brown meadows, the green coat of a CTA bus, the elegant lines of the tall buildings along the river, the purposeful movements of *HG* staff in the city room, muffled by the thick carpets required by the word-processor-dominated newspaper.

He turned on his CRT and hammered out his column, chuckling to himself while he worked. He had dictated most of it in his head on the bus ride. Merry hell would break loose. He should be able to do two or maybe even three more in response to those humorless ideologues who missed his point.

He checked his watch. Seventeen and a half minutes. He called City Hall and informed the Mayor's Press Secretary. "Seventeen and a half minutes today. I thought Hizzoner would want to know."

"Thanks, Red, I'll tell him."

"When he comes in." Red hung up, considered whether in his new life he should continue to tweak the Mayor's nose, and decided that the man would be disappointed if he stopped.

He told his miracle machine to print out hard copy; it breathed deeply for a couple of seconds and then fulfilled his request. He glanced over it and set it aside. *Do a few other things first and then do another revision.*

How long is it since you revised a column?

He punched in Harv Gunther's number. The womanly voice at the other end was willing to acknowledge his existence this time.

"Mr. Gunther will speak to you now, Mr. Kane."

"Red?" A hearty boom. "How are you!"

"Do you have your tape on, Harv? Volume up?" Red tuned his cassette recorder and heard the officious beep which Illinois law required when phone conversations were being recorded. There was an answering beep from Harv's machine.

"Always joking," Gunther laughed.

"Filled with Christmas cheer already, Harv?"

"You didn't call to ask that kind of question, did you?" Santa Claus turning ogre.

"What do you hear from Paul O'Meara lately?" The question had detonated in his unconscious like a terrorist bomb. Had he dreamed it last night?

"What kind of a question is that?" sputtered Gunther. "Paul's been dead for twenty years."

"Officially dead for seventeen years," Red snapped back. "But you know better than that, don't you, Harv? You know that he's still alive and where he is, don't you? Give him my best when you talk to him, will you?"

"You're drunk, Kane," Gunther snarled.

"Is he in Brazil?" That's where Rita Lane was hiding, a big country.

"Or maybe out of your mind!"

"Come on, Harv, you know where he is. He worked for you for ten years before he disappeared."

"You can't prove that!" Gunther was hoarse with rage, and perhaps fear.

"There were others"—a demon had taken possession of Red Kane and was using his voice—"kept reporters. You kept them like you kept women and mostly for the same reason. You enjoyed owning them. Poor devils pretended to be fearless servants of truth, and really were your whores. I know them all, Harv, every one. Tell that to Paul the next time you phone Brazil."

"I'll kill you, Kane!" Gunther screamed.

"You're smarter than that, Harv. You know it wouldn't do any good. Do you think I'd be talking like this to you if I didn't have a doomsday machine somewhere? You'd better hope I have a long life."

"You're bluffing!"

"Try me! And when you call Paul, tell him I was at the graduation of his youngest from Notre Dame. Bye, Harv."

He eased the phone back into its cradle before Gunther could hang up on him.

Harv is slipping, he's a tired old man. A year ago I couldn't have bluffed him on such a wild shot in the dark. He forgot I had a tape running. A threat of murder. Harv is worried, and he'll be more worried when he remembers the tape. If I throw Rita Lane at him, he might crack completely.

Red was numb, drained, exhausted. His shirt was soaked with sweat, his head pounding.

So you tricked a man on the edge of senility, big-deal investigative reporter.

A man who is still capable of murder, a man who will be a threat to society until he's in the tomb. Hunting the Harv Gunthers of the world is your job, Kane.

Then he let himself think about Paul O'Meara.

Paul was still alive. He'd been fed up twenty years ago, sick of his job, sick of his wife, sick of his wailing kids, sick of his own corruption. Probably he had turned over a stone and found lots of worms, all with Harvard Gunther's brand on them. He'd threatened Harv with exposure, not a gross threat, hints mixed with pleas for help, appeals for gratitude. He'd had some money, probably a lot, from Gunther's payoffs. All he'd asked was a chance to escape, maybe a salary—don't call it blackmail. A doomsday machine somewhere.

He'd been taking a chance. Harv Gunther might have thought he was bluffing and killed him. Paul might have been so sick of his life that he didn't care. A woman involved? Not likely. Paul would've wanted a new one, but only after the financial matters had been arranged. Gunther would have decided that Paul alive was less a risk than Paul dead. Probably not much more expenditure. And worth it to get him out of the city.

Cheaper than killing him. Harv was a cautious man. He only killed as a last resort. That's why Red wasn't worried, not yet.

He punched another number on the phone.

"Hi, Annie, is your husband around the gallery? Red Kane."

"Casey," said the former Deputy Superintendent of Police, now gentleman artist.

"Mike, Red Kane. See you later today? Some information I want to pass on. No, not the gallery, let's say on one of the bridges over the Potomac."

Casey laughed. "Oak Street Beach?"

"Fine."

Casey would know what to do with a copy of the tape Red was already making. He would also advise about some undercover protection for Eileen and the kids. Harv wasn't ready to kill yet, but when the Rita Lane time bomb exploded, Red and his family might need instant protection.

Paul O'Meara. Still alive. Wherever he is, probably still playing the Board of Trade game. Maybe a millionaire now, if he made the right moves in the early seventies. Maybe with a whole bunch of new kids. Paul O'Meara, the miserable son of a bitch. He taught me the ideals and he taught me the cynicism you need to live with the gap between ideals and reality, and then he ran out on all of us.

Red picked up his column about girl watching. It didn't seem so funny anymore. The warmth of his experience on the banks of the Chicago River was fading. What the hell difference did it make? Why bother with one crooked reporter and one prostitute-killing old man? Would nailing either of them make the world a better place?

Try as he might, Red Kane could not escape the certain answer that resonated in his brain like echoes in a canyon. Not to nail them would make the world a hell of a lot worse place. Later when his world had fallen apart, Red acknowledged to himself that there were other issues to which he had not paid sufficient attention.

He had taken Gunther's threat too lightly. It was not enough merely to inform Mike Casey. Although he would not admit it to his nasty shrink, he had been running on a supply of energy that was something more than natural; just as in Korea, he was convinced of his own invulnerability.

Once more he was inviting an explosion to send him spinning toward oblivion. Along with those he loved.

21

"Do you want to glance over this, Wils, before I lock it in? We might have a few angry hornets, female variety, buzzing around here after it appears."

He laid the copy for tomorrow's column on Allen's desk. From the corner office, which was the status prerogative of the editor of the *Herald Gazette*, the madam's room in the Danish brothel, one could look down the row of buildings on West Wacker and see the green ice palace where all this had started.

"Sure, Red, if you want me to." Allen grinned nervously, surely expecting another Red Kane joke of which he would be the victim.

He glanced over it once, his habitual frown deepening. Poor Wils, he was so dumb. He'd missed the point completely the first time. It would take three readings for him to comprehend the irony, and then he wouldn't realize that it was irony.

"Going after Hefner is not a bad idea," Allen said guardedly. "I hear there's a film coming out about him."

"About the playmate that was shot by her boyfriend." Red examined the large empty lot, which the staff called Wils's Wonderland. "Bob Fosse is the director, the fellow who made the movie in which Jessica Lange plays God."

"Yeah," Wils agreed, neither understanding the column nor remembering *All That Jazz*—and probably, poor man, not knowing who Jessica Lange is.

Red had not realized that the angel in *All That Jazz* was God either, not until Eileen whispered in his ear, "It's his particular judgment, of course, and she's God."

Matter of fact, why would not Eileen think it at all plausible that a sexy woman would be God?

Were memories of the film involved in what happened yesterday? That is an interesting question.

"This is really very good stuff, Red." Wils frowned even more deeply. "If you do a series of these, it could mean another Pulitzer."

"No room for it on the shelf," Red said airily. And then he added, with a compunction he did not ordinarily feel when he put down his boss, "I appreciate the compliment."

Poor dumb Wils. Wonderland had been his big journalistic triumph when he first arrived. As part of the North Loop project, a national hotel chain had agreed to construct a major convention center, if the city could get it a long-term tax break. The Assessor went along with the proposal. Such breaks were routine when the city needed a new facility that otherwise would not be built. The justification, sometimes phony, sometimes real, was that the business brought into an area by the facility would more than compensate for the tax benefits given to those who built and managed it.

When Wilson Allen discovered this deal, he promptly initiated a crusade in the editorial and news pages against it. The County Assessor, who had to run for reelection every four years, figured it was no skin off his anatomy if the hotel was never constructed and he canceled the tax break. The hotel company, baffled by the stupidity of the reversal, canceled the hotel. The site, from which several worn-out warehouses had been cleared, remained embarrassingly vacant.

Allen and Bradford Winston congratulated themselves in editorials for their big victory and applied for a Pulitzer.

There wasn't any award and Wonderland continued empty, much to the amusement of the *HG* staff and the fury of City Hall. Eventually another national chain would build the facility, with an even bigger tax break—so much for modern crusading editors.

"And I appreciate your showing it to me, Red. By all means run it. First-rate."

Some people you can't help even when you want to. There would be an internal uproar from the feminist ideologues on the staff, and a couple of score nasty phone calls and angry letters. Wils would have to take the heat and he would have to admit that he had seen the column beforehand.

What the hell, Red murmured to Jessica Lange or Whoever it was that had been "all calm and curled" in the green ice building, *I tried.*

He went back to his desk, called up the manuscript of his novel, and began working on it again.

It has to be comedy, he agreed with himself. *Why didn't I realize long ago that as comedy it all makes sense? The Helga story is pure slapstick. And Marian? Can I make that a slapstick story too?*

22

As he opened the refrigerator door and peered inside, in search of some Thüringer sausage, for which he had an irresistible craving, Red was suddenly aware that there was someone else in the house. Too early in the afternoon for Eileen or the kids. Gunther striking back so quickly?

Leaving the door open, he tiptoed over to the sink and removed the largest of the razor-sharp carving knives from the block Eileen kept on the counter.

I'll kill the bastard.

Footsteps, soft and tentative, in the corridor. How had he got in the house? Was he setting a bomb? Or maybe spreading gasoline for a fire?

The footfalls paused at the kitchen door. Throat tight, heart thumping, mouth dry, Red tightened his grip on the knife and prepared to spring. Why had he let himself get so horribly out of shape?

The door swung open and Red lunged.

At the last fraction of a second he averted the path of his charge and crashed into the kitchen table.

"Redmond Peter Kane"—hands on hips, head thrown back, Eileen was laughing at him—"what are you doing on the kitchen floor with a carving knife in your hand?"

Red wanted to be offended, but her laughter was contagious. She was wearing one of John's gray college T-shirts, her hair was tousled, and her face suggested sleep abandoned only a few moments before. A strong, appealing woman aroma floated around her.

"Defending my castle against an invader." He struggled clumsily to his feet. "My wife couldn't possibly be creeping around this hour of the afternoon."

"I thought one of the kids was home from school and stealing supper early. Put the knife down and kiss me. Uhm ... that's better. I came home early because the judge had to see his dentist and I needed some sleep after my exertions last night. I didn't say you could kiss me again. What were you doing in the icebox? Hungry? I can't imagine why. If you let me go for a minute I'll make you a pastrami-and-coleslaw-on-rye sandwich. Red, please, the children could come in any time. What do you want to drink? Beer?"

"Diet Coke."

An ever-so-slight lift of an eyebrow. She revealed, as she reached into the refrigerator, a symbolic white bikini bottom, the kind her daughters might have worn.

"Do you normally sleep in teenager dishabille?"

"Don't be gross, ouch, Red, do you want to paw me or eat?"

"Do I have to choose?"

"One at a time. And to answer your question, I do when I half expect my teenager lover."

Fair enough. He took the plate of cold meat out of her hands and set it down, eased her against the counter, and pushed his hands under her sweatshirt, up to her breasts. He imprisoned them leniently against her ribs.

Eileen leaned back, eyes closed, jaw sagging, fully ready to be taken in the kitchen or anywhere else. Then he thought of what he had done with Helga in the kitchen of her house. Prudery quickly asserted itself.

"I'll have you for dessert," he said, reluctantly releasing her.

"Fair enough," she laughed with what he thought was disappointed gaiety. "You take the sandwiches and I'll bring the drinks."

"Hey"—she balanced the tray—"kiss me again. Someday you'll do it in the kitchen."

"You have weird fantasies, witch lady." He touched her lips with his.

"A real kiss, please . . . hmmm . . . that's better. Your green-eyed witches, once they get turned on, can be really kinky."

What kind of fantasies do you have? I really don't know. I've been afraid to ask. Now that I'm getting hints, I'm even more afraid.

I may have been mousetrapped.

The two sandwiches and the two Diet Cokes, the former on a tray, the latter in tumblers with ice, were borne in solemn procession into the living area. Eileen directed Red to his easy chair and curled up next to the fireplace.

"Why didn't you make love with me in the kitchen? You could have, you know."

Red gulped a large bite of sandwich.

"On the kitchen counter? You would have liked that?"

"I'm getting old, Red." She waved her hand in a matter-of-fact courtroom gesture. "I'm afraid of aging, I'm afraid of death. I'm afraid of the decisions I've made and can't unmake. I'm afraid of my husband, and I'm afraid of myself. I'll try anything."

"Anything?"

"Anything." She rubbed his calf with her hand. "I've never been screwed in the kitchen before, as you well know. I wonder what I've missed. I've missed so much else in life...."

"Oh." Red finished his sandwich and told himself that he might have made a mistake coming home early.

"Sounds like a *Playboy* fantasy?" Her tone was objective, clinical. "An aroused wife who is ready to try anything?"

"When fantasies become real, they become scary."

"I don't get it, Red." Now she was caressing both legs. "I mean, I could understand a prudish husband. I gather that most men are really prudes. And I could understand and appreciate a husband who figured out most of my secrets the first night we were together. But the combination—"

"Prude and artist?"

"Yeah." She rested her head against his knees. "Last night you were so good as to be almost beyond comprehension. Then today—I don't mean to hurt your feelings—when the poor aging lawyer woman is ready for almost anything, you munch on your damn sandwich. What gives?"

He had a sudden and powerful impulse to tell her about Helga, a subject he had discussed only once before—with the priest on the military flight over the Pacific.

"Do you mind if I tell you something from my distant past?"

"Course not." She relaxed against a pillow. "The more I know about my husband the better."

"You might not like it."

"Nonsense," she dismissed this possibility with a brusque wave of her hand.

"I couldn't help but think of it after last night."

She nodded sympathetically, as though she understood, when she certainly did not. "Of course."

So he told the story of his sexual initiation.

23

"You like to watch me, don't you?" Helga stood over him, fingers on the zipper of her housecoat, calmly considering his embarrassment.

"No...," he stammered, conscious that he was alone in the cottage with her and frightened as well as embarrassed.

"Your eyes followed me when I walked up from the beach like you were taking off my clothes." She played with the zipper, moving it up and down. "Do you want to take off my clothes?"

She spoke with a slightly guttural accent, American indeed but with a touch of either Dane or Teuton still lurking in it.

"I'm sorry, Helga," he said miserably, mentally cursing his own clumsiness.

Helga taught at the same school as his mother. She was about thirty, a tall blond from Gaylord in the top part of the Lower Peninsula of Michigan. Her horse face was thin and hard, accentuated by a mane of blond hair tied severely behind her head. But she had a gloriously voluptuous figure, a Danish Juno with impressive bust and buttocks and a flat belly she loved to display in one of the few two-piece swimsuits visible at Twin Lakes in those days. It was in that light blue suit, matching her flinty eyes, that he had hungrily watched her walk up from the beach.

Helga had, he heard his mother tell others, "family money." She'd come to Chicago, his mother reported, because of an unhappy romance in college and was not interested in men anymore.

Nonetheless, she stirred up interest in a lot of men at Twin Lakes. Yet she was active in events of St. Ursula's and was considered a respected member of the parish (her father having converted to Catholicism when he married her mother, a good German Catholic woman from Detroit). To Red's mother she was a loyal and realistic friend in years when Mom was hearing superstitious nonsense from the biddies who flock to an Irish widow like salmon to the river of their origin.

Red's mother had agreed to three weeks at Twin Lakes that summer, by way of exception, but brought Dav and Parn back to Chicago for dentist appointments twice during that time, leaving him alone with Helga. Red was sure his mother had had no intention, as mothers do in French novels, of leaving him in the care of an older woman who would accomplish his sexual initiation. Sex, much less sexual initiation, was something that by definition did not exist in his case. Still she must have had some instincts about Helga, if indeed the woman had not confided in her. And it was hard not to notice that Red was now a big if ignorant and inept kid.

Thus he was defenseless in the room he shared in the small cottage with Parn and Dav, sweating in his swimming trunks as Helga towered over him, an amused smile on her lips and a hard glitter in her eyes.

"You dream of me, don't you?" The zipper fell to her waist. "Does a woman in underwear amuse you more than a woman in a swimsuit?" She shrugged out of the housecoat and stood in the armor-plated "foundation garments" that were required wearing in those days. His eyes bulged, his throat dried up, and his palms were sweating.

When he thought about that scene years later, Helga in pink, hands on her hips, taunting him, he realized that he could have simply left the room, escaped, run away. The truth is that he hadn't wanted to. Despite his fear and his shame, he was fascinated.

"If you look at a woman in a certain way for long enough" —she unbound her long yellow hair and let it fall over her shoulders and chest—"you stir her up and make her want more than looks."

"I'm sorry," he muttered, dreading what was about to happen but filled with a wonderful feeling of wicked sweetness.

"You like my breasts, don't you?" She reached behind

her back and unhooked her bra, a vast and complex garment. She flipped the straps teasingly against his face. "Perhaps you want to touch them?" She sat next to him on the bed, drew his face to hers and kissed him. It was not like brushing lips with Emily or Jane. Rather, it was a sweaty, salty, challenging invasion.

"So, let us see what you look like without your clothes." She pulled away his trunks, completing his humiliation and his enslavement.

Nakedness did not occur and was not discussed in the Kane house after his father had died. Red had absorbed prudery long before he knew the word, a disgust for the human body that alternated with fascination. Eileen was much more relaxed—modest enough, surely, and unpredictable, as Red thought most women were, but not ashamed of human flesh, her own or others'. She had long since given up fighting with Red on the subject. "And you say I'm erratic," she had once exploded at him. "You have ten hang-ups for every one I have."

The hang-ups had come before Helga seduced him, but the shame of those early moments of nakedness remained, fighting perpetually with his memories of the pleasure of the same moments.

So it had started and so it would go on for two years, an undergraduate education in sexuality that he supposed few young men of his generation experienced. When it was over, there was not much about the mechanics of coupling that Red did not know. Nor were there many tricks that might bring satisfaction to a woman that he had not learned.

At first the question of sin didn't arise. What happened between Helga and him was such an astonishment and such a delight that sin/not-sin categories didn't seem to apply. He knew they shouldn't be doing it, but it did not occur to him that he had finally found the unspeakable sin about which the nuns had warned him.

He tried to compartmentalize his life. In one segment there was the seminary and the priesthood, his daily rides on the Chicago Avenue streetcar with his taciturn buddy Mike Casey, his new friends at the seminary who enjoyed his wit even more than the St. Ursula crowd, a disturbing conversation with Anne Marie about Mike, his clumsy and slowly improving ventures in basketball, the death of Roosevelt on a quiet day in April of 1945, the first atomic bomb, the end of the war, his brothers and his mother, his plans for the future. In the other compartment, surrounded by a high wall, was Helga, once or twice a month perhaps, sometimes more often.

For her it had begun, probably, as a cruel perhaps but diverting summer amusement, the initiation of a rather obnoxious young man who was afraid to be caught staring at you. It changed quickly enough, not to love surely, but to an addiction.

When he finally admitted to himself that this was indeed a sin that could damn him to hell for all eternity (and that came some time before it dawned on him that it was also the way babies are conceived), he tried to will himself to stay away from Helga.

She and his mother would not permit it. She would ask his mother at school to send him over to shovel the snow or cut the lawn or put up or take down the storm windows. At that time in her life, Mom was perfecting the technique of control through complaint. He would not be asked to cut Helga's lawn. He would, rather, be assaulted with the complaint that he was lazy and indifferent, did not care about the financial sacrifices she was making for him, spent all his time reading books, and was so useless that if his poor father were alive, he would be ashamed of him.

So despite his firm resolutions to stay away from her he went back, time after time, even when he was certain that he was committing mortal sin, a lamb eager for the slaughter. Once there was no choice, he could scarcely contain his anticipation. It was evil, but it was more enjoyable than he thought anything could be.

Much, much later, on a long plane flight across the Pacific, a priest explained to him that in those circumstances he lacked the freedom and the maturity to give the kind of consent necessary for mortal sin. Oddly enough, if he'd known that then, it might have been easier to stop. The feeling that you are already damned does not give you much motivation for change.

The priest also said that Red was a victim. Maybe he was. In an era when there was a payoff in being a victim, Red was reluctant to accept the label. Perhaps Helga had exploited him. Perhaps he was her victim. But he was a willing victim. He'd enjoyed it, oh, God in heaven, how he'd enjoyed it!

The spiritual direction at the seminary was not much help. The spiritual director talked to the seminarians individually about sex, mostly an obscure and technical explanation that in fact explained nothing. If Red hadn't already been through the reality, he would not have understood what he was talking about. As it was he merely learned some technical terms.

"You're a very handsome young man, Red," the spiritual director said to him in his kindly, sympathetic tone, a wise old father (though he was still in his late twenties). "Girls must find you very attractive. Have you had any problems with them?"

"None in particular, Father." Helga wasn't a girl, she was a woman.

"Any special friend?"

"Not since eighth grade, Father. There was a girl at Twin Lakes the summer before that whom I liked a lot, but I have not seen her since."

They were warned about avoiding young women, told that they were flighty and fickle and that their personalities were tied to the cycle of the moon (a reference that baffled him completely). A retreat master warned them that Samson was the perfect example of what women do to men.

"A married man may have to lose his manliness to them occasionally, for, remember, it is better to marry than to burn. But priests and future priests? ... NEVER! Avoid them, young men, avoid them. They will deprive you of your manliness and virtue. Beware of them, for it is especially the forbidden fruit of the celibate they wish to taste. If they can cheat you of your self-control, it is a special victory for their flirtatious vanity. A woman who wants to unman a priest is as deadly as a black widow spider!"

Red was in no position to disagree.

Helga had amused herself with him at the beginning but,

toward the end of their "affair," Red, displeased with his subordinate role, became the dominant partner. He was stronger than she was and smarter. He didn't like being her slave. Without quite knowing what he was doing, he slowly modified the relationship so she was making love on his terms. They did what he wanted to do, not what she wanted to do. Then she tried to quit. It was his turn to insist and then to force.

"Please, please," she begged. "No more."

"Keep begging, Helga," he laughed, passionately enjoying his new power over her and reveling in her tears. "I like it."

Then, completely in control of the woman, he fell in love with her. At the very end he felt toward her as he did toward Jane or Betty Lou. She became a person to be loved. Puppy love, of course; but unlike most of the puppy loves of his contemporaries this was combined with intense sexual activity. The last time he forced love upon her, she sobbed like a lost soul. Clumsily he took her in his arms and told her that she was beautiful and wonderful and should not weep. He would take care of her and protect her—obviously idiotic promises.

She must have needed tenderness desperately to have settled for it from such an inept punk. Her face softened, her eyes became gentle, and, cuddled in the protection of his arms, she told him about her father who had beaten and abused her and the lover who had deserted her. So the affair became a love affair, a foolish warped love affair, but one in which there was at least the giving and receiving of kindness.

Then Helga wanted to stop the kindness and tenderness. As a slave he was amusing; as a master he was perversely tolerable; as a clumsily tender lover he was terrifying. She moved to San Diego to escape from him. In a curious irony, he did her a favor by driving her out of the neighborhood. In San Diego she met a Navy Captain, a widower home from the war, and married him within the year. They had five sons in seven years and, if his mother was to be believed, it was a happy marriage.

For years Red blamed his sexual troubles on Helga. Then he began to suspect that it might have been an incident without much meaning for the rest of his life. After she had departed on the Union Pacific for California, he did without women until Japan. And after Lindy, he stayed away from them until his engagement to Marian exploded. He was not a satyr. He did not receive all that much pleasure from his love affairs. That they kept happening probably was less the result of sex itself than of other problems in his life.

For the next two years he trudged off to St. Mel's every day in his ROTC uniform (the only Catholic high school in the country with ROTC, because the chairman of the House Military Affairs Committee was an alumnus), acquired enough grace to be second string on a losing basketball team, made a few new friends but remained pretty much a loner (still playing poker with Mike Casey and his former seminary classmates), and dated Betty Louise, a sophomore from Siena of whom by 1983 he would have no very clear memories except that she giggled frequently and was reputed to be pretty.

Anne Marie asked him to a dance in the fall of their junior year, before she fell in love with a Fenwick senior who was killed in the Hürtgen Forest. Red was a stand-in for Mike, of course, but that did not lessen his delight when he discovered that young women had minds as well as bodies, wit as well as pretty faces. Annie was too much for him then. He avoided women like her in the years after that—until he met Eileen.

His confusion about sex, and the mess he made of his sexual life, were probably more influenced by his relationship with his mother than with Helga—his mother who had left him alone with Helga, his mother who had nagged him into going to Helga's house, and his mother who had tongue-lashed him because he did not show more affection for Helga when she bid them a tearful farewell at Union Station the week after Easter.

"Ya, you will pray for me, Redmond?" she asked as she bussed his cheek.

"Sure," Red said, trying to sound uninterested.

His mother called him a cruel beast with a heart of stone. "That woman is the best friend you ever had and you treat her like dirt. You'll be a terrible priest unless you change.

Your father would be disappointed if he knew how insensitive you are to women."

The day after she left, Red went to the spiritual director and spilled out all his sins. The sentence was quick and merciful—leave the seminary at the end of the school year. Tell your mother that it was recommended that you take time off to think about your vocation. Maybe in a few years, you will want to try again.

There were hysterics at home, but Mom could not reverse the seminary's decision. She stormed down there to challenge the rector and the spiritual director. They stuck to their guns and at the same time protected his secret. Reluctantly, she agreed to his enrolling in St. Mel's High School.

"You'll have to find work to support yourself. I'll never spend another cent of money on a son who is so bad that he was thrown out of the seminary."

He had learned all the techniques, but with time he would also learn that technique doesn't matter if that's all you have. After you make a woman glow with physical satisfaction and well-being, what do you do next for her?

24

While he was telling the story, Eileen, pillow in hand, moved from the fireplace to the side of his chair, curled up again on the pillow, embraced his knees, and lay her head on his lap.

"Dear God, Red," she said when his voice had trailed off, "what a terrible experience for an innocent little boy. It's a miracle that it didn't do any lasting harm. I've known you were a tough customer, but to bounce back from something like that ... you were a molested child, that's what you were. And your mother cooperated. Of course she knew, at some level, what was going on. I'm so glad you trusted me enough to tell me...."

Red was disappointed. No lasting harm? What made her think he'd bounced back? Hadn't he said that he was a failure as a man except in bed?

"It's why I degrade women, I guess."

"Don't be ridiculous." She slapped his thigh gently, punishing a baby who was playing with an electrical outlet. "You simply have to learn that your self-image is wrong about this as about everything else. I've never felt degraded when you make love to me."

"No?"

"Course not. You treat me like you're a priest touching a sacred vessel, not exactly a chalice"—laugh and green eyes searching his face—the witch girl was now cavorting—"I'm not thin enough for that. Maybe a monstrance—or what did we call it?"

"An ostensorium?"

"Right." She buried her head again in his lap and squeezed his knees. "If anything, too much reverence and respect."

"But—"

"You're a wonderful lover, Red. You know that."

"Yeah...but..."

Could one so easily describe the agony of the past and exorcise it? Red was afraid that one could. Not nearly enough suffering.

"I love you, Redmond Peter Kane." She hugged him harder. "Now more than ever."

They huddled in silence. *What the hell,* thought Red, *I might as well enjoy it.*

Then Eileen stood up, removed the empty sandwich plates and tumblers to the mantel over the fireplace, knelt by the fireplace and lighted the fire, and then vanished into the kitchen. She returned with a bottle of apple cider and two clean tumblers.

"Autumn atmosphere," she said mysteriously; and, with the marvelous crossed-arm gesture that always tore at Red's lust, pulled John's shirt over her head and off her shoulders.

Her glorious breasts rose and fell over him. She paused deliberately to have the full impact on him. GREEN-EYED WITCH, he imagined the headline, GOES ON RAMPAGE. SEDUCES KANE. "I spoke too quickly, Red, when I said no harm was done. I meant you survived and can still love. But you were hurt terribly. The pain is still there. It always will be. I'm sorry...."

"I enjoyed it, kind of."

"Sure, there was pleasure." The frown of sympathy on her face deepened. "You were a healthy young male animal. And they used you, the two of them. What's more, you knew you were being used." She kicked off her panties and knelt next to him. "You treat me like I'm someone sacred, but has anyone, me included, ever treated you the same way?" She touched his lips with her fingers.

"Uh, well, I don't think—"

"I will absolutely not tolerate any more prudishness from you, Redmond Peter Kane." Her fingers did devastating things to him. "Not after what you started last night. Understand?"

"How can I argue when you do that to me?"

"Precisely," the lawyer who had won a decision. "I'm not so foolish, my darling, to think I can completely heal the hurt that's been there all these years. But maybe in the time ahead of us, I can ease the pain a bit."

"Well, I don't know that it's necessary...."

"Yes it is," she insisted, and began to unbutton his shirt. "We women know that men need gentleness more than we do, and we need it a lot. I don't know why we're so reluctant to act on that knowledge. Damn it, Red, hold still. Did you hear me say that prudery is out between us from now on?"

Her touch was as light as a mother's with a small child. *OH, oh, Red Kane, you're in for it now. You'd better relax and enjoy it because you're going to be smothered with affection whether you want it or not.*

"I said last night that I fell in love with you"—her lips flickered against his face like a fleeing butterfly—"because you were so compassionate. And so gorgeous. And I didn't say because you so badly needed someone to love you."

Red tried to talk, but a hand was firmly applied to his mouth. "Quiet, I'm doing the talking. No one ever did really love you, did they, Red? No woman, anyway. They used you. So I decided I'd be the one to overwhelm you with love. I guess I haven't done very well, have I?"

Red could not have answered now even if he knew how. But in that part of his brain that was still working, red lights went off. He was the one who had failed, not Eileen.

Then he succumbed completely to her compassionate ministrations.

And I thought she'd be disgusted with me.

For a fraction of a second he thought he heard the cosmic baseball bat. Irritably he told it to go away. The Holy Ghost ought not be a voyeur. Ought He? Or She?

"What if the kids—"

"We'll run." She tossed his shirt aside and knelt next to him, fingers on his belt buckle. "I don't know what's happening, Red Kane, but you started this and I"—she opened the belt and at the same time pressed a breast, warm and slightly moist, against his face—"I intend to love you from now on the way you deserve to be loved."

"That's my line."

"Be quiet and relax, my beloved, I intend to bury you in the sweetness of your malted milk and blot out for a few moments all the pain. Stop squirming and hold still while I undress you properly." She finished her task with quick skill. "There, now, that's better."

"Whipped cream too," he sighed.

"Of course." Her fingernails began, with infinite delicacy, to outline his flesh. "It really will be different this time."

"Tell me about it," he tried to say, but couldn't.

Marian would never do this for me, Red thought, and wondered why another of his failed loves would rush into his imagination. At this moment of all moments. Perhaps because long ago he had fantasized, foolishly, of the same scene with her in front of a fireplace.

25

With Marian Tracey, Red's innocence, lost in Helga's cottage at Twin Lakes, seemed to return. Sweet, dainty little Marian was an exquisite ceramic doll with a delicately formed face, carefully turned out by her fastidious mother and her rich father and polished by those skilled finishers of young ladies, the Religious of the Sacred Heart.

The Madames, as they were called with unconscious ribald humor, had changed dramatically since the 1950's. If you want to know the kind of "training" Marian received from first grade to college graduation, you must read Antonia White's *Frost in May*, as scary an account of the perversion of Catholic Christianity as one could imagine. The Madames—female Jesuits, they were often called, and not without reason—specialized in the religious and intellectual formation of wealthy young ladies. Their ideal product was a well-mannered woman, a loyal and enthusiastic daughter of the Church with a discreet sense of social responsibility (for "the poor"), a faithful and hardworking wife and mother, and a frigid automaton on the marriage bed.

Red had no personal experience to judge Marian on the last characteristic, but he would bet on it.

Eileen had had four years of the Madames at Barat and seemed to have been quite unaffected by the experience. But she had been immunized by the loud and bawdy Ryans; and, when she was at Barat, the Madames had already begun, like the rest of the Church, to change.

The "Convent" of the Sacred Heart, where his daughters went to high school, was merely a first-class secondary school, demanding and getting work from their students that a public school wouldn't dream of requiring. The Madames who administered it (now called Religious instead of Madames) were concerned neither with relevance nor with character formation. Academic excellence seemed to be enough. Not a bad idea, but the old mystique was gone. And so were the vocations.

Loyola Tracey, Marian's mother, completely accepted the old Sacred Heart world view, so there was no chance of family-based resistance to the Madames' molding of her daughter. Mrs. Tracey was a Cullen, a name that in her neighborhood of the North Side of Chicago meant the upper crust of the Irish middle class—chief clerks, department managers at Sears, senior court bailiffs. Lew Tracey had struggled through the Depression with a machine shop that made replacement parts for Packards. Doubtless he had to scrape and save to pay convent school tuition for their pretty and adored little daughter.

Lew made millions during the war; when it ended, Tracey Electric (later renamed Tracey Electronics) was a prosperous company in a key position to profit from the coming TV explosion. Like a lot of other men who were just plain dumb lucky in the defense industries, Lew thought that his success was evidence of great personal intelligence and God's special predilection (a term Marian picked up from the Madames) for him. Marian was one of the first Catholic debutantes, bowing at the elite Passavant Cotillion while Red was writing letters to Maryknoll in Japan.

He met her at a summer school class in Loyola in 1952, a radiantly pretty child with light blue eyes and short blond hair, dressed always in a skirt and high heels and never without a hat or gloves. Red fell in love with her the instant he saw her crinkly little smile.

It was his first tumble into normal love since Jane. Betty Lou was a date, Annie O'Brien was a dazzling haunted mystery, Lindy was an orgy partner, Helga was, well, Helga. He had somehow escaped the adolescent experience of falling in love with the girl of his dreams. So he was ready for the big flop on his face when that smile turned in his direction.

"Buy you a drink after class?" he asked hesitantly.

"A Coke?" She smiled again.

"Anything you want."

Red was as always a loner. His grammar school and high school classmates were still in the service. Mike Casey, having "lost the faith" (that was thought possible in those days), was at the University of Chicago. Red was living at home, of course, and going to school on the G.I. bill, despite his mother's hints that if he were not a lazy oaf, he would be "bringing money into the family." The government check, earned in the dust of Korea and the pain of the evacuation hospital, apparently did not count. Parn, now safely through four years at Quigley Seminary, had replaced Red as the family hero, Distinguished Service Cross notwithstanding.

Marian, diminutive angel from another planet, captured him with one flutter of her long eyelashes.

They swam at the North Shore beaches, talked about Catholic novelists—Greene, Mauriac, Waugh, Bloy—eagerly analyzed the social implications of the Gospel in their Young Christian Students meetings, and, with the passage of the months, began to discuss, in cautious circumlocutions, their future together.

Marian had no experience of life, but she was intelligent, possessed excellent literary taste, and could put sentences together on her feet that were both simple and clear. Later he would discover that many graduates of Catholic women's colleges were like her: Their classroom intelligence was first-rate, but it evaporated under the pressure of life experienced outside the classroom. They stopped thinking the day after graduation, partly because intelligence might be an obstacle to marriage and partly because their intellectual training wasn't flexible enough to stand up against life's complexities. Twenty years later feminism would capture their rage, some in favor of it, some, bitter because they had been cheated, adamantly against it.

Red was a war hero and a Captain in the Army Reserve (from which he would later escape as soon as possible). Loyola Tracey could see no objection to him as an escort for her daughter, though there were occasional hints from that refined, dignified little matron that Marian Angela (as she was always called at home) was still "very young."

Red had enough sense to know that this was a child to be treated with respect, not an orgy partner to be ravished. Moreover, the bright young Jesuit who taught his Moral Guidance class explained that God had put sexual pleasure in the world not as a temptation but as a reward. It was meant to be enjoyed as a payoff for the struggle and the difficulty and the expense of raising children. To enjoy it outside of marriage and outside the possibility of raising children was to violate God's plan.

Someone asked about people who were too old to have children and he replied that at that age most people were no longer interested in sexual pleasure, marriages were held together by other, stronger, and more important ties, and that, in any event, having raised their children, those men and women who still had the need for sex had earned the right to enjoy it.

In the middle 1950's he was prepared to buy the deal that their teacher promised. Hold off on sex till Marian and he were married. Then enjoy it, with proper respect for her, of course, as a reward for producing children. And he wanted kids then as badly as he wanted Marian.

So their kisses were at first tentative and brief, not much different from kissing Emily in eighth grade. Red was so much in love with Marian that even a peck sent him to the stars. Later they were passionate: burning kisses, and prolonged petting, though within clearly delineated boundaries. Red later wondered whether Marian felt anything during those romantic interludes. She would have faked satisfaction in intercourse after marriage to be the docile and loving wife that the Madames said she should be. Perhaps she faked passion when they kissed because she thought it would make him happy.

"Frigid little bitch," Eileen said when he told her about his romance with Marian, uncharacteristically catty, especially about a fellow Barat alumna.

"You bet," he responded. "Typical Barat graduate."

He was kicked in the shins. Lightly of course, so he would not be hurt.

He held Marian's delightful little body in his arms on Christmas Day in 1953, both of them trembling with intense emotion.

"I love you, Marian, I want to marry you."

"I'm so happy, so happy. I love you too."

They might have been happy together. He would have

become a typical suburban husband and father, country club member, golfer, who overworked, drank too much (some things are true in all possible scenarios), and fooled around only on conventions. They would have made a Cana Conference, turned out seven or eight kids, and come close to a divorce only once, and that after most of the kids were raised.

It would have been a more simple life.

Marian's father, doubtless egged on by her mother who probably wrote the script for him, saw that it did not happen.

"You actually enjoy working with the press?" Lew Tracey's lip curled with mild contempt. "I find that hard to believe."

It was early autumn of 1954. They were in Lew's study—shelves of leather-bound books that had never been moved since they were installed, mahogany furniture polished to mirrorlike radiance every day—in their lakefront home, in the most exclusive section of Lake Forest. The lake was calm and gold in the setting sun.

Red was nervous, but confident. Marian had assured him that "everything is all right." They lived after all in the second half of the twentieth century now. A young man spoke with his love's father, perhaps, but he certainly didn't ask for permission.

Waving his Havana cigar like a scepter, Lew lectured Red about the dangers of the international Communist conspiracy, pointing out how it was strong enough to threaten even that stalwart tower of Americanism, Senator Joseph R. McCarthy.

"If this country is going to survive, Joe McCarthy will have to be our next President," Lew said solemnly, flicking the ash from his cigar with a quick movement of his heavily jeweled fingers.

"Ike is not a good Republican candidate?" Red asked.

"He's naïve"—Lew Tracey dismissed the General with a wave of his hand—"and a captive of the pro-Communist, Jewish element in our government."

"Men like Sherman Adams and Charles Wilson," Red didn't reply. Nor did he tell Lew that every political reporter in the country knew that Tail Gunner Joe was a hopeless drunk.

"In my opinion"—Lew Tracey used the phrase when he was about to make a statement that was as certain as a solemn papal definition—"the press are the worst kind of garbage collectors, they live off the excrement of our country."

"Yes, sir." Red's face flamed and his fists clenched.

Lew sighed and set aside the now-extinguished cigar, whose acrid smell lingered in the room. His fingers, restless for something to control, played with the fountain pen on the icelike surface of his massive desk. "So you can see why we would have some reservations about our only child marrying a reporter."

"I'm not a garbage collector, sir." Red kept his voice under control. "There is corruption in every profession, business included. I hope by my work and example to raise the standards of the journalistic profession."

"That sounds very pious." Lew's face, much like that of an aging and ailing bulldog, curled into a sneer.

"I feel it's my vocation, Mr. Tracey."

Lew drew in a deep breath and changed his tack. "You understand how much we love Marian, our only child. She will inherit the company when Loyola and I pass on. She will be a very rich woman. Every house in America will have a TV set in a few years and our circuits will be in at least half of them. It would not be appropriate for her to be involved with the company—women are useless at that sort of thing. Perhaps you would be interested in coming on board now? As a vice president, with commensurate salary? That way you could learn the business from the inside."

He must have been contemptuous of me from the first time we met, Red thought. *Naïf that I am, I had missed it completely.*

"I don't think I'm cut out for the business world, Mr. Tracey." At that point Red might have made a deal. He detested the man, but he was hopelessly in love with his daughter. If he'd left it there Red might have come around. Lew Tracey was too dumb to leave well enough alone.

"Your background concerns me, too." He continued to fiddle with his fountain pen, as though he wanted to write something. "Rather radical, isn't it?"

"My father fought for Irish freedom against the English."

"And was killed in a riot, wasn't he? Organizing a union? Was he a Communist?"

"A picnic the police turned into a riot." Red was fighting desperately not to lose his temper. "I don't think anyone has ever claimed that the United Steel Workers was a Communist union. Phil Murray, their president, goes to Mass every day."

"Uhm. . . ." Lew was unimpressed. "What's the most important place in the country for an . . . er . . . reporter to work? Surely not Chicago."

"New York, of course." He wondered what his next tactic would be. "The *Times* or the *Herald Tribune*. Someday in the future perhaps Washington."

"You ever think of going to those cities?"

"You don't have to worry about that, Mr. Tracey." Red thought now that the clouds were about to lift. "I won't take Marian away from Chicago. I like the city too much."

"Let me suggest a compromise, young man." With a grandiose gesture, Lew removed a large checkbook from the center drawer of his desk. "We will not oppose Marian's wishes. However, we feel that she's still very young, too young to make an intelligent choice of a husband. If you will go off to, let us say New York, for two years, and during that time have only minimal contact with our daughter, then at the end of the two years we will give our blessing to the marriage. As a sign of our good faith, we will provide whatever financial assistance you might need to begin in New York."

He opened up the checkbook and began to write, his pen weaving eloquent circles in the air before it touched the precious paper—a gesture of a man for whom the contact of ink and check was a religious ritual. *Good heavens, doesn't the man know that I've seen this act in at least a dozen movies?*

"How much would that be? Twenty-five thousand? Fifty thousand?"

"I'm sorry, Mr. Tracey." Red stood up, playing out his role from the same films. "I love your daughter and I intend to marry her. I hope that eventually I'll have a good relationship with you and Mrs. Tracey. But I'm not for sale." He did not tell him what he could do with his checkbook. Later he deeply regretted that oversight.

"Cheap trash," Lew muttered as Red slammed the door.

"See you tomorrow at lunch when I calm down," Red told an anxious Marian at the door.

"All right," she said sadly.

Red was convinced that she would stand up to her father. If they told him that they were going to be married in the spring, no matter what her parents said, Lew and Loyola Tracey would cave in. It would be difficult perhaps for a few weeks, but they'd get over it. There was little chance of their disowning her. Even if they did that, love was still strong enough to survive; that was part of the movie scenario too.

The next day was Saturday. Red and Marian met at the Berghoff, a fashionable luncheon spot, it seemed to Red in those days.

She came into the room fifteen minutes late. Red rose from the table to greet her, shocked by her red eyes and her tearstained makeup.

"It'll be all right, Marian," he said, holding her arm tenderly. "We love each other enough to see this through."

He imagined quickly all the marvelous young-male fantasies in which he had reveled: an Asian paradise of sensual delights with a cheerfully naked Marian. Somehow they seemed improbable there in the Berghoff.

"I don't think you love me at all." She pushed his arm away and sank into the chair at the opposite side of the table, a little girl whose Christmas doll has been broken. "If you did, you would have been nicer to Daddy. Why can't you leave that old newspaper job, anyway? Do you love it more than me?"

This was not the way it happened in the films. End of scenario. "Are you on my side or his?" he asked coldly.

"I'm on both your sides." She started to cry again. "I wish you'd be more considerate of his feelings. Daddy only wants to help."

They talked for two hours in the restaurant and another hour walking over to Northwestern Station but did not get beyond the first exchange. Marian would accept either of her father's alternatives, though she much preferred that he stay in Chicago and go into the company with her family.

"Please don't ever say again that he was trying to bribe you. He only wanted to help." Once more the tears flowed.

Red was too stunned to be able to think. He loved Marian so much that he probably would have quit the *Herald* and gone to work for her father if she had reacted differently. Like the old man, she overplayed her hand.

"We have to settle this now," she insisted in the vast zeppelin-hangar waiting room of the station, as the monotonous voice on the public-address system announced the departure of trains to Los Angeles and San Francisco and Des Moines and Kalamazoo. "Poor Mommy and Daddy can't sleep at night, they're so upset."

"Let's talk about it again," he said, wondering whether his sleep mattered in her calculations. "I'll call you tomorrow."

"I'll talk to you only if you're ready to accept one of Daddy's alternatives." Her lower lip turned out stubbornly, much like her mother's. "Otherwise I'll know you don't love me."

Marian boarded the Northwestern that afternoon, brokenhearted but confident that by tomorrow he would have come to his senses. Red didn't call the next day or the day after. Each succeeding day, it was easier not to call, although the emotional pain seemed as bad as the physical pain caused by the hunk of North Korean shrapnel.

If she had called him and changed her tune ever so slightly, she probably would have won. Then later she could have manipulated him however and whenever she wanted. He would have been satisfied with even a token declaration of independence.

Even if she had made the token declaration of independence, nothing would have changed. It would have been one more cliché in a romantic comedy. But she didn't choose him over her father.

Instead she wrote him a long and tearful letter, one designed to break his heart. It pledged undying fidelity and love, blamed herself for the "misunderstanding," pleaded with him to forgive her, and begged that he try to understand how Mommy and Daddy felt.

Only one sentence was missing: "I'll marry you no matter what."

Of course, she could have no more written that sentence

than she could have flown to the moon. Or undressed for him in front of a fireplace as his wondrous green-eyed witch and accidental wife had done.

On her own initiative, God help him.

26

Melissa was waiting for him at the Arts Club, punctual as TV anchorwomen had to be. Sitting at a table next to the giant windows whose filtered sunlight glowed on the black marble floors of that elegantly old-fashioned establishment, she was almost indistinguishable from the Gayles and the Terris and Candis and the Tinas who had been part of his life intermittently for almost thirty years—some of them probably grandmothers by now. She was tall, lithe, blond, ambitious, brittle, lovely, undersexed, slightly overdressed in a cream-colored suit, and fascinated by Red.

Rarely did he have to end the relationship. They would gradually drift away, bored and perhaps disappointed when they learned that he would neither marry them (in the first fifteen years) nor move in with them (in the last fifteen years). While it was always supposed to be clear that they would make no demands on one another, it was in the nature of repeated human sexual acts, Red finally came to believe, that demands be made.

Such women were not exactly permanent lovers, certainly not mistresses in the old sense of that word. They were rather women with whom Red occasionally had lunch and with whom he sometimes fell into bed.

Or that's what they were supposed to be.

What did they get out of it? It was hard for him to understand. Not sexual pleasure, surely. And not permanent emotional security. Maybe the last, Terri, had put her finger on it when she said, "You're fun for a while, Red. Then I realize how much older you are."

Well, that was clear enough.

What did he get out of it? Guilt, self-hatred, loathing for his own vices, an escape that took his mind off his failures with Eileen—and an adolescent delight in the chase. The first night together, the first unveiling, the first claim made on the captured one's body—these were the high points for Red. After that came boredom while he waited for her to decide that there was no future with him or that he was too old or that she loved someone else.

How many in thirty years? Seven or eight maybe, one or two others less serious. Years at a time without anyone, then two in a row. Months when he was sure it wouldn't happen again, and then a pair of trim legs in a bar and, trancelike, Red was back in the game.

This was the first time that he would have to explicitly call the game on account of darkness—or perhaps on account of light. The affair was winding down, perhaps to be revived temporarily in the Doral Plaza apartment of a colleague who was off to Africa till the first of the year and had entrusted the key to Red in exchange for a promise that he would check up on it occasionally.

Virtue was not so strong yet in the "new" Red Kane that he did not lament the waste of the apartment. Perhaps Eileen...

He dismissed the fantasy. That would be going too far.

There was little fear of encountering Eileen at one of his lunches with the current girlfriend. He would schedule them when she was on trial and at restaurants too far from the Richard J. Daley Civic Center or the federal courthouse for there to be any chance of Eileen's coming upon his tête-à-tête.

Moreover, she told him each day where she would be, in case something should arise with the kids. At least that was her explanation. Red often wondered whether she was not as eager to avoid a chance encounter as he was.

She must have known. Yet she never threatened, never complained, never even mentioned the subject. Why not?

Why the hell not?

He would have to find out. That which had possessed him twenty-four hours before was demanding a clean start with Eileen. Before that frightening prospect, he must say farewell to Melissa.

She made it easy for him—at first.

"Thanks for the memory, huh, Red?" she said as he joined her at the table. "I ordered you a drink." She pushed the vodka martini in his direction. "Let's drink to the good times that were."

They touched glasses. Red sipped a drop or two. The tears in her eyes wrenched at his heart.

"She doesn't love you, Red." The tears streaming down her cheeks were bitter and angry. "If she loved you, she would fight for you or leave you."

There was no reason why Melissa should understand Eileen's peculiar psychology since Red didn't understand it either.

"I think you're wrong, Mel." He fiddled with his water glass. "But I won't argue the point."

"Poor bitch." She gulped the rest of her martini. "I feel more sorry for her than I do for you.... 'Cuse me, Red. It's been lots of fun and I'm grateful for the chance to know you. I don't want to make this any harder than it has to be." She rose unsteadily, the vodka already having its effect. "There's no elegant way to end an affair. You do it better than any of the others." She bent over and kissed him, rather sloppily. "See you around."

"Good-bye, Mel." He bowed his head sadly. "I'm sorry."

"Really."

She weaved her way uncertainly through the crowded dining room and out the door into the sunshine of Delaware Place.

"Miss Spencer will be coming back? Mr. Kane..." The waiter hovered uncertainly.

"No, Arthur, not today. She has a taping over on McClurg Court. Would you take away this martini and bring me the fruit salad and a cup of coffee?"

Arthur did not quite contain his surprise at the perfectly good vodka martini being dismissed from Red Kane's table.

Why the hell did you bother with me? he asked the Cheshire smile that had ambushed him on Wacker Drive as he walked across the river now to the *HG* building.

I've hurt all the others. Do you know with whom you're getting involved?

The presence that had lurked in the green ice refused to take his self-loathing any more seriously than his self-pity.

Red paused near the monument to Wacker and the other men who had built the drive back in bathtub-gin days and leaned on the railing overlooking the river. *Dick Daley, God be good to him, promised that someday we'd be able to fish in the river during our lunch hour. It will need a lot of cleaning up before that can happen. Divert more water. International treaties, damn Canadians fouling up my river because they won't let us pump more water from my lake....*

He reached for a notebook. Good column idea.

And saw Adele Ward rise up out of the river, her flesh disappearing from her bones as though being eaten away by invisible piranhas.

He shook his head. The vision refused to clear itself away as it usually did. Instead it slowly faded, leaving its traces on Red's brain.

Anxiously he looked at the men and women hurrying along Wacker Drive returning for their afternoon's work after lunch. None of them had seen Adele.

I may be losing my mind, he thought. *I am not a psychic. I don't have these experiences. I don't see dead women in the river. I don't get beat over the head by cosmic baseball bats. Maybe I have some sort of brain tumor.*

Or maybe I should have stayed away from the Amazon.

27

Red's imagination carried him from the banks of the Chicago River to the banks of the Amazon, a weird journey, as he admitted to himself—from tiny river to mighty.

The day he met with Rita Lane at seven in the evening,

the switchboard of the Tropical phoned Red's room, woke him from drink-bemused sleep in which he had dreamed about Harv Gunther killing Adele Ward not in his lakefront apartment but in Rita Lane's house in Manaus.

The señora at the switchboard told him in a voice that was working hard on its English but couldn't help sounding lovely that the Varig plane would not fly to Miami tonight. Mechanical difficulties. Of course the señor would remain at the hotel as the airline's guest.

Impulsively Red phoned Chicago and suggested that Eileen join him in Brazil. "Great country," he murmured. "Green hell and all that sort of thing."

"Is there anything wrong, Red?" she asked cautiously.

"I don't think so. The plane isn't flying tonight. This place is not exactly O'Hare. Can you come?"

"You know I have a trial," she said mildly, in the tone of voice reserved for trying to figure out whether her husband was drunk or how drunk he might be.

"That's right," he sighed. "The long flight and the tropical humidity made me forget. I just woke up."

"Oh."

In fact, he was not drunk. Only slightly hung over. But he would never tell Eileen that.

"Some other time. You'd love it here. Well, I expect I'll get out tomorrow night."

"Stay away from those man-eating fish...." She had figured out that he was not drunk.

"Piranha. The river is jet black, even the bathwater in the rooms...."

"Maybe next year."

Yeah, he thought as he hung up. *Or the year after.*

The Ryans did not like to travel. The women did not trust airplanes. The men were too hooked on Chicago. Perhaps if Eileen and he had traveled together more...

But that was absurd.

He showered, shaved, and went down to the bar, pausing to consider the birds who lived in a glass enclosure in the atrium. None of them seemed very friendly. After two drinks, he ate a huge Brazilian dinner, beef of course, drenched with spice and batter, consumed half a bottle of wine, and wandered into the pool area for coffee and liqueur.

Of course, señor, we have Baileys.

Naturally.

The pool was filled with noisy tourists, mostly German, even though it was ten o'clock at night. Red grew weary of the noise and stumbled back into the dimly lit arched corridors of the hotel.

And bumped into Adele.

Only it wasn't Adele, but a German preteen who looked like her and muttered something guttural which he took to be a reflection on the morals of elderly Americans who have had too much to drink.

Afraid to go to his room until he had sweated off the excess alcohol in his bloodstream, he crossed the road and walked down the dimly lit path to the steamy beaches of the Rio Negro. No bugs—the chemical that made the river black was a natural bug repellent. Sticky-sweet tropical smells assaulted his nose, his shirt was already drenched with sweat, his head light from travel disorientation and alcohol. Lightning crackled across the sky. More rain, another downpour in the works, which would make the worst Lake Michigan deluge look like an "occasional shower."

Adele would simply not leave him alone. A runaway, picked up by white slavers, trained, promised wealth, used, discarded. It was a sorry tale, well known to reporters and law enforcement agencies, who were powerless to put an end to the trade. "Supply and demand, chum," Paul had said long ago. "Don't think that reformers could stop it any more than they could stop us from drinking booze in the good old days of Prohibition."

Red had disagreed but, as in most other arguments, had not been able to marshal evidence to change Paul's mind. Now he realized that Paul was probably right. Still you had to do something....

That's the story of my life, he told himself, wishing he had a glass of Jameson's in his hand. *You have to do something.... Only you never do.*

He made up a story for Adele Ward. *A pretty little girl in a well-to-do family. Happy childhood. Mother died. Father remarried. Stepmother made her life miserable. Ran away, mostly to attract attention. Could happen to anyone. None of us are masters of our fate. Maybe she would have died young of cancer anyway. It çouldn't happen to Patty or Kate, could it?*

Of course it could, you dolt. It's not your fault that nothing terrible has happened to them. If Eileen...

He chased the thought away. Too many unfinished thoughts tonight. The mists and the booze were getting to him. Spooky place. Damn, what was the matter with Varig?

He should go back to his room and sleep it off. Then he saw her on the river in a flash of illumination from the lightning—Adele being eaten alive by the fish!

No, it was the German girl—out in the middle of the river, her legs already turned into skeleton bones.

Red Kane, the hero of Taegu, turned and ran back to the Tropical, burst into the lobby to the dismay of the hotel staff, rushed to his room, and vomited into the toilet bowl—filled with black Rio Negro water.

Outside the rain was pouring down in massive curtains. Red staggered out of the bathroom, removed two airplane-size bottles of Canadian from the refrigerator, and gulped them in two quick gasps. He collapsed, exhausted and sick, on his bed. The Brazilians did not make comfortable mattresses. German tourists probably liked them hard. The whiskey began to dull his brain again. Jameson's it was not, but still potent enough to put him to sleep.

The next morning he told himself that the vision had been a dream and promptly forgot about it.

Yet since his return from Brazil, he thought he had seen Adele Ward several times walking rapidly ahead of him on the streets of Chicago and had dreamed frequently about the Amazon. He dismissed such phenomena as a manifestation of aging romanticism.

His imagination left the Amazon and returned him to the banks of the Chicago River, near the green glass tower that—was it only two days ago?—had unceremoniously thrust him into his new life.

Today was the first time he'd had the dream wide awake. The two rivers—were they connected? And was his—he used the words to himself for the first time—his mystical experience somehow related to Adele Ward's death?

Adele Ward was haunting him. Her bones were not in the Rio Negro, but arguably they were in the Chicago River.

He glanced up at the green glass skyscraper for reassurance. Slowly the humid memories faded. Everything would be all right.

The Amazon jungle was surely a green hell. Not the same kind of green, however, as the 333 Wacker Building. That was green heaven. Where God, not the devil, lived. If there was a God.

Well, dummy, if there isn't, who was it that hit you over the head and turned you into Super Lover last night?

He sighed blissfully. The woman was not bad for a slave girl in Jerusalem. Of all places. Come to think of it, she was also quite acceptable as a Mother from Sligo, too. Ah, those Sligo women!

He continued to study the skyscraper. It was indeed almost the same color as Eileen's eyes.

28

"I'm the witch with the green eyes," the girl said bravely. "The one Mom warned you about, you know, the hot-tempered one...."

Mysterious, magical eyes, imponderable and yet vulnerable, red now from weeping and watery with tears. Yet glowing with a smile. And a hint of laughter.

"I think I knew without being told," he said, holding the young hand firmly. "Your mother was the finest woman I've ever met. I'm sorry I didn't get to know her better."

"I know." The eyes overflowed again. "I am too."

Red often remembered the picture of those flooded green eyes. Despite the pain in them, there was so much promise—hope, vitality, the energy of youthful dreams and enthusiasms. She had deserved so much better than what life had dealt her. Yet Eileen was a great one at making the best of a bad bargain. The frustrations of her marriage to a man who was essentially a good-looking and sometimes charming bum would have destroyed many other women. Eileen bent but she did not break. She was a pragmatist in an age of ideologues, just as her mother had been an ideologue in an age of pragmatists.

Typical Ryan.

She could have done worse, of course. But she could have done so much better.

It was her grave misfortune to be in the wrong place and with the wrong man the day John Kennedy died. Well, none of it could be helped now.

Since her mother's wake he'd looked into those witch's eyes thousands of times. Often he told himself that he romanticized them. They promised magic and mystery, but it was all an illusion. The woman was an able attorney, a superb mother, a faithful wife—under difficult conditions—and a more than passable infrequent bed partner. She was matter-of-fact, down-to-earth, ordinary, the most nonsupernatural of women.

It didn't do any good. Red knew better. As the woman in the *Sun-Times* had said, Eileen was special. And not because she was the best woman trial lawyer in town and not because she made the most of a very bad bargain named Red Kane.

Kate Ryan's wake had been quintessentially Irish, displaying that weird mixture of fatalism and hope, of tragedy and joy, of despair and laughter that was imprinted on the Irish psyche long before the missionary monks showed up and that merged so easily with Christianity that not even the monks realized that it was a little weird.

In the old days in the mother country, before the Church finally eliminated the wake (something it did not try to do in this country), men and women would make love in the potato fields outside the house where watch was being kept over the dead. The message was loud and clear—"Fuck you, death!"

They don't make love in the potato fields these days,

though Red did not want to deny the possibility of anything in the Ryan clan.

Kate's early death was a bitter tragedy for her husband and children and young grandchildren. Though they'd known it was coming, they were devastated by grief. Yet the sorrow mixed with festivity. The Ryans could not assemble for any purpose without it turning into a party.

"Mom would have been furious if we were gloomy," his wife would say to him many years later, tears spilling out again. "I'm sure she would have come back to haunt us."

Red confessed that he came to the wake partly out of respect for a remarkable woman and partly out of curiosity. How, he wondered, would this spectacular clan cope with death? Were they as Irish as they pretended to be?

And he was also a little curious about the green-eyed witch, a girl now in her late teens, he supposed. A wake would be a safe environment to see what she was like.

Not safe enough, as it turned out. The mixture of curiosity and affection he saw in her witch's eyes haunted him long after Kate Ryan was buried in the ground of Mount Olive cemetery.

When his romance with Marian ended, he was at first hurt, numb, wiped out by pain. Then slowly he became angry. He had been played for a fool. He was an innocent young romantic, taken in by a scheming conniver.

His mother was not much of a help. "What happened to your pretty little sweetheart?" she would demand at least once a month.

And that changed into, "When is your pretty little sweetheart going to marry her handsome young doctor?"

His mom had disliked Marian from the first time she met her. "An empty little nothing," she said with a sharp cut of her hand, as if chopping off Marian's papier-mâché head. Later she would hate Eileen venomously. "A fat worthless tramp, you can see it in her eyes."

His mother also hated the Ryan clan. "Trash that put on airs." In fact, Eileen and the Ryans were guilty of something much worse than putting on airs. They threatened his mother with the loss of all that was left in her life.

Marian did marry her doctor, a man ten years older than

she was and handpicked, he was sure, by Mommy and Daddy. Years later he was arrested on a narcotics charge. The divorce that followed was noisy and messy. She remarried in her early forties, a Harvard Business School grad who was vice president and controller of the company. Red did not feel vindicated, only sad.

When his anger abated about a year after his last conversation with Marian in Northwestern Station, he continued to be frightened—both of another rejection and of another trap. So he stayed away from the kind of woman with whom he might fall in love and consorted, in one way or another, with those whom it was fun to pursue and relatively easy to lose.

Gun-shy? Hell yes. His fragile masculine pride had been hurt. He would be cautious before exposing it again. He was well on his way to becoming your stereotypical Irish bachelor who does not marry until he is almost fifty—if then.

So fascinating and mysterious and strong women like Eileen were off-limits. He had routed a wheedling manipulator like Marian. An Eileen, a creature of light (which is what her name means in Irish), if permitted to get too close, would overwhelm him.

A hasty judgment made of a teenager at a wake? Sure, but as it turned out, a very accurate judgment. He saw those green eyes again in the bar of the Marina City restaurant in the spring of 1963, when the missile crisis was over and the March on Washington yet to happen. Marina City was at that time a fashionable new complex on the river, picture on the cover of the Chicago phone directory and similar honors. He thought correctly that the towers were two ugly corncobs. Time, and such monuments of the Fourth Chicago School as the John Hancock Center and the Sears Tower would do in Marina City in a few years.

When she saw that he had recognized her, the eyes lit up with amusement. A shadow of an impish smile flicked across her intriguing round face, framed by long, ebony hair, falling on her dress like tar on snow.

It hung in the balance for a few seconds. This was not his leggy blond prey. This was a glorious and dangerous black-haired buttermilk-skinned Celtic virgin.

Dangerous. Vulnerable perhaps. Imponderable surely.

And irresistible.

"What's wrong with the world that you're drinking alone?" He eased onto the barstool next to her. She seemed very young up close, too young to be alone in what he would later call a singles bar.

"Stood up for a date."

Already the fear and curiosity and affection, all undeserved, shone on him—and broke his heart. "How tasteless."

"I think I scared him off. Women law school students can be a bit much." Her whimsical smile suggested that it was no great loss.

"Might I fill the vacancy? Dinner and movie?"

"We were supposed to see *The Leopard*; it's here in the Marina City Theater. You won't have to take me home. I live in the building."

"I am reduced to awed worship by Claudia Cardinale."

"That's the kind of woman you like, is it?"

The chemistry of flirtation was surging back and forth between them, carried on the same air as her scent, feminine enough to be enticing, discreet enough to be elegant.

"Would you go without me?" He munched on a huge handful of popcorn, to hide his embarrassment. The girl already saw through him.

"Certainly. Have you read the book? Wasn't it a shame that the poor man didn't live to see it published? I hope he knows now."

He was indeed awed by the sumptuous young Cardinale that evening. And even more awed by the sumptuous young woman next to him. She had finished college a year early by attending both summer school sessions for two summers and had then enrolled in Loyola's law school, in those days less than eager for women students. He gathered that the rudeness of her male classmates did not bother her in the least. Ned Ryan had remarried, as all the family thought proper. Eileen insisted on an apartment of her own, to give Ed and Helen the privacy to which they were entitled. She wanted to work for Bob Kennedy when she graduated. Hunt organized-crime types.

The witch's eyes flared when he lightly kissed her good night.

Red was as much in love at that moment as he had been at his worst with Marian. More. He was older and lonely. And he had met the perfect woman.

He fought it every way he could. Sometimes during the spring and summer he would catch her watching him with an amused smile, perhaps like an angler who has hooked a big fish. Later he would think that it was like the smile of a mother for a wicked but entertaining little boy. Or like that of her daughter, Patty, grinning at some dumb caper of Luciano the Labrador.

He kept his distance, dating her only once a week. He made no passes, conscious that this was an impressionable young virgin, even more entitled to his protection than Marian had been. Eileen did not push. She was young and in no rush. Her family did not seem to object. They were certainly cordial when he was dragged to their summer compound at Grand Beach. Yet even then he tried not to like them. He didn't object if this gorgeous Irish goddess—mind-boggling in a bikini—found him amusing. He objected when her relatives smiled at him in the same way.

It was a big summer for the family. Helen, Ed's new wife, was pregnant. Cathy Collins, a cousin, was about to enter the convent—and begin a tragic pilgrimage which would end in the torture chambers of Costaguana. Blackie was home from the seminary for his first summer vacation. Red was permitted to participate in these festivities as though he were a member of the family, even constrained to learn how to water-ski.

Eileen was the quietest of the Ryans, like her father in that respect at any rate. Until the singing began. With hardly a word of encouragement, after the required family viewing of *Twilight Zone* she would bound to the piano and lead the family choir. That summer the big musicals were, as he remembered, *Carnival* and *How to Succeed in Business without Really Trying*. Eileen sang with a clear, sweet, and disciplined voice and clowned at the piano like an uninhibited professional performer. The clown would later seem to be buried in the lawyer. Except when she would sing with the girls. And except sometimes when she and Red would make love.

"One would think she would do well on the musical stage," Blackie whispered in his ear during a summer song session.

"One would."

"One would wonder why she pursues the law instead."

"One would."

"One would be surprised that a Ryan thinks she's not good enough."

"Astonished."

"Humph..."

Eileen was born, he would later learn, while her father was away on his destroyer fighting the Japanese. Somehow that made her the most serious of the Ryans. And deprived the stage of an appealing and talented performer.

Who would never have married Red Kane.

He resolved at the end of that summer to stay away from her. She was ten years younger than he was. He'd be an old man when she was in the prime of her maturity. Yet he did not avoid passionate embraces on the beach at night—God, should there be one, has designed summer beaches for capturing the male of the species. Red would begin the necking and she would end it with a skyrocket of passionate affection that made him want to spend the rest of eternity on the beach in her arms.

"All in all, you're not bad, Redmond Peter Kane," she said one Saturday night when they strolled back from a particularly mind-bending interlude of embracing. "Not nearly the sexless Irish bachelor you pretend to be."

"I'm glad to know that I suffice," he said, brushing sand off his slacks.

"That," she said, touching his cheek, "remains to be seen."

He might have held out for a long time. He might even have escaped. His Irish-bachelor credentials were pretty good.

Neither Eileen nor he realized how deeply involved their emotions were, how strong the ties had become, even that first night at *Il Gattopardo*. They both thought they could proceed carefully and leisurely. They did not understand how compelling love between man and woman is once it has been set in motion, especially when they find themselves sharing cosmic tragedy.

29

Pat Moynihan was on the TV screen, a young, black-haired Pat. "If you're Irish you know the world is going to kick you around. We'll laugh again, but we'll never be young again. We thought he had more time. So did he."

"Turn it off, please, Red," her head burrowed against his chest. "I can't stand it anymore."

Red walked over to her tiny portable TV, glanced out the window at the silent Chicago River, seemingly mourning under the darkness of the autumn sky. Pat was right, he would never be young again.

He returned to the couch and took the weeping Eileen back into his arms.

The President was dead! The city room had been frozen in shock when it came over the AP wire. It could not be. Their gallant young President who was about to lead the country into a new era. It was impossible.

With clumsy hands and leaden feet, automatically like zombies, they had turned out their special editions, many of them convinced that the right-wing/John Birch element in American society was about to stage a coup. It could not be the madness of a single crazy man, could it?

There were a few free hours. Red literally ran across the State Street Bridge to Marina City and rode up in the elevator to Eileen's apartment. Dressed in jeans and a man's-style white shirt hanging outside her slacks, she was watching the TV screen with hypnotized fascination, as they all were doing that day, tears streaming down her cheeks.

Later they would try to explain to their kids what it was

like. The kids would listen solemnly and nod their heads. But they wouldn't understand. They couldn't understand. Moynihan had said it all. A single evil man, with a single evil bullet, had destroyed the best hopes of a generation.

Eileen and he clung to each other in grieving silence. Then, imperceptibly, something in their embrace began to change. It became both more intense and softer. Perhaps it was two mourning Irish Catholics defying death, reasserting life. Or maybe it was only lust, unleashed by grief. He moved Eileen's head so he could look into her face. In the back of his brain, he heard a voice warning that he was exploiting an innocent virgin. But her smile, shining through tears, invited Redmond Peter Kane to do whatever he wished. The sweetness of the moment was beyond resistance. He began to unbutton her shirt.

An inexperienced virgin she surely was. But she was also a woman who knew instinctively how to give herself completely in an offering of love. For a short time that tragic evening, Red forgot all the other foolishness in his life and encountered his first and only lover.

Afterward, guilt already enveloping him like poison gas seeping from a leak in a pipe, he kissed her good-bye and raced back to the city room. She followed him to the door of the apartment, shirt modestly clutched at her breasts, face radiantly happy. "I love you, Red. Never forget that."

"I won't," he promised.

The next morning he called her, sick with grief and loathing for his own vileness. "I'm sorry, Eileen," he pleaded, "terribly, terribly sorry."

"I'm not," she said firmly. "Not in the least."

"Didn't we sin?"

"Why don't you take it up with your confessor?"

There didn't seem to be any suitable reply for that.

About then or perhaps shortly thereafter, a fertilized ovum that would grow into John Patrick Kane was implanting itself in his mother's womb. The John was for his father and her brother who was studying to be a priest and for their dead President. They never discussed whether the Patrick was an oblique tribute to the now-senior Senator from the Empire State.

Something died and something lived.

Two weeks later John Patrick Kane's mother missed her period. A week after that, she was sick three mornings in a row. Self-reliant and sensible woman that she was, she went to see a doctor. Then, she waited till after Christmas to tell Red. He contended, with some sincerity, that their child must grow up with her as its mother.

"It doesn't have to be that way, Red," she argued. "The kid will be much happier if he does not grow up in a marriage that started on the wrong foot."

So insistent was she that there was no need for them to marry, that he started to wonder if she did not want to marry him. A nice blow to his arrogant generosity that would be.

"Would you rather not be my wife, Eileen?" he asked tentatively.

"I've wanted to be your wife since Mom's wake. Maybe even since I read your article about her when I was a dumb high school sophomore. I don't want it to be this way. I didn't mean to take away your freedom. Honestly, Red, I am so filled with regrets. I knew what was happening. I knew what time of the month it was.... I lost all willpower and character. I want you to be free."

He folded her into his arms. "I've never felt freer, woman. And don't dare think differently."

That should have settled it. Or maybe it shouldn't have. Had Eileen ever forgiven herself for forcing him into a marriage? They didn't talk about it—or about anything else in their twenty-year relationship. Would they have been more open with one another if their approach to the altar had been less precipitous?

There was never time. Maybe there would never have been time even if they had not been lovers that night.

His brother, Father Parnell Kane, home from Rome and working at the Chancery, found time in his busy schedule to take care of the paperwork and to officiate at their marriage in Holy Name Cathedral. Blackie Ryan, beaming owlishly next to him, acted as the altar boy. Eileen, at Red's absolute insistence, wore full bridal white. They left for Acapulco on their honeymoon, a mixture of unbearably sweet passion and morning sickness, and an occasional outburst of temper followed by delectable love, Eileen's way of apologizing.

It's been that way ever since. No more morning sickness and much less frequent passion, but two strangers living together.

They were godparents for Chantal, Helen Ryan's first child, "a little girl who looks and acts just like Blackie," by common agreement. Red envied Ned and Helen their love and wondered whether he was doomed, for his past sins, not to be able to love a woman.

Red was faithful to his wife until the birth of Patty. The pregnancy was difficult, with numerous threats of miscarriage, and the delivery terribly painful. Eileen was worn out and overwhelmed by the burden of two babies in the apartment. Red was striving to prove that he could be as good a political editor as Paul O'Meara.

Red was less sexually driven than bored, not with his wife, not with his children.

But with himself.

30

Automatically Red Kane reached for his cigarettes as he hung up the call to Brazil. Damn Third World telephone systems didn't work half the time and the other half they worked badly.

Rita Lane was still alive, however, and relatively serene. There had been no more messages from Adele Ward. And no sign of agents of Harv Gunther hunting her down. How good were her contacts with the Brazilian police?

They were excellent, thank you. If anyone was looking for her, they would know.

Red hoped the Brazilian cops were better than the people who maintained the Brazilian long-distance service.

His cigarettes were not in his shirt pocket. What had he done with them? Damn and double damn. Had he run out?

Then he remembered that in the first fervor of his reformed life a couple of days ago he had given them up. It seemed easy then. How long would it take before the hunger ebbed? He'd read somewhere that the first week was the hardest.

He poured himself a cup of herbal tea instead.

There was something missing in the Harv Gunther picture. He opened his locked file cabinet and considered the Paul O'Meara and Harv Gunther files—next to each other. Obviously they belonged together. But Paul was only part of the Gunther story and, all things considered, a small part for everyone but Red and maybe Paul's family. Most of the young journalists in town had never heard of him. Even if Red could prove that he was still alive somewhere, it would make little difference to the citizens of Chicago. Linking him with Harv Gunther would have almost no impact. So there was a journalist who once was in Gunther's pay and had disappeared a long time ago. So what?

So why the death threat from Harv?

He was an anxious and irascible old man, perhaps still worried about the Adele Ward murder. Later Red blamed himself for not taking the threat seriously enough. But at the time, his enthusiasm was sweeping all obstacles aside. Nothing and no one could stop the new Red Kane.

What possible link, he wondered, could there be between the disappearance of the old journalist and the young girl? Paul had disappeared in the winter of 1963; Adele had been murdered in the spring of 1983. She had not even been born when Paul took his walk across the snow-shrouded bridge.

And why the threat from the limo on Wacker Drive over the Pulaski Demolition investigation? If that was a threat and not a random traffic mistake.

Red reached for his cigarettes again and then diverted his hand to the teacup.

At the outer fringes of his consciousness there was a hint of a connection. Gingerly he removed the Adele Ward envelope. Everything was still there—the pictures, the statements, the unsigned handwritten note. He pondered them and then replaced them in the file and locked the drawer.

There was a piece of the puzzle that must be found. No,

not found. It must be uncovered. Somehow, somewhere, he had it.

Lord, he needed a drink. He glanced at his watch. Four-thirty. They'd be gathering at Billy Goat's or Ricardo's.

So, Cheshire smile, all calm and curled, I won't have a drink. I'll betake myself to the East Bank Club, ogle the young women, and swim a half mile. Much more healthy than a half bottle of Jameson's at the Old Town Ale House.

Wonderful.

The new life had its ups and downs. For forty years he had prayed intermittently that God would tell him what to do. So God had told him.

It turned out to be damnably hard. Perhaps impossible.

Eileen was problematic. Yesterday, she had phoned him from her office in high dudgeon. "Red, do you want my colleagues and associates to think I've taken a lover?"

"Yes."

"It is NOT funny. I repeat, NOT funny."

"What's the difference between a colleague and an associate?"

"One is a . . . God damn it, Red. Will you listen to me? I am totally embarrassed when I come back from court to discover another two dozen roses in my office. What will people say?"

"Like *totally* embarrassed?"

"Humiliated too." She ignored his hint that she was talking like his daughters.

"The card said, 'Love, Red.'"

"People don't see the card."

"Okay. I won't do it again. I'll bring them home instead."

"I don't mean to sound ungrateful."

"You do though," and he hung up, incensed.

Hey, I hung up on her. How about that. I'm fighting back. Restrain them, like Joe Murphy said.

The worst part of it was that he was deliberately putting her on. He knew that the roses would embarrass her at the office. Fine. It had been a long time since he'd been playful with her. She'd have to get used to it.

They both had forgotten what falling in love was like—hours of serenity and peace, followed by more hours of anxiety and depression. Absolute and total confidence in the beloved, alternating with the most absurd jealousy—of Nick Curran now, God save us all. Unspeakable happiness at the top of the roller coaster; and the restless melancholy at the bottom of the roller coaster.

"We're both too old for that," he argued, but that didn't change anything. No matter how old, infatuation was infatuation, even if the object was your wife of two decades.

She snapped at him more in an hour than she had in months before. The big difference was that now it was Red's turn not to snap back.

"Take your hands off me," she would snort. "I am not a thing to be used."

Dutifully he would remove his hands, perhaps commenting, "I thought you said you were willing to try anything."

"I didn't say that." A guilty grin would sneak across her face.

"And you didn't say I could feel you up anytime I wanted."

"CERTAINLY not. And if you say I lie as much as Kate, I'll KILL you."

Usually his hands would be recaptured at once. Sometimes it would take her an hour or even a half day to apologize. "Nervous old woman afraid of sex and death," she would whisper into his chest. "Red, I don't understand. Why do you put up with me?"

He assumed that it was a rhetorical question. Later he would not be so sure.

He was still, as Kate had remarked with bemusement, doing his "practically-perfect-Daddy bit": emptying the garbage, taking Luciano for his walks, keeping the refrigerator filled with Diet Coke and Diet Pepsi in the proper amounts, even putting up the last of the storm windows ("No Thermopane for this house!").

"Why don't you do something wrong!" Eileen had barked, half fun and full earnest.

"Practically perfect Daddy," Kate marveled.

So I'm outrageous, Red thought, considering his CRT. He grinned to himself. *Part of courting a woman is to be a little bit outrageous.*

So he had crept down Wabash Avenue to Marshall Field's and into the lingerie section, which he had not visited for twenty years, and sent—on her charge card of course—a collection of delicate peach-colored garments to her at the office. To his surprise he remembered the right sizes.

He was even less successful with the kids. Katie sulked when he asked her how school was ("Boring") and who she was dating ("No one"). Johnny mumbled on the phone when he asked about the prospects for the basketball team at St. John's. Patty flounced out of the room when he asked if he could read her term paper on Gerard Hopkins.

So he had come to work that morning feeling pretty grim about his new life. The foul-ups of the Brazilian telephone system had caused him to lose his temper and swear at the operator, the sort of behavior that had been typical enough before the Feast of All the Saints, but that was supposed to have been left in the past.

He messed with his novel, somehow not finding it very funny anymore and fended off irate calls from readers about his column on women that had appeared that morning.

In the early afternoon, after eating two oranges and a banana, he tried the call to Brazil again. Still no luck. The operator would call back.

Sure.

Some of the women staffers seemed to want to talk about the column but were frightened off by his glare. He told the switchboard that he was not in for readers.

The phone rang again. Goddamn Brazilians.

"I don't want to hear about your problems," he shouted into the phone.

"Red..."

A soft, female voice.

"Eileen," he snapped.

"I enjoy being courted. Totally. Thank you."

"Put them on in the women's room. Give your colleagues and associates a thrill."

Why is she bothering me?

"I already have. And you knew my sizes, too."

She objects to roses and she doesn't object to frilly underwear. What the hell!

"I've had two decades," he softened considerably, "to examine the dimensions of your body, woman. Besides, while I have nothing against it, they kind of beat the St. John's T-shirt."

Eileen Ryan Kane actually giggled. "You're sweet, Red. I don't know what's happening, but right now I think it's wonderful."

"I can send lingerie but not roses to the office," he said, still testy.

"You can send anything you want, darling."

So he tried the call to Brazil again and finally talked to Rita Lane. At the end of the day he had for his efforts a page and a half in the novel, a weak column for the next day, a headache, hunger for a drink, and a pleasant phone call from his wife.

Better, he supposed, than nothing.

He would have to stop back at Field's on his way to the East Bank and buy her something else. One could spend a lot of money on a new lover.

He grinned. Maybe a bad day, but it would be a good night. Very good.

As he was leaving his cubicle, the phone rang. He hesitated and then answered it.

"Red? Nick Curran. I'm here at Northwestern Hospital with Eileen. I'm afraid there's been an accident."

From the Kane File

November 3, 1983

Kane's Corner

HEF IS RIGHT ABOUT WOMEN

by Redmond P. Kane

The 30th anniversary of *Playboy* being just around the corner, it seems appropriate to admit that Hugh Hefner is right about women. They are designed for the entertainment of men.

Hef is wrong, however, about entertainment.

On the face of it, women were assembled to entertain

and delight us. Their faces, their bodies, their voices, the touch of their hands, the sympathetic glow in their eyes, their laughter, their tenderness when we're sick, their encouragement when we're down—I defy you to find more entertaining material anywhere in the world. They beat music, painting, sculpture, fiction, even food all hollow.

There may be a better way of passing the time than girl watching (or woman watching, as far as that goes), but I don't know what it is.

There will be cries of outrage from feminists about this column. Many of them resent their own entertainment value. They do their best not to be entertaining themselves and to persuade other women that they should abandon their entertainment role.

Short of self-mutilation of one kind or another, that's impossible.

I'm not saying that this is the way things should be. Whoever put the cosmos together may have shown singularly bad taste in the matter, but S/He arranged things in such a way that women delight men, endlessly, amazingly, delightfully.

The evolutionary folks tell us that the "secondary sexual characteristics" —which, God forgive us for it, we men admire so much—and our (men's and women's) constant preoccupation with sex are all part of a conspiracy to keep the male and the female together long enough to raise offspring that require a long period of parental care and protection to mature into adults.

In other words the Conspirator designed women to entertain us, scheming that we would be so delighted with them as to cleave to them indefinitely and help them to raise our children.

Maybe it should have been done some other way. Take it up with Herself. When the feminists demand that we do not enjoy womanly beauty they are demanding that the evolutionary process be reversed.

That will take a while.

The problem with the *Playboy* philosophy is that he doesn't really understand what is satisfying sexual entertainment. In the early days when Hef and his photographers left something to the imagination, the magazine had some small entertainment value, in addition to satisfying the inevitable curiosity of adolescent men. (And all men are more or less adolescent; otherwise, I suspect, the species might discontinue itself.)

Now it's strictly dullsville because Hef and the bunch of revelers up at the Playboy Mansion don't understand that entertainment involves people. Only a rare music lover will be satisfied with a picture of Sir Georg and the CSO. I don't know a single Chicago Bulls fan who gets his kicks from staring at a newspaper photo of Reggie Theus.

A record of the orchestra or a TV replay of a Bulls game is better than still photos. But those who look to music or basketball for their recreational entertainment will tell you that the real thing can be enjoyed only when human persons perform with peak efficiency in response to the challenge of doing what they alone do best—you have to be there at the Horizon or at Orchestra Hall, and deeply involved as a human person with the human persons who are performing.

Girl watching is mildly more entertaining than watching the clouds drift by. Enjoying the fresh young bodies on a beach beats snorkeling, as far as I'm concerned. I guess I'd look at a current, no-imagination-required *Playboy* centerfold before I glanced at the smokestacks out at Commonwealth Edison.

But more than a day or two on bikini beach is a bore. Girl watching does not fill up many of the empty spots in a day. The centerfold loses its allure pretty quickly. Striptease acts pall after a couple of visits. The porno film business soared a few years ago and then collapsed. I'm not saying these entertainments lack appeal, nor that there are not men for whom they are enough.

I'm saying that you only get full entertainment value out of a woman when you're involved with her in a relationship in which you can fight with her and then make up. Reconciliation with a woman is the best entertainment bargain in the world. Murder, yes; divorce, no way, as someone remarked the other day in a competing paper.

Again, I'm not saying that this is the way it ought to be. Personally, I wouldn't mind if the Conspirator had arranged things in such a way that I was designed to relate with a harem of gorgeous creatures who were not as completely human as I am. Mind you, it would probably not be as interesting as the present system, but then in the hypothesis, I wouldn't know that.

I'm simply saying that's the way it is. Hef and his bunch don't understand that without a relationship of equity and commitment you simply don't get full entertainment value out of your woman.

Is the reverse true? Do we entertain women?

It's hard to know because they won't say. Sometimes I think that they don't need as much entertainment as we do. Other days, I think their principal entertainment is laughing up their sleeves at us. Yet other days, I think that they are more willing to settle for second-rate entertainment than we are.

My own personal hunch, and don't tell Hef or his mob of sybarites this, is that the greatest injustice in the struggle between the sexes is that it is relatively easy, in our present state of physical evolution and emotional sensitivity, to keep a man entertained.

And damn near impossible to really entertain a woman.

The male of the species has only begun to learn how it's done.

31

"It was only a simple mugging, Red. Routine, it happens every day."

Eileen was sitting up in the hospital bed, pale but composed, more worried, characteristically, about her distraught husband than about the bump on the back of her head on which a large ice pack rested. Had nothing changed since 1968?

I'll kill Harv Gunther if he hurts her, Red thought. *I'll kill the bastard with my bare hands.*

"In the Dirksen Federal Building?" Nick Curran asked. "With your dress slashed?"

"We live in a jungle, Nick." She shrugged. "Life in jungles is especially hard on women."

She had left the courtroom, entered an empty elevator, and could not remember anything more until she woke up in the hospital with a vicious ache in the back of her head. The doctors saw no sign of concussion or fracture, but were keeping her in the tiny, disinfectant-smelling hospital room overnight for "observation."

"A federal marshal found her," Nick explained again to Red, "when the elevator opened on the first floor. Unconscious, with her dress slashed and her purse missing."

"Torn to shreds, you mean." Red paced the room, like an angry grizzly bear. "Mike Casey said that the guy must have liked to use his knife."

And that there was no hint that Gunther was behind the attack.

"Well," said Eileen, "he didn't use it on me. Anyway, it's either a random mugger or someone who is angry at me about the Houston case or something else. I'm not going to be terrified into changing anything. I hope that's clear, gentlemen?"

Mike had promised some discreet surveillance. A mugger? A nut? An angry client? Harv Gunther?

No reason to choose any of them. Except that the skill of the caper suggested a message sent by a professional.

Or perhaps only a lucky amateur nut.

"Make it good surveillance, Mike," he had pleaded.

"We should perhaps take precautions," Nick said tentatively.

"Of course we will." Eileen adjusted her hospital gown. "Now, Red, if you would go home and reassure the children."

"I'm staying here with you for the night."

"No, you're not," she replied with some asperity. "You're going home to be with the children."

"Annie Casey is with them," he turned on her fiercely. "Don't try to order me around. I said I'm staying here with you and, God damn it, I'm staying here with you. The matter is settled."

"The doctors."

"To hell with the doctors!"

Eileen laughed, winced with pain, and then laughed again, more carefully.

"I'm glad you're staying, Red. I would have been terrified here by myself."

Nick chuckled genially. "You're in good hands, Eileen. Take it easy."

"See you tomorrow, Nick."

"Only if I think you're well enough to go to the office tomorrow," Red snarled.

"Of course, Master." She smiled at him, vastly amused.

I've never given her an order before. She seems to like it. "Well, I'm glad you're listening to reason."

"I'm tired, Red," she said. "I have a terrible headache. The painkillers make me sleepy. The dratted nurses will come in every few hours to shine lights in my eyes. I hope you don't mind if I sort of pass out on you?"

"No." He dragged the single, straight-back metal chair close to the bed. "You have my permission."

"Hold my hand, please."

It was a weak, fragile little hand; a defenseless, trusting child.

"Uhmm...."

"Sleep well."

"Uhm-hmm....Oh, Red, the knife didn't damage your present...."

Forget about Harv Gunther. Protect Eileen. Forget about everything. No, I can't do that. God in heaven, again I ask You. Don't let anything happen to her. She's all I have.

Please.

32

The pinch was not hurtful, not even all that lascivious. It was, however, "fresh." The woman clinging to the edge of the pool reacted with appropriate outrage, both feminine and feminist. She swung her strongly muscled arm, elbow first, at her attacker.

Red ducked under the dangerous elbow and grabbed her solid forearm. "You should wear contact lenses in the swimming pool." He pushed in vain against the immovable limb. "Otherwise you might hurt some poor harmless husband."

"Red!" she exclaimed. "What are you doing here?"

She was wearing a black tank suit, whose purpose was purely functional, save that on Eileen's body nothing could be merely functional.

"It's a family membership, isn't it? Do you mind taking that lethal weapon out of my face, woman?"

Gradually her arm changed its posture and its attitude; soon it was resting affectionately against his chest. Only a small lump on the back of her head and an occasional headache reminded them both of the attack a few days ago in the Dirksen Building.

And her lingerie collection was growing exponentially, as the economists would say. The first phase of Red Kane's reconquest of his wife had been successfully completed. It did not follow, he told himself, that the courtship could stop now. Maybe it could never stop. Anyway, it was too much fun to think about stopping.

"Red Kane in the East Bank Club?" She still didn't quite believe it. "What will your public say?"

"I'm disguised as a lawyer's spouse. Maybe no one will recognize me."

She shoved him away, none too seriously. "Does Dr. Klein know you've become an exercise freak?"

From another woman it would have been a nagging question. From Eileen it was a request for information. Whatever worry she might have felt was hidden in her businesslike tone and matter-of-fact voice.

An insight about his wife flickered in Red Kane's brain and then died before he could identify it.

"As a matter of fact, I saw him yesterday. We did a stress-test thing. I'm afraid you'll have to keep working. No insurance money from Red Kane's estate for a long time."

"You've stopped drinking and smoking." A simple statement of objectively noted fact.

"You've noticed?" He tightened his grip on her waist. "A few other changes too . . . ?"

"What annoys me about you"—a quick, by no means displeased intake of breath and no answer to his question—"is that you are able to stay thin without any effort." Her forearm brushed against his chest. "God knows what kind of a hunk you'll become if you work at it."

Red floated closer to her, his body brushing hers. His fingers probed delicately.

She broke away and swam, with sure, powerful strokes, across the pool. Awkwardly Red pursued her, spitting out the thickly chlorinated water as he clung to the pool side next to her.

"It's all right for lovers to play around here at the East Bank," she grinned at him, "not husbands and wives. It's considered vulgar."

You're a little weird, Eileen, but I'm crazy about you anyway.

"All right," he feigned reluctance. "I suppose you've already used those medieval torture machines."

"No, I had to get the dirt of the federal courts off my skin. Do you want me to demonstrate? Promise you won't overdo it? I can't stay home from work this week to nurse an aching husband."

She pulled herself out of the pool, grabbed a towel, and bolted for the women's dressing room, a young plains animal, rejoicing in her gracefulness and strength.

Jimmy Carter would call it lust in the heart, Red reflected as he climbed out of the pool after her, much more slowly.

Fifteen minutes later he watched intently as Eileen, in forest-green leotard and hose, seemingly imprisoned in a jungle of black bars, swayed back and forth against some of the bars, which reluctantly gave way under strong pressure from her body.

"This builds up the stomach muscles," she gasped, "not that you need it all that much.... Red, you're supposed to be studying the machine, not me."

"I know." He wet his lips with his tongue. "You're more interesting."

"*Entertaining* is the word you're groping for." She blushed deeply. "Come on, tough guy, let's see you do this...."

Red tried the rowing machine, complained inordinately about ruining his new sweat suit, moaned that he was too old for such nonsense, and began to enjoy the unaccustomed demands on his muscles.

"Time for the day," Eileen announced, sounding like a track coach. "We don't want a paralyzed Pulitzer pundit on our hands."

"Alliteration," Red mumbled as she pulled him out of the machine. "Will I be in any more trouble if I say you look gorgeous in a leotard?"

Another blush. "You have to be a full partner in the firm to afford the clothes and the jewelry to jog or exercise here. I'm almost ashamed to be seen with you in that exercise suit. No class."

"Buy me one with class for Christmas." He dried his sweaty face with a towel.

"Sure," she said, hesitating slightly.

"I'll still be here at Christmas, Eileen." He threw the towel at her.

"I didn't mean..." She looked at the floor, doubtless wishing that she could cut off her tongue.

"Come on." He put his arm around her and squeezed her affectionately. "I'll buy you supper."

"I pay the bills for this place.... You're embarrassing me, Red."

"That, woman, is the general idea. Now hurry up and dress. I've worked up an appetite."

"For food, I trust?"

"Among other things."

Red, conscious of the astonished glances as he strolled through the East Bank's dining room, found a table by the window overlooking the north branch of the Chicago River. *All we need now*, he thought, *is a fishing platform out there. It would make heaven perfect for Dick Daley.*

As he waited for Eileen's appearance, Red reflected on the genius of combining an exercise center with a singles bar. Loud, noisy, vulgar, snobbish, but undoubtedly functional and commercial. He jotted a few notes for a column and looked up to see the same magic witch's eyes that had captured him at Marina City several centuries ago.

"Is this place taken?" she asked, her voice hinting at sultry nights under the tropic sun, very much at odds with her black flannel one-button suit and jacquard blouse with cowl neckline. "My God, Red," sudden alarm, "what's wrong?"

"Huh?"

"A new blazer..."

"Double-breasted, you should excuse the expression." He feigned surprise at her surprise. "Navy, with gray flannel slacks. Shirt and tie match too, if Mike Casey is to be believed. As for the underwear, you'll have—"

"You haven't bought a new suit in three years!" Her hand remained on the chair. She was not only surprised but worried.

Red stood up and eased her into the chair. "I decided I wanted to look like a male sex object."

"Sometimes," she sighed, "I think it would be easier if you weren't so sexy.... Anyway, you look wonderful. The girls won't believe it."

She had never before accused him of being sexy. "I hope I'm sexy enough to hold your attention through dinner. I've been waiting for my wife, but you'll do."

"I cannot stay long," she spoke in her long-forgotten Kim Novak voice, "a few moments."

"Enough to ask when you started to read my columns."

"We take the public position that we don't read them." Eileen dismissed the question with a flip wave of her hand.

"That doesn't mean we don't sneak a peek now and again, especially when everyone in the Dirksen Federal Building is talking about it."

"You see, Eileen"—he leaned forward eagerly, determined to explain—"when I use the word *entertainment*, I don't mean it in the same sense...."

"I am not totally illiterate, Red," she laughed, touching his hand. "I know what you meant. I may not read Richard Wilbur riding to work, but I AM capable of noticing an occasional journalistic paradox."

"Speaking of Wilbur"—he pulled from his jacket pocket the paperback book, which was folded open at "Objects"—"listen to this:

"The trench of light on boards, the much-mended
    dry

Courtyard wall of brick
And sun submerged in beer, and streaming in glasses,
The weave of a sleeve, the careful and undulant tile,
    A quick
Change of the eye and all this calmly passes

Into a day, into magic."

Then he read the passage about the Cheshire smile floating in the leaves, "which sets me fearfully free."

She listened attentively, as though it were not the first time in twenty years of marriage that her husband had read poetry.

"That's lovely, Red. We don't like to think of God freeing us, do we? But that's what God's for."

"Right." He stuffed the book back into his pocket. Too damn perceptive by half. Should he tell her about his experience at 333 Wacker Drive? Why not? Now was the time.

He hesitated and the opportunity was lost. Later when she wanted to lock him up in a booby hatch, he wondered whether it would have made any difference if he had discussed his "experience" with her early instead of late, before she had some grounds for thinking that he was around the bend.

"You should write poetry," she said with an unerring instinct for what he was thinking.

"That'll be the day."

The electric tension that was building between them was broken instantly. Eileen tipped her Perrier glass, to her enormous embarrassment.

Again the elusive insight. What was it?

They ate fruit salad and drank Perrier water and felt hungry and disgracefully virtuous.

"You know what we're doing after you sign the check?"

"Let me guess." Her green eyes glittered mischievously. Even lustfully.

"You'd guess wrong." Red thought uneasily that he'd never quite seen that glitter before. "We're going down to the Fine Arts to see the reissue of *The Leopard*. I called home and left Patty in charge. I explained that we were redoing our first date. She seemed a bit astonished that they still showed movies that old."

"Red..." The hunger faded from her eyes to be replaced by tears.

"It's the uncut version. Three and a half hours."

"More Claudia Cardinale."

"I hardly noticed her that night."

"Baloney, not to use more scatological language.... Was Patty rude to you?"

So she did notice the veiled animosity between her husband and her elder daughter.

"She did the bored-teenager bit at first. Then when I explained about *Il Gattopardo*, she goes—you should excuse my using her word; as you know the verb *to say* is now archaic—she goes, 'Like totally awesome.'"

As she was signing the check, she considered him seriously.

"Wondering whether I'm worth the cost of the dinner?"

"Cheap date." She returned her felt-tip pen to her purse. "No, wondering..."

"What?" He took her hand.

"Whether you're happy."

"Huh?"

"I mean..." She made a face of displeasure at herself. "I mean are you happy now because of us, or if things are good between us because you are happy."

"That's pretty philosophical, Ei." He raised her hand to his lips.

"Lascivious hand-kisser." She kept her fingers against his lips. "I know it doesn't make any sense at all. I need a purpose in life, I guess."

"Lawyer, future judge, mother, wife, lover—not enough? Supermom has to be something else too?"

"Come on." She rose. "Let's go to the movie. I'll figure the question out later. No feeling up your date, remember, it's a mortal sin."

"Right!"

On the way out of the East Bank they met Mike Hermann, a young feature writer from the *Tribune*. New Yorker, of course.

"I never thought I'd see you here with the swingers, Red." He shook hands cordially.

"Looking for some ideas for some columns about entertainment."

"And I don't believe"—he took Eileen in appreciatively—"that I know this young woman."

"Eileen, this is Mike Hermann, one of the more promising talents at the opposition. Mike, my first wife, Eileen Ryan."

They exchanged greetings, Mike as if he were meeting royalty. "Your last wife too, I daresay."

"So far." Red felt his body freeze, as though he'd bumbled into a cold-storage locker. Melissa entered the door of the club and walked by them, her face a mask of sadness.

If Eileen recognized who or what Mel was, she gave no sign.

Nothing lives but something dies, he thought as he watched the slow elegiac beginning of *The Leopard* and remembered Mel's agonized face. *Dear God, forgive me.*

He and his first wife held hands during the film. Halfway

through it her hand found its way to his thigh and then moved backward and forward gently.

"Trying to distract me from La Cardinale?" he whispered in her ear.

"Definitely."

Eileen, he reflected, *is a witty, intelligent, and uncomplaining date—just like she was twenty-one years ago. What happened to all the fun we might have had together?*

At last the insight alighted in his brain long enough for him to codify it: *You're as much a mystery to her as she is to you.*

How can that be? You're as transparent as the plastic around a bouquet of fresh flowers. Why should you be a mystery? Maybe she thinks she's transparent too. What the hell is going on?

They were both tired when they finally parked the VW in front of the house on Webster. Red was prepared to forgo love. Eileen was worn from another brutal week of her defense of the hapless Hurricane. But moonlight flooding their marriage bed through Johnny's skylight settled the matter.

He wrapped his arms around her from behind and drew her to the shimmering bed. They remained motionless, fully clothed for a long time. There was no need to do anything more than be together. Red smelled the fragrant sweetness of her hair and listened to the smooth, peaceful rhythm of her breathing. Should he tell her that he wished she'd let her hair grow long again?

"Fallen asleep on the poor woman?" she murmured. "She's not what she was twenty years ago, is she? Fading away into a hag. Scared of her own shadow. Incoherent half the time."

"Not rushing. It's Friday night." He fumbled for the zipper on her skirt, found it, and tugged. She pretended not to cooperate in the rest of the disrobing; and he pretended to be half-asleep and confused about how the various fastenings worked.

"You're a wonderful lover, Red," she sighed. "But I've told you that, haven't I?"

"Can't tell me enough. By the way, I read somewhere

that the line in the poem in which he says the Daughter of Jerusalem is like a mare with Pharaoh's chariots—"

"How many times must I tell you"—her fingers were leisurely undoing his buttons—"that I will not be dragged into court when you fail to give proper credit in one of your columns for an idea you read somewhere."

He put his hand over her mouth. "Let me finish. The point is that there are no mares with the Pharaoh's chariots. Only stallions. So when he says that his wife is like a mare among the chariots, he means she has the same effect on men that a mare in heat would have on an army of stallions. Now I'll let you talk."

"That's an utterly chauvinist metaphor ...," she argued with little conviction. "No one would notice me if I walked across your city room."

"Every man in the room would lose his train of thought and fantasize for an hour or so about doing to you what I'm about to do."

"A mare in heat indeed ...," she breathed softly.

Their love was in the mood of the film, slow, gentle, nostalgic, a sensuous day on a humid tropical beach—the kind of beach Red had only visited in fantasy.

And as he, serenely happy, floated away into another night of exceedingly pleasant dreams, Red heard his wife weeping again.

Book THREE

A ray of sunshine started down between the tree trunks. It touched the pool with liquid gold. The pool became transparent to its green depths and her self was plunged in those depths and yet upraised with joy upon the rushing wind. The light grew stronger and turned white. In this crystal whiteness there was ecstasy. Against the light she saw a wren fly by; the wren was made of rhythm, it flew with meaning, with a radiant meaning. There was the same meaning in the caterpillar as it inched along the rock, and the moss, and the little nuts which had rolled across the leaves.

The significance was bliss, it made a created whole of everything she watched and touched and heard – and the essence of this creative whole was love. She felt love pouring from the light, it bathed her with music and with perfume; the love was far off at the source of the light, and yet it drenched her through. And the source and she were one.

The minutes passed. The light moved softly down, and faded from the pool. The ecstasy diminished, but in its stead came a serenity and a sureness she had never known.

– Anya Seton

33

"I don't understand," said the little old lawyer, a wizened gnome in his tiny, dusty cave, as he fidgeted with a manila folder. "Paul has been gone for twenty years. Why can't you leave the dead in peace?"

"He was in Harv Gunther's pay, wasn't he?" Red leaned forward on the shabby, pockmarked desk. A hint that Paul was still alive was the most he could expect from Alfie. "C'mon, Alfie, and you were the go-between, weren't you?"

Alfonsus Ligouri Walsh had moved into his small office in what was then the Conway Building the day he passed the bar exam in 1935 and for forty-eight years, without secretary or partner, Alfie Walsh had plied his trade, the political lawyer, in that office, without apparently ever either dusting it or throwing out a scrap of paper. The world had changed in forty-eight years. The governmental offices of the city of Chicago and the county of Cook could no longer be contained within the old-fashioned classical City Hall–Cook County Building across the street from Alfie's office, its gray bulk dimly perceptible through the office's unwashed windows. The old Morrison Hotel, onetime headquarters of the Cook County Democratic organization, and reportedly the place where Alfie had eaten lunch when he still ate lunch, had been torn down and replaced by the dark brown rust and glass rectangle of the Richard J. Daley Civic Center.

"I dunno," Da Mare is alleged to have said. "Dey tell me that after a few years the color'll stop looking funny."

(In Da Mare's vocabulary "dey" were always the people who gave him bad advice.)

In the unlikely event that Alfie should put aside the aged manila folder he always seemed to clutch and stir from his desk to gaze out the window of his office, he would see where his beloved Morrison used to be, the Picasso sculpture in the Civic Center Plaza frequently surrounded by "demonstrators and hippies," in Alfie's world view, the abomination of desolation. The Conway Building was now part of the Chicago Title and Trust Building and Miro's woman had taken refuge in its courtyard, desperately trying to peer around the corner of the courtyard so she could stare balefully at her Picasso rival across the street in the Civic Center Plaza. Red Kane doubted that Alfie Walsh noticed any of the changes. His world was frozen in 1935 and his political hero was not Da Mare but "Mr. Nash," Pat Nash, the Eddie Vrdolyak of the 1930's. As far as Red knew, Alfie had no life outside of his office. If there were a Mrs. Walsh and Walsh offspring, they were never mentioned. And if Walsh left the office and its musty smell of dead paper to eat lunch or go home at night, no one had seen him on the streets or in the restaurants, not since the Morrison Hotel had disappeared. He never appeared in court, never visited other lawyers' offices, probably had never been in the Daley Civic Center.

His brown double-breasted three-piece suit may very well have been the same one that the young Alfie Walsh wore on the October day in 1935 when he first walked into the Conway Building, and the expensive diamond rings on his knobby fingers were surely purchased before the beginning of the Second World War. Alfie Walsh was as much an unchanging part of the Chicago scenery as the locks at the mouth of the Chicago River—and about as important, if you were a politician. Alfie's reliability, discretion, and instinctive shrewdness were beyond question. If you wanted something done, informally, off the record, and with no footprints left, you called Alfie, usually from a pay telephone, and he arranged that whomever you wanted to communicate with would call him also through a pay telephone. You and your counterpart might be at opposite ends of the country or merely opposite ends of the Civic Center Plaza talking to one another through Alfie, whose only interest in the negotiation, as he whispered in his soft, mortician's voice and rustled old papers, was to help his "two friends" reach an agreement.

Alfie also was Paul O'Meara's lawyer, a fact that should have made Red suspicious a long time ago.

"Paul was a good friend of yours, wasn't he, Alfie? He gave you a lot of business, didn't he?"

"I had a lot of friends." Alfie raised his hands as if seeking heaven's protection from Red's persistent demand for information. "A lot of them are dead now, God be good to them. I tried to help as many of them as I could."

"You handled Paul's account at the Board of Trade, didn't you?"

"Glory be to God! Is that a crime, Red Kane? He was a friend of mine who wanted to make a few investments. Being as how he was a public figure and a reporter and all that, he wanted to do it privately. I found a broker for him. Is it wrong to do something like that as a favor for a friend?"

"You didn't wonder where the money came from?"

"You sound like Don Roscoe. You think you're the United States Attorney for the Northern District of Illinois, or something like that?"

The little old man's dry lips moved slightly in what might have been a smile. Alfie Walsh was joking. "Anyway, he's been dead for a long time. What difference does it make?"

"You were the go-between in the triangle, Alfie." Red pointed an accusing finger at him. "The money came from Harv Gunther. You passed it on to the broker, probably in the same envelopes in which it came, and kept some sort of records of the investments for Paul so he knew where he stood."

"Is any of this a crime?" the old man demanded, doing his best to answer questions by asking more questions.

"You knew that Paul O'Meara, the political editor of the *Herald Gazette*, was in the pay of Harvard Gunther, for maybe fifteen years."

"Was he the only one? Weren't those the days when the salaries were so lousy that reporters had to earn money some other way? Weren't a lot of them, especially the big ones, making a few dollars here and there on the side? Don't some people still do it today?"

Red sighed. "To continue your litany of questions, Alfie, am I not old enough to stop worrying about such things? Maybe even old enough to be on the take myself?"

"Did I say that?" Alfie asked defensively.

"How long, and for how much?"

"Is money worth what it used to be?" The lawyer's nervous little hands caressed the weather-beaten manila folder he was clutching. "A few thousand dollars a year over fifteen years. Does that seem like a lot of money now?"

"Fifteen years." Red sighed. "Even before I went to work for the *Herald Gazette*."

"Are you going to find any records to prove it, Red?" the little lawyer asked. "Are you going to drag me before the grand jury or write a column about me to get at Harv Gunther because twenty years ago he gave a few gifts to a friend of yours?"

The answer to the question was obvious. The name Paul O'Meara meant nothing to a new generation of newspaper readers and Assistant United States Attorneys. They couldn't care less about the bribes that had passed through this office. Red was looking for clues and hints, not evidence.

"You haven't been telling me the truth, Alfie." He leaned back in his chair, feigning relaxation. "Who was the other broker? Joe Dowling handled the account that was in Paul's and Sally's names jointly. But there was another account, wasn't there? And another broker? An account that Paul closed a couple of weeks before he disappeared. It was under an assumed name, practically impossible to trace. You're the only one who knew for whom the broker was trading. One day you were told to close the account and collect the money in case. Paul stopped by late in the afternoon, picked up the cash, swapped a few stories with you, and then went over to the Morrison Hotel for a drink. You never saw him again after that, did you, Alfie?"

The little old lawyer's weak blue eyes narrowed to pinpoints. "I don't know what you're talking about," he barked, sounding like a pet poodle yapping at a mailman.

I've got him, Red thought. *My hunches are still on a roll.*

"Then one day you read in the newspapers that he'd disappeared. You were suspicious, of course, because you're Irish and a lawyer. But you did what you were supposed to do with the official estate, and you asked no questions and gave no hints to the cops. Deep down inside, Alfie, you thought he was still alive, didn't you?"

"I'm not saying a thing, Red."

Ah, but you didn't deny it, Alfie. Like Harv Gunther, you're an old man. Not as quick as you used to be.

"It was a long time ago." Red stood up and removed his raincoat from the cluttered table by the window. "I don't think you know where Paul O'Meara is. But I think you hear from him occasionally, a voice on the phone, a long-distance call from far away, nothing important. Paul's got other people handling his money now. Just a voice from the grave. Paul having his little joke. And somehow or other, you have a way of getting in touch with him in emergencies. You call somebody who calls somebody else who passes the word on to Paul and then he calls you. As soon as I leave the office, you're going to start that chain, aren't you, Alfie? You're going to let Paul O'Meara know that Red Kane is on to him and he's going to start to worry real bad, isn't he, Alfonsus Ligouri Walsh?"

"In God's name, Red, why are you doing this?" Alfie rose from the desk and bustled across the office to help Red on with his coat, an astonishing phenomenon because Red had never seen Alfie leave the desk before. "Why can't you leave the dead in peace?"

No easy answer for that question. He hesitated at the doorway. Why not probe Alfie about the Adele Ward murder?

Why not? Obviously that would tip his hand to Harv that he knew about the young hooker's death.

Or did Harv know already? Was that the reason for the Wacker Drive limo and the attack on Eileen?

"Read about it in the newspaper, Alfie." Red laughed as he departed the musty office. "And don't worry, I've got nothing against you."

As he walked across Daley Plaza to Dearborn Street, hunched against the cold November rain and biting wind, Red still searched for an answer to Alfie Walsh's question. The target was Harvard Gunther, murderer of teenage prostitutes and corrupter of the press. But Paul O'Meara was a target too, a surrogate father who had deceived his substitute son. Somehow it fit with what happened to him on the Feast of All the Saints. Red Kane was searching for integrity again, maybe this time his own integrity.

He had not been able to get through to Harvard Gunther since he had tricked the old man into admitting that he had paid off Paul O'Meara. But Gunther knew that he was trying, and Gunther would know in a few minutes, if he didn't already, about Red's visit to Alfie Walsh. Harv would be worried, and wherever he was in the world, Paul O'Meara would be worried too. Red would let them both worry. He would ease off for the next few days, no calls to Harv, no more probing in the Paul O'Meara story. Let the other side sweat.

The most likely scenario would be a threat of some sort from Gunther, followed up by a peace offering. That would be the time to spring the Adele Ward murder on Harvard—and then move very quickly to get the story in the paper, before Gunther decided to kill again.

Gunther's back was to the wall, and he knew it. He was probably cursing himself for the murder threat on tape. It wasn't enough to send him to jail but it was certainly enough to smash his reputation, if Red brought it over to Channel 2, for example, and asked Walter Jacobson to play it on the ten o'clock news.

At the corner of Dearborn and Wacker, the mist swirling down the river from the lake made it impossible to see more than a block away—hiding the incredibly ugly State of Illinois Building (it looked like Governor Thompson but wasn't kinky enough to be a good resemblance) and also the green tower of 333 Wacker. The effects of his religious experience, if that's what you call it, did not seem to be wearing off. He was exercising regularly and felt no compulsion to either drink or smoke. He was continuing his courtship of his wife, an adventure with emotional ups and downs that required constant concentration and effort and rewarded him with immense pleasure. And he was searching, he hoped skillfully, for ways to reopen communication with his children. That required even more effort. The kids seemed to sense that he was trying to modify the patterns of his relationship with them and were stoutly resisting even the first step in a change. Kate sulked; Patty flew into rages; John mumbled on the telephone. Maybe it was necessary and good for children to revolt against their parents.

Or maybe the kids figured, with ample reason, that the Irish adage was right: Better the divil you know than the divil you don't know.

There was no rush. If he blundered about, like a bull in a china shop, he might make matters worse. The quizzical expressions, which continued both in the city room and at home, suggested that those who knew him were uncomfortable with the new Red Kane, troubled perhaps that the sudden flowering of virtue might be the sign of physical or mental illness. He had to reassure those he loved at the same time he was pursuing them.

The closest anyone had come to a direct question was Eileen, a couple of days ago on Sunday morning, when he brought her breakfast in bed. Coffee cup in one hand, sheet held at her throat with the other hand, she looked at him curiously. "I am being courted and seduced and I love it, Red, but I'm not sure why."

"Because I love you, that's why," he said, kissing her chin. "Can't a man change? You yourself said it was different this time, didn't you?"

"I didn't expect it to be this different."

"You gotta take your chances," he said, buttering her toast.

"I guess." Apparently she was abandoning her cross-examination. "Would you give me my robe, please? It somehow seems indecent to read the Sunday *New York Times* in the nude."

He made a show of reluctance as he draped the white nylon robe around her shoulders, protesting that the *Times* never looked better. She laughed at him, an inviting and affectionate laugh that would never be heard in the courtroom. She leaned forward and kissed him.

Red removed the robe, took off her glasses, snatched away the *New York Times* for which she tried to reach, and pried the rumpled sheet out of her fingers. Eileen, her posture completely changed, sat rigidly upright like a marble statue, head adverted, fists clenched, submitting to him but not responding.

"Something wrong?" He held her arms lightly. Eileen of the even disposition, Eileen the self-possessed, was being replaced by an occasionally moody and frequently unpredictable woman.

"You didn't say why you are courting and seducing me." Her eyes were tightly shut, as though she could not bear to look at him.

"You started it." He backed up, uncertain and hurt.

"That is not true and it does not answer my question."

"Well, if it's an answer you want, because I love you." He brushed her lips, also tightly closed, with a quick kiss. "Must I say something more than that?" *Like I had a profound religious experience in front of a skyscraper?* "You are a bit of an invitation, sitting in bed that way." He touched her throat cautiously, expecting it to be ice-cold.

She threw her arms around him, as fervent now as she had been aloof a few seconds before. "Of course not, my darling. Lawyer lady is just acting crazy. The Ryan in her surfacing again."

Eileen was baffled, curious, and a little uneasy, he told himself after they had made love. He must be cautious as he moved into the next phase of the second courtship of his wife.

Second? Hell, he'd never really courted her the first time around.

And she had been acting a little strange, indeed more like a Ryan for a long time.

She had called him at the office earlier in the day, before he left to see Alfie. "I hope you won't mind abandoning your study this weekend," she said brightly. "Johnny's bringing a visitor home from Collegeville."

"I haven't been spending many nights there," he replied. "I thought you had noticed that."

"The bedroom has seemed crowded lately," she laughed.

He made an explicit and graphic observation about his intentions toward her for that night, detailing an unusual posture for lovemaking. She responded with a delighted snort. "I'd like to see you try THAT."

"You will certainly see it and you will certainly like it," he promised. Horny teenagers. "I didn't know Johnny was coming home this weekend."

"Nor did I. Apparently his friend wants to see Chicago."

"Well, he's welcome to my study, unless I should get turned out of my bedroom this weekend."

"I don't think that's about to happen, Red. Incidentally, it's a she, not a he."

"A girl?" Red exclaimed. "Johnny's bringing a GIRL home for the weekend?"

"Her name is Lois," Eileen said mysteriously. "She may have a last name but I haven't been told it yet."

Be real nice to the girl, he told himself, *and maybe that way you can get through to your son again. How the hell did you lose him in the first place? No Boy Scouts, no Little League, no Cub games with him? But Johnny was never interested in Boy Scouts or Little League or Cub games. And as far as you could tell, he's never been interested in politics either. What do you say to a kid whose principal activities, besides playing basketball, are fooling around for hours in a darkroom and wandering around the house with patches of colored fabric in his hand?*

Preoccupied with John, Red strolled into the *HG* city room after his visit to Alfie's office.

"Your daughter Patricia called you a couple of times, Mr. Kane," said the attractive young black woman at the switchboard. "She wants you to call her back as soon as possible."

Red hurried back to his desk and dialed his home number. The line was busy, so he called the second phone, which Eileen had had installed for the two girls—and to calm Red's intermittent fits of outrage about busy signals when he tried to call home.

Sure enough, there was no busy signal on Patty's line. Only a couple of weeks ago he would have chewed her out for not using her own phone. Now he realized how ridiculous such complaints were.

"Hi, Patty, it's your dad."

"Well," a haughty, contemptuous young voice responded, "I'm glad you FINALLY got around to calling back."

"I was out on an interview," he said easily.

"I'm SURE. Well, if you want to leave Katie in jail all afternoon and evening, I suppose there's nothing I can do about it."

In the back of his head he remembered the phone call from Dav when Parn had been picked up by the Oak Park police for drinking beer in Skeleton Park.

"Katie in jail?" He sat up stiff and straight and anxious. "Where is she? What's she in jail for?"

"She's at the Shakespeare Station." Patty's tone suggested that Red himself had somehow been responsible for his daughter's arrest. "She and Mark are there for stealing the Volvo."

"How could she steal our family car?" Red demanded.

"I'm SURE she knows what she did," his elder daughter replied venomously. "She called on the phone and she goes, 'Mark and I were arrested by the police for taking the Volvo. Call Mommy and tell her,' and I go, 'I'll try to get Mommy but she's in court,' and then she goes, 'Well, then, get Daddy.'"

"You haven't been able to get through to your mother yet?" Red was already on his feet, buttoning his raincoat again.

"I'm SURE that if I was able to get Mommy, I wouldn't have called you."

"Fine, keep trying to reach your mother. We may need a lawyer."

"For SURE I'm not going to stop calling Mother."

Red could not resist the last word. "Really!"

34

"Daddy, Daddy, Daddy!" Katie sobbed, embracing her father. "It was terrible in there. Those women said such GROSS things to me!"

"They couldn't be gross enough, you stupid little fool." Red shoved her away. "When are you going to grow up?"

The cops grinned. They knew they had another irate parent to manipulate.

When the woman juvenile officer brought Kate into the interrogation room in the police station, which like most police stations smelled like an ineffectually disinfected public washroom, Red saw in his daughter's eyes a look of pure terror, more afraid of him than she was of the cage in which she'd been locked up with pickpockets and drug addicts and whores. Her fear made him even more angry.

He and Katie were saved by the cops' complacency. He recaptured his daughter quickly.

"Sorry, kid," he murmured. "I think I'm the juvenile delinquent for saying that. Let's start over."

Katie hesitated, considering perhaps the advantages of total martyrdom. She rejected that typical Irish woman's escape and embraced her father again. Red noted with considerable satisfaction that the cops were disappointed.

He stroked his daughter's long blond hair and dabbed with tissue at the tears on her slender and lovely face, so much like that of her wondrous grandmother, Kate Ryan. Yet she seemed pathetically fragile in her rumpled blazer and plaid school uniform skirt, more fragile than her grandmother would ever have been.

"Easy, easy, easy, kid. It's all right now."

Please, God, he prayed silently, *let me do the rest of this right.*

"Hello, Mr. Kane," the young man in the doorway said hesitantly.

"That's Mark, Daddy," Kate said between sobs.

"You must have a last name, Mark?" Red couldn't help but like the looks of the young man, frightened, but neatly dressed, clean-cut, and respectful.

"Mark Doherty, sir," he said sadly. "My father is a surgeon on the staff of St. Joseph's."

"You probably are in a lot more trouble than Kate," Red said, doing his best to grin reassuringly.

"Yes, sir." The young man shook his head dejectedly. "I sure am."

"We have a very serious problem on our hands, it seems, Mr. Kane," said the arresting officer, whose gold badge revealed that his name was Phalen.

"Your daughter has very serious problems, Mr. Kane," agreed the thin, horse-faced woman probation officer whose name, it seemed, was Stewart.

"We thought it best to have a little conversation, Red, first... before things get out of hand," said the Sergeant who apparently had been assigned to supervise the conversation.

"Yes, indeed, Sergeant Finnerty." Kane led his daughter to one of the chairs arranged around a steel table and sat easily on the edge of the table. "I presume the charges are fairly serious to put a juvenile in the cage with adult offenders."

"Well, now, Red," said the Sergeant. "That might have been a mistake."

The three cops and the two kids and Red arranged themselves around the table, next to the window of the interrogation room, whose dirty beige walls had doubtless seen much more serious human misery than two juveniles brought in because they had allegedly stolen the car from one of the juveniles' families. Finnerty was a wiry little fellow in his early forties with salt-and-pepper hair and a thin beagle's face. Phalen was a fat ponderous oaf, and Stewart a lean and very nervous juvenile officer playing in a league that she didn't understand and didn't like.

In the twitch of an eyelid Red remembered that a couple of times when Kate had been a noisy and difficult baby, he had risen from his bed, taken her from Eileen, and walked back and forth in their bedroom, soothing the angry little ball of girl child into accepting tranquillity. "You don't make a bad Madonna," Eileen had said.

The special relationship between the contentious little blonde and her father had lasted a long time. When had it ended? Ten years ago? No, more like five—about the time of her tenth birthday.

Now he'd have to play Madonna again to his daughter.

"Suppose you tell me, Officer Phalen," Red promptly took control of the conversation, "exactly what the charges are against my daughter and this young man."

"We can't afford to be lenient on these kinds of offenders, Mr. Kane," he said pompously. "There's more drugs in this district than you'd believe possible. We have little girls in grammar school that are pushers. Unless we take a hard line, every kid in the district might be in danger."

"I understand," Red said patiently, letting him play his cards.

"I'm sure you know the statistics on fatalities from teenagers driving under the influence of alcohol," the juvenile officer chimed in.

"No, I don't, Ms. Stewart. Suppose you tell me."

"It's a bad combination of offenses, Red." The Sergeant hunched over, salvaging his juvenile officer from embarrassment. "Admittedly they're first offenders—"

"Fucking serious offenses just the same." Phalen blew out air in his cheeks. "Fucking serious."

Red resisted the temptation to comment on the cop's language. "I repeat my question, Patrol Officer, what are the charges for these, ah, dreadfully serious offenses?"

Katie, whose head had been bowed over the table, looked up and grinned, despite herself, at Red's choice of words.

Don't laugh now, kid, he pleaded with his eyes. Instantly she sobered up.

"Well, sir." The fat cop shrugged his massive shoulders expressively. "We haven't exactly made any charges yet. You see, we apprehended these juvenile perpetrators for a moving traffic violation and then discovered that the young man was driving your car. We smelled beer on his breath and we searched the car and found some traces of marijuana in it."

"Why did you search the car?" Red demanded. "Because of the moving violation? Do you normally search cars that you stop for moving violations?"

"Your daughter has very serious problems, Mr. Kane," Officer Stewart interjected.

"Perhaps she does, Officer Stewart," Red replied smoothly. "I'm not sure, however, that I would look to the Chicago Police Department to solve those problems. Let me ask another question. What was the moving violation of which Mr. Doherty is charged?"

"Running a stop sign," Phalen said ponderously.

"There were other cars on the street?" Red demanded.

"No, Daddy," Kate interjected, "and the sign is like kind of hidden by the trees."

"So, Officer Phalen, you apprehend a young perpetrator

for going through a stop sign, bring him into the station, put him and his passenger in detention cells, and search their car for marijuana because he ran a stop sign. Is that usual procedure?"

Sergeant Finnerty, by far the smartest of the three, saw which way the conversation was going and interjected to reassert Chicago Police Department control. "There have been no formal charges, Mr. Kane," he said, raising a soothing hand. "Mind you, we had no reason to think the young man had permission to drive your car."

"Did he have permission, Mr. Kane?" Officer Stewart asked.

"If my daughter said he had permission"—Red studied Kate's face carefully—"then he had permission.... Don't you think it would have been more appropriate to check with me about the permission before bringing two juveniles into a police station and putting them in cages with adult offenders?"

"We think your daughter was driving the car." Phalen was now red-faced and angry. The conversation wasn't going the way it was supposed to go. "We think they changed places when they saw my blue light."

"Sergeant Finnerty." Red ignored the angry cop, figuring it would make him even more angry and easier to deal with. "Sergeant Finnerty, was young Mr. Doherty given a Breathalyzer test?"

"We didn't want to do that, Mr. Kane," the Sergeant scratched his head.

"And you've searched the two of them for traces of marijuana?" Red continued to drive his point home. "You searched the car. Did you search them? Did you look in their purses or their wallets or their pockets?"

"We haven't done a strip search yet," sulked Officer Phalen.

"Your daughter has very serious problems, Mr. Kane," Officer Stewart observed.

"I believe I've heard you say that, Ms. Stewart." Red smiled at her benignly. "It won't be necessary to say it again."

The door of the interrogation room opened and Captain Dermott O'Neil leaned against the doorjamb negligently, giving the impression of someone mildly interested in the conversation.

"Let me review, Captain O'Neil," Red said with a genial smile, "what I have been told. Mr. Doherty was driving in my Volvo with my daughter. Through inattention or negligence he ran a stop sign. Officer Phalen apprehended him, demanded his driver's license, I presume, and the deed to the car. He discovered that the car was my property. The young woman accompanying Mr. Doherty claimed to be and doubtless provided evidence that she was my daughter. I'm sure that Officer Phalen checked with the computer to ascertain whether the car had been reported stolen. There is some suspicion that Mr. Doherty was driving under the influence of alcohol. However, no Breathalyzer test was made. Moreover, my car was apparently impounded and searched, for reasons that are not clear to me yet, and some traces of marijuana were found in it, though as I understand, not in my daughter's purse or Mr. Doherty's wallet. Is this an accurate summary, Sergeant Finnerty?"

"I'm certain we can work something out, Red," the Captain said lightly.

"I'm sure we can," Red said, every bit as lightly. "Someone is going to have to explain to me why my daughter, against whom, as far as I am aware, no charges have been made, was locked in a cage with adult offenders. To tell you the truth, Captain, that's going to take quite a bit of explaining."

"She was driving the car," Phalen said sullenly.

Juvenile Officer Stewart opened her mouth as if to remind him once again that Kate had problems and then decided against it.

"Were you close enough to the car to be able to testify to that in court, Officer?" Red asked with his most genial smile.

"Seeing as how it's you, Red," Sergeant Finnerty said nervously, "we might be ready to reconsider this matter."

"Though your daughter is very lucky that the charges are not more serious," said Officer Stewart, and then lapsed into silence in the face of Captain O'Neil's baleful stare.

"Captain O'Neil," Red said in his best seminar voice, "my

father was shot in the back by a cop; my stepfather was a cop who shot himself through the brain. I know cops. I know what was going on here. I don't like it. I don't want any favors, but I'll tell you what's going to happen. We're going to drive away. We're all going to forget about this incident completely. Do I make myself clear?"

He saw Katie's eyes widen in astonishment and the back of her hand rise to her mouth in a gesture of horrified surprise. *I never did tell them, did I?*

The Captain nodded glumly. "If that's the way you want it, Mr. Kane."

A few minutes later Red and the two young people climbed into the Volvo. "Were you driving, Katie?" he asked.

"Yes, Daddy," she said sadly, embracing him again. "And I was smoking pot, but only part of a joint."

"And, Mark, how many beers did you have?"

"Only two, sir." The young man bowed his head in remorse. "I'm a quarterback, so I can throw the cans pretty far."

"And then the two of you changed seats with remarkable dexterity. Your gymnastics training, I suppose, Katie?"

Katie continued to hang on for dear life. "Yes, Daddy, we did it real quick."

"Doubtless. Very quick thinking. Very quick reaction. You beat the rap this time."

The two guilty teenagers agreed in unison.

"Yes, Daddy."

"Yes, Mr. Kane."

Red sighed loudly. How much life had changed since the days of his childhood in South Chicago. Was it the same cosmos? Maybe he ought to drag out the two fragments he had written about those years.

They were part of a memoir that he told himself he would someday complete. He had worked very carefully on those fragments, revising and revising again. He had almost memorized the paragraphs. Mentally he reviewed them. Why show the fragments to his kids? They couldn't possibly comprehend his childhood. "Boring!" they would say. Or think, if their mother frowned a warning at them.

What was a man his age with his past doing with three

teenage children who were born and raised in a different universe? Well, time to say something. "The two of you are suffering from a very serious problem."

"What is that, sir?" Mark Doherty looked at him curiously.

"Terminal assholism."

They all laughed, the two children uneasily.

"Daddy, such awful language," Kate howled, "even if it is true."

35
From the Kane File

First of two undated autobiographical fragments

My oldest memories, happy images before bloody ones, are of the Chicago World's Fair of 1933–34. They are hazy, but splendid recollections of open-air buses, vast esplanades of buildings, an "enchanted island" especially for kids, and the twin towers of the sky ride. I have a hard time linking the pictures in my memory and the pictures in the books about that far-off event. In my memory the world's fair was glorious, magical, almost otherworldly. The pictures in the books, however, suggest that it may have been cheap and tawdry and rather pedestrian. I wonder if my memories are not of the fair itself but rather of later dreams that I would have when I heard my mother and my father talk about the fair.

My father, an open, expansive man, predicted even more progress for Chicago in the next century. My mother, who had been a schoolteacher before she married, lamented that the city could spend thousands of dollars on Sally Rand's "sinful" dances and yet pay schoolteachers only in scrip, which most Chicago banks would not accept.

I even remember standing in the backyard of our two-flat at Ninety-third and Coles in South Chicago and watching the seaplanes of Marshal Italo Balbo flying over our house on their way to the world's fair and proclaiming to my laughing father that someday I would be an airplane pilot too.

Balbo's planes may have been a dream. The house at Ninety-third and Coles, however, was not a dream. It actually existed; it still exists, or it did the last time I drove through South Chicago, a battered wooden structure more than forty years old, even when we lived in it, and now incredibly small as compared to my memories of it as a big house with a vast backyard.

My memories, vague, chaotic, dreamlike, of the first seven years of my life in that house are all pleasant, warm, happy. Rory Kane, my father, was a skilled workman. They couldn't run No. 2 blast furnace at Republic Steel without him, he boasted. So even in the depths of the Depression in the early 1930's he had a job and we had vegetables and meat on our table. There was no thought of Mom going back to her job teaching, and our house was filled with his loud and happy laughter.

A giant, burly redhead, my father was not much over thirty in those days, but I think as I look back on that time that his infectious enthusiasm and good humor and optimism must have made him seem even younger. My aunts, I'm sure, did not approve of him. My mother, schoolteacher that she was, was constantly trying to remake him so he'd be a little more "presentable" and "respectable," but even she could not resist his laughter for long. She disapproved of the drinking and gambling cronies that used to fill the kitchen on Saturday night, yet I can distinctly remember her taking beer bottles out of the icebox (and it was an icebox, the iceman coming every couple of days with a slab of ice that kept the inside of the box cold) and passing the bottles around the table, dodging, not always successfully, my father's massive paw. He was probably too much for her and I'm sure that her unmarried sisters, Mae and Maude, were instant in their warnings that she ought to bring him to heel—an impossible task, I suspect, for any woman. Yet as long as he was alive Mom's passion for respectability was overwhelmed by his high-spirited enthusiasm. She must have been very happy, because I was so happy in those days. A boy cannot have blissful memories of a home in which mother and father were not utterly content with one another and with their common life.

Dav's memories were even more obscure than mine, though he did mention in our conversation the day before Tet, in Viet Nam in 1968, that way back in the beginning of his recollections there was "grace."

The towers of the world's fair, Balbo's planes, the elm trees in front of our house (long since the victims of Dutch elm disease), flowers in springtime in the backyard, riding around on my father's shoulders, laughter and happiness in the house, grace before meals at Christmas and Thanksgiving, somber parties on St. Patrick's Day, when the cause of Ireland was remembered, angry men in the kitchen when the steel union was organizing and my father's voice bellowing above all the others, shouting optimistically that they couldn't possibly lose—these are the memories of the world before Memorial Day, 1937. I often ask myself, if I had had seven or eight or even ten more years in that environment, whether I would be a different man today. It's a foolish question, maybe one more attempt to escape responsibility for the mess I've made of my life. I suppose I should be thankful for what I had—many of my contemporaries spent the first seven years of their lives in homes that were far more impoverished physically and emotionally than mine.

Dad's origins were obscure. Mom didn't know much about his youth or didn't want to tell us after his death. He was born, I knew, in south County Dublin and had gone to school with the Jesuits, indeed the same school that James Joyce attended. He was supposed to attend the university, but became involved in the "Troubles" and had to leave the country, apparently very quickly. He was not, my mother often insisted, an illiterate peasant from the west of Ireland but the son of a prominent Dublin family forced to go into exile because of his Irish patriotism.

For most of my life I was willing to leave it at that and not to wonder why a witty and presumably literate man would live in South Chicago and work in the steel mills. Why did he never return to the Ireland that he loved so much and for which he had fought, if my mother was to be believed, so bravely?

I managed to find his name in the records of the Jesuit school and to discover that he had been the best student in his class. The Jesuits had no idea whether any of his family was still alive, so I drove out to Dun Laoghaire and found the address where his family lived when he was in school. It was a big elegant place, mid-Victorian in style, only one street away from Dublin Bay. Amorphous clouds of mist drifted lazily in from the water, hiding and then revealing an azure sky that would have been more appropriate for Amalfi. The thick smell of brine hovered all around like formaldehyde at a funeral home. The house was owned then by a Dublin banker in his early forties named Paul Laverty and his handsome wife, several years younger. They were friendly, comfortable people, with the Irish obsession for tracing history. They had purchased the house from the McLennans and they believed that before the McLennans the owner's name was Hardy. The wife thought an old woman in the fish market in Bray had once remarked to her that long ago the Kanes had lived there, "The son was with Michael Collins, you know."

"Does the name Michael Collins mean anything to you?" Paul Laverty asked.

"Of course it does," I replied. "But why would my father have left Ireland in 1922? Collins's side won the civil war, didn't they?"

"Ah, but Collins and Kevin O'Higgins were both killed," said Maeve Laverty.

"Men were close friends one year in those days, and bitter enemies the next year. O'Higgins signed a death warrant for the friend who had been best man at his wedding. They were bad times."

She and her husband both sighed the characteristically Irish sigh, which sounds like the beginning of an asthma attack, and I joined them.

"I can put you in touch with someone," said Paul Laverty. "You're at the Shelbourne? A man may call and say that I told him to call. You can trust him."

Sure enough, the call came. I was to meet a friend of Paul Laverty's at a certain public house in Dundrum and I was to come alone.

Feeling very much like a character in *The Informer* or

Odd Man Out, I sat at a scarred and battered table in the far corner of the room in the pub and wondered how long it would take to grow accustomed to the pungent smell of peat in which the old place had been steeped for decades, maybe centuries. A little old man, cap pulled down over his face, glided up to the table, sat down across from me, and peered at me intently through the gloom.

"Ai, 'tis Rory's son you are," he said sadly, lighting an ancient pipe. "I can tell it in the eyes and in the mouth and, sure, in the shape of your shoulders. You have the looks of a man that Rory would be proud to call son."

I didn't learn very much from the old-timer. My father was sixteen at the time of the Easter Rising, left school at the end of the academic year, and sometime not too long thereafter signed on with Michael Collins in what was in effect the first urban guerrilla army of the twentieth century. He broke with Collins when the Free State treaty was accepted and was on De Valera's side during the civil war. "He did a lot of damage to the turncoat Free Staters," said my informant. "Mind you, he had nothing to do with the big fellow's death. Collins deserved to die, of course, because he betrayed Ireland, but he was a great man and Rory Kane wept when he heard about his death, and himself a fool for leading a patrol in the west of Ireland, even though he was Defense Minister and a General."

There were too many allusions, too many winks, too many long and significant pauses (whose significance I didn't understand) while the pipe was being relit, for me to grasp more than half of what the old man with the peaked cap was saying. "Why did not my father return to Ireland when De Valera came to power in 1927?"

"Ah well, now, that would be asking for trouble, wouldn't it? And was Rory Kane the kind of man who would ask for trouble?"

So he must have had enemies on Dev's side too; and, in any case, his parents, my informant told me, were dead by then and he was their only son—"Were they not after marrying very late in life and having himself as a bit of a surprise?"

So Rory Kane had fought against the Black and Tans

and in the Troubles and on the losing side in the civil war. He had left Ireland hastily when the civil war ended, never to return, perhaps because it wasn't safe for him to return and perhaps because with both his parents dead there were too many memories in Ireland with which he did not want to have to live.

The old-timer removed a frayed, dirty brown envelope from his pocket and passed it across the table to me with the solemnity of an aging Bishop distributing Holy Communion. Inside the envelope there was a picture, a tall, bespectacled man, perhaps in his early forties, who looked like a schoolteacher. De Valera, of course. And next to him was my son Johnny, a tall, broad-shouldered young man, almost certainly still in his teens, an old Lee Enfield rifle in his hand, an enthusiastic gleam in his eyes.

I brought the picture home but I've never shown it to Eileen or to the kids. Maybe someday I'll try to explain to them the twisted and tragic lines of history that brought him to the prairie near Republic Steel Works on Memorial Day, 1937.

36

"Shall we talk about it now, or after supper?" Red asked Kate as he opened the Volvo door for her, half a block down Webster from their house.

"We'd better get it over with," she said glumly. "Daddy, why did you help us to beat the rap?"

They had dropped Mark off at his parents' high-rise lakefront fortress. "You'd better tell your father the truth, Mark," Red had told the young man gently. "He'll hear it eventually anyhow. If he wants to call me, I'll be happy to talk to him."

"Thank you, Mr. Kane," the young man said respectfully. "Good-bye, Kate, I'll see you around."

"You egged him on, didn't you, Kate?" Red eased the car

away from the entrance to the apartment building and into the mainstream of Inner Drive traffic.

"I guess so," she agreed. "He's so crazy about me, he'll do almost anything I ask him. Poor geek."

They had driven down the edge of the park to Webster in silence. Red put his arm protectively around his daughter as they walked through the dusk to the family home. "There wasn't any rap to beat, kid. They had nothing on you. They might have given Mark a ticket for running a stop sign. When that dummy Phalen saw whose car it was, he thought he could play some games. Finnerty and O'Neil will chew his hide off for being so dumb."

"Did they want a bribe?" she asked. She did not ask why he had changed his mind about her when he came into the police station. Thank God for that. Red had no idea how he would have phonied up an answer.

"No, not really, kid." He glanced up the steps to the house. The front door was already open, Eileen waiting anxiously. "Phalen thought he could hassle me a little and then brag to his buddies that he'd made life difficult for Red Kane and that now Red Kane owed him some favors. In the scenario, you see, I was supposed to come in screaming mad at you and not even notice that Phalen had no grounds at all for dragging you into the police station."

"I was like totally freaked out that you didn't come in screaming." Katie examined his face carefully, as though she were not altogether sure that this strange man was her father.

"Disappointed?"

"Like totally freaked out," she said again.

"You two don't look like you need a lawyer." Eileen stepped aside so they could come into the house. "I must confess I'm terribly relieved."

"We like totally beat the rap." Red winked at his wife. "And Kate is, I mean, really freaked out."

"Ah, that explains everything," said Eileen.

"We're going to talk about it before supper." Red devoutly wished that the confrontation could be postponed until after supper and preferably until after Judgment Day. The physical and emotional strain of acting like an intelligent and sensitive father instead of an angry and outraged father had exhausted him. "Do we want Patty in the conversation too, kid?" he asked Kate.

"I don't care," Kate said sullenly.

"Well, if you don't care, then we won't ask her," Red said smoothly. "And, like, I'm not going to turn into a nerd now, not after repressing all my nerdiness this far."

"You'll never be a nerd, Dad," Kate giggled. "Only a geek once in a while....I think it'd be a good idea for Patty to listen to our talk."

Eileen rolled her green eyes in astonishment, dazzled by her husband's newfound wisdom in dealing with adolescents.

So Red Kane and the three women in his family sat around the empty fireplace on John's Technicolor cushions (which seemed to attract women much more than chairs and sofas—maybe John knew something that Red didn't about how women relax), sipping Diet Pepsi while Red continued his campaign to carve a path through the jungle that separated him from his offspring.

"Like how long do you think we ought to ground you?" Red began the conversation.

"Maybe till Easter," Katie said shyly. "I deserve at least that much."

"Do you think we could make it stick that long, Kate?" He grinned at her over the top of his Pepsi bottle.

"No...I'd really flake out, like maybe by Ash Wednesday. Till Christmas?"

"Would you believe two weekends?" Red cocked an eye at his wife to see if she approved.

Eileen smiled faintly, as if to say, "It's your ball game, buster, play it your way."

"That's not much punishment," Kate said dubiously.

"I think those couple of hours in the cage at the Shakespeare Station might count for a little bit of punishment."

"Oh, Daddy." Kate's eyes filled with tears. "That place was so terrible. Those poor women...Am I going to end up like them?"

Eileen winced and bit her lip. Red groped desperately for the right answer. "You're a very lucky young woman,

Katie. Not merely because Mark has a good throwing arm and you're an agile gymnast and can change seats in the front of the car very quickly. Even if Phalen had found beer cans and marijuana joints, nothing too terrible would have happened to either of you. Most of those poor women never had a chance, not really, at anything else in life. No, you're not going to go that route, Katie. But that doesn't mean that you won't hurt yourself badly and that you won't waste the intelligence and the beauty with which you've been blessed."

"Really," murmured Patty, from her silent corner of the room.

"I suppose so," Kate replied dubiously.

Maybe I've overplayed my hand, Red thought. *Making the moral points too quickly. What do I say now?*

The same instincts that told him Paul O'Meara was still alive whispered a response in his ear.

"It's hard having two famous people for parents, isn't it, kid?"

Kate's face lit up, astonished and delighted that her daddy seemed to understand. "WELL, like I totally don't want you to STOP being famous," she said briskly. "I mean, that would be totally a geek-out."

"But still, people give you a hard time about it. And you wonder if you're anything else besides the daughter of a famous lawyer and a notorious columnist, and sometimes you're not even sure that the famous lawyer and the notorious columnist really think you're anything besides the daughter of two famous people who might embarrass them by some nerdy thing she does."

"Well, sometimes...."

"So it really freaks you out when I show up at the Shakespeare Station and am on your side and even, like, kind of say that you had permission to let Mark drive the Volvo...."

"REALLY!" Patty commented from the bleachers.

"Totally freaked me out," Katie agreed solemnly.

"Okay. Eileen, do you have anything you want to add?"

"The defense rests," Eileen laughed.

Both her daughters laughed with her, obviously with very great relief.

"Patty?" he asked, glancing at the bleacher seats.

"Like wow!"

"Okay, both of you go wash your face for supper and we'll eat the pizza your mother put in the oven for us."

"Spaghetti and meat balls," Eileen said mildly, as their daughters raced up the stairs.

At supper, a chastened Kate, her face twisted in a pretty but puzzled frown, trying to work out a deep problem, sprang the biggest surprise of the day. "Daddy, was Grandpa Kane as good with teenagers as you are?"

"One question at a time," Red gulped, wishing he could trade places with Luciano. "We didn't have teenagers in those days. My father was good with kids, but he didn't live long enough to know his sons when they were in their teens."

"How did he die, Daddy?" Patty seemed ready to call a truce for the moment, on grounds of curiosity if nothing else.

"I wrote it down a long time ago, kid. I thought someday I'd read it to you or your mother. May I?"

All he'd ever told Eileen was that his father had died in an accident in the mills. Somehow it did not seem fair to impose the horror on her. Would she be angry because he had kept it a secret?

All three of his women nodded solemnly. Red rose to find the buried document in his study. Generations. Parents and children. Children become parents. Make the same mistakes. Foolish chances, foolish decisions. *Dear God, if you're really out there swinging Your bat at me, help me to be a good father.*

"How DID he die?" Patty persisted as soon as Red returned, impatient to know the heart of the story.

"He was murdered. By cops."

37 From the Kane File

Second of two undated autobiographical fragments

The heat came early that summer. And with it the permanent fetid stench of the paint factories and oil refineries east of us in Hammond. Memorial Day was blisteringly hot and, even in the morning, heavy with humidity. Mom didn't want to go to the picnic in the prairie near Republic Steel. "It might be dangerous," I remember her saying.

"Nonsense, woman." Dad patted her head reassuringly. "Mayor Ed Kelly himself has promised there'll be no police there today. It'll just be a holiday picnic and a peaceful little parade."

There was nothing scary or threatening about the crowd in the prairie. A number of people carried American flags, strikers and their families were eating picnic lunches, ice-cream and lemonade vendors were selling their wares as fast as they could put them into people's hands, a typical Memorial Day celebration, only a few signs with slogans like "Win with the CIO."

My memories of that day are now so mixed with the newspaper photographs and the newsreel film that I have seen many times since then that it's no longer possible to separate the images, not that it matters. My father was a member of the strike council, and a dedicated believer in the SWOC (Steel Workers Organizing Committee). I remember him arguing in the house with dubious friends that Tom Girdler, the president of Republic Steel, had to be beaten. He was the most antiunion businessman in the country, and if he was beaten, then opposition to the rights of the workingman would disappear.

I don't suppose my father could have ever imagined that a time would come when intellectuals and liberals and journalists and professional leftists would turn against the labor unions, in great part because the unions had been successful in making room for blue-collar workers in America's middle class, thus offending the snobbery of the professional left-wing intellectual.

I can't say that there was any feeling of fear or any intimation of violence that Memorial Day morning. Kids my age and older were running around chasing one another, tossing sixteen-inch softballs back and forth, beginning to organize a softball game. Little girls were playing with their dolls. Young workers and their dates were flirting mildly with one another. In the distant haze at the other end of the prairie there were the Browning .30-caliber machine guns at the gates of Republic Steel, manned by the strikebreakers. No one paid any attention.

Then the atmosphere changed, for a long blue line of Chicago policemen filed around the corner of Republic Steel and took up a position between the plant and our picnic, as if defying us to march in the peaceful parade that Ed Kelly had authorized.

No one ever learned who it was who ordered those five hundred cops to line up in front of Republic Steel on Memorial Day morning.

I saw my father, red hair streaming in the hot wind, gathered with several other members of the strike committee, debating whether to cancel the march. I don't think there ever was a vote. Some of the men, my father included, merely grabbed banners and flags and began to walk toward the plant. Off on one wing a group of strikers' wives formed up and began their march. Kids trailed along behind, after the main body of marchers, spectators at what still seemed to be an innocent parade.

The cops did not back off. The march across the thick weeds of the prairie slowed but continued forward as it approached the line of grim men with clubs in their hands. Suddenly a group of cops broke ranks and rushed toward the women, smashing at breasts with their nightsticks. The women screamed and began to run. Later, on the newsreels, I would see a woman trip and fall as four cops pulled her on the ground while they smashed her face with the butts of their pistols. Then some of the workers, furious, threw pop bottles at the police, a "provocation" (as the papers said the next day). There was a popping sound, tear gas being fired into the crowd. For some reason I broke away from my mother and ran forward into the reeking cloud of gas and the swirling mass of confused men, crying and clawing at their eyes. Then there were more popping sounds, not tear gas this time, but revolvers. Around me some men fell on the ground and others began to run. The blue-coated line charged toward us, nightsticks raised in the air.

I was searching for my father, determined to drag him out of the mob and lead him home to our house at Ninety-third and Coles. Suddenly a breeze blew away a patch of the tear gas smoke and, my eyes smarting, tears running down my cheeks, I saw my father's giant red head only a few yards away. Before I was able to reach him, the police were upon him, slashing at his head and body with their clubs.

Dad fell on one knee, struggled to stand, and then collapsed on the ground when a policeman hit him viciously in the neck with a nightstick. Then another cop calmly pointed his revolver at my father's back and blew a gaping hole in it.

Everything else is a blur—the geyser of blood from Dad's back, my mother's hysterics, the wake, the funeral, the terrible lonely pain in the house that seemed empty, all blur together.

I've watched the newsreel perhaps a score of times. I think that perhaps six or seven seconds of it show my father's death, though ten men were shot in the back that day and it's hard to know whether the Paramount camera team actually did capture Rory Kane's last moments of life. The look on the cop's face as he fired bullets into the back of the prone striker is very much like the look I remember on the face of the cop that killed my father. I suppose the man is long since dead, as all of us eventually are. Even now, should I see that face it would be very hard for me not to choke the life out of it.

The Chicago newspapers the next day blamed the Memorial Day Massacre on the strikers. Those of us who were in that unarmed holiday parade were described as "lusting for blood" by the ineffable *Chicago Tribune* of Colonel Robert

R. McCormick. For many months Republic Steel was able even to suppress the Paramount newsreel. Tom Girdler and the Little Steel (a term used for all the companies besides U.S. Steel—Big Steel) companies won the battle and, indeed, they won the campaign. The Little Steel strike was lost. My father's fellow workers, beaten, frightened, and humiliated, went back to work.

But the CIO won the war. The National Labor Relations Board and Franklin Roosevelt beat Tom Girdler, and a couple of years later the CIO won an election in Republic Steel. The plant has been union ever since. Ten men were killed on that Memorial Day; ninety others, including women and children, were hurt. Eight more men were killed before the strike was finally broken. Senator Robert La Follette, of Wisconsin, launched an investigation that finally forced the release of the Paramount newsreel. My father had not, then, died in vain.

They sang "Solidarity Forever" on that bright, hot, humid Memorial Day as they marched toward the gate of Republic Steel, and Solidarity did, indeed, win in the end. Unfortunately Rory Kane was not alive to enjoy the victory, and the memory of his last moments are branded in the brain of Rory's eldest son, never, never to be forgotten.

Even now I think that it would be appropriate if God should have damned Tom Girdler to the bottom pits of hell for what he did to my father.

There isn't much memory in Chicago of the Memorial Day Massacre at Little Steel. It's conveniently forgotten, like the Fort Dearborn Massacre and the Chicago Fire and the influenza epidemic of 1919. I don't even think the steelworkers' union recollects it, except perhaps as a fuzzy symbol, as pertinent to present problems as the Battle of Antietam in the Civil War. The police department, the same police department whose discipline broke down again in front of the Conrad Hilton in 1968 and beat my pregnant wife—thirty years later—did everything it could to cover up and forget its own ineptitude. And if there is any sorrow in the Chicago journalistic profession about the distorted reporting of the Memorial Day Massacre in all the Chicago papers for the next several weeks, I have never heard it expressed. Indeed, younger reporters are simply not interested when I try to explain the Little Steel Massacre as one of the deep-rooted historical causes for the animosity Chicago workingmen have against newspapers.

Workers, you see, are hard-hat, blue-collar, superpatriotic, racist chauvinists on whom the young reporters can look down with supercilious contempt. Sometimes I think not all that much has changed since Memorial Day, 1937.

Even now I can feel the sting of the tear gas in my eyes, see the policeman's club smashing into my father's head, blood even redder than his hair spilling out. I watch his back explode as the cop, with an expression of beatific joy, empties his revolver into the man that I worshiped so much.

And even now I feel guilt, unreasoning absurd guilt that I did not get to him in time to pull him away from the blue-coated killers.

38

Red closed the manila folder and glanced at his watch. A little less than ten minutes. About a thousand words. He had not read it too rapidly. He was drained of all emotion. His father's death might have happened yesterday.

The three women were stony faced, as exhausted as he was.

"Grandpa Kane was a hero," almost-eighteen-year-old Patty, who couldn't imagine a violent steel strike, breathed softly. "I'm so proud of him."

"You must publish that sometime, Red." Eileen's voice was choked with emotion. "Does my father know?"

"I told him. He seemed to understand."

"I hate cops." Kate spit the words out violently.

Red put his arm around the blond sophomore, loving

her more at the end of this turbulent day than he ever had before. "I know the feeling, kid, but it's not right." *Good God, Kane, you're beginning to sound like a saint.* "There are good ones and bad ones just like everybody else."

39

"Dad, this is Lois... Lois, this is my father..." He hesitated and then finished in a tone that suggested both reverence and embarrassment, as if the old man were a *capo de tutti capi*, "Red Kane, the columnist."

John drew thick blond eyebrows together in an anxious frown and set his jaw both defiantly and fearfully, wanting Red to like this young woman from the wilds of northern Minnesota he had brought into their house. He probably hoped for rudeness because that would confirm his permanent animosity toward his father.

John's persecution complex had its usual effect on Red: it inclined him toward the behavior that the complex expected. He nodded without looking up from his careful perusal of the Song of Songs in the Bible.

Then he realized the inconsistency in being rude to a young woman while you were reading about the charms of the Shulamite.

He bounded cheerfully out of his chair. "I'm delighted to meet you, Lois. 'Cuse me for being preoccupied with the most erotic book in the Bible." John's jaw dropped. "Come on in, sit down and tell me what you think about Chicago." He grinned wickedly at his son. "I promise you it'll all be off the record."

Lois was unquestionably attractive, long fine brown hair, brown eyes, brown skin, a lithe, deftly sculpted, and appealing young body in a brown sweater and skirt that reminded Red of how young women dressed when he was that age. Much better taste than John had ever demonstrated before. She was also terrified, quite literally trembling at the prospect of encountering John's father, the notorious Redmond Peter Kane.

"It's the first time I've been to Chicago, Mr. Kane." Lois sat on the edge of the lemon-colored cushion next to the fireplace in which Eileen was busy lighting the fire, hands on her knees, like a novice talking to a Bishop, a novice wearing cranberry-colored slacks and sweater in keeping with the season. "I've only been to Minneapolis twice. I think Chicago is a breathtakingly lovely city. You can read all about the various Chicago schools of architecture, but you have to really see the buildings to know how wonderful they are."

"Did John show you the 333 Wacker Building?" Red decided on the spot that he would interview Lois Schwartz, not indeed for an article that would ever be written, but because an interview might be the best way to put this obviously intelligent as well as attractive young woman at her ease. "As I remember, I attacked it in my column, but it's still one of my favorite buildings."

"The one that looks like a slab of artistically carved green ice?" she said, locking her fingers together so they wouldn't tremble. "I think it's beautiful too."

"You're from Bemidji, are you not?" Red leaned forward, concentrating on her as a good interviewer always concentrates.

"Not exactly," she blushed. "I live outside it in a little town called Nebish which is seven or eight miles off the main road between Bemidji and International Falls. My father owns a ski resort and a Ford dealership in Bemidji."

Yes of course the town would be called Nebish. Poor John, don't look so embarrassed.

"That's the resort kind of near the Red Lake Indian Reservation, isn't it?" Red asked.

"That's right." The young woman glowed as brightly as a Christmas tree. "Some of the Indians from the reservation work for my father."

Eileen looked up from the fireplace in astonished disbelief. Her husband's knowledge of the Red Lake Indian Reservation just might possibly have been the most incredible phenomenon in twenty years of erratic marriage. She rolled her green eyes appreciatively and returned to fire logs, pushing Luciano's nose firmly out of the way.

Nothing to it. A call to the president's office at St. Ben's, a glance at a road map.

A few more questions about her mother and her father, her two brothers and her sister, and Lois was completely at ease. Patty and Kate drifted into the room, taking their place in the bleacher seats, while Red delicately and gently learned just about all there was to know about Lois Schwartz.

And there was, it turned out, a good deal to know. Until she had enrolled in St. Benedict's College the big events in Lois's life were a monthly trip to the shopping mall at Grand Forks, a visit every year or two to Duluth, and one trip to a cousin's wedding in Minneapolis. Nonetheless, she was a well-informed and well-educated young woman. Her family, indeed, lived in the woods on the shore of a lake so far away from the main road that they had to generate their own electricity and pump their own water. Nonetheless, she was an enthusiastic participant in the "museum without walls" that was modern culture. Television brought the world into their log home, and the U.S. mails brought *Vanity Fair* and *Vogue* and *Harper's* and *Mademoiselle*, and the *Smithsonian* magazine, and *Time* and *Newsweek* and the *New York Times*—"three days late"—and the *Wall Street Journal*.

The bookstores in Grand Forks either sold or could order for her the Abrams Art Books and recordings by the New York Philharmonic, the Chicago Symphony, and the Berlin Philharmonic. Lois Schwartz was a backwoodsperson, a peasant among those sophisticates, awed by the great city of Chicago and frightened by her boyfriend's family. But she was a well-educated and cultivated peasant who had studied and read and reflected and listened to music and knew more about culture than ninety-five percent of reporters who worked for the *Herald Gazette*—and probably a good deal more than the *Herald*'s professional critics.

"I feel like I'm being interviewed for a feature story, Mr. Kane!" she laughed at a break in the interview, as Eileen tiptoed softly around the room filling everyone's wine-glasses—everyone's but Red's. Without being told, Eileen knew that all he wanted was soda water. The green-eyed witch was biting her lip to keep from laughing at Red's smooth charm with Lois.

He gave her his best "just-wait-till-I-get-you-in-bed-tonight" look. She turned away with an expression that said, "I will shortly have hysterics if you keep this comedy up."

"I'm not going to write you up." He toasted her with his refilled soda water tumbler. "But I think you're a very interesting young woman and I'm delighted that my son has the good taste to invite you to come to Chicago and meet us. Tell me, given your druthers, would you rather raise your own children in a place like Nebish or would you prefer to live in Chicago? That's not a loaded question. I think a good case can be made for Nebish, and you're excellent proof that, at least in the United States, no one need be outside the 'museum without walls.'"

"I've thought a lot about that, Mr. Kane." Lois turned the glass of white wine thoughtfully in her long delicate fingers. "And if you really want to know what my 'druthers' are, I guess I'd like to spend six months each year in both places—summers in Nebish and winters in Chicago!"

The whole Kane family laughed enthusiastically and Lois laughed with them, not altogether sure of the joke, but still feeling that they were laughing with her and not at her.

Later his son stopped Red on the stairway, his eyes shining. "Thanks, Dad," he said simply.

Uneasily, Red wondered if he might have contributed to the feelings of inferiority toward his father that Eileen claimed troubled John. *What the hell, you do what you can.*

"There are two ways to handle a nervous stranger, John." Red hoped he wasn't sounding too pontifical. "You either ignore them completely or make them the center of attention. There's no better way of doing the latter than an interview, because an interviewer, if he's any good at it, must concentrate totally on learning about and understanding the person he's interviewing. There was something in those lovely brown eyes that suggested to me that your friend Lois had a lot to say."

"I'd never heard her say so much." John was trying to make up his mind whether to be offended. "I learned more about her tonight than I have in the last three months." He paused and then rushed ahead impulsively, "Do you like her, Dad?"

"Lois"—Red poked his son's massive arm—"is the sort of young woman who makes me feel very sorry that I'm not twenty years old again."

John strode down the corridor to his own bedroom, the confident walk of a delighted young man who, much to his astonishment, has won approval for a project that he was sure would be rejected.

He'd be resentful again by morning, but they'd made a beginning. The only thing harder than a beginning, Red was learning, is a continuing.

Red paused a moment before walking to the other end of the hallway. There was little chemistry between John and Lois, no electric current leaping back and forth. In contrast, between him and Eileen there was now white heat. A simple kiss of greeting or good-bye, once empty marital routine, could turn into a passionate embrace. Passing each other on the stairs, as romantic normally as two cars passing in the opposite direction on an expressway, might become a tryst. Eyes would lock, hands would touch, a pat, a caress and then, especially if the children were not around, the games would begin.

"Lots of gazelles and young stags on the loose in this house," she would observe with a complacent giggle.

Eileen was now normally an exuberant and uninhibited, if skittish and giddy, partner. Not always uninhibited, however. Sometimes, despite her refusal to tolerate his prudishness, she still became momentarily a bundle of anxious inhibitions. She talked about herself as though she were two different women; the self-deprecating "lawyer lady" had been joined by a "comedy lady" who she claimed was "sluttish."

Earlier in the week a tryst had been developing after a chance encounter in the hallway outside her study.

"Have to go shopping at Treasure Island with Patty. She'll be home in a few moments," Eileen had murmured as he held her against the wall and began to fondle her. "Fixated on my boobs, aren't you?"

It was an observation, not a complaint.

"All Irish men have the same fixation. Anyway, you'd be disappointed if I wasn't. Besides, YOU pinched ME."

"Regardless ... which lady is better in bed? Lawyer lady or musical-comedy lady?" She bit her lip to contain her racing emotions. "You have your choice, you know."

"Same wife."

"Regardless ... lawyer lady tends to be a frigid pig." She squirmed as oh-so-tenderly his fingers worked their way into her flesh. "Oh, Red ..."

Her skin was warm and moist. He bent his head to kiss her bare chest. He knew he should challenge her separation of herself into different people. Later. Now, as tongue touched hardened nipple and Eileen, sighing contentedly, dug her fingers into his hair to hold his head in place, he thought that to hesitate here for all eternity, between arousal and fulfillment with the woman he loved, would do very nicely as heaven.

"Mo-THER!"

"Damn," he muttered, reluctantly trying to withdraw his lips from her breast.

"Little bitch looks at me like I'm a sex fiend." Eileen would not free him from her grip. "Can't hide a thing from her. Was the lawyer lady a good lay ever?"

Lay? Not Eileen's language.

"You'd better believe it.... Maybe you should talk to Patty about us."

"Mo-THER. I'm SURE they won't keep the store open all night."

"Only when she asks, and she won't ask. COMING, Patty." She disengaged from Red. "You'd better be here when I return, buster."

Red pulled her back. "Your blouse ..."

She couldn't get the straps and buttons in the right places. "Comedy lady tends to be a slut," she snickered.

Red pushed her hands out of the way, readjusted her clothes, and fastened the buttons properly. He promised that he would be waiting when she returned.

Since then both the lawyer lady and the comedy lady had reappeared, usually in incoherent, Ryanish babble. Perhaps they should have acted like sensible veterans of twenty years of marriage instead of like horny adolescents. It was too late now. The love affair would have to run its course.

When he left John to figure out whether he was pleased or displeased with his father's charm, he wondered whether the lawyer lady or the comedy lady (perhaps her counterpart of his green-eyed witch) would be waiting for him?

He sighed. When he tried to analyze their scorching romance, desire always exorcised thought. He hurried to their bedroom.

At the door he thought of Harv Gunther and the mugger in the Federal Building elevator. *Is Gunther still a threat to Eileen? I'm so deliciously happy these days I've forgotten about him. Should I call Mike Casey?*

Then he forgot about the Gunther threat—a mistake he would later have good reason to regret—and pushed through the door.

"Why would he think that we might not like her?" he asked Eileen when he entered. Glasses perched firmly on her nose, she was reading Stephen King's *Pet Sematary* in bed, very much the lawyer lady.

"No particular reason." She closed the book, removed her reading glasses, put her glasses and the book on the table next to the bed, and demurely readjusted the thin strap on her pearl-gray nightgown. Tonight she was the old familiar Eileen, a lovely matron indeed but not a wanton bedmate out of an adolescent fantasy. Very much the lawyer lady. "John has never had much confidence in his own judgment. He just sort of assumes that most of the decisions he makes are mistakes. Bringing Lois home was a big decision and he was about ninety-five percent certain that we wouldn't like her."

"Do I criticize him that much?" Red sat on the edge of the bed and took his wife's hand. "If I do, I can't remember it."

"You hardly ever criticize him." She touched his chin with her fingers. "When the boy grows up with such a competent and well-informed father, he kind of naturally feels inferior. You were wonderful tonight, Red. Truly wonderful."

"Two down, one to go." Red guided her fingers to his lips. "So far so good."

"Two?" Eileen raised a dubious eyebrow.

"Katie and John. Now I have to cut my way through the jungle with Patty."

"The children's mother doesn't count?" She raised a mischievous eyebrow.

"The children's mother has been asking for trouble all day long."

"Really? Red, stop looking at me that way!"

Overcome again with the power of the enormous love he felt for her, Red disposed of Steven King, pulled back the sheet, swept his wife into his arms, and quickly dispossessed her of her nightgown. Her resistance was perfunctory and insincere.

"The children's mother," he said, hugging her tightly, "is a far more serious problem."

She became a worse problem during the next half hour. Red was contentedly nibbling on the firm flesh of her breasts, enjoying himself enormously and in no hurry to end the foreplay. Eileen, still the lawyer lady with her glasses back on, was absorbing his ministrations like a purring kitten.

"You really are a terrible prig, you know that, don't you?" she said.

"Huh?" Red demanded.

"He's my husband. He married me." Her voice changed. "The hell he did. He thought he was getting a wild actress woman and instead he got a stodgy lawyer."

"What's going on?" Red demanded.

"You be quiet," she informed him, he wasn't sure in which character, "this is between me and her. You go back to eating my tits. That's what you're supposed to be doing now."

"I—"

"Be quiet." It was the comedy lady. "What kind of a dolt are you? You had to be a serious professional, calm, responsible, in charge. Don't you dare blame your family. They all supported me."

"I didn't want to lose control. I was afraid...."

"And now you think you've wasted your life?"

"Maybe I have!" The lawyer lady was close to tears.

"And you think you can let me out of the box by playing the slut. How can a prig be a slut?"

"You're the slut!"

"You tell him to stop being a prude and you're worse than he is!"

"I am not!" Now she was in tears.

"I don't know whether I want to play. I don't trust you. Take off your glasses, anyway. How can a man enjoy the tits of a woman wearing glasses?"

"God damn it, Eileen," Red yelled. "Stop it!"

"It think it's pretty good dialogue for spontaneous drama. Don't worry, Red." She took off her glasses and pulled his head back to her breasts. "I've chased the lawyer lady away for the rest of the night. Now we can have some fun."

"You're not drunk?"

"Course not," she sniffed. "Just a little psychodrama. Storytelling as foreplay. Which did you like better?"

"I like them both."

"That's because you're my husband. Please don't stop."

"One more question."

"All right." She shifted in her bed, the kitten upset because the affection had been diminished.

"Why didn't you become an actress?"

"'Fraid I wasn't good enough." She turned her head so he couldn't see her face. "I'd rather be the naked mare in your city room than talk about it."

"That's an honest admission." He turned the stubborn jaw back. Her eyes were tightly closed and her face taut with shame. "Were you good enough?"

"That's an extra question."

"God damn it, woman, I'm your husband." He kept his fingers on her contentious jaw and laid his other hand firmly on her belly, gently but authoritatively forbidding evasion.

Silence. She thought she could wait him out. Not the new Red Kane. He increased his pressure on jaw and belly.

"You're going to be stubborn about it?" She opened one eye.

"Yes," he insisted, thinking that he had never dared be so masterful with her before. He pushed even harder against her, stopping just short of hurting her, and balanced his demand for truth with an affectionate kiss.

"All right. I might have been." She opened both eyes,

considered him gravely as Patty had done but with something that might even be called respect. "Now I'll never know. Satisfied?"

"What does Blackie say about your career choice?"

"Oh, HIM! That's none of your business." She pushed him away and bunched the sheet up over her body, chin-high.

"I know what he says." Savagely Red pushed her shoulders deep into the mattress.

"What, Mr. Smartass?"

"Exactly what I say: it doesn't matter whether you're a lawyer or an actress, so long as you're Eileen."

"Oh, Red..." She burst into tears. "I've wasted my life. In four years I'll be the age Mom was when she died."

He wrapped his arms around her and waited patiently till the sobbing stopped. So that was it?

"Feel better?"

"A little. Are you sure you love me?"

Feeling very proud of his assertiveness, he pried her fingers away from the sheet and delicately resumed his work on her breasts. "I repeat, I love both the lawyer and the actress because they're both my wife Eileen."

She nodded and sunk her fingers into his hair so that he could not pull away from her again.

He removed his lips from her breast for one last word. "And right now you're thirty years younger than your father, who is very much alive."

"I was wondering," she sniggered, "when you'd think of that."

Later Red would ask himself why he did not seize that opportunity to talk seriously about their marriage. Why was he content with admiring his own performance as the challenging husband instead of continuing the performance to its logical conclusion?

He defended himself with the argument that his wife was not quite ready to talk. Psychodrama, yes; talk, no.

But that defense came after it was too late.

40

Patty was the hardest nut to crack.

"I'm really just not up, like totally, for some airhead serious talk, Daddy!" Red Kane's middle child insisted. "Can't we let it go to some other time? WHY DO WE HAVE TO TALK NOW?"

"Because I said so, God damn it!"

Red had a throbbing headache. His dreams of Adele were stronger and more vivid. He was worried about Harv Gunther. He had learned from Mike Casey that Eileen was receiving anonymous phone calls at her office—heavy breathing and muttered obscenities. He had ranted at her because she had not told him. She replied coldly that she was more than capable of taking care of herself.

Eileen and he were quarreling often, as the Houston case occupied more of her time and the Gunther and O'Meara files became an obsession with him. Perhaps their fighting was nothing more than lovers' quarrels, but Red now was wondering whether, Holy Ghost's bright wing or not, he was fouling up his last chance with his wife.

"It's gross to take God's name in vain!" Patty stamped her foot. "And I have a term paper to write."

Red needed a drink so badly that he thought he might have a heart attack without one.

Stupid cop-out.

It was Thanksgiving week, and for almost a month Red Kane's rejuvenated life had persisted. He had assumed that as God's kick in the ass receded it would be more difficult to sustain his well-intentioned resolutions. Rather to his surprise, he did not cave in when the pressures mounted. Not once had he stepped inside the Old Town Ale House, and while he didn't swim or exercise every day, he still was at the East Bank Club often enough so that his presence there no longer surprised anyone. The revision of his novel was almost finished. He was biding his time with Harv Gunther, waiting for Harv to make his next move. He continued to be positively charming in the newsroom and virtually a bosom buddy of poor, confused Wilson Allen. He and Katie were good friends again, entertaining one another at supper each night with ethnic stories that Patricia dismissed as "totally gross."

Virtue was no longer as easy as it had been in the first couple of weeks after IT happened. Now he had to work to be patient and kind, self-restrained and thoughtful. Endless effort. Not fair, he complained. As usual, no response from the cause of all his problems. And not enough help from the other members of his family yet either.

He had yet to visit a parish priest to straighten out his life with the Church; nor had he begun serious conversations with his wife or reestablished diplomatic relations with Patty.

Nevertheless, he was, on the whole, pleased with himself. In his mind he had made up a column about the "new Red Kane," in which he compared his own metamorphosis to that of Richard Nixon, insisting that the only difference was that the old Nixon came back and that the old Red Kane had not come back.

Yet.

Patty was a much tougher problem than he thought she would be.

"I want to know why we're not friends anymore." He turned down the music of WFMT and leaned on the desk in his study. Patty, clad in her teenage uniform of jeans and sweatshirt ("Property of the Athletic Department of the University of Montana," it said) was curled up in a tight little knot on the only chair her brother had seen fit to put in the study—assuming, no doubt, that only one person at a time would want to use it.

Luciano, inevitably, curled up at her feet in a pattern not unlike his mistress's.

"I dunno." Patty's response was the standard all-purpose evasive adolescent answer.

"We used to be good friends," Red said gently. "I don't think we're friends anymore and I wonder why. It seems that you don't even like me anymore."

"Oh, I still LIKE you, Dad." She uncurled herself and sat upright in the chair, resigned to the conversation. "I just totally don't RESPECT you."

"I'm sorry to hear that, Patty," he said, trying to sound not too threatened. "Maybe if you tell me what I've done to lose your respect, I might be able to win it back."

"No way," Patty said grimly.

"No way you'll tell me, or no way I can win it back?"

"No way you can win it back."

"That's kind of unforgiving, isn't it, Patty? No second chance?"

"I, like totally, can't respect you because you are so geeky with Mom." His daughter's face was locked in a tight, hard, angry frown. "You don't respect her, so I don't respect you. Right?"

How much did she know? Did she know about the other women?

"Most of the time, Pat, I am pretty unhappy with myself in the same area. Your mother is much too good a woman for someone like me. Yet I do try, and I've been trying harder lately...."

"I don't see how you can be such a GEEK to her...." Patty shook her head angrily. "It isn't fair, it just isn't fair."

"Marriages go through cycles." He moistened his lips with his tongue, groping for words. "We had a bad time of it, all my fault; at the same time you're going through a critical—"

"Life-cycle change," Patty said bitterly.

"I think I'm getting better at it," he began tentatively, "in the last couple of weeks—"

"Teenage lovey-dovey shit!" Patty exploded.

Despite their outbursts of anger, Red and Eileen were now hopelessly in love with one another, more in love, in fact, than they had been during their courtship, which was really not a courtship at all. When they were apart they could hardly wait until the time came when they could be together again. They called each other more often during the day on the phone in a single week than they had done in five years before in their marriage. When they were together they could not keep their hands off each other, and when they were alone in their bedroom they could not tear off their clothes fast enough to begin yet another round of lovemaking.

Eileen seemed to be undergoing a transformation of her own. Her cool self-possession slipped occasionally into either sudden irritability or transient giddiness. Frequent physical love was perhaps thawing icebergs inside her too.

There were two ways to deal with her, Red was discovering. You needled her or gave her orders. The first made her giggle even more and the second amused her enormously. Both required courage and determination from Red, who had never in his life made fun of or ordered about a woman.

"You giggle more than your daughters," he informed her in bed one night.

"Gazelles tickle." She giggled again. "To say nothing of your young stags."

"Not the woman I read about in the *Sun-Times*."

"Castrating bitch."

Soon, very soon, he would insist that they begin their serious conversation about how to rearrange their marriage. Falling in love, he told himself, is a great beginning, but it isn't enough.

That evening in his study, however, he felt compelled to defend himself against the devastating charge of his daughter. "Your mother and I are at a stage in our marriage, kid" —he shut his eyes, trying to imagine how he should put it— "when we are very strongly attracted to one another again. That's a phase. It's part of the cycle in any marriage. When falling in love over again with your spouse goes out of a marriage, there isn't much left. I suppose we do look pretty silly at times—"

"Like totally icky," Patricia insisted.

"It's all right for you and Jeff to freak out over one another, but not all right for Mom and I?"

"Forgodsakes, Daddy. You and Mom are MARRIED. You're not SUPPOSED to act like gelheads with one another. It's SO embarrassing!"

"Do you want us to stop, hon?"

"Course not!" she snapped back at him. "It's better than not talking to one another. Besides, I don't see how any man could NOT be in love with Mom."

Ah-ha. He was being faulted both for loving his wife and for not loving her enough.

"We're at a turning point, your mother and I, and I think if you give us, or maybe I should say give me, a little more time—"

"DADDY," she said impatiently, shifting around in the chair again and tucking her legs under herself, "I don't care what you and Mom do, so long as you RESPECT her. When you respect her, I'll respect you again."

"You don't think I respect her now? Is there any way I can persuade you that I respect her more than anyone else in the world?"

"Katie thinks the two of you are CUTE—geeky sophomores like her and Mark. Just because you're sweet on Mom now doesn't mean it's going to last. Will you still be sweet on her at Christmas or Easter or next summer or when I go away to school?"

"Are you going to give me a chance?" He hunched forward on the desk, resting his chin on his hands. "Or have you already figured that I'm just another nerd sophomore who will let your mother down in a few days, a few weeks, or a few months?"

"WELL..."

The rigid righteousness of an adolescent, the same kind of rigid righteousness about which Paul O'Meara had teased him when he was an adolescent reporter in his middle twenties.

"Well?" he said. "What now...?"

"Candidly, Daddy, to use your favorite word, I think you are really sophomoric most of the time...."

That was the issue, nailed down after traveling the characteristically twisted adolescent trail: Patty, like most teenagers, was ambivalent about emotions between her parents. They were both EMBARRASSING and CUTE. Her objection was deeper than just embarrassment, however. Red had not treated her mother with sufficient respect before. Their current love affair wouldn't last. He would go back to his old ways, and her mother would be hurt again.

"You mean that I have not paid any attention to your

mother for a long time, and now, all of a sudden, I'm a lovey-dovey teenager? And that won't last, so in a little while I'll be as bad as I ever was? Is that about it?"

"You don't respect her, Daddy. She's the most wonderful woman in the world. Everybody else respects her and you treat her like she's part of the furniture, or maybe like she's Luciano—a pat on the head or on the butt and a nice word is supposed to keep her going for a couple of months."

"And you don't think I'm going to change?"

"No way. And next year I'll be away at college, and you know how quiet Katie is when she's in one of her moods. Mom won't have anybody to talk to."

"Do I get a chance to do better?" he asked meekly.

"I like you, Daddy," she said firmly. "I just don't respect you anymore."

"We'll have to wait and see, won't we? Both of us."

Patty slipped out of the chair and bounded to the door of the room, Luciano padding quickly after her.

"You're giving me a little bit of a chance but not much, is that the idea?"

Patty turned at the door, hands on her blue-jeaned hips, a youthful goddess of justice reluctantly making a concession. "WELL, at least you didn't deny anything."

Luciano turned around too, panting eagerly, ready to follow in whatever direction his mistress led.

"Thank you for your candor." Red bowed his head politely. "We'll see how I do on probation."

"REALLY!" She sailed forth from the room, Luciano in dogged pursuit.

Red slumped wearily over his desk. Worse even than interviewing Richard J. Daley, against whom you could never win, God be good to him. Somehow he had forgotten how rigidly righteous an adolescent woman could be. Patty was intelligent and sensitive; she would mellow as she matured. But would she ever get over her disillusionment with her father, that all-powerful, all-wise hero of her childhood who had turned into a stupid bum, lacking even the elementary intelligence to love his remarkable wife?

She didn't know about the other women. Thank God for

that. If she had ever found out about them, her father never would have been granted the chance to regain her respect. As it was, he had been granted, none too graciously, another chance and warned that she thought he'd blow it.

"You never said," he murmured to Whoever it was that had launched him in this perhaps quixotic attempt to salvage something from his life, "it was going to be easy. I sure hope You don't turn out to be a seventeen-year-old girl."

There was no comment from the dialogue partner. There never was. *Well,* thought Red, *if You made judgments like a seventeen-year-old girl You certainly would have warned us.*

Wouldn't you?

He lifted his tattered Gucci briefcase—bought at the Rome Hilton during a terrible rainstorm—from the floor and opened it on his desk, removing the hard copy of the most recent one hundred pages of his novel. The second draft was completely different from the first. He had written out most of the biographical material, afraid that he had provided his protagonist with too many excuses, too many escape hatches, too many loopholes. The hero was now a kind of Irish Catholic Woody Allen, clumsy, bumbling, ineffectual, relatively innocent, and to be salvaged by a wife and family who never gave up on him. High comedy instead of grim tragedy.

Patty, he felt, would not like the hero very much, but she'd probably like him a lot more than she liked her father.

He worked through the first ten pages and then shoved the manuscript aside, emotionally drained by the confrontation with his daughter.

I really do need a drink, he thought. *If Patty should hear me think that, she'd want to know why any man in his right mind would want to go out of the house for a drink when he has a wife like Eileen waiting for him in his bedroom.*

The love that was all calm and curled in the glass building welled up within him, permeating his blood vessels, his bones, his muscles, and every cell in his body. As long as that love was with him, he could cope with angry young women like Patricia Anne Kane.

But he might be losing Eileen again. What could he do about that? She was so tired and irritable that she might resent his making a pass just now. The lawyer lady was in charge again.

Hell, what else do I have to offer her? A little bit of distraction from her rage at Don Roscoe.

Eileen was in the shower. Again. The woman had a cleanliness fetish.

Briefly he thought of his mother, who was also Patricia Anne. She was not a Patty, however, but Patsy Anne. Her outrage about the injustice the world had worked on her was not completely dissimilar from the outrage of her granddaughter. *Dear God in heaven,* he thought as he undressed, *what would Patty be like if she had to go through what Mom went through?* He considered the question and decided that Patty, no fault of his, God knew, was much better equipped to deal with crisis and tragedy than her grandmother had been.

The shower water was still running. An impulsive and indeed impudent fantasy raced through Red's mind. *I've never done that before. Why don't I do it now? Why not indeed.*

He opened the thick glass door of the shower and stepped in. "Remember that movie, *Psycho*?"

"Red!"

Eileen, shampoo tube in hand, backed up against the steaming shower wall, water and soap streaking her firm white flesh, shoulder blades pressed defensively against the wall. Captured, embarrassed, delicious.

And ready, to judge by the outrage on her face, to go into her spring-thunderstorm routine.

"Sorry," he mumbled. "I'll leave. It was just a crazy idea...."

His wife hesitated, words of ridicule on her lips.

"Don't you dare," she gulped, changing her mind and grabbing his arm. "You surprised me and you scared me, but that doesn't mean I don't want you to be here." She handed him the shampoo tube. "I told you once, I'd try anything. And I've always had this fantasy about a man giving me a shampoo in the shower."

"You're sure?" He considered the shampoo tube dubiously.

"I'm sure," she laughed. "And delighted and flattered. And also happy that you've finally given up some of your prudishness."

Her hand tightened on his arm. The tilt of her jaw was like Patty's. He would not be permitted to sneak away.

So Red squeezed the tube and gooey gelatin squirted out on his wife's hair. "I'm glad I saw the eye doctor this afternoon about contact lenses." Eileen drew him closer so that their bodies were touching. "If we're going to do this sort of thing often, I want to see more than foggy shapes."

"What do you think our teenage daughters would say if they knew we were doing this?" His wife's head was now a thick snowy mountain of suds.

"They'd be embarrassed and delighted, I suppose," she answered promptly, collapsing her whole weight against his chest, as if she no longer had any will of her own.

Then she began to sing "Sunrise, Sunset," from *Fiddler*, in her clear, light, and joyous voice.

"You never sing in the shower, Eileen." Red hesitated. Was she about to mourn for her lost career again? How was he supposed to deal with that problem?

"I do when my husband is washing my hair and driving me out of my mind with desire. What are you waiting for? This hair washing is serious business. Next song is 'Tradition.'"

He continued his task, distributing the huge surplus of suds all over the familiar and yet always mysterious landscape of his wife's body.

It was scenery he knew well, all the valleys and hills, all the secret paths, the rivers and streams, the mountains and the forests. Yet it was still a surprise at every new exploration. Not as perfect a landscape as it used to be, marked despite the excellent preservation work, he admitted again, by the erosions of time and gravity, but all the more appealing for that fact.

The steam and the water and the suds seemed to wash away all the rottenness and corruption of his past. His world spun around him. The designated hitter was coming out of the dugout. Red waved Him off, like a manager not ready yet for the slugger.

"I liked your hair when it was long." He rubbed in a giant glob of suds, breaking the spell that almost possessed him.

"Really?" She interrupted "Matchmaker," stayed his hand, and looked up at him in surprise. "Why didn't you tell me? I'll let it grow long again."

He kissed her affectionately. "Don't do it just for me."

"What better reason? No, not that way, Red. Here, let me show you." She guided his hands into her hair. "You'll make a good hairdresser with a little practice."

"It's hard to pay attention for some reason."

"I can't imagine," she chuckled. "Please concentrate on my hair for the moment, anyway...and, by the way, what were you and Joe Murphy talking about when you were ogling us at Blackie's party?"

He knew it would come up eventually.

"We weren't ogling. We were admiring."

"What?"

"Two matron/goddesses." He wiped some suds off her breast.

"I bet. WELL, what did you say about them?"

"Who?"

"The goddesses with the big tits."

He might as well tell the truth. "Joe said that Ryan women demanded that they be adored, cherished, protected, restrained, and enjoyed."

"How beautiful..." Her eyes began to tear. "Restrained is the important word, of course. That's what we need most."

What the hell did that mean?

Tube still in one hand, he gripped her waist, thumbs on her belly, and held her against the shower wall. "Like this?"

"That's nice too." She drew her breath deeply. "And you can kiss me now too, while you're at it. But I mean restrained all the time because otherwise we think you don't care how flaky we get."

"I don't think you're flaky, Eileen," he said dubiously. "And I think *cherished* sums it all up."

"How sweet! But please, please Red, kiss me and tell me you love me."

He brushed her lips.

"No, I mean a real kiss."

So he crushed her against the wall and devoured her with a supremely passionate kiss.

"All right?"

"Well, better. The lawyer lady is on the run. Now your line, please."

"I will cherish you always, Eileen. Always."

"Forever improving on my scripts. Could I have one more kiss, pretty please?"

Somehow it seemed a plea for survival. Red could hardly refuse. Under the circumstances.

That night he dreamed again of the Amazon—steamy mists, samba drums, dark rivers, and a woman, sometimes his wife, sometimes his mother, pushing him into a swarm of piranhas.

41

"Pretty soon you're going to have to take up that collection for the marble urinal, good buddy," Harvard Gunther toasted Red. "These mortal remains aren't going to remain much longer."

"Then what, Harv?" Red asked crisply, biting his tongue so as not to suggest a reunion with Adele Ward in the hereafter. A reception at the plush, green-and-beige Ritz Carlton with its lobby fountain rumbling uneasily in the background, as if threatened by the implacable tower of the Hancock Center across the street (*How would you like to have that for a next-door neighbor?* Red asked himself), was not the environment in which to play his ace.

The case against Harv was now almost airtight. Checking the national list of missing children he had found the name Arlene Warren, from Toledo, Ohio, age twelve at the time of her disappearance. The accompanying photo was of a winsome little tyke who seemed ten years instead of two years younger than the anguished girl whom Harv was destroying in Rita Lane's pictures. It was, however, the same sad, empty face.

He had asked a trusted Toledo journalist to trace her family background—steel-mill family, harsh parents, poor grades in school, runaway—and to search for a link with Rita Lane's child-prostitution racket. The information was not essential, but it would be helpful in the story he would finally write.

And the prize he would surely win. Was that the real motive for it all? Reestablish his journalistic reputation? He needed to talk it all out to be sure of his reasons for pursuing the evil old man who grinned at him like a Marx-Brothers-comedy imitation of Satan.

"Nothing, I hope." Harv drained his glass. "If there is any judgment, you know what the verdict will be on me."

"They allow last-minute plea bargaining." Red sipped his Perrier—now ordered with two twists of lime.

"Even that sexy broad you're married to couldn't get me off," Harv chuckled.

The cocktail party was a celebration of the publication of a special Chicago issue in a national travel magazine. Red had drifted into it because the editor of the issue had worked at the *HG* after she graduated from Northwestern. Long ago they had flirted briefly. As he congratulated her with a perfunctory hug and kiss, he wondered why he had been interested.

Harv explained to Red that he owned part of the company that published the magazine. "Leisure industries are a big thing, Red. You ought to put some of your fortune into a good one."

He no longer looked like a big bald wizard. Rather, now he looked like a model for the fellow who pilots the boat across the River Styx, sunken, hollow, bent, Charon ready to pilot his craft down the lower level in the dark of night. Red shivered. He would not want to ride on Harv's boat; you'd be robbed on the way to Hades.

Only the shell of the great magician remained, clad in a thousand-dollar dinner jacket and flaunting expensive diamonds, despite his yellow face and protruding eyes.

The face of death was on Harvard Princeton Gunther.

He was a harmless, dying old man. What right did Red have to anticipate God's judgment?

Yet Gunther's voice was powerful and his eyes flashed with manic delight. Harv would go down into hell twisting the last pleasure out of life, pleasure that might involve pain for someone else.

Was he the death rider from the Apocalypse Red had conjured out of the terror he thought he saw in his wife's eyes and who now haunted his dreams with Adele and his mother and the man-eating fish? Was Harv Gunther death? Or was the Holy Ghost death?

"Looks to me like she's going to get that nigger Houston off." Harv grabbed another glass of champagne from a passing tray.

"Who? Oh, Eileen . . . I suppose so. . . ."

"Don Roscoe's a horse's ass"—he swallowed half the glass—"going after a poor nigger for the publicity."

"Like people used to go after poor cops. . . ."

Harv threw back his shrunken bald head and roared with laughter. Then the laughter turned into a wrenching cough, which he cured with the rest of the glass of champagne.

"You're lucky to have a woman like that," Gunther continued. "In another age, some rich and powerful baron would take her away from you."

"Would he?" Red felt his throat tighten. "Fortunately, today men don't take women."

"Balls!" Gunther exploded with another half cough, half laugh. "That's what women are for. Don't pay any attention to this feminist bullshit. It's all window dressing. The bottom line is still that you take a woman and do what you want with her." Gunther's rheumy eyes shone with anticipation. "You make her like it. A few rough lessons and she likes it anyway. Right, good buddy?"

"I wouldn't know." Red clenched his teeth, disgusted and angry. "I'm not a sick, senile phony."

"Sure you know." Gunther pounded him on the back. "I bet you have a great time pushing around that fat green-eyed bitch of yours. She's the kind that loves it."

"I don't believe so, Harvard." *If I weren't after a story about this man, I'd hit him in the teeth.*

"Shows how much you know. I'd love to have her underneath me, tied up if you know what I mean, and pleading for mercy—pleading for more of the same, of course." He licked his lips appreciatively. "A man could have a lot of fun messing up those tits."

"I don't like your fantasies, Harv." Old man or not, he was about to be belted in the jaw.

"A dying man has the right to a few"—Harv found another champagne glass—"no offense, Red. You don't appreciate what you have, that's all."

"I think I do."

"Yeah?" His eyes hardened. "Well, we'll see. If you don't stay on your good behavior"—he nudged Red's chest with the glass—"I might have to arrange a little demonstration for you. Mother and daughters both, that's a great combination." Spittle drooled from his lips. "Ever try any of that action, Redmond?"

"You leave them alone, Harv," Red said coldly, "or I'll kill you. I mean it. I'll cut off your balls and stuff them down your throat."

"If you do," he toasted Red again with a manic laugh, "I'll come back from the grave and cut them up in little pieces. See you, good buddy."

Leaving Red dumbfounded, Harv strolled away, his body shaking with a grating mixture of coughs and laughter.

Civilization leaves those who more or less keep its rules at the mercy of those who do not. In the Dark Ages, rough feudal justice would have disposed of a robber baron such as Harv early in life. Now, a man devoid of principles, he preyed on those whose principles kept them from fighting Gunther's ruthless fire with fire of their own.

He wouldn't hurt Eileen. He wouldn't dare.

Yet, dying old man that he was, he might mutilate other women. The desire to inflict pain, which must have been the driving force of his life, was now all that kept him alive. He was as dangerous as a dying Bengal tiger.

Red fled to one of the elegant washrooms, walls covered with blue-gray fabric, and was briefly but violently sick.

As he leaned against the washbasin, fighting for calm nerves, he remembered his sickness in the Tropical Hotel on the banks of the Rio Negro. Black water in the toilet bowl.

As he struggled to regain his breath, Red remembered that other horrible experience.

The morning after his vision of Adele—or was it the tourist Fraülein—being consumed in the dark river, he had made quiet inquiries to learn whether anyone had perhaps died the night before.

"Of course not, señor. Why would you think that?"

"Because I'm crazy that's why."

The assistant manager fortunately did not understand enough English to comprehend what he had said.

Dutiful and responsible tourist that he'd always been, Red signed up for a ride down the Rio Negro, beyond Manaus, to the confluence with the Amazon—brown and black mixed in some kind of sick gravy. He tried to work up good liberal guilt about the rape of the rain forest but decided that if he lived in the shantytowns built on platforms along the river above Manaus he would vigorously support any measures that might improve the standard of living of Brazil—not that much would filter down to the shantytowns anyway.

He ate lunch at the Tropical, beef again, and drank a couple of glasses of Brazilian beer that was not nearly as good as Harp or Guinness, though almost as dark as the latter.

Then, still playing the tourist, he boarded the hotel bus for another ride into Manaus—to see the opera house where Caruso sang, he told himself, and where Klaus Kinski and Claudia Cardinale appeared at the beginning of *Fitzcarraldo.*

He also told himself that he did not want to respond to the implicit invitation of Rita Lane to accept his reward for taking the burden of Adele's soul off her conscience. Still, the compulsion to taste of that sick and forbidden fruit was growing stronger. Damn, why wasn't Eileen with him?

Not that her presence made any difference when compulsions were upon him.

I pursue women, he insisted, *they don't offer themselves to me. Well, maybe Eileen did. Maybe she still does.*

Then as he walked up from the massive steel floating dock—constructed by the English at the turn of the century—toward the opera house (following Claudia's footsteps, so to speak) he saw Paul O'Meara.

In an immaculate white suit, with carefully trimmed silver hair, and carrying a jaunty cane, Paul was only a few feet in front of him. Repressing an urge to pounce on him, Red followed him cautiously to the Cathedral square. Then as Paul fiddled with his key while opening the door of a Benz 280SL, Red put his hand on the man's shoulder.

"A long way from the Wabash Avenue Bridge, isn't it?"

He was rewarded with a baffled stream of Portuguese. The man was not Paul, but even as he tried to apologize in English and to accept the man's totally inappropriate apologies in a mix of English and Portuguese, Red did not completely believe it was not Paul.

I am in bad shape, he thought, as he sunk into a seat toward the rear of the Tropical bus. *If I don't get out of here quickly, I may spend the rest of my life in a Brazilian loony bin.*

The Varig flight was canceled again that night, but he was assured that he would be on the flight to Mexico City the next morning. He called Eileen to tell her that he would be home by the end of the day.

When Rita Lane called to invite him for cocktails, he virtuously declined. He wasn't up to sex anyway.

He never did succeed in persuading himself that Paul was not in Manaus. Yet if he was alive in that frontier city and in the pay of Harv Gunther, why was Rita Lane still alive?

None of it made sense. Paul was dead. Rita Lane would be dead eventually. So would he. So would Eileen.

That thought disturbed him as he slipped unsteadily out of the men's room of the Ritz Carlton.

Perhaps it was not Red's death but her own that Eileen saw over his shoulder. Sex, God, death—were they all the same thing?

42

Red dreamt often about his mother. She would come into the house and denounce his family for extravagance and waste. Have they forgotten, she would demand, that they are poor? Does he not care that people will think they are living beyond their means? Is he so thoughtless—always the charge of thoughtlessness—as to suppose that the poor need not live poor?

In the dream Red never succeeded in explaining that they were not poor anymore before he woke up, perhaps because in the world of dreams he was not convinced himself.

They had worn thick sweaters through the winter of 1937–38 because they could not afford enough coal to keep the temperature over sixty. Red learned how to line his shoes with newspapers before he trudged through the snow to school. They ate potatoes and fish, meat no more than once a week, because they could not afford "expensive" food. There was no tree at Christmastime. He was withdrawn from St. Patrick's parochial school and sent to public school, and Dav began first grade at the public school. When it came time for First Communion, he wore a badly fitting white suit that the sisters of the parish borrowed from a family whose son had made his First Communion the year before. They rode the Stony Island streetcar downtown and then the Harrison streetcar out to the Loyola Dental School on the Near West Side, where a student dentist poked and probed at their mouths and Mom complained about the bad teeth they had inherited from their father. Even though he was only eight years old, he sold Father Coughlin's paper, *Social Justice*, in back of the church on Sunday mornings—not realizing then, of course, that the paper was turning anti-Semitic, or, for that matter, even knowing what anti-Semitic meant.

In his mind Red knew that the comfort of his adult life was not responsible for the starvation in sub-Sahara Africa, but every time he saw the poor children from such countries on a television screen he saw himself at Ninety-third and Coles in 1937, 1938, and 1939—a clumsy, overgrown, shamefaced young man, clad in ill-fitting clothes and hiding behind the role of class clown. That poor kid made others laugh to exorcise his family's shame.

Like a lot of Depression children, Red was now useless with money. He gave it away recklessly. He didn't keep accurate records. He couldn't budget to save his life. He refused to buy himself new clothes and ordered shirts out of a cut-rate catalog. Eileen turned shrewish at tax-return time, as often at his penury as at his carelessness. She was dismayed that he didn't fly sleeper on his trip to Brazil. "It's a tax deduction, Red. If your health isn't worth a few hundred dollars to you, it certainly is to me."

"I never thought of it that way," he admitted ruefully.

She looked as if she was going to tell him that he OUGHT to think of it that way. She held her tongue, knowing how useless such a reprimand would be.

Periodically, he lectured his children on the horrors of poverty. They listened silently, embarrassed by their own affluent, comfortable lives and unable to respond to his harangue. The last time he tried it, Patty challenged him. "Why are you guilting us, Daddy?" she demanded hotly. "It's not our fault we're not poor, and it's not our fault other people are poor."

"Guilting?" he asked, mystified by the use of the word.

"It's a transitive verb as well as a noun," Eileen said. She, too, listened in silence to his orations on poverty, probably feeling as helpless as the kids.

"I'm not trying to guilt you, Patty. I merely want you to realize that not everyone has as easy a life as you do."

"You sound like a parent," she scoffed at him contemptuously. "It's your fault, not ours, that we don't have to work for our clothes and our school and our food. Guilt yourself, don't guilt me."

Eileen was watching him intently, wondering, perhaps, how he was going to handle his middle child's defiance.

"I guess I do sound like a parent," he admitted grudgingly.

"If you want us to praise you for protecting us from the poverty you suffered when you were a little boy," Patty was remorseless, "just tell us what day each week you want us to do the praise bit, and we'll do it." In a singsong voice, she began, "Thank you very much, Daddy, that we don't have to wear heavy sweaters in the wintertime like you did back in the 1930's!" Her lip curled contemptuously.

"Patricia ...," Eileen said warningly.

"I don't care." She spit out the words. "I'm sick of being guilted every time I buy a new dress. So the 1930's were bad, so this isn't the 1930's. So what!"

"That is QUITE, QUITE ENOUGH!" Eileen commanded in a voice that suggested that, almost eighteen years old or not, Patty would shortly be banished to her room.

By now Red felt very foolish, for he was guilting Patty and Kate the same way he had been guilted himself forty years before. "Maybe I should write a column," he conceded, "about dumb parents who don't realize the world has changed."

"Really!" Patty agreed.

"I know it's hard for you to understand, Patty," Eileen tried to soothe her ruffled feelings. "The men and women who lived through the Great Depression will always feel different about money than those who did not, just like those who lived through the Viet Nam War will always feel different about war."

"WELL THEN," Patricia huffed, "what am I going to complain to MY children about? How am I going to guilt them?"

"Maybe"—Kate looked up from her pizza—"maybe you can guilt them about not growing up with a father who grew up during the Depression!"

Red often wondered whether any of it had been necessary. When Aunt Mae, an angry, chirping little canary (and Aunt Maude was an angry, screeching little parakeet) moved in with them, Mom began to teach again as a substitute, and after the first six months she became a more or less permanent substitute at a public school in the neighborhood. There was no company or government pension, but his father had had an excellent life insurance policy and several thousand dollars in the bank. They could have made do for several years without embracing all the trappings of poverty the way they did. His mother was probably punishing herself and them for having survived while Dad died. The country went into another "slump" in 1938, and, remembering the days when schoolteachers were paid with worthless scrip, she was firmly convinced that the worst of the Depression was going to come back. Indeed, she confidently predicted the return of the Depression until the middle 1950's.

In 1939 she had just turned thirty and was a very pretty young woman—short, slender, curly black hair, a thin, appealing face and sparkling eyes in a picture in the family album. Red could not relate the attractive young woman in the picture to his memories of unhappiness, misery, complaint. Yet he could see why Sergeant Martin O'Riordan had wanted to marry her, though he failed to understand why she settled for someone so ponderous and dull as Marty. Perhaps she felt that she was only entitled to one happy marriage. Perhaps she had been guilted by her mother and by Aunts Mae and Maude into feeling responsible for Dad's death. Perhaps Marty O'Riordan was expiation, the price that was to be paid to discharge her guilt and to provide some sort of security for her three sons.

They moved from South Chicago to a little bungalow on the West Side. The three boys transferred to St. Ursula Grammar School, where he once more became, almost on arrival, the class comedian and mimic. Both his aunts told him that they were much luckier than they deserved to be, that Sergeant O'Riordan was a very important man and had great political influence, particularly with his boss, Captain Carmody, a man who was later celebrated in the Chicago newspapers as the "richest cop in the world."

The days of poverty were over. For a couple of years they had the good life. Even when Marty put a bullet through his skull, after talking to a grand jury (under the restless questioning of the crusading young Assistant State's Attorney Harvard Gunther), there was enough money to heat the bungalow in the winter and for the clothes, often hand-me-downs, that kept Dav and Parn only a little bit more shabby than the other kids the same age at St. Ursula. Marty was a big man, broad-shouldered, fat, heavy-footed, plodding. His silver hair and red face made him look like a has-been Irish wrestler. As if to compensate for his clumsiness, he spoke very softly, a voice hardly above a whisper even when, as was often the case, he was beating them with a razor strap (which was never used for sharpening a razor) in order to "teach you kids some discipline."

It was a losing battle for Marty O'Riordan. He was one, they were three, and he was slow while they were quick. After a couple of years he gave up on them and tried to pretend they didn't exist. Marty was not a bad cop, as cops went in those days. He was never drunk, refused to fix traffic tickets, and risked his life a couple of times chasing burglary suspects. The graft he took, Red heard him explain to a young parish priest once, was "honest" graft. "I can go to Communion every Sunday morning and hold my head up high," Marty whispered proudly, an elephant preening himself. "I've never touched a dime from a prostitute, and I've never taken any money that they haven't wanted to give me."

Marty was disingenuous on two counts. He did take a lot of money from pimps, and it was by no means clear that the tavern owners, policy kings, pimps, and professional gamblers in Captain John Joseph Carmody's police district did indeed want to make their weekly contributions to sustain the Captain's reputation as the richest cop in the world.

Marty was Jack Carmody's bagman. His principal responsibility, indeed his only responsibility, was the weekly visits to the Captain's "friends" in his precincts and the delivery of those contributions on Friday afternoons to the Captain's office. There the two of them counted the money, and Carmody scrupulously gave ten percent to his faithful Saint Bernard dog; then sent Marty O'Riordan home to them, a happy and contented man.

It was the way things were done, as unexceptional as the White Sox's spring training in Pasadena, California, and the Cubs' over on Santa Catalina Island. One would no more question "honest" graft than one would question that George William Mundelein always was and always would be Cardinal Archbishop of Chicago.

Then someone decided that there should be reform. "As

if we didn't have enough trouble what with the war going on and all," Marty complained to Mom.

Jack Carmody had overplayed his hand, demanding too much of a bookie whose "outfit" (as they called the crime syndicate in those days) connections were stronger than Captain Carmody had believed. Tom Courtney, State's Attorney, and Tubbo Dan Gilbert, his chief investigator, began a highly publicized investigation of police "irregularities" in Carmody's district. (Courtney and Gilbert, a few years before, had done the syndicate a big favor by framing Roger "Terrible" Touhy on the false charges that he had kidnapped a lesser mob character named Jake "the Barber" Factor. Almost two decades later, the conviction was reversed and Terrible Touhy and his gang were released. Touhy himself was executed shortly thereafter by the mob, because he knew too much.) Carmody backtracked quickly and made his peace with the mob, doubtless paying a heavy indemnity for his mistake. But Courtney, Gilbert, and Harv Gunther, who was Courtney's bright young crusader, still required a victim to "throw to those wolves at the *Herald-Examiner*," as Marty complained when he found out he was the victim.

If he had accepted his scapegoat role, Marty would have done all right. He might never have been convicted, he certainly wouldn't have gone to jail, and would have been rewarded with a job to replace the one he had lost in the police department.

Unfortunately, somewhere Marty had achieved a passion for respectability. A homeowner in North Austin, a dutiful usher at St. Ursula, a diligent member of the American Legion, Marty forgot that he was the son of an immigrant hod carrier. He was proud of the prestige that his wife's training at "Normal" (later, Chicago Teacher's College and, still later, Chicago State University) gave her. Not very bright, betrayed by his patron, ridiculed in the press, humiliated before the grand jury, Sergeant Martin O'Riordan ended his life in June of 1943, the day Red graduated from grammar school. The body was found in the squad car in which he had diligently carried the weekly bag for Jack Carmody for most of a decade.

It was a very neat job. A single bullet fired into his ear.

At the wake everyone marveled at how "natural" poor Marty looked.

His death was the end for Mom. She was still a young and attractive woman in Red's grammar school graduation pictures. Nine years later, when he came home from Korea and Japan, though she had barely turned forty, she was already an old woman, devoid of all womanly appeal.

Younger than Eileen, he'd often mused.

"Her life ended on Memorial Day, 1937, didn't it?" Dav had asked Red in Saigon, shortly before his death.

"Or maybe when Marty died?"

"Yeah, maybe." Dav looked up from his hands. "I almost forgot about him. He wasn't all that bad a guy after all."

"Yes he was, Dav," he said heavily. "He ended her life as well as his own."

Red's mother lived until 1964, twenty-one years more after Marty's suicide, attending Mass every morning, doggedly teaching at the Ella Flagg Young School, complaining about the kids in her class—always worse than last year's class—and nagging Red. All the pent-up wrath and fury of those long years of loneliness exploded when he told her he was going to marry Eileen Ryan. She refused to come to the hastily arranged dinner at the Ryans' house in Beverly Hills and adamantly rejected the possibility of attending the marriage at St. Praxides' Parish, a refusal strongly supported by her now-aged maiden sisters, Mae and Maude. If he had married a Moslem from darkest Africa, his mother would not have been more angry, although she was never very clear as to the specific reasons for her objections, other than the Ryans' "pretensions."

"If you were not such an asinine fool," she hurled at him, "you wouldn't have to ask why I hate that hard little bitch."

Despite her hatred for Eileen, she assumed that they would begin their married life in the bungalow on Massassoit Avenue.

"It was good enough for your stepfather and me. Why isn't it good enough for you and your fancy little bitch?" she demanded hotly.

"We simply can't live on the West Side, Mom," he pleaded. "Eileen has to live near school until she finishes."

"Maybe when there's a grandchild around," Eileen whispered at the wedding banquet at the Beverly Country Club, "your mother will be reconciled. She never had a chance to see Davitt's children. I bet all her love will be showered on your kid."

"Our kid," he insisted. "I'm sure you're right. She'll get over it by then."

His mother did not live to see John Patrick Kane. Walking home from school on a dark March afternoon during a snowstorm, she stepped in front of an automobile driven by an eighteen-year-old senior from Austin High School (black, as Mae and Maude were quick to point out in the hospital). The kid slammed on his brakes, but the car skidded into and over her. She was unconscious when the ambulance brought her to St. Anne's Hospital and dead forty-five minutes later. The driver was charged with reckless homicide, but the charges were dropped.

Red was certain that in whatever moments of consciousness she may have had at the very end, she blamed him for the accident. Just like his father, he had failed her.

What a happy young woman she must have been when she brought him home, a helpless little infant, to the house at Ninety-third and Coles, put him in the arms of the big, laughing, red-haired Irishman who was his father. Those were the best moments of her life, hints and promises of happiness that neither his father nor he were ever to fulfill.

43

The Brazilian dream remained in Red's head the next morning, a tantalizing and troublesome fantasy that somehow suggested, like a grim, gray spirit, that there were dismal shadows matching the dazzling light that had leapt out of the green ice building and enveloped him on the Feast of All the Saints. In addition to an amused smile, all curled and warm, that lurked in that building, there were other and much more malign smiles prowling the world.

For the first time since November first, Red was troubled, as if by a toothache that might or might not be real: If there were good angels, he supposed, there must be bad angels too.

Why should he be worried? Was he not pursuing Adele Ward's murderer with all the skill and resourcefulness of which he was capable?

Impulsively, he placed a phone call to Manaus. With more efficiency than the Brazilian telephone system normally demonstrated, he was connected with Rita Lane's home. A young woman's voice, in fractured English, assured him that Señora Lane was shopping but would be back later in the afternoon. No, there was no message, merely Señor Kane had called and would be in touch with her again.

Rita Lane, then, was still alive, as yet untouched by Harvard Gunther's fears. If he ever tricked Gunther into commenting on the Adele Ward matter and hence making the whole story a legitimate matter for newspaper coverage, he would have to warn Rita instantly. Once the materials were in the pages of the *Herald Gazette* she would be safe, because killing her would have become pointless.

He ground out a column complaining about the arrogance of the television journalists who exploited the sorrow of families whose Marine sons had been killed in the bombing in Beirut. "Pretty soon now the media world is going to discover how intensely it is hated by ordinary Americans. When the 1960's punks who run around with cameras and microphones begin to wonder why the rest of the country so despises them, they might replay the tapes of their disgraceful invasion of the homes of the Marines' bereaved families."

Not bad, he decided. Perhaps a little more nasty than the new Red Kane normally permitted himself to be. Still, those who brought cameras and microphones into the homes of grieving families merited a touch of nastiness.

His phone jangled. Johnny calling from Collegeville. Would it be all right if Lois ate Thanksgiving dinner with them?

"Sure, Johnny," he said, "as long as her family doesn't object."

"Lois is mature enough to make her own decision about such matters, isn't she?"

Red took a deep breath. "I'm not laying down conditions, kid. Of course it's up to Lois. I'm just making an observation. Maturity means considering the feelings of everyone and balancing them as best you can."

"I understand." Johnny relaxed. "I might like kinda have to be there at her house for Christmas or New Year's."

"Would I get in trouble if I said it sounds kind of serious?"

John was not sure how serious it was. They were both still pretty young. Maybe all they were trying to do was to find out how serious it was. A long pause. "You and Mom don't object to her?" A troubled, anxious, uncertain question.

"Your mother will have to speak for herself, John. Lois strikes me as an intelligent, attractive, vulnerable young woman with considerable resources of strength and integrity—more like your mother than she might seem at first. No marriage is ever easy, and you both still are, as you say, young. No way, however, would it be a terrible mistake."

How much like Polonius did I sound? Red wondered.

"Thanks, Dad. I appreciate that. I guess I'm kind of hopelessly in love with her."

"I know the feeling," Red replied.

"I've noticed." John seemed to think that that comment was hilariously funny.

When you and Lois play the kinds of games in the shower that your mother and I played last night, Red reflected mentally, after he had hung up, *then maybe you'll be able to laugh at us.* He felt extremely complacent, both about his wife and about his response to his son's phone call.

He called up the manuscript of his novel on the CRT and began the revision of the final chapters. His phone rang again.

"It burned up on me, Daddy," wailed a young woman's voice. "It just caught fire and burned up!"

"Kate?" he asked, rigid with fear.

"No. Patty. The Volkswagen burned up in the parking lot at school."

"Are you all right?" Red screamed into the phone.

"I'm okay, I guess." The young woman's words were coming between sounds that were half gulp, half sob. "It just caught fire in the parking lot and burned up. Honest, Daddy, I didn't do it!"

"I'm not blaming you, Patty. Are you sure you're all right?"

"I'm fine, Daddy." Frightened, Patty was desperately trying to control her emotions. "Worried that you'll be angry with me."

"Patty," he said, trying to control his own emotions, "I'm sure you didn't set fire to the VW."

"Oh, Daddy, I'm so glad you're not angry with me!"

"I'll be right up. Are the police there?"

"Yes, Daddy, they're here, asking all kinds of questions. Uncle Mike the Cop is here too."

Red began to relax. If the former Deputy Superintendent was lurking on the grounds of the Convent of the Sacred Heart, Patty and Kate were at least as safe as they would have been in a Trappist monastery.

"Fine, I'll be right up."

It required several eternities for the Yellow Cab to make the trip from the *Herald Gazette* building to the grounds of the Convent of the Sacred Heart, even though the late-morning traffic was light. Red gave the driver a ten-dollar bill and did not wait for the change. The family Bug, innocent of resale value with its 110,000 miles, was pathetically obvious in the parking lot of the school, a charred and broken toy, smelling of burned rubber and acrid smoke. If one of his daughters had been in it when it had burst into flames, she would have been reduced to ashes. A cop and two firemen were poking around inside it.

Red turned away with a shiver, rushed into the school, and exploded through the door of the principal's office like a man escaping from prison. Patty, the stern hanging judge of the previous night, threw herself into his arms sobbing inconsolably. "Oh, Daddy, Daddy, Daddy!"

"Everything's all right, hon," he said reassuringly, sensing for perhaps the hundredth time how like her mother Patty felt when he embraced her. "Everything's all right. It wasn't your fault, it was just an accident. Don't worry about it. Relax."

Slowly, the young woman calmed down, and her hysterical sobs became soft weeping.

Katie, the principal (a religious of the Sacred Heart, about his age, in lay garb), and the slender, elegant Michael Casey stood respectfully, waiting for father and daughter to reassure one another. "I guess we're just going to have to get a new car, Daddy," Katie said calmly. "That one wouldn't have lasted more than a couple of months anyway. I don't think it would have survived winter."

"It was my poor, wonderful little love Bug," Patty wailed, edging toward hysterics again.

"We'll get another love Bug and this one will be reincarnated in it." Red patted her back. "There's a reincarnation for VWs even if there isn't one for people, isn't that right, Sister?"

"Absolutely, Mr. Kane," the nun agreed, "especially if they're driven by young women."

"We might call Eileen," Mike Casey said tentatively. "Somebody should be at home with these two young women."

"Mom is on a trial," Kate insisted. Usually the more unstable of the Kane daughters, Kate was as serene as an elderly sister fingering her rosary beads in the chapel. Patty the sensible and reliable child had become a nearly hysterical little girl. "She's going to save poor Hurricane Houston from that awful Don Roscoe."

The former Deputy Superintendent grinned impishly. "A worthy cause if there ever was one. I could call my wife—"

"My column is finished for the day," Red interjected. "If some of your blue-coated friends would drive us back to the house, I'll take care of them."

Before they left, Mike took Red aside, his voice gentle, his pale blue eyes as calm as a lake on a windless day in summer.

"It was a judgment call, Red. We saw the three men planting the incendiary device. They're not Outfit pros, just bumbling amateurs working for Harv. Obviously, he's out of favor with the mob. We would have stopped the kids before they got in the car. I thought it was better to let Harv's thugs think that no one was watching. I'm sure all they wanted to do was to destroy the car. Harv thinks he's sent you a message."

"God knows he has," Red said tightly. There HAD to be a link between the Paul O'Meara disappearance and the Adele Ward murder. Who cared about a reporter that no one remembered? But was the connection in Harv's failing mind or in the real world?

"He'll be waiting to hear from you, either with threats or with capitulation." Casey's hands were jammed into the pockets of his double-breasted Italian suit. "You're calling the shots."

"I think we'll let him wait," Red said slowly. "As long as you and your friends stay this close to my family, that seems to be the best strategy."

Mike nodded. "I agree. Don't let it last too long, though. He's a frightened old tiger, wounded, cornered, and dangerous."

"If he doesn't move in a day or two," Red said, "then we'll go after him."

44

Red removed the last of the family's pizza from the freezer and served it to his daughters for lunch. They both agreed, under the circumstances, that they would drink a little bit of red wine, a beverage that they normally dismissed as "yucky." They did not object to their father's limiting himself to Pepsi. They insisted that they would watch a film on the VCR. Both the girls, in a strange, perverse, adolescent obsession, argued that they simply HAD to see *Fitzcarraldo*, the Klaus Kinski film their mother had purchased in the summer and which they had both resolutely refused to watch. The pictures of Manaus and Iquitos and the Amazon River were not exactly what Red needed to see.

Brian Sweeney Fitzgerald and his band of silent Indians dragged the riverboat up the side of a mountain. The phone rang.

"I'll get it," Red insisted, though there was no sign that either of his daughters had any intention of answering the phone. "It's probably your mother."

"Red Kane," he said as he picked up the phone in the kitchen.

A long silence at the other end. Harvard Gunther making his move.

"Go ahead," Red said softly. "I'm listening."

An equally soft laugh from out of the past. "You know who it is, old buddy."

"I thought it would be you," Red replied to Paul O'Meara.

"You always were a quick one, Red. Sometimes a little too quick for your own good.".

"I'm listening," Red said tersely. He was not shocked. He felt little emotion of any kind. He'd never really believed that Paul had died. Since the day after Paul walked across the Chicago River in a blinding snowstorm, Red had known in the depths of his soul that his mentor and ideal was somehow corrupt. The familiar voice on the phone presented not a shocking revelation, but an old truth finally acknowledged.

"I wonder if you really are, old buddy."

"Go ahead." Red would be damned if he would give the bastard the satisfaction of sounding frightened.

"Drop it, old buddy, and there'll be no hard feelings on anybody's part. Forget the past. Worry about the Pulaski case if you want. Forget about me."

"Oh?" Harvard Gunther was proposing a deal and using a voice from beyond the grave to make it clear how important the deal was. No mention of Adele Ward and Rita Lane. So he still held the high ace.

"He's not going to last much longer, Red," Paul said. "He's an old man. Leave him alone and everything will be all right."

"I hear what you're saying," Red replied.

"And leave the dead in their graves. Bringing them back to life wouldn't help anyone."

"I suppose not," Red admitted, thinking that he was so far the more devious of the two.

"You understand the message, old buddy? Everything stops now and there's no hard feelings on either side."

"I understand the message, all right," Red said, stretching the suspense out so that O'Meara wouldn't think he was a coward.

"And you accept the conditions?" Now it was Paul's turn to be nervous.

"I don't have much choice, do I?"

"Not really, not if you don't want anything worse to happen."

Red waited about the same length of time that Paul had made him wait in the beginning of the conversation. "I guess we have a deal then."

"Fine," Paul laughed amiably, "just fine. Nice to talk with you again."

"Heaven is a pleasant place?" Red asked lightly.

"Paradise."

Red could imagine the old crooked smile on his mentor's face.

The line clicked. Softly, Red returned the kitchen phone to its wall cradle.

After *Fitzcarraldo* ended with the spectacle of an opera company singing *I Puritani* on an Amazon riverboat, Red left his daughters to munch popcorn and drink yet more Diet Pepsi and raced around the corner to a public telephone booth in a bar on Clark Street. He reported to Mike Casey the substance of the message though not the identity of the messenger.

"Are you really going to abandon the story?" Mike, who knew his friend well, sounded skeptical.

"I'm going to let Harvard P. Gunther think I have."

"Ah."

"One or the other of us is not going to survive, Mike. I promise you that. Either Harv or I will take the big fall."

Back in the house he wondered with a shiver why he had said that.

Book FOUR

I had been ploughing all day in the black dust of the Lichtenburg roads, and had come very late to a place called the Eye of Malmani—Malmani Oog—the spring of a river which presently loses itself in the Kalahari. We watered our horses and went supperless to bed. Next morning I bathed in one of the Malmani pools—and icy cold it was—and then basked in the early sunshine while breakfast was cooking. The water made a pleasant music, and nearby was a covert of willows filled with singing birds. Then and there came on me the hour of revelation, when, though savagely hungry, I forgot about breakfast. Scents, sights, and sounds blended into a harmony so perfect that it transcended human expression, even human thought. It was like a glimpse of the peace of eternity.

—John Buchan, "Memory Hold-the-Door,"
in F. C. Happold,
Adventure in Search of a Creed

45

Thanksgiving was the high-water mark for the new Red Kane. Or so he thought as he prepared to lead the family in grace before meals at the Thanksgiving dinner table—"dining area table" to keep Johnny happy. He was in the process of making a decision to seek help from his Church on his two major problems—Harv Gunther and Eileen Ryan Kane. Thus he felt in a religious, not to say spiritual, mood.

"I'm going to make up my own grace," he announced.

"Has Daddy become a Protestant, Mommy?" Kate asked in a stage whisper.

"Silence, young woman," he commanded.

"Really," she giggled.

His life of love and virtue had persisted for almost a month. The novel, tightened, revised, transformed, had been sent off to Great Western Books. It read well, Red decided, even if he did say so himself. Perhaps it was not very profound, but he felt it would be a page turner, and that the ending had a very neat twist.

Favorable mail was pouring into the *Herald Gazette* on his most recent columns. His pursuit of Harv Gunther was on track. The jungle separating him from his children had been partly cleared away. Even Patty, after the death of the old VW Bug and the discovery of a new one, was no longer "totally" hostile. She watched Red and Eileen intently, as if analyzing and pondering and evaluating their love affair. Kate was still mostly silent, but not sullen, and her occasional comic remark brought down the house. Lois and John, closely but discreetly monitored in far-off Minnesota, seemed to be very much at home with one another and with the Kane family. The love affair with his wife continued with distracting but pleasant intensity, marred occasionally by spectacular fights that led to yet more love. Eileen, despite the difficulties of the Houston trial and the obstructionist bullying of Don Roscoe, the U.S. Attorney, often glowed with happiness.

So, coward that he was and fearful of losing her, he made love and not talk.

He had shoved to the back of his mind the slashing of Eileen's dress, the burning of the VW, and the phone call from Paul O'Meara. He had outsmarted Harv Gunther and would nail him eventually, maybe exposing Paul O'Meara too—though he was not certain about that. Mike Casey would protect the family.

Later, when this happy scenario collapsed, Red would charge himself with culpably naïve self-deception. He had convinced himself that there was no danger because he wanted the happiness of his rebirth to be unsullied and complete. For that presumption he would pay a heavy price.

"We want to thank God," he informed both the Deity and his family before they dug into the turkey, "for all the good things He has given us, including the victory for the Detroit Lions and Lois to enhance the already dazzling glamour of our dinner table...."

Sniggers from his two daughters and a flattered blush from Lois.

"We want to thank Him for the food we eat, the air we breathe, the sky, the grass, the waters of the lake, our family and our friends, all the wonderful relatives we have, the love that binds us together, and the opportunity He provides us every day to renew and strengthen that love...."

"Will he be as long as the sermon at St. Clement's?" Kate doubled up, trying to control her laughter.

"Shush," Eileen said, her green eyes sparkling stars of admiration.

"It is very hard to talk to You, God, because, as You know, there are always distractions around this supper table—mostly from loudmouthed teenagers. But we're grateful for all the blessings You've given us in the past year and we hope You will keep us safe and together in love for the next year. Through Christ our Lord."

"AMEN!" They all shouted enthusiastically.

"I get no respect," Red complained, reaching for the carving knife.

I don't know what You started, he muttered internally to the bat wielder of Wacker Drive, *and I'm not sure where it's going to end, but I've never been more grateful. Help me to keep it up.*

Eileen chattered happily through the meal and downed three glasses of claret, two more than her usual maximum.

"Mom, you're going to be like totally soused," Katie warned her.

"I'm making up for what your father isn't drinking," Eileen blurted, and then turned scarlet. "I'm sorry, Red...."

Red found it very funny. He toasted her with his Perrier glass (Powerscourt, Waterford). "You have a long way to go to catch up."

Tears welled up in her eyes; then, seeing that he was neither hurt nor angry, she grinned wickedly and toasted him back.

A couple extra glasses of claret and she is very like her mother.

Red normally hated holidays because they were always unhappy times at his mother's house, particularly after the death of her second husband. Perversely, he even managed to spoil holidays in his own family despite the indomitable Ryan ebullience, which always salvaged something of the holiday spirit for the children. This Thanksgiving, however, Red was the most joyous of celebrants. Confidently and eagerly he looked forward to Christmas, the first happy Christmas since 1936. The new Red Kane, he was convinced, would be irresistibly happy during the joyous season.

The agenda called for a songfest in the "parlor area" after dinner, with Eileen presiding at the piano and leading the songs in her clear, sweet voice. Later, Mike Casey—Uncle Mike the Cop to the kids—and his new wife, Annie, would join them for "a sip of something and a song or two."

Mike had phoned Red two days after Red's conversation with Paul O'Meara and reported laconically, "It seems the heat's off. Harv isn't worried anymore."

"You'll still keep an eye on us for a while?" Red asked.

"Certainly," Uncle Mike agreed. "We have a pretty good line on his people now. Any move they make our informants will hear about. But, Red ... let me know if you decide to go after him. Things could get very tacky about then."

"I sure will," Red breathed fervently. "Maybe halfway through next week I'll begin."

Red was procrastinating on the Gunther case, collecting more information as an excuse for avoiding the final confrontation. He was less frightened by Gunther (after all, he held the Adele Ward high card) than he was uncertain about his ethical obligations. Why go after an old and probably dying man? Did not the Bible say that we should let the dead bury their dead? And was not Harvard Princeton Gunther almost dead? What good was vengeance against the man who had corrupted his hero? Was he not as bad as the young punks on the *Washington Post* or the *Wall Street Journal* who dug around in the past for the sheer notoriety of destroying the rich and the famous and the successful?

His obligation to defeat Harvard Gunther was much deeper, more powerful, more solemn, and in its own way more religious. Red had no illusions about his own goodness. But Harvard Gunther was evil. Did that evil have to be exorcised to justify Red's newfound happiness with his family? Was it proper for Red to be enjoying his wife while Adele Ward—who had become interchangeable with Kate in his dreams—was unavenged?

If I were not such a guilt-ridden Irish Catholic, he thought as the Caseys joined the songfest, *I'd forget about Gunther. Why should he be my obligation?*

After the Caseys went home, Red and Eileen left the kids to watch Clint Eastwood and his monkey on the VCR and stole off to their bedroom. As frosting on the Thanksgiving cake, or maybe whipped cream on the pumpkin pie, his wife was a particularly compliant and luminous lover—like a sanctuary lamp in a darkened church.

Yet despite the fervor of his kisses, he thought he saw terror in her eyes during their romp—terrible fear at what she saw lurking behind him.

He was too tired, too happy, too satisfied to ask what she saw. And too afraid.

He knew what she saw. Or rather whom. The pale rider. Death.

46

On the bright and cheerful morning of the Saturday after Thanksgiving, Red decided that the time had come to consult with the priest. The excuse for this decision was a romp with his wife the night before, a replay of the Thanksgiving-night adventure with less intensity and more laughter.

Eileen had fallen asleep quickly. Red twisted restlessly, profoundly satisfied with their romp and yet anxious about what might come next. Sexual high jinks with his wife were great fun. They were also threatening. Could he keep up with her indefinitely? And it was disconcerting to realize that his chaste and proper wife was as capable of manic sexual hunger as Lindy. Or even Helga.

Moreover he was now haunted by the blasphemous fantasy that when he screwed Eileen he was screwing God. The Invader who had lurked behind William Pedersen's green ice tower was the One who had intruded into him, not vice versa. Or so it had seemed at first. Now sexual roles were confused and so were God and Eileen. When she would squirm under him or over him, her wet body straining for release, grunting and moaning in a desperate lunge for pleasure, he would be obsessed by the imagination that he was now invading God.

It was blasphemous, wasn't it, to identify a woman in the final stages of sexual arousal with God?

Or was it?

The question was interesting enough. But it was not the real reason for Red's turning to the Church for help.

Once more he thought that at the height of her passion his fey wife had seen a figure from the Apocalypse lurking just over his shoulder. Was it death who had swung the cosmic baseball bat and not the bright-winged Holy Ghost?

Had the last month been a preparation for death?

As he pushed the doorbell at Forty Holy Martyrs' rectory (and whatever had changed in the Church, the long wait before rectory doorbells were answered had not and would not ever change), he acknowledged ruefully to himself that he was suddenly frightened. He expected his Church to reassure him about his renewed life. Would it soon be taken from him?

In the shower he had asked himself, whom should he see? The pastor of his parish?—A brilliant and gifted man, but he knew the family too well. The young priest? Fine man, but... well, too young still. Blackie? Red hesitated. He conceded that the nearsighted little Rector of Holy Name Cathedral was one of the most gifted men he had ever met. But ...but Eileen was his sister. Would it not be indelicate to discuss their sexual relationship with her brother?

Besides, Blackie was on his annual retreat at the Trappist monastery in Kentucky—"catching up on last year's prayers," he would say owlishly.

So on Saturday morning, before the Kane family and Lois piled into the Volvo and drove around the end of the lake to Grand Beach, Red stopped by the rectory of a neighboring parish and talked to Larry Moran, a classmate of Parn's and, as Red remembered him, one of the more intelligent members of the battered class of 1960. Larry had done graduate work in psychology, though Red seemed to remember hearing somewhere that he had given it up for the Hispanic apostolate on the North Side of Chicago. Moran had aged shockingly. His long hair was snow-white, his face lined, his body thin, almost emaciated; he seemed as run-down as his rectory, the inside of which had not seen a paintbrush since John Kennedy was President. His pale blue eyes, however, still glowed with intense life, and his rich baritone voice seemed cheerful and enthusiastic—a basso singing one of the arias from Handel's *Messiah*.

"It's good to see you again," Larry said, bringing a brief ten-minute conversation to an end and hinting broadly that there were other things to be done on Saturday morning besides discussing Red's brother and family (about whom Red had precious little information) and their other classmates and friends who had left the priesthood.

"It's sort of a business call." Red resisted the impulse to stand up as Larry had. "I've had a kind of personal problem I wanted to discuss with you."

Somewhat reluctantly Larry sat back in the chair, absently brushing dust off a stack of ancient baptismal record books piled on the floor next to his chair. "Sure, Red, always glad to help."

So Red Kane poured out the story of the new man who had been born after Mass on the Feast of All the Saints and the transformation that had occurred in that man's life. He did not mention Harv Gunther or the novel, and only delicately alluded to the intensification of the love for his wife. He decided that he would not talk about his sudden fear of death unless the priest asked about it.

"I have a hard time thinking of myself as a mystic," he summed up. "I have to say, nevertheless, that it's been an extraordinary month."

Larry nodded his head in understanding. "I've been away from psychology for a long time, Red. That was a bad part of my life. I let myself think that academic game playing was a substitute for the service of the poor. Still, I'd be happy to talk with you a couple of more times so you can sort this out. I suppose I should say at the beginning that the Church has historically been very skeptical of private revelations, alleged ecstasies, and self-diagnosed mysticism."

"I know that," Red agreed, "and I'm with the Church in that matter, at any rate. Yet we've certainly had our mystics, and I suspect lots of ordinary people have had experiences like John of the Cross but never got around to writing about them."

"My feeling," Larry said, "is that the Church hasn't been skeptical enough. John of the Cross, Teresa of Avila, that whole bunch were clearly schizophrenic. That's all right, I suppose. In other eras schizophrenia was perhaps more functional than it is today. Maybe society was better off when it knew how to utilize schizophrenics. But I think it's a mistake to confuse schizophrenia with Christianity. Ours is a religion of service to the poor and not mystical experience."

It was not exactly what Red had expected to hear. Yet he felt obliged to persist, just as one feels obliged to continue poking at a sore tooth even after one is convinced that the tooth has a cavity. "Isn't it possible to have both? Somehow I remember learning in college that Saint Thomas argued that the Christian ideal was a blend of contemplation and action."

"Fuck Saint Thomas," Larry Moran said derisively. "What did he know about the meaning of poverty in the modern world? The only measure of Christianity, Red, is the extent to which an individual Christian identifies himself with the cause of the poor, the suffering, and the oppressed. Anything else, any private devotion, any so-called religious experience, any kind of liturgical revival is simply worthless. If we are not identified with the poor, we are positively evil. Maybe when we have finally brought a world of liberation and justice into existence, we can afford again the luxuries of mysticism and contemplation. I'm not sure about that, to tell you the truth. I think they've always been a cop-out to escape the demands of justice, to rationalize the oppression of the poor."

"You make a very strong case ...," Red said, wondering why priests now said "fuck" as often as cops did. It was a perfectly good Anglo-Saxon word, describing a pleasurable human activity. But when it was mindlessly repeated, Red thought that someone was trying to prove something. "In Latin America, as in Poland, the Church is certainly the only opposition party."

"Fuck Poland," Larry shouted, banging his hand on the desk. "I'm sick and tired of hearing about Poland. The misery and suffering right here in the city of Chicago and in the Third World are far worse than anything that happens in Poland. Political freedom is a luxury we can afford to worry about only when the hungry people in the Third World and out there on the streets of my parish are fed." He gestured angrily at the unwashed windows of his office. "The Poles have full stomachs. Jesus came to free us from misery and oppression, not to promise us nice comfy, cozy mystical experiences, a fulfilling sex life, and liberal democracy."

"The charismatics ... ?" Red asked tentatively.

"Some of them are all right," Larry conceded. "At least they're open enough to listen to the claims of the poor. But they tend eventually to contemplate their own spiritual navels, just like middle-class Christians have always done. And you know what, Red? When you're gazing at your own navel, you don't see Christ in the least of his brothers and sisters with their hands outstretched toward you pleading for something to eat."

Red, always guilty when confronted with injustice and poverty, felt like a debased hypocrite because of his preoccupation with his own emotional and psychological state. What the hell had happened to his compassion and his social awareness?

"I guess you're right," he agreed. "I've paid too much attention to myself."

"Not necessarily," Larry simmered down. "It's perfectly proper for you to want to discuss your experiences with a priest. I'm sorry if I gave you my standard white-middle-class sermon." Larry grinned crookedly, though Red suspected his heart was not in his smile. "I'll be happy to listen to you if you want to come to talk about it again—as often as you want. I thought I should tell you where I'm coming from these days, and perhaps also warn you that one can slip into quasi schizophrenia without hardly realizing it."

It was the first time Red would hear the words "quasi schizophrenia." He would hear them often in the next couple of weeks.

He made an appointment to return to Larry's rectory the following Saturday and drove back, confused and uneasy, to the house on Webster Street for the pilgrimage to Grand Beach. Larry Moran was not some starry-eyed punk; he was a mature, sensible, dedicated parish priest, the kind of person Red had always admired since his first encounter with Father John Raven at St. Ursula's forty years before. Larry had thrown a whole bucket of ice water on Red's dreams. It was an unpleasant experience, Red figured, but one that was good for him.

Later Blackie Ryan's judgment on Larry Moran was different: "As G. K. Chesterton remarked long ago, 'A heretic is not a man who denies the truth but a man who knows part of the truth and thinks it's the whole truth.'"

They had not come even close to discussing the sickly figure on the white horse whom Red thought his wife saw when she made love with him.

47
From the Kane File

February 14, 1975

Kane's Korner

THEY DON'T WANT US TO HAVE FUN
by Redmond Peter Kane

Rome.

You never see anyone in the Vatican smile.

Maybe that's why the leaders of the Catholic Church are so vehemently obsessed with sex. They're not having any fun in life and they want to make sure that married men and women don't have fun either.

They don't want us to enjoy our pilgrimage through the mystery of the attraction between men and women because they don't enjoy anything.

They won't help us when we get lost on our pilgrimage because if we find our way we might experience pleasure, brief but delightful. They have never experienced any pleasure at all—except maybe in spoiling our pleasure.

Sit on the sidewalk cafés along the Via della Conciliazione, which runs from St. Peter's to the Tiber (created by Mussolini, incidentally, in an urban renewal project in which the homes of the poor people were traded for a vista of St. Peter's), and watch the various scruffy Vatican bureaucrats shuffle down the street, an occasional one with soiled purple piping on his hat and a few more wearing black suits and dirty black ties instead of cassocks. You wait in vain to see a single smiling face. Bureaucrats don't smile, not even in the city hall of Chicago where it is not required that you work for a living. But it doesn't seem unreasonable to expect ecclesiastical bureaucrats to look at least mildly happy. They are, after all, in the service of Jesus of Nazareth, who came to bring Good News—or so I'm told. None of the Vatican creeps seem to have been let in on the secret of the Good News. They don't exactly radiate the kind of happiness that would make you want to follow after them and find out what their secret is. They bumble along the Conciliazione, looking neither to the right nor left, utterly oblivious to the rest of the human race.

You gotta admit that the Roman citizenry, with long memories for the years when their ancestors were part of the papal police state, aren't particularly friendly to their clergy. Indeed, a typical encounter between someone in the Vatican and a Roman is a ritual in which both participants make it clear to all around that it is only with enormous difficulty that they can avoid spitting on one another.

So you begin to understand, here on the Conciliazione, why the Catholic Church puts most of its available energy into denouncing sexual pleasure: the Vatican bureaucrats are very unhappy men, and they don't want anyone else to be happy.

If you consider the problem for about five minutes, it becomes obvious that the human body is designed for sexual coupling, a process which at least intermittently is pleasurable (perhaps not as often or not as intensely as the Vatican types might fantasize). Whoever was responsible for this interesting but relatively awkward scheme to continue the species made our inclination for periodic coupling fairly powerful. Hence, it is not surprising that we humans mess up rather often in our intimate relationships.

Why could not a Church say, "Hey, fellows and girls, this is a good thing, even though you're going to have lots of trouble with it and you're going to make some mistakes; but do your best anyway, and remember that God loves you regardless"?

It seems to me that that approach would be as effective as any other in minimizing the number of ethically inappropriate sexual couplings—not that any religious approach is going to have much effect once the blood gets heated up.

If the Catholic Church should adopt such a policy on sex, it would be free to devote some of its energies toward the other sins in which the species engages, even to preaching the Good News of God's love, which, I have been told occasionally, is what was on Jesus's mind in the Gospel.

You get the impression, however, from the first day you step into catechism class up until the last papal document, that the Kingdom of Heaven has been identified with a set of stringent sexual prohibitions. The Gospel is that and nothing else.

In my generation, at any rate, the Catholic Church accompanied us through life whispering in our ears, "Sex is dirty!" or "It's all right now since you're married, but don't enjoy it too much!"

Now I submit that that's weird. The folks around here are all upset about something they call "natural law." I fail to understand how they can escape the obvious fact that there are few things more natural than men and women enjoying sexual intercourse. Yet, if you read the stream of hand-wringing documents emerging from the brown palace down the street (this being a family paper I can't tell you what the color is like), you have to conclude that the Roman Church goes into a paroxysm of grief every time a man and woman have a pleasant night together. You got to wonder whether their joy is all that offensive to the God who allegedly designed them as sexual creatures.

The curial creeps are eager to tell you that there's more to marriage than sex, as though that is a brilliant discovery on which the Catholic Church has a monopoly. Nobody, apparently, has suggested to these aloof celibates that it's very difficult for a man and woman to live together, and that if it weren't for sex, most of us would probably give it up. Or to say it a little differently, maybe a husband and wife can renew their love without sex, but it sure as hell is a big help, and you kind of suspect, when you consider the anatomy and the psychology of our species, that that was precisely what the Designer had in mind.

The crusty fellows up in the Vatican Palace will tell you that they strongly support the renewal of married love. Sure, but they don't want us to enjoy it much. "The laity," as one of the bureaucrats told me the other day, "must be warned of the dangers of 'unbridled passion.'"

It has been my observation that the problem in marriage is far more likely to be that there is too much *bridled* passion.

I don't blame Catholicism's drumbeating obsession with sexual ethics on celibacy. Most parish priests nowadays, I'm told, are sympathetic to married people. I blame it on the joylessness of this terrible place that for so many years has almost but not quite perverted the joy that's in the Gospel.

You want to know something? If the Bishop of Rome could gather together these characters some morning and tell them that the celibacy rule and the sixth commandment had been suspended for 48 hours and that they could go out and make love with the most beautiful Roman women they could find (and, by the way, they ARE beautiful), most of them would simply stumble back to their offices. The prospect would not appeal to them at all. Nothing that involves joy or pleasure or fun would appeal to them. Their mission in life, their vocation, is to drive joy out of the world.

You have a hunch that Jesus would not approve.

48

"Mr. Gunther is out of town this week, Mr. Kane," the sultry telephone voice at Gunther Enterprises informed him. "He will be back the first of next week. However, he did tell me that if you wanted to discuss the Pulaski case with him then, he would be happy to answer all your questions, at your convenience."

"Thank you very much," Red said brightly. "Write if you find work."

Harv was in one of his genial moods, confident that he had scared Red off and happy to pick up the threads of the Pulaski case, knowing full well that the threads were now so completely tangled that there was not the slightest chance of either Red or the United States Attorney for the Northern District of Illinois ever straightening them out, even should that worthy suddenly acquire the ability to read and write.

Red's ace was Adele Ward, a card that had to be played at precisely the right moment or it would not be trump. Gunther had doubtless been astonished that Red had guessed the truth about Paul O'Meara. Somewhere in the back of the old man's head would be the suspicion that Red knew an enormous amount about him.

In this hunch, Harv would be perfectly correct. The stringer in Toledo had discovered that Adele/Arlene's family had abandoned the search for their daughter shortly after the murder and that large sums had been deposited in their bank account from a check signed by a "Frances X. Jones." Somehow, by means about which Red did not inquire, the reporter had managed to get a Xerox of the bank's Xerox of the check. It was the same handwriting as on the note to Rita Lane.

Harv's gofer was not taking a huge chance. With Arlene's parents silenced and Rita Lane out of the country, who was there to fear? Who cared about a butchered teenage hooker?

Who besides Red Kane?

Sick, frightened, and confused, Gunther was vulnerable to a sudden assault about the young prostitute's murder. It was a long shot. A younger Harv Gunther would never have let himself be mousetrapped by such a patent trick. Even the present, feeble Harvard Gunther might be sufficiently on his toes to laugh off any charge Red might make.

It had been a frustrating week. The cheerful confidence with which he had sent the bundle that was his novel off to Great Western Books diminished rapidly when he didn't hear from them. Maybe it was too happy a book, too cheerful, too funny. Maybe its heroine was too glamorous, too intelligent.

No reaction to the novel, no confrontation with Gunther, no new chances to improve communications with his children. Less time with Eileen, who was now fighting her way through the final phases of the Hurricane Houston trial.

He glanced over once again his columns on the Catholic Church. Only a half dozen or so in fifteen years of column writing, certainly not one of his major themes. Nonetheless, they reflected neatly the love/hate relationship that existed between Red and his Church.

When I needed the Church's help, he told himself angrily, *it was never there. And when I didn't need its help, it was all around me, harassing, threatening, warning, disturbing.*

Now that I may need it more than I ever have in my life, the best I can find is a priest-psychologist turned alienated radical.

He put the columns back into his file and locked the drawer. He glanced at his watch. Eleven o'clock and no idea for a column. *I might as well take my daily walk now, and do the column this afternoon.*

He donned his London Fog raincoat, which had not seen the inside of a cleaning establishment in five years, rode down the elevator and walked over through the Loop to St. Peter's Church, a noisy, bustling ornate marble supermarket of traditional Catholic religious services that always seemed to smell of incense—probably as artificial as the electric votive candles.

For the last week or two, Red had been stealing over to St. Peter's almost every day. It seemed a good idea to spend some time praying. Moreover, now that the novel revision was finished, there was little to occupy his time in the course of a day, particularly since he no longer efficiently consumed the end of the day at Ricardo's or Billy Goat's or the Old Town Ale House. He wasn't sure that he actually did that much praying when he went through the glass and marble portal of St. Peter's. In fact, he didn't know quite what he did inside the church. After a few moments, the bustle and the murmur of busy ritualists faded away and Red was as alone as though he were marooned on a desert island. Some days he lost all track of time; glancing at his watch when he stepped out of St. Peter's, he would realize that he'd been there for an hour or even an hour and a half, more time praying in one day than in ten years.

As a young man he had learned that the Catholic faith could not be separated from social worship or social responsibility. Whatever the hell happened between him and Whoever Else in St. Peter's, it was not very social. Larry Moran wouldn't approve. Red wasn't sure that he approved either. Might not St. Peter's become an addiction as compulsive and as debilitating as the addiction he had left behind at the Old Town Ale House, an addiction that still tugged at him several times every day?

Today, Red told himself, *I am a little confused.* He stepped aside at the door of St. Peter's to avoid being trampled by a group of elderly women who, having made their daily peace with the Lord, were now charging enthusiastically back into the world prepared to smite all their enemies. *I'm rushing through life like they are, only maybe faster. Perhaps the new game is to slow down. I'm not sure I know how to do that.*

If You are up there, and if it was You who sandbagged me over on Wacker Drive, You'd better come up with a new idea for me.

A half hour later Red left St. Peter's with his new idea, a dazzling, shocking, prurient idea.

"Shame on you," he told the possessor of the Cheshire smile. "What would the sisters say if they knew you were putting that kind of idea in my head in church, while Mass was going on up at the altar!"

49

"I'm glad I didn't meet you after I had married someone else," Eileen said fervently as she and Red, shivering in the early-December cold, walked down Monroe Street past the

Dirksen Federal Building, with its defiantly cheerful "red lobster" Calder mobile, toward Michigan Avenue.

"Do you mind explaining that characteristic Ryan-family observation?" Red tightened his grip on her arm. The strain of the Houston trial was taking its toll on Eileen. Her cool, matter-of-fact conversational style was giving way to kooky Ryan-like comments. Red decided not to tell her that she was sounding more and more like her gifted but spacey sister, Mary Kate the Shrink. (The Ryans tended to add titles to their given names as though to distinguish themselves from someone else with the same name but a different job—Mary Kate the Shrink, Blackie the Priest, Mike Casey the Cop, Eileen the Lawyer. Red suspected that their code name for him was Red Kane the Hack, but he had never asked.)

"If I had married someone else and then met you"—Eileen huddled closer to him as though to escape the chill wind that was bouncing off the Loop canyon walls—"and become addicted to you like I am, I'd commit adultery almost every day."

"I'm flattered, I think."

"And you also think that I sound more like Mary Kate every day, don't you? It's all your fault, Redmond Peter Kane, you're cracking me apart. The facade is crumbling; the real Eileen Ryan is about to pop out of the box. She'll make Mary Kate look self-possessed and rational. And she's going to do her malted-milk thing for you this afternoon because she loves you so much."

"Heaven forfend that there would be two Mary Kates," Red laughed, more or less sincerely.

Tumescence seemed to twist Eileen's speech into the form of Irish bulls.

"I thought I saw you on Monroe during the lunch hour."

"No, I ate at the *Herald*."

"I know." She squeezed his arm. "By the time I caught up with you, you weren't there."

And in the lobby of the building, "There's so many people waiting for this elevator that if we all get on it there won't be room for half of us." Then dizzy chuckles, as though she realized she was talking nonsense.

The last time they were in bed together, she had lain next to him on her stomach, apparently asleep, face buried in her arms. Red was dozing, one wayward hand at the small of her back.

"It's not merely that you're so sexy," she'd begun, in her legal-argument tone.

"Oh?"

"Or that you know more about my body than I would want even my husband to know..."

"Eileen." He patted her rump, mostly to get her attention. "I AM your husband."

She tilted her head in his direction and opened a quizzical eye, as though this were a new idea, worth considering perhaps but by no means self-evidently true. "Regardless... where was I?...Please don't interrupt, darling."

"I won't," he promised, kissing her back.

"Uhm...that's nice...don't stop...the point is..." She was now driving home her point to the jury. "The point is that it's always fun. Like being a little girl again. I was a very playful little girl. Did you know that? You make me young again. Isn't that wonderful?"

"It sure is," he agreed, wondering what she would say next.

"I think I better nap now," she sighed.

Red abandoned his exploration of her back. The poor woman was trying to survive on four hours of sleep. He drew the sheet up to her neck and settled back to continue his doze.

He was almost asleep when she assaulted his face and chest with fiercely passionate kisses. "I love you, I love you, I love you," she said between each kiss, in a voice that suggested tears.

What the hell...?

Their love affair was now so steamy and intense that it had become for both of them an obsessive preoccupation. For Red a pleasurable burden, but a burden nonetheless. What it was for Eileen, one minute somber and distant, the next minute deliriously giddy, he had no idea. He was afraid to ask.

How long could this boiling sexual intensity possibly

continue? Might not it be appropriate to call the game on account of darkness? Or at least seek a prolonged time out? It was not rational or proper, was it, to become sexually obsessed with a wife of twenty years?

The answer to the questions was always the same: He loved her too much to stop. Lust and affection, pleasure and tenderness, were feeding on each other's flames—like a match and a gas jet alternately enkindling one another—making him utterly powerless to turn off the fire.

If it was death that Eileen sometimes saw in the room with them when they were loving each other, death would have to wait.

He was unable not to suggest to her the brilliant idea that Someone had planted in Red's head inside the nave of St. Peter's, an idea that would have profoundly shocked the elderly women kneeling around him in the church: Dick Garvey's apartment in the Doral Plaza on the north edge of Grant Park. "I won't mind if you bring Melissa along when you check out the apartment," Dick had said with a wicked grin when he tossed Red the keys before his overseas assignment.

No, he should not invite Eileen to visit the Doral studio apartment with him. But he loved her so much that he could not silence his lascivious tongue.

She listened calmly to his suggestion and responded without changing her expression. "A love nest at the Doral? Kind of a glittering, plastic place, isn't it? Still, it sounds like an interesting experiment."

An interesting experiment it certainly was. The strange apartment, dry and airless, in the middle or the end of a cold December afternoon created a sexual ambience in which all restraints and inhibitions, all shyness and fears were as quickly peeled away as their clothes.

"I get up in the morning and I tell myself I ought to be ashamed," Eileen continued. "I'm an animal, a she-beast in heat, King Solomon's mare—no, it was the Pharaoh's mare, wasn't it?—my behavior is gross, obscene, disgusting for a responsible trial lawyer with a successful professional career. I have a difficult and important case in which a poor victimized black man depends on me almost completely to keep him out of jail, so I permit myself to degenerate to a violent voluptuary who wants nothing but sex, sex, and more sex."

"I like that alliterative phrase, violent voluptuary." Red opened the door to the Doral Plaza for her. "Is this affecting your performance in the trial?"

"God no." Eileen looked up at him with worshipful eyes and tightened her grip on his arm. "I've never been better. Maybe you could arrange a sexual orgy the final week of every one of my trials. Still, it's like flourless German chocolate cake. You know you've had too much of it, but you can't stop eating it."

Red took her hand and pulled her away from the elevator door.

"I've been called many things in my life, woman, but flourless cake, you should excuse the expression, takes the cake."

"Flourless GERMAN CHOCOLATE cake . . ." she insisted, dragging him toward the door of the empty elevator. "You may taste just a little better."

"A heavy burden though?" The door closed on them.

Eileen kissed him. "He's not heavy, he's my husband."

"I do my best." Since they were the only ones in it, he put his arms around her and felt her body give itself completely to him. His own desperately hungry self responded with a matching gift.

"Some one of these days," she said huskily, "we're not even going to make it through the door of the apartment."

That gave Red another idea: *Next time I'll start undressing her in the elevator.* While there was still time, he assigned the blame for this disgraceful idea to the lurking Cheshire smile.

It was four-thirty. Today they had about an hour and a half between end-of-day recess in the federal court and the meeting of the trial team in Eileen's office. Nick Curran would brief Eileen on technicalities of the banking act that she must know, letter perfect, the next morning.

When their first round was over and he had been buried once more in the healing sweetness that he'd experienced for the first time the day he told her about Helga, they lay exhausted in each other's arms, sweating, disheveled, complacent, and triumphant, and watched the Chicago skyline light up for the night, as Eileen hummed tunes from *Camelot*.

"I sing while we're making love," she had informed him primly, "because you like it."

"I do?"

"Certainly. You think it's kinky and crazy and you like to bed a kinky crazy woman. Don't you?"

"So long as it's you."

"Regardless."

That late afternoon in the Doral while they admired the skyline, Red realized that once again, as happened whenever Eileen tore his sanity away with such gentle, overpowering love, he had sensed a hint of a cosmic baseball bat flailing around nearby, a Cheshire smile about to float by the window. He firmly exorcised such lurking traces of Whoever. It was fun, but you didn't want to do it twice.

"You're wonderful," Red murmured, too blissful to think of anything more imaginative.

He heard a faint sniffle and glanced at his wife's face. Teardrops were gently falling on either cheek. She was no longer svelte, he observed, but thin, frail, Irish linen that had been cleaned once too often.

"I didn't hurt you, did I?"

She shook her head negatively, as though it were absurd to imagine that he could possibly hurt her.

"What's wrong, Eileen?" he asked affectionately.

Suddenly she was sobbing hysterically again. This time the grief was more desperate, the agony more hopeless, the pain more destructive. Red held her in his arms, her unresisting body pressed against his until the worst of the weeping was over.

"This time you're going to have to give me an explanation."

She shook her head decisively. No way.

"You're not getting out of this apartment, woman"—he gripped her chin firmly—"without a beginning of an explanation, and THAT is final."

Her tearstained face, showing every one of her forty-two years in the dim light of the room, pleaded with him for a reprieve.

"You heard me," Red insisted. "That's an order."

"All right," she half sobbed, half snarled, twisting away from him and leaping out of the bed.

For several moments she stood at the window of the studio apartment, gazing at the snow-dusted brown meadows of Grant Park, a beautiful nude woman contemplating ...what?...the end of a dream?

Wearily, she turned in Red's direction, leaning against a drape. The nearest apartment buildings were as far away as the University of Chicago. Even the most high-powered binoculars could not violate her modesty.

"Stop looking at me that way," she demanded roughly.

"C'mon, Eileen, you're too beautiful not to admire."

"I'm sorry, Red," she said simply, "terribly, terribly sorry."

"You said that before." Red sat on the edge of the bed. "Sorry for what?"

Adulterous love? She must know that he was in no position to denounce anyone for that.

"For tricking you into marriage." Slow, gentle tears reappeared on her cheeks. She rushed on recklessly, charging up the hill like Pickett at Gettysburg. "All the bad things that have happened to our family ever since are God's punishment for the terrible wrong I did then."

"My God, Eileen." He could hardly believe that was the problem. "We settled that twenty years ago on Saint Stephen's Day. I wasn't tricked. I wanted to marry you."

"Don't be ridiculous, Red. Of course you were tricked. I knew there was a good chance I would conceive that night and I went ahead anyway."

"I repeat, Eileen"—he tried not to sound impatient with such foolishness—"what I just said. We talked about THAT in 1963 too."

"No we didn't." She rubbed her hand over her face, as though trying to remove terrible scars. "We didn't resolve it at all. You accepted the accomplished fact. Like a loyal, honorable Irish Catholic, you made the best of a bad bargain and married the woman that seduced you, even though you knew then, as you certainly know now, that it was a terrible mistake."

"A mistake?" Red rose from the bed and tried to take

her in his arms. "You think what we've just been doing is what a man does with a wife who is a mistake?"

"Please, Red." She slipped away from his grasp. "Don't touch me now. I can't bear to be touched . . . it took twenty years for me to become the kind of wife you needed, even in bed, and that doesn't solve any of the other problems."

"What other problems?" The world in which he was now walking was a strange mixture of Lewis Carroll's Wonderland and Franz Kafka's Castle.

"The problem is that you're a great man"—she opened her purse and shuffled through it and pulled out a tissue—"with enormous talent and dedication. You needed a wife to strengthen you. Not a frigid bitch who would stand by helplessly as your confidence in yourself and your talent faded away. I gave you three children, I maintain a reasonably presentable household, I make love to you occasionally." She shrugged hopelessly, sending a movement through her naked body that stirred the embers of desire in Red. "Anyone could do that. You needed a special woman so you could continue to be the special man that you were. There never has been anything special about me. I'm merely a dull, dry, shanty-Irish lawyer who isn't nearly good enough for you."

"You have it all wrong," Red said, feeling as helpless as he had at the side of his mother's casket. How could such an intelligent woman deceive herself so badly about him? "I'm the one who's not good enough for you. I've been a drinker, a poseur, and a lecher, a disgraceful husband and a failed father. I told you a long time ago that you were the perfect woman for me, and you still are. It's my fault that only in the last month or so I've been able to respond to a perfect wife."

Eileen collapsed to the floor, curling herself into a pathetic heap. "Don't blame yourself for those other women. If I had been the kind of lover that a man like you needs, there wouldn't have been other women."

Oh my God, Red thought to himself. *She's blaming herself for my adulteries.*

"That's not true!" he exclaimed aloud. "The things that are wrong in our marriage are my fault, not yours."

"They are NOT your fault!" she shouted. "You are the one who made the best of a bad bargain. Our problems are MY fault!"

"They are NOT your fault," he shouted back. "And don't try to tell me that I made the best of a bad bargain. You did!"

"Typical Irish male! You don't understand a thing!" she screamed at him.

"My God, Eileen, do you realize what we're doing?" He sat on the floor next to her and stroked her back lightly. "Most husbands and wives blame one another and fight about that blame. You and I are each blaming ourselves and fighting because the other won't give up responsibility."

"But it IS my fault." She pulled away from him, leaned against the wall, and covered her breasts protectively with her arms.

"I should have begun conversation about our relationship when we came back from the honeymoon," he argued sadly.

"That shouldn't have been your responsibility," she insisted, drawing her legs up beneath her chin, armoring herself with her own body. "I should have done it. Only I was afraid."

"Of what were you afraid?" He sat next to her and tentatively took one of her hands in his.

"I was afraid—" She gulped. "Oh, Red, I was afraid that if we ever talked about things you'd realize how worthless I am and I would lose you. Even now I'm afraid I'll lose you. The only reason I might keep you is that you feel sorry for me."

"And I was afraid that if we talked seriously I would be worthless in responding to the needs of a strong and powerful woman." He put his arm around her waist. A strange idea teased the back of his brain. Eileen was somehow linked to the Wacker Drive Raider. Was that One also afraid to lose him? It was an absurd idea. But it implanted itself in Red's mind and remained.

"That's stupid," she insisted weakly, leaning her head against his shoulder and permitting her temporary armor to collapse.

"I know you feel that way," he agreed. "Will you at least concede that I feel that everything you say is fully as stupid?"

"I dunno," she sniffled, sounding exactly like Kate the day the police had picked her up. Now Eileen was the girl child who needed a Madonna to mother her.

Mother your wife? Now there's an interesting idea!

Red's lips lightly touched a now-undefended breast, cold as a granite statue. "Well, at least we've begun to talk, and you haven't lost me yet. And we're going to keep on talking, however belatedly, and I'm not going to let you get away. Even if everything you say about yourself is true—and it's not—you're still a better roommate than any man has a right to expect, and I'm going to keep you on the payroll for that reason if no other."

She sighed helplessly. "You're terrible."

And the sigh turned into a giggle.

"What is it you see behind me when we're making love?" The question had leaped out of his mouth before he had time to reflect on it. "It terrifies you."

"You've noticed." She pulled away from him.

"Is it death?"

"Course not." She turned toward the wall.

"Well, who or what?"

"God. Telling me that I am an evil woman who has no right to be so happy and that I will have to suffer for my happiness."

In 1983? She sounds like my mother.

"That's not what God is like." Red took both her hands in his to draw her back to his arms. She resisted, straining to keep him at a distance. "You ought to be ashamed of yourself. God has grounds for slander action against you."

"All right, wise guy." She was furious at him. "You know so much. What is God like?"

"God is a tender, passionate lover, like me at my very rare best." Had he really said THAT? "Or even more when you heal me like you did today. God's a chocolate malted milk, with two squirts of whipped cream. He's not waiting to zap us. Rather He's standing around patiently biding His time until we are ready to return His love."

Red Kane, theologian. Well, you don't have to practice what you preach. Or even believe it.

"Do you really believe that?" The tension went out of her arms.

"Of course." Red's lips returned to the breast he had been kissing. It was not nearly so cold. "Deep down you do too."

"You sound just like my brother."

"So I have to be right. You owe God an apology." He kissed her other breast. She sighed in resignation.

"Oh, Red." She held his head against her chest. "I'm so sorry. Dumb menopausal lawyer woman went and had hysterics."

"Once in twenty years of marriage...you're entitled." He enveloped her in his arms, for reassurance and love, not more sex. Well, not necessarily.

"Two or three times, actually," she sniffed, now limp and passive in his guardianship.

He held her as close as he could, as though contact at every point on their naked bodies would give him access to her troubled glorious soul. Katie in his arms again, an exhausted girl baby, accepting completely her father's maternal affection.

Is this what they expect from us? Now, isn't that interesting? A woman would risk limitless fucking if she wanted a maternal husband. Not a bad idea, come to think of it. Red Kane, Madonna and stud at the same time.

As if she had read his mind, she drew away from him.

"Aren't we going to continue to talk?"

"Not now," she pleaded. "I'm too beat out, and I do still have a trial." She reached for her glasses on the bed stand, always the first step in dressing.

"It doesn't have to be now," Red agreed.

Later, when everything had fallen apart on him, Red would wish he had insisted she call Nick Curran to tell him she would be an hour late.

The day after Eileen fell apart at the Doral Plaza, an uncertain and troubled Red Kane sat at his desk in the *HG* city room, wondering what to do about his wife and about Harv Gunther. Both adventures had turned sour. Harv was dangerous and Eileen was coming apart at the seams. Harv was not worth fighting. Eileen was worth saving, all right, from whatever demons he had unleashed within her, but how was he to do that?

It was late on a dark winter afternoon; eddies of snow flurries obscured the river and hid completely the 333 Wacker Building. The warm breast and bright wings seemed to have deserted him.

The phone jangled; Red jumped anxiously and lifted it from his desk with a trembling hand, as though he had been waiting for bad news.

"Red Kane."

Silence.

"Red Kane here."

"I know." A disguised voice. O'Meara again? No, someone else.

"Who is it?"

"You want more on Gunther?"

"Who is it?"

"Eat your supper at Billy Goat's tonight."

The line clicked dead.

Red hesitated, called home, and told a disinterested Patty that he was going to eat downtown.

"Like, no one comes home for supper anymore."

"So you have no one to fight with?"

"Really, Dad, don't be gross."

"I try." Red waited till she hung up.

Brat.

He sat in a corner at Billy Goat's, consumed four medium-rare lamb chops, three glasses of Perrier water, and two dishes of chocolate ice cream. Despite serious attempts to seem invisible, he was cornered by Lee Malley, who reported the latest gossip about the *Sun-Times* and Rupert Murdoch.

"Newspaper people are the worst complainers in the world," Red mumbled.

"They have a lot to complain about." Lee was offended.

"Only when they forget that what they do beats working."

Finally about nine o'clock, Lee took the hint and drifted off, doubtless, Red thought, to the arms of his live-in girlfriend, poor woman.

He ordered another dish of chocolate ice cream.

The waiter brought a note with it.

"Thanks," Red said, tossing it aside with deliberate unconcern while he finished the ice cream. He'd swim an extra quarter mile tomorrow.

Then he opened the note. A crude scrawl. "Meet me around the corner on the Lower Level."

A trap?

Casually, Red signaled for his check, paid the bill, and drifted over to the public phone.

"Mike? Red. I'm at Billy Goat's. Don't worry, nothing but French Fizz. I'm supposed to walk out of here and turn the corner into the Lower Level.... Yeah, Charon is probably waiting for me. Suppose you park your car at the Grand Avenue entrance.... No, I won't take any chances."

Which is just what he did five minutes later, the biggest and dumbest chance since he fired the bazooka at the North Korean tank.

He strolled out of the café and around the corner. The Lower Level, empty of traffic, looked like a set for a modern version of one of the less pleasant places in the Inferno—close to the bottom, to judge by the slush on the black street. The hideous yellow lights on either side reminded him of a morgue. Or maybe a clearing in a haunted forest with the half-dozen parked cars being the wolves gathering for a kill.

Maybe werewolves.

He shivered, and adjured his superstitious imagination to calm down.

Why am I not home in bed with my wife?

Because my wife is at her office working on a trial, that's why.

No one appeared. He glanced at his watch. Ten minutes. A false alarm. Someone's idea of a joke. They knew what the Lower Level did to his Irish dread of the uncanny.

The headlights flickered in a car on Illinois Street to his left. That's where the contact was. *All right, let's see what he wants.*

Then Red took his stupid chance. He walked down the steps to the street.

The headlights came on again and stayed on. The car began to move, tires squealing against concrete as it roared toward him. Paralyzed, Red watched as it closed in.

Seconds, violence was always quick, his father's death, Korea, Viet Nam, there was never enough time to think.

Then he thought of Eileen and threw himself behind one of the immense pillars that supported the Upper Level. The car screeched by him; its bumper brushed his trench coat.

Now a creature of instinct, Red ducked around the pillar and fell to his knees. A light patter of explosions reverberated in the Lower Level Canyon. Pinging noises like snarling mosquitoes buzzed above his head. The car raced across the Michigan Avenue Bridge and left into the darkness of the Lower Level of Wacker Drive.

Trembling with terror, unable to move, Red cowered against the pillar until Mike Casey's voice cut the darkness.

"Red . . . it's all right now."

"The hell it is." He stood up and brushed off his coat. "Go on, tell me I was a damn fool."

"Not necessarily. If they wanted to kill you, they would have. You were supposed to be frightened, not killed."

"They got what they wanted. A little calling card from Harv?"

"A gentle reminder. Red, think about whether you want to continue this cat-and-mouse game."

"I'll switch the metaphor. I'm holding the high card."

"He doesn't know that, does he?"

"Not yet."

"Play the damn card as soon as you can."

Red agreed, but still he hesitated.

50

"I pulled out your column the other day, Red," Larry Moran said, his chin resting on his crossed fingers as he leaned on the rectory office desk. "You know, the one in which you tore apart the damn fool from the National Council of Priests' Federations who let you pick up the tab at his public-relations lunch."

"I remember." Red felt dimly guilty about that column now. He was seeking help from his Church and one of its priests, though he could tell the priest nothing about the terrors from which he needed protection. He should not have attacked the priesthood in that column. "I guess I was taking out a lot of my anger at the Church on the poor guy. I have this damn fool obsession that the Church is responsible for most of my problems. Intellectually I know it's not true, but whenever I get a chance to stick it to them, I do."

"You have every right to be angry." Larry's high forehead furrowed in a doubtful frown. "The Church DID let down the enthusiastic Catholic Action laity of the 1950's. But that isn't why I read the column. I was afraid you might think I was like that kid and be upset with me for saying pretty much the same things when you were here last Saturday."

Red was confused, tired, and unaccountably lonely. The strain of the enthusiasm over the last five weeks was beginning to have its effect on him. The new Red Kane was in serious trouble.

Later he would use the image of a Mississippi riverboat to describe what had happened. "The paddle wheel was spinning more rapidly than ever, but the boat wasn't moving."

"Why not?" The shrink drew deeply on her cigarette.

"The rudder wasn't working."

"You were impotent, in other words?" She ground out her cigarette with a vicious twist.

"Sometimes a rudder is a rudder." Red tried to laugh.

"It is not a humorous matter, Mr. Kane."

In fact Red meant that the voice of Paul O'Meara from "beyond the grave," the horror scene with Gunther, Eileen's collapse in their Doral Plaza love nest, and the shooting incident in the Lower Level had convinced him that his experience on Wacker Drive had not eliminated evil from the world.

More bluntly, he was scared.

First of all, he was worried about the telephone confrontation with Harvard Gunther early next week. He had heard not a word from Great Western Books. The Hurricane Houston trial was dragging on, closing arguments on Monday, case to the jury Monday night or Tuesday morning.

Eileen was nervously uncertain about the outcome. Putting Hurricane on the stand in his own defense was a calculated risk, but finally she had little choice. Don Roscoe's picture of Hurricane as an irresponsible spendthrift clearly offended the respectable lower-middle-class black women on the jury. She had warned the former basketball hero that he could simply not afford to play "cool cat," "laid-back dude" on the witness stand. He ought to be hurt, contrite, dismayed. There was no phoniness in such an image: the "cool dude" act covered up Hurricane's terror in the courtroom and his own monumental ignorance. "Poor man," Eileen had said sympathetically, "his I.Q. certainly isn't much over 85."

"He sure can dunk," Red observed.

"Roscoe had a guilty verdict sewed up," she said as she readjusted the ice pack on her head before Red's visit to Forty Holy Martyrs' rectory. "I was trying desperately to figure out a way to plea-bargain. Then like the world's all-time great dummy that he is, he tore Leroy apart in cross-examination and reduced him to a clumsy, inarticulate bungler who couldn't even put verbs in his sentences. Roscoe's assistants tried to call him off. He wouldn't listen. Those women in the jury box saw a smartass little white man ridiculing a poor black street kid who had already been taken in by white sharpies. Roscoe gave us a new lease on life."

"What are his chances, Eileen?"

Eileen rearranged the ice pack again over her eyes. "Better than even, considering the government has an airtight case against him. Our argument has always been that Hurricane was exploited by his business associates and did not understand what he was doing when he filled out those loan applications."

"Did he?"

Eileen rearranged the tattered old robe that she was wearing and shifted her position on the bed. It didn't seem to help the headache much. "He's certainly innocent until proven guilty. It's a toss-up, Red. If I weren't a superstitious Irishwoman, I might be inclined to say we'd probably win. Now all I want to do is to get rid of this damn headache."

By the end of next week he would know about the novel and Harvard Gunther, and Eileen would be free of the trial. It would be a big week.

Eileen was worn out from the trial and from the agony of her emotional outburst in the Doral Plaza. She had stopped using makeup, the first time in over a decade. She had never used much, but it was always applied with characteristic precision. Now, rather than smear her face sloppily because she was so tired, she ignored her tubes and jars.

And showed her years, much to Red's dismay. He might grow old and die, but not Eileen. She was supposed to be perpetually young.

This weekend was surely not the time to raise again the question of where their marriage might go in the years ahead. There was, after all, no rush. Perhaps after the trial was over and after he had finally made up his mind about whether to move against Harv Gunther and after Christmas they could get away someplace where there was a patch of sunshine and work it all out.

"He was not a bad kid, Larry." Red stirred himself out of his reveries about Eileen and tried to concentrate on the priest. "He meant well, but I would hardly put you in the same class of social-action enthusiast."

"They call it 'peace and justice' now, not 'social action.' Look, Red, I'm intelligent enough to know there are no simple answers. You can't dismiss economics with enthusiasm. A just society can't be built overnight." He took his head off his fingers. "We must put all our efforts and our energies into work for the just society, no matter how long it may take to create it, no matter if we are absolutely certain we will never live to see it. Jesus demands nothing less from us. I read the papers, I watch the television news, listen to the politicians, and say to myself that it's all bullshit. None of it makes any difference as long as there are little kids right here in my parish who don't have enough to eat and who are going to shiver with cold all winter long."

Red remembered shivering in the house on Coles and a stomach that, if not exactly empty, still craved for more food. "I don't disagree," he said.

Then, self-consciously aware of how ridiculous he must sound in a parish like Larry's, he described (leaving out the erotic details) the quandary in which he and Eileen found themselves (leaving out, too, the calm, curled, and perhaps vulnerable reality that might still have been waiting in the vicinity of the green glass skyscraper).

There was a long pause when he finished. "Do you want to know what I think? What I REALLY think?"

"That's what I'm here for, Larry."

"This'll sound strange coming from a psychologist." Larry drummed his fingers on the old desk. "I think you and Eileen ought to forget about your relationship. Remember the line we used to use in the old Cana Conferences—well, maybe you don't remember them. I keep forgetting that you never were a priest. 'Love doesn't mean two people looking at one another, it means two people looking in the same direction.' That was not a half-bad idea. Tom Wolfe said that the 1970's were the 'me decade.' I think that the 1980's are the 'we decade,' in which couples or small groups of individuals zero in so totally on their own interpersonal relationships that they completely forget the rest of the world. You and Eileen should find something useful, something relevant—God, Red, those are the wrong words—something socially challenging to do. Open a soup kitchen somewhere, if nothing else. Get out of the courtroom and away from the typewriter and out into the streets of the city where the poor people are and where you can make your own personal contribution to alleviating misery and suffering. Take the first steps in your own life toward committing yourself to the building up of a just society. The careers at which you are both so good are, after all, worthless; they don't really help anybody." He rose from the desk, as a sign of dismissal. "You write entertainment; she defends people who probably ought to be in jail. No wonder you have spiritual and marital problems."

"That makes a hell of a lot of sense," Red said, temporarily fired up with enthusiasm for the modest, simple, generous life. "Incidentally, one last question on a totally different matter?"

"Sure." Larry sighed patiently, but remained standing.

"I have a kind of ethical problem as a reporter." Red stumbled, trying to make it sound important but not as important as world poverty. "Should I do an investigative piece on a wicked man who may not live much longer?"

"Why is that a serious issue?" Larry knotted his forehead painfully. "Why shove the poor man into the grave?"

"Well, he did many terrible things...and he is capable of a few more before he dies...and he represents an evil in the world."

Put that way it sounded trivial. How else did you explain a man who lived in a world that Larry Moran, indeed almost any priest, did not understand and could not imagine?

"The systems that need to be changed, Red, are structural." Larry walked toward the door. "Reform capitalism so that it's no longer capitalism, and problems like your old man will take care of themselves. Won't they?"

What would Harv be in a socialist society? Either dead or the chairman of the politburo.

"I suppose."

As soon as he left the rectory, however, Red wondered how he would be able to explain to Eileen that she ought to give up, for a while anyway, defending gelheads (as the kids would say) like Hurricane Houston. Maybe, however, on that warm sunny beach somewhere the two of them could work out a way of simplifying their lives and devoting some of their time and energy together to goals that were not irrelevant or useless.

What did Larry Moran mean when he said that he kept forgetting I was never a priest?

And he was no help at all on the subject of Harv Gunther. In Larry's vision of things, the savage murder of a teenage prostitute was merely one of the inevitable evils of a capitalist society. A price on anything, even a young woman's life.

He was, perhaps, not completely wrong. That vision, however, was no help to Red in making the decision of whether to go after Harv Gunther before God had a chance to demand an accounting.

"I should think," Blackie would say later, lifting his eyes to heaven as if in fervent prayer, "that every use of the word 'relevant' since 1965 earns the user at least seven quarantines in purgatory."

"What is a quarantine anyway?" Red asked.

"I haven't the foggiest, but indulgences used to get us out of seven years and seven quarantines in purgatory. Or maybe they substituted for seven years and seven quarantines of public penance, which somehow or the other seems inequitable. In any event, Redmond Peter Kane, with all due respect for my colleague in the clergy Laurence Joseph Moran, about whose zeal there can be no disagreement"—Blackie raised his eyes heavenward again—"might I make the gentle suggestion that anyone who thinks that law and journalism are not socially useful professions is full of what my beloved sibling Mary Kate the Shrink would picturesquely call 'horse manure'!"

"I don't know." Red was too confused at this stage of the struggle to know anything. "I think what he said about the simple life was very wise."

"Depend on it, esteemed brother-in-law, anything that is proposed under the banner of blessed simplicity in the contemporary world is surely to be distrusted. Any churchman who urges us to return to simplicity, however sincere and pious he may be, is urging us to immaturity and irresponsibility. And don't argue with me about that, because I'm right and you know I'm right."

Red did not urge the simple life on his wife when he returned to the house on Webster Avenue. Eileen, still clad in the tattered old robe and with the ice pack still held on her head, was bent over the kitchen table with a legal-size yellow pad, scrawling notes for her closing summary to the jury of Hurricane Houston's peers. Although Johnny had provided a small and elegantly feminine "library area" for his mother on the third floor of the house, Eileen, almost superstitiously, insisted on working at the kitchen table as she had when they lived in the tiny apartment on Belmont Avenue near the home field of the hapless Chicago Cubs.

Red kissed the back of her neck gently. "How's it going?"

"A little bit of it is beginning to take shape." She looked up and shoved her glasses onto her forehead. "I thought there was no point in waiting until the headache went away, because the headache won't go away until I've finished my first draft."

"Smart girl," he agreed. Had that look of adoration always been in her eyes? After twenty years together, was he only now beginning to notice it?

"How was the conversation with Father Moran?"

"Interesting." He opened the icebox and removed the last bottle of Diet Pepsi. "The damn brats have killed the Diet Pepsi again!" Instantly he regretted his outburst of temper. That was the old Red Kane sneaking into the family kitchen and disturbing his headache-wracked wife. "Oh, well," he sighed. "They're only kids. What are daddies for except to put Diet Pepsis in the icebox?"

"They're for going to the store and buying more Diet Pepsi." Eileen actually seemed to have laughed. "I don't know what's got into you, Red Kane, but your patience with the brats has become positively saintly."

"Funny thing happened with Larry." Red zipped up his Varig Airlines windbreaker. "He was talking clerical gossip and then he sort of laughed. Said it was hard for him to remember that I hadn't been a priest once."

"What's funny about that?" Eileen glanced up at him from her yellow notepad.

"I left the seminary after my second year, and my life has not exactly been priestlike."

Eileen returned to her notes, pushing her glasses back into place. "Sometimes when we go into a restaurant together I have the terrible feeling that people—older people, I mean—are staring daggers at me because they think I'm a woman on a date with my parish priest."

"And what do you feel like when that happens?"

"Hmm...Oh, I don't know. I guess I want to make love with you as soon as I can."

"What the hell does that mean?" Red snapped.

Eileen lifted her eyes from her notes, sad, tired eyes. "I can't talk about it now, Red, I have to do this dratted outline. I suppose I'd have to think about what I mean. Just now I can't think about anything but Leroy Houston."

"Well, maybe I ought to get some more Diet Pepsi and earn my spurs as a useful daddy."

As he gathered together empty bottles to return as a good Lakeshore Limousine Liberal citizen should, Eileen spoke again, mumbling at her notepad. "Pardon? Oh, what I said was..." She did not look up. "...I suppose it has something to do with the fact that you kind of look like a priest. So much compassion—something like that."

As he bought the Diet Pepsi, Red pondered the interesting change of roles between Eileen and himself. Now he was the teetotaler and she the tipsy lover of champagne.

Virtuously he purchased two twelve-packs of Pepsi for the Doral apartment, but nothing stronger. No way, as the kids would say.

He'd brought a bottle of champagne one afternoon and Eileen had polished two-thirds of it off while delivering a monologue on what was happening to them.

"There is a much greater burden to falling in love with a spouse than with anyone else." She held out the paper cup from which she was guzzling his present. "Thank you, it's very good. Sure it doesn't bother you?"

"I'm not an alcoholic, Eileen. I've stopped drinking, that's all."

"Where was I? Oh, yes. When a man and woman are married for twenty years, has it been that long, yes it has, there is an agenda which climbs into bed with them, isn't there?"

"If you say so."

"I do and it's true. More anger and more happy memories. More regrets. And more fear of the erosion of time." She gulped a large swallow of the sparkling white drink. "We can't let ourselves fall out of love this time, like we did all the other times, we both know that."

"Love requires work," he said tentatively, brushing his fingers against her flank.

"And how much work"—she sipped more champagne and pointed an accusing finger at him—"have we put into our marriage?"

"Not much, passion and silence."

"Terrible."

"We love the things we love for what they are."

"Wallace Stevens?"

"Robert Frost."

"Wrong again." She extended the paper cup toward the bottle. "Last drink. We both know that this is our last chance, don't we?"

"Do we?" He nibbled at the breast which was closest to his lips. "Of course we do. Unless God is crazy enough to give us another chance."

"Stop that! Well, not completely. I mean, can you imagine me drinking this wonderful stuff stark naked in a love nest with my husband when I was twenty-one?"

"I enjoy the image now."

"Of course. Well, I should hope so. Why don't you put your arm around me? It's difficult to try to talk these problems through without some emotional support."

"Is that what you want?"

"For the present. We'll see about later. Now then ... well, why do you think we are so much more obsessed with each other, physically obsessed, than we were twenty years ago?"

"More love?"

"That merely restates the problem.... You will stop me when you think I will drink so much that I'll become ill?"

"Yes."

"Well, then fill the cup again, please ... with your left hand, silly, I need your right arm around me. Now, O all-wise Solomon, tell the poor tipsy Daughter of Jerusalem what love is."

"Passion and affection, feeding on one another? Or maybe blended judiciously, like in a skillfully made martini?" Where had he heard that line?

"Oh, that's good, very good, but why passion? And why now? And why so goddamn strong now"—she tilted uncertainly in one direction and stiffened her back—"that it turns into an obsession and right in the middle of a trial?"

"I suppose that passion heals, Eileen. Maybe we both want more to heal and to be healed."

"You're a goddamn poet, that's what you are." She threw her arms desperately around him. "Dear God in heaven, I love you, Redmond Peter Kane. I don't want to lose you."

"That," he said, cuddling her close, "is not on the agenda." She was much too thin, no longer capable of arguing, as all the Ryan women did, that she was five pounds overweight. More like seven or eight pounds underweight.

"We're besotted because we're afraid of death, you know that too," she sobbed into his chest. "Two middle-aged lovers fighting against the cold of the night. That's why falling in love is so much more passionate now."

"Now who's being the poet?" He stroked her back reassuringly.

"I love you, Red. I don't want ever to lose you."

Occasionally in their marriage it occurred to Red that Eileen's expression of love was not merely a polite convention between a husband and wife, nor even part of the rhetoric of marital sex. She meant it.

Whenever Red thought that, he felt suddenly as if he were on the sky deck at the Sears Tower in the middle of an attack of acrophobia. He wasn't sure whether to run or jump.

This time, like the other times, he ran.

"You'll never lose me," he murmured into her hair.

"You'll die first and leave me a lonely widow."

"Love is as strong as death." He kissed the nape of her neck. "You're stuck with me for eternity."

"Saint Redmond of Lincoln Park quotes Scripture.... I think I'd better sleep a little. You did let me drink too much."

"Always my fault."

"Always."

He took the bottle away and held her in his arms while she napped.

What the hell brought that on?

Okay. In the future it will be Diet Pepsis.

Outside the supermarket after he had bought the Diet Pepsis, like a good and useful daddy, he pondered whether perhaps he ought to buy some more champagne. Never know when you might need it. Christmas, for example. He hesitated, then went into the liquor store and bought two bottles of Dom Perignon.

Just in case.

He looked at his image in the mirror behind the counter. *Do I look like a priest?*

Damn it, I do. A broken-down pastor who wants to go back to being an associate again.

When he returned from the supermarket, heavily laden with a variety of sugar-free and caffeine-free sodas, Eileen had disappeared and Patty was sprawled on her stomach on the "living room area" floor, surrounded by class notes.

"History test?" he asked.

"Physics shit," she said glumly.

"I never liked it either. But that was a long time ago."

"Really." She turned over a page of notes and glared at it, as though it couldn't possibly have been her own handwriting.

"Do I get three cheers for being a good daddy because I have replenished the family supply of Diet Pepsi, Tab, Diet Coke, and sugar-free Dr. Pepper?" he asked brightly.

"TWO cheers for a useful daddy," Patty said with a mischievous grin.

He went upstairs, hid the champagne in his study, and returned to the kitchen.

It was their first conversation about death. Maybe the next time Eileen was a bit tuned they could talk about other serious things.

Like life. The rest of.

As he was stuffing some of the precious nectar into the refrigerator, Patty yelled from the front of the house, "There's an operator-six call for you on the bulletin board."

A 213 area code. Someone calling him from Los Angeles. Could it possibly be Parn?

It was indeed.

"Hi, Brother," the former Monsignor Parnell Luke Kane said cheerfully, "how'ya doing?"

"Struggling along," Red replied uneasily. Cheerful weekend calls had never been in Parnell's line.

It was not a cheerful weekend call. Parn had lost most of his money in a big land development scheme that had folded "about three weeks before the Reagan recovery would have salvaged us." He still had a few dollars, of course, and no one in the family would starve. His marriage was on the rocks. Lorraine and the kids had already moved out; she had turned out to be a bit of a bitch anyway. There was a new woman in the picture, he might marry her someday—not right now, however, not until he got back on his feet again.

Parn was no longer a little boy. Forty-seven years old and a failure in two careers. Yet the voice at the other end of the line was as boyishly enthusiastic as ever, the same indefatigable charm that had conned his mother and hypnotized ecclesiastical authorities.

"Coach, the thing is," Parn went on blithely, "that I need a little bit of money to tide me over for a couple of weeks. I'll be able to arrange a bank loan soon and get everything straightened out then, and, of course, I'll pay you back. I wonder if you could help out?"

"Of course. How much do you need?" Parn had cadged money almost all his life, as a little kid in grammar school wanting to buy a Good Humor, a seminarian needing money for a summer trip, a young priest wanting to buy presents in Rome. When his spectacular rise in the Chicago Chancery began, Parn no longer asked Red for money—perhaps because he had found more affluent patrons. Now the cycle was beginning again.

"A thousand or two, say, twenty-five hundred?" Parn said in the same tone of voice in which he had once asked for a nickel Good Humor bar.

"I'll get a check off to you Monday morning," Red replied. After all, he did have the money. Neither he, Eileen, nor the kids would suffer because of the gift.

"Great," Parn said enthusiastically. "Hey, would you send it express mail?"

"No problem."

"How're things going in the diocese?" Parn asked, much as he would ask how the Chicago White Sox looked for next year.

"I'm not all that close to what's going on in the diocese."

"Hell, I don't know why I asked you that. For a couple of seconds I thought I was talking to the priest. I'm the priest in the family, not you. Funny, isn't it?"

"I left after my sophomore year," Red said lamely.

"Well, great to talk to you again, Bro. Let's stay in touch. And don't forget to send it express mail."

He didn't even say thanks, Red noted to himself. Of course, he never said thanks for the Good Humor bars either.

In one day, two people momentarily think I'm a priest, one of them my brother; and my wife, who obviously knows about most if not all my adultery, says that I look like a priest. I need a drink.

December 6, 1983

Kane's Korner

THE USELESSNESS OF MEN

by Redmond Peter Kane

It may be that the world cannot dispense with men. We will still be required, unless Herself intervenes with a new dispensation, to make a biological contribution to procreation. Beyond that we are becoming increasingly obsolescent.

I walk down Michigan Avenue on a cold winter day and see a kid (girl-person variety) 5′1″ tall shivering in the cold, directing traffic. She reminds me not so much of my seventeen-year-old as of my fifteen-year-old. Instantly I want to protect her. It's not right that this poor young woman should be braving the elements on Michigan Avenue on a frigid December day. Some strong boy-person type should be doing it. That's what men are for. Women should be home where it's warm.

I'd probably feel sorry, because there's still a bit of the

bleeding-heart liberal left in me, for a cop of either sex of any age suffering from the winter weather on Michigan Avenue. Can't we get computers or something to do that kind of work? Yet to tell you the truth, I am still sufficiently a male chauvinist (or whatever) to be especially sorry about the plight of the girl-person cop.

And if I offered her my sympathies, she would probably drag me over to the Chicago Avenue Police Station for publicly insulting a police officer.

All of this is by way of introduction. Yesterday, I wended my way to the Everett McKinley Dirksen Federal Building, slipped by the grinning Calder Lobster, which does not ever seem to be affected by the cold, and rode up the elevator saying a prayer for the repose of the soul of Everett McKinley Dirksen, who is probably putting them to sleep in heaven even now, to watch the closing arguments in re *United States of America* v. *Leroy "Hurricane" Houston*. I went, not because the Hurricane was one of my favorites when he was dunking them for the Chicago Bulls and dozing whenever the other team had the basketball. I went there because The Woman was heading the Hurricane's defense team.

It was the first time I was ever in the courtroom when The Woman was arguing a case and I sort of scrunched down in the farthest corner so that neither she nor any of the other legal geniuses from Minor, Grey, and Blatt would know I was there. Everyone tells me that The Woman is a superlative trial lawyer. I don't doubt it. As far as I can tell, she's good at absolutely everything.

I've stayed away from her courtrooms for the same reason, I presume, that she does not sneak into the city room of the *Herald Gazette* and watch me peck out this column (I report a couple of days each week to City Hall how long it takes, so that the Mayor won't worry about my overworking). If your spouse is in a career, you want to stay away lest you embarrass said spouse. It's a very Irish way of doing things.

Hurricane Houston's crime, if you've been following the case in this distinguished journal or on competing media, is that he is not very bright and, relatively speaking, a celebrity. He messed up a couple of loan applications when he was trying to fend off the vultures who pick clean the bones of celebrities who are not very bright. It's not at all clear that anybody would have lost any money through these omissions of LeRoy "Hurricane" Houston's if the United States of America, in the person of its Attorney for the Northern District of Illinois, had not decided to drag the Hurricane before a grand jury.

An absolutely certain way to push someone over the edge into bankruptcy is to drag him before a federal grand jury.

Why go after an unfortunate like Leroy "Hurricane" Houston? The answer is that he is a celebrity. If you are Donald B. Roscoe, the aforementioned United States Attorney for the Northern District of Illinois, and you want to get to be Governor the same way Jim Thompson did, i.e., by piling up a record for convicting celebrities, then you indict folks like the Hurricane, drag out the trial, make it a courtroom spectacular, take a strong and stern stand in favor of honesty, integrity, and virtue, and sadly lament the bad example given to young athletes by the Hurricane's offenses. That absolutely guarantees you 90 seconds of coverage on both the five o'clock and the ten o'clock news for several weeks.

What better way to move into the Governor's Mansion when Jim Thompson finally decides that it's not nearly as big as the White House?

Not to put a too fine edge on the matter, Donald B. Roscoe is a bully. He's pushing around Leroy Houston, not because that poor unfortunate is any threat to the aforementioned United States of America, but because it's a splendid way for an ambitious young political hack to obtain free publicity.

Roscoe lives up to his advance billing. He storms, he pouts, he slams on the table. He protests, he laments. Outside of Yuri Andropov, Leroy Houston is undoubtedly the greatest single living threat to the welfare of the Republic. You watch the faces on the jury. Nine of them are black, and all nine are embarrassed by what this grown-up black juvenile delinquent has done. Don Roscoe is a bully and a ham actor but, mostly by luck I suspect, he has bullied these black jurors, especially the six women on it, into thinking they will have to answer for gross negligence at God's Judgment seat unless they send the Hurricane off for six months on the basketball team at the Federal Correctional Institution in Lexington, Kentucky.

So long, Hurricane, it's been good to know you.

Then The Woman begins her summary. You have to confess to yourself she does indeed look like a nun college president, and talks like one too, soft, gentle, apologetic.

At that point you want to leap up, charge down the aisle, break most of Don Roscoe's buck teeth, and expose, as only the Poor Man's Mike Royko could, the frivolity of the United States of America wasting its time and money in a ridiculous effort to put Hurricane Houston behind bars.

You restrain yourself, but with difficulty. It ain't fair that this sweet, lovely woman should have to fight such a nasty bully. When you calm down it dawns on you that the jurors are listening attentively, and the women jurors are kind of nodding in agreement. How clever of The Woman. But she's always been clever. Don Roscoe may be a bully, but he's not nearly a clever enough bully. Hooray for The Woman!

There are more summaries and then a bitter procedural wrangle between Roscoe and The Woman. Roscoe does his thing again—apparently he has one thing—he shouts, he laments, he protests, he pounds, he outrages. The judge turns to The Woman. She says a few words so meekly and softly that you can't even hear. Roscoe is now so outraged that you're afraid he will go into convulsions. You're half out of your seat, ready to storm down the aisle and throttle the bully: How dare he hurl such abuse at Your Woman? The Woman spins on her heel, and hands on her hips stares at Roscoe with calm amusement.

"Really, Mr. Roscoe, His Honor, the jury, and counsel for the defense have had ample opportunity during this trial to observe your histrionics. Don't you think it would really be much wiser for you to dispense with them now?"

The jury laughs.

Honest! They laugh. You sink back into your chair. No need to throttle anyone. Don Roscoe was probably going to lose anyway. Now he's blown it sky-high. The judge, suppressing his own smile, admonishes The Woman mildly. One black woman juror is grinning broadly. They have not exaggerated. The Woman is indeed a superb trial lawyer.

She can handle bullies like Donald Bane Roscoe all by herself. She does not require you to charge down the aisle and work mayhem on such bullies. Atta girl!

Or maybe atta person!

You feel quite proud. And thoroughly useless.

The Lord God began to screw Redmond Kane, as he saw the matter, on December 7, the forty-second anniversary of the Japanese attack on Pearl Harbor. Two sneak attacks. Having frustrated Red's final endeavor to find out what the Lord God wanted him to do about Harvard Gunther and Eileen Ryan from one of his priests, the aforementioned Lord God began to play games.

When Red looked back on the events of the day, he could not find any clues of what was about to happen. The emerald, of course, was a big mistake. But how could he have known that beforehand?

Troubles had been mounting rapidly, piling up in great big mountain chains of worry. Yet there was no hint in the troubles of what would happen to bring Red's world tumbling down.

He was restless, nervous, impatient, uneasy about the outcome of the trial, troubled by Eileen's failure to comment on his column about her, fretful about the silence of Great Western on the book, concerned about the delay of the final confrontation with Harvard Gunther. He found himself periodically itching for his cigarettes and longing for the quiet afternoon hours in an alcoholic haze at the Ale House. He snapped impatiently at the food editor when she brought him her customary (since the Feast of All the Saints) morning cup of herbal tea and was brief and curt with Lee Malley when that worthy stopped by to gossip about the implications for journalistic employment in Chicago with the Murdoch takeover at the *Sun-Times*.

"We'll let the *Trib* pick up Mike Royko without even making a counterbid," Malley said, jamming his hands into his tight-fitting jeans pockets in disgust.

"What need does the *Herald Gazette* have for a Rich Man's Red Kane, anyway?" Red stabbed, spinning back to his CRT. "Maybe Brad Winston could arrange a straight player trade. No, they're so cheap upstairs they'd expect Murdoch to give them Royko and next year's first-round draft choice for me."

Lee took the hint and drifted away.

Yet Red did not notice at the time how tense and excited he was. Later he would say to Blackie, "... teetering on the edge."

Not having heard a word from Eileen, he called Nick Curran at Minor, Grey, and Blatt. "Nick? Red. Is the jury still out?"

"Still out," Nick responded. A decent man as always, Curran did not express surprise that Eileen had not phoned him. "Judge Neenan is very upset. You know how he is. Kept them up most of the night and hasn't ordered lunch for them yet. There's a rumor floating around that they may hand it down this afternoon. Eileen thinks there's one or two holdouts on the jury."

"Against conviction?"

"Hell, no, against acquittal. The question now is whether there is going to be a hung jury and another trial for poor Hurricane. I don't think any of us could take that."

"Don Roscoe would love it," Red snorted. "Another chance to appear on the evening news denouncing the corruption of sports figures. From Roscoe's perspective a hung jury may be even better than a conviction."

Red debated whether he should eat lunch, go over to the East Bank Club for a swim, or sneak into the back of the courtroom at the Dirksen Federal Building. He left his office, convinced that his destination was the East Bank Club, but somehow he ended up at the far corner of the plush, paneled courtroom of Judge John Francis Neenan, the punctilious, difficult, and fussy man who, like most other federal judges, assumed that his appointment to the federal bench was proof of his superior wisdom and virtue (when in fact it was only proof of his superior political connections). The courtroom was tense and expectant when Red slipped in. "They're coming back in in a few moments," a young reporter from the *Herald Gazette*, whose name Red didn't quite remember, whispered in his ear.

Judge Neenan's attitude toward the jury as it filed, or rather stumbled, into the courtroom was that of a parochial school primary teacher dealing with tardy students. His "Have you reached a verdict?" implied that whether or not they had, they were bound at least for Sister Superior's office and, quite possibly, for Monsignor's.

It was the first time Red had ever been in a courtroom to listen to a jury verdict in one of his wife's trials.

"And what is that verdict?" demanded Judge Neenan imperiously. It turned out that the jury had decided that the United States of America had failed to prove its case against Hurricane Houston. "Not guilty!"

Hurricane exploded into the air as if he were dunking from the left side of the basket, and then did a little dance in front of the jury bench, much as a wide receiver would after catching a touchdown pass. His family and friends yelled their enthusiastic support. For a few terrible moments Judge Neenan's courtroom seemed remarkably like Chicago Stadium. Red thought the judge might have apoplexy on the spot.

Hurricane kissed Eileen solidly and spun her around in a victory whirl, as if she, perhaps, were the cheerleader for the team. Naturally she did not lose her composure, not even when he kissed her and swatted her rump as if she had made two free throws.

Red waited in the corridor at the back of the press mob waiting to hear statements from the winners and the losers. "It was a hard-fought case," Don Roscoe said, his protruding teeth gleaming brightly. "The important thing is that we have taught the young people of America that their athletic heroes, even the most famous, are not above the law."

It was, Red believed, what was commonly referred to in limousine-liberal circles as a "moral victory."

"We done stomped 'em!" Hurricane hollered. "We done

stomped 'em real good!" which for Hurricane was a fairly elaborate sentence.

Eileen was tired and drawn, a mother who had spent the whole night with a sick child. "A jury of his peers has found Mr. Houston not guilty of the crimes with which he was charged," she said quietly. "Unfortunately, no jury will be able to sit in judgment of why he was ever brought to trial. No jury will ever render a verdict on the question of whether the crime Mr. Houston committed was that of being a celebrity. No jury will ever decide whether the money of the American taxpayers was wasted in an unseemly search for prosecutorial publicity."

"Are you saying that Don Roscoe sought this indictment just for publicity purposes?" demanded a young woman reporter from Channel 2.

"I don't believe that's what I said," Eileen replied mildly.

"You implied it!"

"I don't think I did." She permitted herself a small smile. "If I thought that, I might advise my client to seek redress for malicious prosecution in a civil suit."

"Are you going to file such a suit?" the woman reporter insisted.

"I doubt it." Eileen allowed herself another smile. "Now if you will excuse me, I have to return to my office and catch up on the mail."

"Nice goin', kid," Red said as his wife strode by him.

She stopped and turned in surprise. "Red! I didn't know you were here."

"Stopped by for the two-minute drill." He shook hands solemnly with her. "And in case you needed help to climb down off the tree after that Bantu dance!"

"Looking for material for another column?" she asked calmly.

In the weeks ahead Red would ponder often that question. It was a hint that the romance between the new Red Kane and his wife was in trouble. At the time he missed the significance of her question. He thought only that it was a shame she had misunderstood the point of the column, but that he could explain it later on. Moreover, her mood changed almost at once to affectionate gratitude. "Already two days ahead. I wanted to tell you that the kids were doing fine. I also wondered if I might buy you supper?"

"Before or after a session at the Doral Plaza?" Her mysterious green eyes probed at him as though he were a stranger she was trying to analyze.

"That's up to you," he said quietly.

"I'll have to spend some time with my client and his family." She nodded. "I'll see you in a couple of hours."

"I meant it." He kissed her forehead. "You were sensational in there."

"It was really a very simple case," she shrugged off his compliment. "Often it's much more difficult to defend a case against a stupid prosecutor than against an intelligent one."

"You understand, then, what it's like to work for editors."

At last she laughed, a beat-out laugh, but still a moderately happy one. "I guess so. And you, poor man?" She touched his hand. "You have to put up with it every day, not just during trial. See you soon. I do want to be with my husband." She smiled weakly. "He's such a sweet man."

"Meet you in your office and walk over?" he asked lightly.

"Wonderful. I'm so tired I might not be able to find it."

"Maybe you should sleep first?"

She touched his lips with her finger. "Second."

She returned his kiss on the forehead and then edged her way into the melee of fans celebrating around Hurricane Houston. The Hurricane had been found not guilty by a jury of his peers, but the jury had not returned any of the money that had been, quite legally, removed from his pockets by his agents, advisers, and fair-weather friends. The best the ex–basketball star could hope for was an assistant coaching position at a high school or possibly, if he were very lucky, a small college. The best trial lawyers in the country could not salvage him from that fate.

And the worst? Drugs and an early death.

An all-American sports success story.

Red considered writing a column on the subject and then decided that he would hold off for a while, at least until he could sort out why Eileen objected to the piece he had done about watching her in the courtroom.

Uneasy, but not terribly worried, Red checked in at the

Herald Gazette and discovered that there were no phone messages for him from Harvard Gunther.

Somehow, he had made the decision that he knew all along he would have to make. He would accuse Gunther of the murder of Adele Ward and see what happened.

He made sure that his present had not been stolen from his pocket. Wouldn't do to lose it now. Then he tossed two crank phone messages into dead center of the wastebasket and, confidence in his masculinity reassured, strode out of his pastel cubicle.

His phone rang. He hesitated, then decided to answer it.

The Toledo reporter, with more information on Adele's parents. "The Warrens have been acting strangely, Red. I followed your instructions and stayed away from them. But the paper tried to get an interview as part of a series on missing children—it's a hot subject this year after that TV program. They wouldn't talk to our reporter and then skipped town. Does any of this fit with what you know?"

Red's heart skipped a beat and lunged toward his throat. If the Warrens were nervous, might that make Harv nervous?

"Maybe, Ted. If there's a story about them, I'll give you first shot at it in your territory."

His head pounding from both lust for battle and lust for woman, he walked back to Jackson Boulevard and Eileen's office.

She leaned briefly against him. "Maybe I should have stayed with musical comedy."

He held her close. "You're sounding like you lost, kid."

"I'm sounding like someone who isn't sure that the whole shitty game is worth it."

"Tsk-tsk, such language."

"Wash my mouth out with soap."

"I have a better suggestion."

"Oh?" She grinned wearily. "Let's get on with it then."

Her comment did not seem to be a complaint, however. Quite the contrary, she leaned on his arm during the walk back to Michigan Avenue in the near-zero weather and praised him.

"You've been so sweet through all this mess, Red. I can't tell you how grateful I am."

She sagged in his arms as soon as she had entered the Doral studio. "Take me someplace where I can sleep in the sunlight for six weeks," she said wearily.

"You'll have to pay for it, of course."

"In a number of different ways, I'm sure." She tittered and leaned on him even more heavily. "I'm sorry if I seemed short over at the Dirksen Building. I was glad to see you and very happy you came. It meant a lot to me."

"You were sensational." He hugged her as tightly as he could. "When they go after me, I'll insist that you be my lawyer. It'll be fun throwing you up into the jungle trees when it's over."

Eileen needed reassurance of her worth as a woman and a human being. It was a night for sweet and leisurely sex instead of manic passion. He undressed her slowly, as she swayed and sighed, removing her pink underwear with almost religious reverence.

Her naked beauty filled him with affection and desire. Slowly, slowly, he told himself.

Carefully he caressed her face, as though he were discovering its outlines for the first time. Eileen's body was taut with expectation, but she accepted his slow play submissively. Then he kissed her as if he were a kid in sixth grade on his first date. Again. And again. And yet again. Eileen quivered with scarcely controlled emotion.

"Red...," she murmured, "I'm going out of my mind."

"Ah, woman," he said in his phony Irish brogue, which always made her snicker, "'tis yourself that doesn't have any more clothes to remove."

"Red." She blushed. "You're embarrassing me."

"Ah, I intend to do a lot more than that. Still, I suppose that, since you're such a famous trial lawyer and all, I ought to put something decent on you before we proceed to the main event."

He removed the emerald from its box, fastened the chain at the back of her neck, and rested it on her chest, just above the joining of her breasts.

"Sure, it's the smallest and the most expensive nightwear that you've ever had."

Her vast green eyes filled with tears. "Oh, Red." She held

the gem in her hand. "It's so lovely. You shouldn't have. I don't deserve—"

"'Twas very dear," he ignored her protest. "But worth it. Sure, 'tis on your account at Tiffany's, but I'll pay for it when the bill comes."

"Thank you," she blubbered, and hugged him enthusiastically. "I love you, I love you, I love you."

"Course you do." He patted her again where Leroy Houston had swatted her, reasserting his rights to that delectable part of her.

She drew away from him and examined the gem again, now unaware of her nudity and their increasing sexual arousal, as though in its green rays she could find some hidden truth.

"It matches your eyes," he said foolishly, as his fingers brushed a breast.

"Does it?" She glanced up at him. "Green-eyed witch, huh?"

"I have evil designs on you, green-eyed witch," he said softly. His hands rushed lightly and quickly from her shoulders to her thighs, then made the return journey more slowly and forcefully.

"No, Red, that's not what I want today. Let me do it to you." She smiled shyly. "My malted-milk thing. A way of saying thanks for all the support during the trial."

"I'll never say no to that." He permitted her to ease him back on the bed and relaxed, as happy as he'd ever been in this, open, trusting, vulnerable. Hers to love however she wanted.

Her fingers and her lips began their sweet, delicate, affectionate pilgrimage. She whispered words of tender affection into his ear. His being began to disintegrate. *Each time this happens*, he thought, *I feel like I'm going to die and at the same time live forever.*

Eileen, creature of light, was blessed with the lightest fingers and the lightest lips, the most radiant smile and the most happy laughter in the world. Her subtle body was wind and air and, alternately, moonlight and sunlight, gentle waves and lazy surf, spring zephyr and winter wind.

Then, as she guided him, drenched in poignant sweetness

and healed of all his hurts and regrets, slowly and skillfully to the shining mountaintops of their lovemaking, Red knew that he had finally unlocked the secret of his magic, green-eyed wife just as she had unlocked the secret of healing his accumulated pain.

He had not yet discovered all the wonderful mysteries that were in her—that would take forever—but he had cracked open the critical mystery of how to love her. He perceived, with absolute clarity, or so it seemed to him then, what he must do and be and say in order to make Eileen a happy woman and keep her happy. His insight went far beyond physical skills. He would not only make love to Eileen, but he would love her, and being loved, she would be happy and his. The pride, the enormous shattering pride that went with that realization, was not a pride of possession, but rather the pride that comes from knowing at long last who one must be and what one must do.

Eileen prolonged their pleasure to the last possible moment and then they passed through the crucible of excruciating delight. Her cry of joy was long and piercing.

Good enough for you, Red thought, thoroughly satisfied with himself.

Then he saw the green gem, glowing between her breasts, as she lifted herself off him. The stone captured his eyes and would not release them. It was part of their pleasure, however, not an obsession. Not yet.

What happened next was utterly distinct from sex, as he told both his shrink, who wouldn't listen, and Blackie, who would.

He was drowsily slipping along the down side of ecstasy into a contented afterglow. He and Eileen, their bodies both greasy with sweat, were more or less automatically disengaging from each other, both of them now seeking a complacent nap as much as they had sought ecstasy a few moments before. Dreamily Red noticed how spectacularly beautiful she was after lovemaking and felt a vague but powerful contentment that he finally knew how to love her in bed and out.

The light from the emerald grew in power and filled the room.

The bed, the room, the Doral Plaza, the Chicago skyline, the cosmos turned into fluid chaos. Desperately Red reached for his wife, a last wild grasp for stability and protection.

Then, again, the swooshing sound of the cosmic baseball bat. It was not exactly a sound, because it was nothing you heard, but rather a signal, an advance warning, a loud primal cry that perhaps might be translated, upon later reflection, "Look out, buster, old Yahweh is here again!"

Red had a moment to wonder how he would explain to his wife what was happening. Then the love that had lurked behind the green glass skyscraper at 333 Wacker Drive swooped with ah! bright wings into the small studio apartment and took possession of him.

No, rather the Holy Ghost, or Whatever, erupted from the emerald and from his wife's swelling breasts. Yes, of course, warm breast. Eileen was not merely the occasion of this new love that invaded their room and their bed of pleasure. She and the love were temporarily bound together in one eternal love.

Later, trying to analyze the experience, Red felt that someone was saying to him, in effect, "You like her, huh? I'm glad you do, because I made her for you. I like her too. She's mine. In fact, she's Me."

So his naked and sweating wife was not exactly a partner, nor a witness, nor even a trigger for the other. Rather she was a hint, an early spring flower promising July warmth.

It was like Wacker Drive: light, heat, fire, overwhelming, invading, possessing love; dazzling truth, beauty, and goodness; confidence, hope, joy, the promise that all would be well; a love so unspeakably powerful that, in the instant it possessed Red, he knew he could never escape from it. Nor would it ever permit him and Eileen to escape from one another. When the joy seemed so intense that he knew he would die, the operator of this transcendental Concorde jet turned on the afterburners and Red thought he had died and was in heaven, a golden city whose ivory walls were his wife's breasts.

Then Eileen was shaking him anxiously. "Dear God in heaven, Red, what's wrong? What's the matter? Are you sick? Red, I love you, I love you!! Oh, my darling, you're not dying on me, are you? I can't bear to lose you! Red, please don't leave me!"

He was aware that he was crying and shouting, that he was caught up in a delirium of happiness. "I'm not going to die, Eileen." He bubbled with laughter. "Neither one of us is ever going to die. And I'll never leave you!"

"God help us, Red." She searched his face anxiously. "I've been afraid for weeks that you were having a nervous breakdown. I'll call a doctor. Dear God in heaven, don't take him away from me!"

Book FIVE

Prayer of Someone Who Has Been There Before
After the last time—
when I finally turned from flight
and from somewhere came the strength
to go back—
I rummaged the ruins,
a refugee picking through bombed belongings
for what surely was destroyed
and began again
I grew my new life
thick and rough
with an alarm system on the heart
and an escape hatch in the head.
It was as spontaneous
as a military campaign.
I loved in small amounts
like a sick man sipping whiskey.
Each day was lived within its limits
Each moment swallowed quickly.
It was not all—our embracement of life
but neither was it the hunched
and jabbing stance of the boxer.
There was courtesy and a sort-of caring
It was not bad.

Now this,
This thing—This feeling
this unbidden intrusion
which had no part to play
but played it anyway.
All those things scrupulously screened out
  want in.
And I can sense it coming,
a second coming,
a second shattering.
Someone—Something
is at me once more,
mocking my defenses,
wrenching my soul.
God damn it!
Is it you again, Lord?

—John Shea

53

The next day the afterburners were still working. Red was as high as a NASA satellite. And moving.

Not that anyone would have noticed. He had learned from his previous collision with the Transcendental Designated Hitter how to mask his reactions, behavior that both the shrink and Blackie, in almost their only agreement, would later tell him was unwise.

With extraordinary difficulty he reassured his terrified wife that he had merely experienced a "postcoital high." Eileen had never heard of such highs (Red had not either, for that matter), but, somewhat reluctantly, she had accepted his glib explanation.

And glib he certainly was. *You may be a voyeur,* he told his persistent Friend, *but you certainly do unloose the tongue of an Irishman.*

Red realized that if he was to keep his secret a secret, he must even restrain his verbal facility, a terribly difficult task. He never asked himself whether the secret ought to remain a secret. It was unthinkable to share it with anyone else. They would think he was crazy.

"You're looking mighty chipper today, Redmond Peter Kane," said Lee Malley, leaning against his desk.

"The Woman won her case," Red said simply.

"Chipper" was scarcely the word for it. Red was bursting with happiness, serenely confident that the love that was still blazing inside of him would enable him to sweep away whatever little minor obstacles stood as a barrier to a happy, creative, productive life.

"Would you really go to work for Murdoch?" Lee sniffed his herbal tea lovingly.

"Do you think he'd want me after I suggested he was an undesirable alien?"

Lee Malley thought that he might. Murdoch was interested in selling newspapers, not in settling grudges. Lee had heard that after he'd bought the paper, Murdoch had sat down with some of the senior people across the river and gone through page after page ridiculing the dullness of the paper. The *Sun-Times* people, he thought, had been too busy for the past five years or so basking in self-praise for their liberalism and their investigative exposés to realize that, take Royko and the comics away and they were dullsville. They'd been resting on their laurels for a long time, hadn't they?

"And on their asses at Ricardo's." Red was drinking his coffee black these days, and only a few cups, too. No more twenty cups a day like when he was the old Red Kane. "Not that they had any monopoly on that. Being a reporter is better than working for a living."

"There will be a lot of musical chairs," Malley observed. "Stars leaving the *Sun-Times* to move across Michigan Avenue to the *Tribune* or across the river to the *Herald Gazette;* and ambitious younger people moving in the opposite direction, if they can satisfy their consciences and risk the barbs of disgruntled liberals at Ricardo's."

Lee was clearly assessing his own position and the possibilities of rising quickly in a Murdoch-owned *Sun-Times*. *More power to him,* thought Red. *Most of the liberals who would complain about the "sellouts" working for Murdoch would themselves sell out if the proper price were offered.*

"I heard that when he met with a bunch of Chicago civic leaders, your friend Harv Gunther was there." Lee tossed his teacup into a wastebasket.

"I'd rather work for Murdoch than Harv." Red blew on his coffee. "Although Harv pays his reporters pretty well."

"You don't really believe those stories about Gunther buying reporters, do you?" Lee's eyes were wide with partially feigned disbelief.

"Come on, Lee, there's no profession that doesn't have some members who can be bought, including, maybe I should say especially including, the priesthood. Ever since Jake Lingle, the *Tribune* reporter, was shot on the way to the I.C. train because his masters in the Capone crowd thought he had betrayed them, there have been bought reporters in this town. Some sell out for money, some for sex, some for a chance to rub shoulders with the mighty, some because they enjoy feeling that they have power and influence, some because it's a quick way to get news leaks and stories."

"I don't know any."

"I do. Mind you, like every other form of corruption, it's easy to kid yourself at the beginning. You're doing a favor for a friend, hushing up something that's not very important, or giving someone a boost that doesn't do any harm. Then you get deeper and deeper, a little bit more dependent on their gifts and a little bit more afraid of blackmail."

"Nobody's ever tried to bribe me." Lee laughed a bit too nervously.

"Maybe you ought to do an exposé."

"And end up like Jake Lingle?"

Immediately after Lee had ambled back to his own desk, the phone rang. A sexy voice announced that Mr. Gunther now had time to talk to Mr. Kane.

"Speak of the devil," Red muttered.

"Pardon?"

"I was talking to someone else," Red said smoothly.

He did most of his interviewing nowadays on the phone, partly because it was easier and partly because people were a little bit more unguarded on the phone. Mostly, however, because it was easier.

Today, though, Red wished there were a way to get around the custom. He wanted to see the expression on Harv Gunther's face when he started talking about Adele Ward, to watch the spittle drool from his twisted mouth. But to propose a personal interview would needlessly alert Gunther that something was up.

He flipped on his recorder. The warning ping elicited a response from its mate at the other end of the line.

Cradling the phone against his shoulder, Red opened his locked file and removed the Adele Ward folder. He placed it on his desk and opened to the first page of Rita Lane's statement.

"First of all," Harv's voice boomed with bonhomie, "congratulations to your wife on saving that poor coon. It was a ridiculous indictment to begin with."

"Eileen doesn't give herself much credit for beating a dummy like Don Roscoe," Red said lightly.

"She's still the best defense lawyer in town. If any of the people in the Pulaski business are ever put in the same treadmill as Houston, I suggest they hire her. Would you think it was a conflict of interest?"

A genuine question or a dodge? A dodge, probably. "I don't make Eileen's ethical decisions for her, Harv. I mean, I wouldn't if I were asked and I've never been asked."

"Fair enough. I'm sorry I didn't get back to you earlier, but these times between Thanksgiving and Christmas are terribly busy—charities all over the place, you know. If you really want to talk about the Pulaski affair, I'll answer your questions; but it seems to me it's a pretty dead horse now."

So Red began once again to trace the tedious and intricate paths of inequity in the demolition business. Gunther's answers were smooth and confident. Obviously, the whole affair had been settled. Most likely anyone who could verify Red's tips had been bought off.

Afterward, Red would be convinced that if the cosmic bat had not pounded against his head the previous night and left him both deliriously happy and at the fine edge of his verbal and intellectual talents, he would not have been able to win the game with Harvard Gunther. And, as he said to Blackie, "It was a damn shame I did win it."

"The good guys don't win often," the Monsignor reflected, as he rearranged the positions of the wise men in the Nativity scene on his end table, moving the black wise man from the last to the first position.

As he neared the end of his list of questions, Red had the sensation of turning on the automatic pilot, moving into passing gear, switching on an altered state of consciousness, unleashing the genie from a bottle. Another Red Kane, not the new one or the old one, took over from the depths of his personality—maybe the Red Kane whose genes were inherited from a father who had fought with Michael Collins against the Black and Tans.

"Incidentally, Harv, what did it feel like when you were killing Adele Ward? Was murdering a sexual partner the biggest thrill you've ever had?"

There was a moment of total and profound silence, a deserted graveyard late at night. Red breathed deeply, waiting for the worst.

"What the hell are you talking about?" Harv yelled at him.

"Did you plan to do it beforehand? Did you tell yourself that you were finally going to find out what a real-life snuff scene was like? Or was it spur-of-the-moment artistry?"

"I don't have to listen to this—"

"It certainly sounds like fun." Red began to read from the verbatim descriptions in Rita Lane's statement, flipping the Polaroid photos as he talked. The manila folder was tilted toward him so that no one else in the city room could see portraits of a young woman's hideous suffering.

"You can't prove a thing." Harv's voice was now raw and shaky. Red had hit him where it hurt.

"Harvard, I've got pictures."

"I'll cut off your wife's tits, throw acid on your kids' faces; I'll hack off your balls and throw you into the river if you try to print that stuff," Harv thundered.

He had forgotten about the two tape recorders, even though they pinged faithfully every fifteen seconds.

"I wouldn't even try that if I were you," Red said, trying to sound calm despite the ice that was rising in the pit of his stomach. "The people of Chicago have the right to know about this crime. Nothing you can do will stop them from knowing."

Gunther then blew his cool completely. "You have those pictures over here in my office by closing time today, or I'll kill you, and I'll make your wife and kids wish they'd never been born."

"Are you threatening me?" Red asked.

"A quarter million dollars for those prints."

"No, thanks, Mr. Gunther."

Red hung up softly. How long would it take Gunther to realize that everything was on the recorder and that he had not only committed indictable crimes on the telephone but given the *Herald Gazette* a perfect opening for printing the story of Adele Ward?

His first call was to Mike Casey the Cop. "Mike?"

"Red."

"Harv blew his cool, gave me enough confirmation of the murder so we can go with the story. Made some pretty brutal threats to me and Eileen and the kids."

"Okay," Mike said promptly. "I'll get my men out and tip off some of the people in the department who might be interested. I won't tell them much, though."

"Fine. I'll be back to you."

"Red . . . don't hang up. It's going to be chancy. Gunther's slipping. He's got bumblers working for him. I think we can take care of it, but don't take any risks that you don't have to. . . ."

"Don't worry about me, Mickey. Take care of Eileen and the kids."

"I'll take care of everybody," Mickey said in almost a whisper.

Then he dialed Eileen's direct-dial number at the law firm.

"Ms. Kane," she said calmly.

"Eileen, we're finally moving on the Harv Gunther thing. He made some threats. I've talked with Mike Casey about security for you and the kids. Be careful."

"Of course," she said crisply. "What do you have on him, if I may ask?"

"A real-life snuff film. He murdered a fourteen-year-old prostitute."

"Oh, my God. Go get him, Red. Don't worry about us."

As Red later tried to argue with Eileen and the shrink, she had behaved that morning just the way he knew she would—calm, confident, supportive, a woman for whom bravery in a time of crisis was a given. If she had said anything, absolutely anything, to indicate that she wished he would drop the story, he would have called Gunther back instantly and called the game on account of darkness. Then he buzzed Wilson Allen.

"Wils, I'm sitting on the story of the decade, maybe the story of the quarter century. It's dynamite. Give me an hour to do it, and then I have to see you and Brad. If we go with it, we must go with it tomorrow."

"You have it all nailed down?" Wils asked anxiously. "We can't afford a mistake these days. You know what the libel suits have been like."

"Believe me, Wils, there won't be a libel suit on this one. Eleven-thirty?"

Fretfully, the editor agreed. If the new Red Kane had not been so dominant that morning, the old Red Kane would have thought that Wilson Allen was truly a shithead. What kind of editor is it whose first worry when promised the story of the quarter century is about the libel laws?

Red rewound the tape and inserted the plug in his ear, searched for the proper spot in the conversation, and began to type his lead: "I'll cut off your wife's tits, throw acid in your kids' faces, I'll cut off your balls and throw you into the river." The piece went on: "Thus Harvard Gunther, distinguished civic leader and renowned Chicago political influential, threatened a reporter who read to him an affidavit describing the murder of a teenage prostitute."

Not a bad lead, Red decided. *Another Pulitzer? To hell with Pulitzers. This is to liberate Adele Ward from purgatory.*

At eleven-twenty, as he was finishing up the third of his two-thousand-word articles, the phone rang.

"How's it going, Redmond?" a familiar voice inquired.

"Not so bad." Red clenched his free fist. "How's yourself, Paul?"

"Middlin', middlin'. I wonder if I could have a few words with you?"

"Sure," Red said guardedly. *I should have expected this call.*

"Not on the phone," Paul said quickly.

"You name it."

"Well . . ." Paul was at his leisurely and debonair best. "I hear you hang around the Old Town Ale House these days. Nobody I know is likely to be there at, say, one-thirty, are they?"

"Not very likely. You have to judge the risks, Paul."

"Not many risks, Red. The young ones don't know me and the older ones wouldn't recognize me."

"It's your funeral, Paul."

"I hope it doesn't end up being yours." Paul was trying to sound ominous. "The old man is really fit to be tied."

"One-thirty at the Ale House. It will be good to see you again, Paul."

"Same here, kid, same here."

Red sat for a moment staring blankly at his CRT. *The most important man in my life. A man whose skill, ingenuity, and, I thought, integrity made concrete my abstract and dreamy ideals about journalism. And now he comes back from the dead to protect the murderer of little girls.*

Shit.

At eleven-thirty sharp he laid on Bradford Winston's vast—absolutely clean—mahogany desk the cheap printout paper with his three stories, the Polaroid pictures, and the affidavits. Then he placed next to the affidavits his black Sony cassette player. "Read the articles, look at the pictures, read the affidavits, and then I'll play the tape. Don't worry, there are the required beeps every fifteen seconds."

Winston and Allen turned pale after the first paragraph of the lead story. Both of them became visibly agitated.

"God, he could kill us in the courts." Allen's fingers were shivering as he flipped to the second page of the printout.

"If you can nail all this down," Winston said, displaying somewhat more journalistic sense than his editor, "it's another Pulitzer for us."

"Don't say a word until you've gone through all of it," Red insisted.

The second that Brad Winston had flipped closed the folder with Rita Lane's affidavits, Red pushed the play button on his Sony. Both men recoiled in horror as if a ghost had leapt at them from the cemetery when they heard Gunther's initial outburst. They listened in silence until Red turned the machine off.

"What do you think, Wilson?" Brad asked, trying to sound casual.

"Gosh, Bradford, I don't know. I think we ought to sit on it for a couple of days, give everyone a chance to calm down, talk it over with the lawyers, make sure we don't go off half-cocked."

"What about the risks to your family?" Winston's steel-gray eyes locked with Red's. "Aren't you putting them in enormous danger?"

"I've taken precautions."

"Is a crazy old man likely to become unpredictable and vengeful?"

"It would be self-defeating for him to follow through on any of those threats now that they're on tape."

"But still . . ." Wilson fidgeted with his Princeton tie. "It's an enormous risk."

"Do we have to make a decision now?" Winston was arranging, compulsively, the file folder, pictures, and the printouts in a neat little stack. "Maybe Wilson is right. Maybe we need a few days to think about it, check out the facts, that sort of thing."

"No way, Brad." Red reached across the desk and pulled the pile of materials toward himself. "I need a decision and I need it now. There are lots of people's lives at stake. My family, my informant, and my own, incidentally. We will all be in danger until the first edition hits the streets. Then Gunther will be powerless, and the police will be falling all over themselves trying to protect us in case he should finally go round the bend totally."

"I don't think there's enough here to convict him." Wilson Allen's trembling finger pointed in the general direction of the evidence, which Red had removed from the table and put protectively in his lap. "I don't think anybody would bring this into court."

"This isn't a Don Roscoe case." Red slammed his fist against the table. "You mean to tell me that you don't think Rich Daley would?"

"Gunther contributed to his father's campaigns." Winston leaned back in his chair thoughtfully.

"If you think that would make any difference, you don't . . ." Red decided to steer away from an argument about Chicago. "Look, I'm not sure about the legalities. Probably they'd need the eyewitness. If I were her, I wouldn't come. But it doesn't really matter whether Gunther's convicted on a murder charge. As soon as this story breaks, his whole empire will collapse, and all his trained canaries will be rushing to the microphones for their chance to sing. Hell, I have enough material in my file for four more stories on him. I'll start working on them this afternoon. If we run this story, Harvard Gunther is finished."

"He's an old man, Red." Allen was now playing nervously with his Cartier ballpoint pen. "Can we do this to an old man?"

"An old man who kills teenage girls and who might do it again? Come on, Wils, age is no excuse."

"He does have a point, you know." Brad Winston's smooth, unlined face was marred by an ever-so-slight touch of a frown, something that Red had never seen before. "He's a civic leader and we will have to live with a lot of heat for going after an old man with such a distinguished record of public service."

"Bullshit!" Red kicked the chair back. "He also has a long record of violating almost all laws of God and man. If the public doesn't have a right to know this story, then it doesn't have a right to know anything."

"Time. Just give us a little more time." Wilson Allen sounded like a teenager threatened with expulsion from high school.

"Maybe run it by the lawyers for a day or two..."

Red stood up and moved toward the door. "If that's the final decision, then all bets are off. You have my resignation effective at once. I will go over to Channel Two, and, if I make it alive, offer it to Jacobsen for the five o'clock news. From there I'll make a call to Rupert Murdoch. Take it or leave it."

"It's up to you, Brad." Allen shrugged his shoulders like the nervous errand boy he was. "I think it's a great story, a sure prize winner, but I think it needs more time."

Winston suppressed a mild yawn, a sure sign in Red's experience that he was anxious. It was the only sign. "You're putting us in a very difficult position. You realize that, don't you, Redmond?"

"You heard what that man said he was going to do to my wife and children, didn't you? Do you really expect me to give you a couple of days while he delivers on those threats?"

"Not really." Winston yawned again. *Damn his glacial WASP soul*, Red thought.

"With Murdoch coming into town, we could be in real trouble if this backfires on us," Allen pleaded anxiously.

"Let's leave poor old Rupert out of this." Bradford smoothed the carefully groomed brown hair. "We really don't have any choice, do we, Redmond?"

"None at all, Bradford."

"Then we're not going to go with it?" Allen said with obvious relief.

"Oh, quite the contrary, my dear boy." Bradford stood up, six feet three inches of slim, languid ease. "Go with it in the first edition."

54

A note was waiting for Red at the Ale House, neatly typed. "There's a house on North Park, half a block up, left-hand side, old Chicago balloon type, being rehabbed. The front door is open."

Red hesitated. *Another trap?*

Probably not. If they wanted to gun him down, they could just as well do it on the street. But they had no way of knowing what Red had done with his evidence. He might well have a doomsday machine ticking somewhere. As in fact he did. He still held the high cards.

And if I tell myself that often enough, maybe I'll begin to believe it.

He tucked the note into his coat pocket, turned up his collar, and walked out into the thickly falling snow.

Eileen and I have to go somewhere warm when this is over.

He considered carefully the house across the street. It was one of the last wrecks on the block, a tattered old wooden A-frame that might well have survived the Fire. Fifteen years ago it could have been bought for twenty thousand. Now the land alone was worth a couple of hundred thousand. Some smart heir had hung on to it for a long time, determined to squeeze the last penny out of oncoming yuppiedom.

Telling himself that he indeed had a doomsday machine, Red ducked his head against the cold wind, crossed the street, and climbed the stairs to the second-floor entrance, a relic of the day when Chicago was still a swamp.

He shoved against the old door. It didn't move, stubborn as all things old tend to become. He shoved again. Locked.

What the hell? He pulled out the note, looked up and down the street, and decided that this was surely the place.

No cars coming, no one with a .22 or maybe an Uzi pointed at his gut. He leaned his shoulder against the door and shoved again, this time with all his strength.

The door popped open.

Inside the house was gutted, no woodwork worth saving here like La Manse Kane up on Webster. Only a few blocks away. *Why am I not there with Eileen in my arms?*

He picked his way across the floor. It creaked and groaned beneath him. They could easily torch the old firetrap with him in it.

Not with my doomsday machine, they can't.

Still pretty confident about that machine, aren't you, fellow.

At the back there was a staircase, narrow and dubious, leading back down to the first floor. It looked like an entrance to a dark and dusty cave.

I've come this far, what the hell!

Red put his foot on the top step, hesitated and then began to pick his way down the stairs.

On the third step he lost his balance, stumbled, and then careened down to the ground floor.

"Careful, Red, a big guy like you could get hurt in this place."

At first Red did not recognize Paul O'Meara. The handsome, tan, silver-haired man sipping a bottle of Heineken's next to the snow-marked window seemed younger than Paul O'Meara was when he disappeared years ago. He looked as if he were Red's age, not more than ten years older. Then Paul tilted the beer bottle in his direction, an ironic salute, and grinned cheerfully. Same old Paul O'Meara grin.

Red could not help himself. "Good God, Paul, it's great to see you again."

"Same here, kid." He embraced Red warmly. "Age doesn't seem to have taken a toll on you at all."

"And it makes you look younger," Red replied honestly enough.

"Sit down," Paul said easily. "Want one of my beers? Or some Jameson's?" He produced a bottle from under the plank on which he was sitting. "Best I have in my office here is a paper cup."

"No one outside in a car with a twenty-two, Paul?" Red glanced out the window. "Or is this a little different from the Lower Level?"

"It was only a warning, kid. Nothing more. Believe me, if we wanted to get rid of you, we could. Easily. Should I open this bottle?"

Red eased himself into a battered mohair couch in the corner of the room. It was as cold inside as out. He needed a drink, if only to stay warm. Again he thought of Eileen.

"I've left the Creature alone. By the way, were you ever in Brazil?"

"I'm not a Nazi war criminal, kid." Paul's merry, crooked grin had not changed. "Only a reporter who needed a second chance in life."

So much for my psychic sense. How did I figure him to be involved with Rita Lane? Probably the Gunther connection. Two people corrupted by the same demon do not have to be corrupted in the same time and at the same place.

Red removed his Sony from his jacket pocket and, with fingers shaking from the cold, placed it upright on the floor between the two of them. "I'm recording this conversation, Paul. If that's not acceptable, then we're not going to have a conversation."

"Is that necessary, Red?" Paul winced as though Red had hit him in the gut. "We go back a long time."

"Back to a time when you taught me how to write a news story and convinced me that even though we were in a profession of whores, it was still possible to have principles."

"Okay." Paul shrugged painfully. "But, like I say, you haven't changed a bit. Still the Boy Scout, still convinced you can make the world a better place."

"No, just trying to keep it from becoming a worse place."

Red played back a couple of turns of the tape to make sure it was recording.

"You must exercise a lot to stay in shape." Paul considered him critically. "A little more gray hair, maybe, and a little thinner on the top, but otherwise you haven't changed much in twenty years."

"Some bit of swimming the last few weeks," Red said lightly. "Not much else. Genetic luck, I suppose."

"Exercise, no smoking, no drinking," Paul was still hiding behind the mask of small talk. "Turned over a new lease on life?"

"I have a young wife to keep up with."

"I hope you still have a young wife when all this is over," Paul said ominously.

"Get this straight." Red leaned forward and pushed the pause button on his recorder. "If anything happens to Eileen or the kids, I'll kill you, Paul. And I'll find your new wife and your new kids wherever they are and do to them whatever has been done to my family."

The afterburners were still working. On his own power, Red would never have said those words—never even thought them—and even as the words popped from his mouth like bullets from an automatic weapon, Red realized that he couldn't possibly live up to his threat.

"I think you mean that." The amusement in Paul O'Meara's eyes was replaced by fear. "So you're not a Boy Scout anymore after all."

"Damn right I mean it." Red released the pause button on the recorder. "You were telling me about what Gunther would do to my family unless I turn over the evidence that he murdered Adele Ward?"

"He's an old man, Red, don't you realize that?" Paul locked his long thin fingers together around the bottle of Heineken's. "He may have only a few months to live. Can't you leave an old man alone for the last few days of his life?"

"Old men can kill and bribe and corrupt, and young men can't? Is that what you mean?"

"What the hell good do you expect to accomplish?" Paul asked wearily.

"Look at these pictures." He threw two of the Polaroids, recaptured from the photography department at the *Herald Gazette* after they had been copied, on the table in front of Paul. "I want to stop that. Do you have a young daughter, Paul? I bet you do. How would you feel if that were her?"

"A runaway?"

"What difference does that make? She was someone's daughter."

"Look, Red"—he spread his hands in a plea—"I don't know what the old man has in mind. He's a tricky old bastard, always has been. All I know is that he's told me he'll give you a million dollars—tax free—in hard cash if you kill that story and give him the pictures. He's not worried about himself, because he knows he could die anytime. He's worried about his wife, his children, and his grandchildren. Can't you have some mercy on them?"

"A million dollars...," Red said cautiously. He had no intention of accepting the bribe and normally would have told Paul O'Meara what he could do with it. But the blazing afterburners made him shrewd. Perhaps he could buy a few hours of safety until the first edition of the *Herald Gazette* was on the streets. "That's a lot of money...."

"Two million, if you realize it's tax free. You could put it in municipals—a lot of different ways of doing that—and earn sixty or seventy thousand dollars a year that would also be tax free."

"Is that the way you did it, Paul?"

"Look at me, man." Paul tilted his chin defiantly. "Twenty years ago I was headed for the tomb. There didn't seem to be any way out. My marriage was a wreck. I was disillusioned and fed up with being a reporter, a fall-down drunk with nothing to live for. There was no way out, or so it seemed. If I could get a second chance, another start, I thought I might be able to stitch together a happier life for myself. Harv Gunther helped me. That's all."

"When did you go on his payroll?" Red demanded.

"About the time you started to work for the *Herald Gazette.*" Some of the firm, Sunbelt posture oozed out of Paul O'Meara's shoulders. "Small gifts here and there, at first without strings attached, then, later, with some strings that didn't make any difference. I never did sit on a story that interfered with what you guys call nowadays 'the public's right to know.' Trivial stuff. Honestly, Red, I was no Jake Lingle. He didn't have me in his pocket. Anyway, that was part of the problem I wanted to escape from."

"And so..." Red watched his friend and mentor squirm with a mixture of pity and contempt. "... So you finally stumbled on something big, something that would have put Harv Gunther behind bars, and you saw your chance. You told them you'd do this one last favor for him, and then asked if he'd do one last big favor for you. Stake you to a new life and help you to disappear so you could begin that new life. Right?"

"You always were a smart reporter." Paul slumped over the unopened bottle of Jameson's. "I'm sorry if I let you down, Red. These last twenty years have been happy for me, unbelievably happy. I'm a new man. Look at me. Can't you see that for yourself? No great harm was done to anybody, except maybe you. I thought you'd understand."

"To me," Red snapped, "and to Adele Ward. She'd still be alive if you had sent Harvard Gunther away twenty years ago."

"How can you say that!" Paul sat up straight, his eyes blazing. "Teenage hookers have a life expectancy of eight months. If Harv hadn't killed her, drugs would have."

"And what about the cops, politicians, and reporters that Harv has corrupted since then? What about the gambling, the vice, the crookedness, the broken legs, and the murders? Do you think Adele Ward's death was the first one for which Harv was responsible?"

"Shit, Red, you sound like a fuckin' reformer! ... Anyway, in a very short time, Harv Gunther is going to be standing before a more powerful judge than John Francis Neenan, and a more merciful judge than you. Can't you leave Harv Gunther to heaven?"

"So the new Paul O'Meara believes in God now?" Red asked with heavy irony. He had mentioned John Francis Neenan. Paul either lived reasonably close to Chicago or, more likely, still saw the Chicago newspapers regularly.

"I think I do. My wife"—his eyes lit up—"is a devout Catholic. Post-Vatican-type, Catholic liberal. She's a wonderful woman, Red." He reached across the table and grabbed Red's hand. "I've often wished that the four of us—you and Eileen, Mary and I—could get together and talk about old times. My kids are about the same age as yours, too."

"So if you believe in God, what do you think He thinks about your disappearance?"

"I did what I had to do, Red." He tightened his hold on Red's hand, his eyes begging for forgiveness. "I'll take my chances on God's forgiveness."

"And what will your family think if they ever find out?"

"All my life is in your hands." He gestured at the tiny Sony, no bigger than a box of cigarettes. "You could destroy my family and myself with that thing."

"A million dollars?"

"Actually, the man said I could go as high as two. Give it to charity if you want. Red, consider it a dying man's expiation."

Red turned off his Sony. "Tell the old man I'll think about it and meet you here tomorrow afternoon."

"You've taken a great load off my mind." Paul smiled with cheerful relief. "Maybe I made the wrong choice twenty years ago, Red. Maybe other people did suffer because of my choice. I dunno. I justify it to myself by saying they would have suffered anyhow. But no one's going to suffer if you let the old man die in peace. His days of doing evil are over. His wife and kids—"

"I have to run, Paul." Red rose from the couch. "Same time, same place."

"I'll tell the old man"—Paul reached for Red's hand—"that everything's on hold. Then after tomorrow maybe there will be some way the four of us can get together. Your next vacation, maybe."

"We'll see," Red said enigmatically.

As he turned off North Avenue and walked down North

State Parkway, by the now unused Cardinal's mansion at the head of that most elegant Chicago street, Red felt no emotions at all for Paul O'Meara. The ghost of a father figure had been quietly buried. How much money, he wondered, was Harv paying Paul to lean on him?

In front of the Cardinal's mansion, a caricature of a Gothic haunted house with more than a score of chimneys, Red stopped dead in his tracks. Suddenly the pieces all fit together. *So that was it! No wonder Harv was so nervous about my search for Paul!*

Red's stomach turned. The taste of bile rose in his mouth. Only his reverence of the Church prevented him from vomiting on Sean Cronin's front lawn.

55

Red reread the letter from his editor at Great Western, not quite able to believe her judgment of his novel. He was the new Red Kane, the "crusading reporter, the loving husband, the sympathetic father, the brilliant novelist." Everything was supposed to be "all right" from now on. Somehow the message had not quite reached Rachel Monroe of Great Western Books.

Dear Mr. Kane:

We are grateful to you for sending us your manuscript.We have read it with considerable interest, but unfortunately it does not fit into our publishing needs at the present time. It may be that a company interested in pious romantic fiction would be interested in your work.

Cordially yours,

Red thumbed through the fanfold paper on which his manuscript was printed. Not a single page was marked, not a single margin crinkled slightly from the touch of a thumb. They had not even bothered to separate the pages so that Xeroxed copies could be made.

Did they expect he would send their advance back? He'd surprised them with a manuscript, so they were cutting their losses. Rachel's nasty letter was doubtless the product of editorial committee group think, rationalization, self-justification, evidence against potential litigation.

Probably they had forgotten about the advance. The way they played musical chairs at the publishing companies, there was no one around Great Western now who remembered their contract with him. Some legal or accounting type would discover the mistake a couple of years in the future and make a halfhearted attempt to get the money back. Red would have to check with Eileen, but he suspected that Great Western wouldn't have a case.

Still, it hurt like hell. No one else would ever see his novel and he would never write another again. He dropped the manuscript into a wastebasket and answered his phone. It was Walter Jacobsen. "No comment, Skip." He hung up.

Then he removed the manuscript from the wastebasket. Throwing it away was an empty, symbolic gesture, after all, unless he was ready to wipe out the *Herald Gazette*'s computer memory of the story, and he was not quite ready to do that yet.

"Save it for the Ryan family archives," he grumbled to himself. "Caitlin might get a few laughs out of it."

He opened the locked file cabinet in his desk, dumped the manuscript into a manila folder, and then hesitated, removing the Paul O'Meara tape from an adjoining folder. He considered the tape for a second. Paul's life in his hands. Throw it away, or make a copy of it for Mike Casey the Cop?

He pulled open the middle drawer of his desk, removed the Sony 510 and a larger cassette player, plugged them together, and made the copy of the O'Meara tape.

I won't use it, he told himself, *unless I have to.*

The day before he had rushed through the newsroom to his cubicle, pulled out the Gunther file, extracted the handwritten note on Regency Hyatt stationery and the Xeroxes of the Warren checks, and searched through his correspondence file for a sample of Paul's handwriting.

A postcard from the World Series: "We're not going to win, but it's a hell of a lot of fun. Stay out of trouble. Paul."

Fingers trembling, Red compared the card with the unsigned note to Rita Lane: "The material is now food for the fishes."

He closed the manila folder as if he were looking at dirty pictures in a sixth-grade classroom and S'ter was descending upon him.

Paul O'Meara, who was so devoted to his new family, could describe the butchered body of a girl as fish food. A runaway, he had said contemptuously a few hours earlier.

Red slumped further into his chair. Paul O'Meara was still Harv Gunther's stooge. He had been bought thirty years ago and was still bought. When Harv needed something dirty done, Paul would do it. Why? For a few extra dollars? College tuition for his kids? Or because Harv could still blackmail him?

The reason didn't matter. Paul O'Meara, presumed dead for twenty years, was an accessory after the fact to the murder of Adele Ward.

Red shuddered. Maybe accessory before the fact. Maybe he was Harv's contact with Rita Lane.

This discovery made the story even more sensational. Red turned on his CRT and then paused to reflect. Why use it? There was enough news, enough slime. Why destroy the new O'Meara family and the Warrens? Was it not enough to sacrifice Gunther's children and grandchildren to the public's right to know?

He clipped the card, the Xeroxed checks, and the unsigned note and placed them back in the Gunther file. They would be insurance in case he needed it.

The first part of the Harv Gunther story had exploded that morning with huge Judgment Day headlines: "Gunther Involved in Teenage Murder." Preliminary reports were that 250,000 additional copies of the paper had been sold, a temporary surge past the circulation of the *Sun-Times* and the *Tribune*. The story was all over the radio and television news. The opposition papers were caught flat-footed. The *Sun-Times* doubtless preoccupied with Rupert Murdoch and the rumored defection of Mike Royko, had ignored it, while the *Tribune* gave it a half column on the sixth page. Don Roscoe had huffed and puffed about possible civil rights violations on recording phone conversations, Roscoe, who presided over the bugging of federal courtrooms. Rich Daley had promised his office would begin an immediate investigation of the charges and pointed out that recording phone conversations was not against the law of Illinois so long as the warning beep could be heard. He added, in a masterpiece of hedging of which the old man would have been very proud, "Mr. Gunther is a very distinguished citizen, but no one is above the law."

The city room had celebrated ecstatically, another triumph for the *Herald Gazette*, just at a time when a triumph was desperately needed. Wilson Allen had scampered around the room grinning, if not quite like a Cheshire cat, at least like a cat who had swallowed a canary. He pumped Red's hand in congratulations at least once every five minutes. Brad Winston actually walked into the city room for a few moments—Red was surprised that he was able to find it—and favored the prize-winning columnist with an aloof smile. "Another Pulitzer, Red. Well done!"

As they briefly shook hands, a column lead had clicked in the back of Red's brain: "All you have to do is touch Bradford Winston's hand to realize that he is the first of the robotic publishers."

Only after the bedlam had subsided did Red notice the large package on his desk with a Great Western Books logo (from Lexington Avenue) on the label. He realized, with sinking heart, that they wouldn't be sending the manuscript back if they had liked it.

After he had returned the original O'Meara tape to his file drawer, Red slipped a copy into his jacket. Later in the day, when things had quieted down a bit, he would sneak up Michigan Avenue to the Reilly Gallery and give it to Mike Casey.

"Holy Nellie!" bellowed Lee Malley from the wire service printer. "He killed himself!"

"Who?" several voices in the room demanded in unison.

"Harv Gunther! He shot himself through the head with a German Luger....Man alive, he left a note blaming Red Kane and the *Herald Gazette*!"

Red rushed to the City News Bureau ticker. The first line simply said, "Gunther dead." Then, a half inch down the page, another line: "Harvard Gunther, attorney, civic leader, and real estate broker, was found dead in his Gold Coast apartment this morning by his maid, Laura McDaniels. He apparently shot himself with a German Luger which McDaniels said was a souvenir of the Second World War."

In which Harvard Gunther had not fought, Red thought ruefully.

Then a headline on the ticker: "Gunther blames Kane, *Herald Gazette.*"

Police sources said a note was found near Gunther's body that read: "I die by my own hand, but the real killers are Red Kane and the *Herald Gazette*, who would not permit an old man to die in peace."

As Red watched the ticker, it began to spit out the letters again, a quick biography of Harvard Gunther, probably a canned obit that was already in the files.

Red was stunned. Gunther had cheated him of his third Pulitzer. That didn't matter. Adele Ward was free now, and the truth, which was also in this case news, had been told.

Yet in a way, Harvard Gunther had won the last round. He would not have to face the press and answer their questions. He would not be alive to see his reputation crumble. He'd escaped, in this life at any rate, any payment for his crimes.

Jack Kennedy was right—whoever said life was supposed to be fair? And he had put Red and the *Herald Gazette* on the defensive. Now *they* would have to answer the questions of others since Gunther was no longer alive to answer questions. It could be very sticky.

"You damned fool," someone shouted into his ear, jarring Red out of his reverie. "You've ruined us."

Wilson Allen was dancing around him, like a Hollywood Indian prancing around a bonfire.

"Huh?"

"You've killed Harvard Gunther! You've made him a

martyr! And we're the ones that martyred him. And with Rupert Murdoch coming into town!"

Red heard his editor's words and saw a handsome, anguished face contorted with fear and rage, but he wasn't really listening. The afterburners were working again. He understood what Paul O'Meara had meant. The old man had plans of his own. He knew his reputation would be ruined. What he wanted was vengeance.

He had promised to hurt Eileen and the girls even if he had to come back from the grave to do it.

Harv intended to keep that promise.

"Get out of my way, you shithead!" He shoved Allen aside and raced back to his desk.

First he dialed the Reilly Gallery. "Reilly Gallery." The quietly elegant voice of its glamorous owner.

"Red Kane. Tell Mickey it's a Mayday."

"He knows. He just left."

"Thanks, Annie." Mike had been even quicker on the draw. *Please God that he was in time.* Then he dialed the Convent of the Sacred Heart. "Sister Aurelia?"

"Sister Aurelia is in conference," said the switchboard sweetly. A novice voice, even if they didn't have novices anymore.

"Red Kane. Total emergency. Put me through at once."

Like a good novice she didn't argue.

"Sister Aurelia." *They must teach 'em to sound musical on the phone.*

"Red Kane, Sister. My daughters' lives are in danger. Get them both in your office with your security man, and don't let them out till you hear from me."

"Of course, Mr. Kane."

As he raced for the elevator Red thought to himself that if Sister Aurelia had been one of the younger generation of nuns, she would have wanted to break up into small groups and discuss his request.

"Dear God," he prayed as he ran down the stairs, despairing of the elevator ever coming. "Please don't let me be too late. Help me to save Eileen."

56

Red raced across the Loop, oblivious of the bitter cold and unaware that he had fled from the city room in shirtsleeves during the coldest December in the history of Chicago. He did not notice the terrible ache in his chest nor the strange glances from pedestrians. His only emotion was anger at himself because he was not in better condition and hence could not run faster.

To the objection he would face later, that he should have taken a cab, Red had a convincing answer. He could run faster than a cab could cross the Loop at lunch hour. To the other objection, that he could have easily made a phone call, Red had no answer at all. Weakly he would protest that he was the only one who had seen Mike Casey's pictures of Gunther's hoods. But he had to concede the truth: perhaps he DID want to be a hero.

Feet torturing him, arms and legs screaming with pain, chest ready to explode, sweat pouring out of all the pores of his body despite the fifteen-degrees-above-zero cold, Red exploded through the door of the LaSalle and Jackson building, knocking over a man who looked like a prosperous commodities broker. "Follow me," he shouted at the surprised security guard, and bolted into a miraculously open elevator door. A crowd of people tried to follow him, doubtless wanting to stop at every floor from two to six. He pushed them out. An overweight and pompous young man tried to resist. "Hey there," he demanded, "who do you think you are?"

Red threw him to the floor of the lobby.

"Let's go," he shouted to the thunderstruck security guard.

"Man, you're crazy," the guard yelled back.

"I'll have you fired," Red bellowed, and let the door of the elevator close.

Its progress to the seventh floor was seven eternities.

He bolted through the glass doors of the Minor, Grey,

and Blatt outpost, all beige and light blue and brown, discreetly consoling when you saw the size of your bills. "Mr. Kane!" shouted the terrified receptionist. "Mrs. Kane—" Red raced by her and down the corridor toward Eileen's office. At the corner of the corridor he bowled over two very senior and very important partners, dark-vested patriarchs of corporation law. *Let them sue for damages later.*

Just as he turned the corner, he saw two men emerge from the staircase opposite Eileen's office and quickly dart in. As they went through the door, one removed a gun from a shoulder holster and the other clicked open a switchblade.

At full speed, like a Lake Street elevated express train in the old days, Red charged into the office, smashing into the backs of the two men, knocking them both over. He caught a quick glimpse of Eileen's face, contorted in terror, and then dug his knee into the groin of the man with the gun.

He rolled over and saw the switchblade poised above his chest. *Dear God, I haven't any strength left. He's going to kill me. He's going to drive that knife into my heart, this man whom I don't know with the stocking cap pulled down over his face is going to end my life.*

Then he heard Eileen scream and he found the strength to hurl the knife-wielder back against the wall. He scrambled to his feet, knocking over a chair. The man with a knife recovered his balance and poised to charge at Red, like a linebacker on a blitz. Now working on his afterburner energy, Red grabbed the chair and slashed at the knife-wielder's face. The knife clattered to the floor.

Red jumped for the knife and beat the masked man to it. Too quickly. The other was not trying for the knife. From pocket of his black jacket he drew a thin plastic container and tossed it, almost casually, at Red.

It's a bomb, Red thought, and grabbed for it, vaguely planning to throw it out the window.

He missed. The container shattered on Eileen's desk. A cloud of steam rose from the desk and the light, transparent liquid flowed rapidly across the wood and papers, eating them like a swarm of ants and filling the office with the smell of rotting eggs.

The man reached into his other pocket at the same moment Red crashed into his knees. The attacker screamed in terrible pain as the acid ate into his hand. He tore himself loose from Red, flung off his jacket, and hurled it at Eileen.

She stepped back and automatically reached for the jacket.

"Drop it!" Red shouted.

Startled, she released the jacket as the fabric disappeared in a puff of acid-created steam. She saw something behind Red. The terror on her face turned to horrified grief.

"Look out, Red, he's going to shoot you!" Eileen screamed hysterically.

Red whirled around, the remnants of the chair still in his hand, and saw the revolver pointed at his head. It was firmly grasped in both hands of the masked man.

Just like a gun in a North Korean tank, he thought.

Red slashed at the wrist of the gunman with the broken chair leg that he still held, deflecting his aim at the last moment. The gun exploded and tore a hole in the wall only a few inches from Eileen's head.

"Get the hell out of here!" he yelled at her.

There was nowhere to go. The man with the gun and the man with the knife now had Red trapped between them and Eileen pinned behind her desk. There was a silencer on the gun, so unless Red's manic race down the corridor and Eileen's screams attracted help, it was all over.

The knife-wielder, one hand twisted under his arm in excruciating agony, closed in behind him. The instincts that had kept Red alive in Taegu and Saigon bugged out. He was cemented to the floor, unable to think or react.

This is the way it ends, he thought.

He did not say an Act of Perfect Contrition. He did not shout at Eileen that he loved her. Rather he vaulted over the desk, knocked her to the floor, and covered her body with his. "Movie-star foolish," he would be told later, since bullets from the .38 would have easily torn through both of them.

"Hold it right there," said Mike Casey the Cop, gliding through the doorway like an America's Cup boat racing for the finish line. "Put your gun on that desk, nice and easy, or I'll blow your head off."

As Mike, resplendent as always in a double-breasted blue

suit, jabbed his police service revolver into the neck of one of the masked assailants, two other men, both lean, tall, and hard like Mickey, subdued the hood with the knife and pinned him to the floor, twisting the glittering switchblade out of his hands.

"The kids are okay! Do you hear me, the kids are both okay!"

"Get off me, you fucking fool!" Eileen screamed. "How dare you risk all our lives for a stupid news story!"

57

From the Kane File

a Commentary on WBBM News Radio

Red Kane has finally gone too far. His irresponsible and undocumented attack on civic leader Harvard Gunther obviously caused the death of that grand old man. Most Chicagoans will turn away in revulsion from a has-been reporter who used to be a spoiled brat and is now the aging youthful prodigy of Chicago journalism.

No one has ever denied Red's talent. His problem, according to many who know him well, is that he was successful too soon, too early in life. He won his first Pulitzer Prize before he was thirty and his second before he was forty, the first because he stumbled into a scandal in traffic court (which is about as difficult as plowing into a snow pile in the wintertime), and the second because he happened to be in Viet Nam at the time of the Tet Offensive. As the Mayor said last summer, "Red Kane is lazy." And he's lazy because success has always come too easily. Red Kane has never had to do the dogged, persistent legwork of a careful and responsible investigative reporter. He has lolled around the city room of the *Herald Gazette* and Near North Side bars waiting for stories to come to him.

It's been a long time since Red won a Pulitzer—fifteen years, to be precise. Obviously, he thought it was time for this third award of journalism's most coveted prize. Someone gave him some dirty pictures (presumably in a North Side bistro). He put together a dubious tape and found some very problematic affidavits and launched an attack on one of Chicago's most distinguished citizens.

No one would claim that Harvard Princeton Gunther was a saint. His political and legal past, his machinations in the real estate market, were, to put the matter charitably, often dubious. But in the last ten years of his life, Gunther was a transformed man, dedicated to the service of the city of Chicago and generous in his personal charities. It was a well-known fact in Chicago that Mr. Gunther's health was poor, that, indeed, he only had a few months to live. But Red Kane, always the smart-mouth mischief-maker, would not permit Harvard P. Gunther to enjoy his last few days in peace. So now Gunther is dead, Chicago is denied the service of a generous community leader, and Red Kane, presumably, is on his way to another Pulitzer Prize.

We said earlier that Mr. Gunther had turned over a new leaf. Isn't it time Red Kane did the same?

I'm John Madigan, News Radio Sssssssssseventy-eight.

Editorial from the *Chicago Tribune*

MEDIA IN TROUBLE WITH PEOPLE

In recent weeks, in the wake of the Grenada invasion, the mass media have agonized over their apparent unpopularity with the general public. The American people, it would seem, were delighted that the press were excluded from the Grenada invasion and affronted by our claim that we had a right to be there. Obviously, our interpretation of the First Amendment and the public's interpretation are different. We were heroes at the time of Watergate and villains at the time of Grenada. It is indeed appropriate that we examine our conscience.

In Chicago yesterday we saw a perfect example of the kind of irresponsible journalism that should disturb the consciences of all those who work in the media. Columnist Red Kane's shameless attack on sick and aging civic leader Harvard P. Gunther was a classic example of why the public has come to distrust and even despise newspaper and TV journalists.

This page is surely not the place to comment on the weaknesses of Redmond P. Kane's sordid attack on a dying man, nor on the irresponsibility of the upper echelons of the Herald Gazette Company for permitting such an attack. Suffice it to say that we cannot imagine Rupert Murdoch, when he comes to Chicago next month, ever being so crassly and cruelly sensationalist.

Commentary on Channel 3 News

Chicago has always had the reputation of being a town of slugging, two-fisted, hard-drinking journalists. Charles MacArthur and Ben Hecht, long ago, celebrated the toughness and the cynicism of the Chicago press. There are many distinguished names in this tradition—Clem Lane, Ed Leahy, Len O'Connor, Mike Royko. There have also been disgraceful episodes which we would rather not remember. For example, there was Jake Lingle, the *Tribune* reporter who was murdered by the Capone mob in the 1930's, apparently because he was demanding more money to stay bought. It is difficult to imagine, however, that Chicago will ever produce anything more sleazy than *Herald Gazette* columnist Red Kane's attack on dying civic leader and philanthropist Harvard Gunther. As is well known, Mr. Gunther was not always a model of civic probity. In days gone by, however, the rules seemed to be different. Gunther more than made up for his past peccadilloes by his civic-mindedness and generosity over the last two decades.

This did not seem to matter to columnist Kane, who has sunk a long way from his two Pulitzer Prizes.

His wildly improbable, his squalidly obscene, tale about the alleged crimes of a man on his deathbed are offensive to all of us at Channel 3. Speaking for the editorial board and for station management, I wish to express our abhorrence and our condemnation of what Mr. Kane has done, and to say that as far as we're concerned, there ought to be no place for him in the Chicago media.

I'm Helen Slattery, editorial director, Channel 3.

Editorial from the Chicago *Sun-Times*

Kane's Kaper

There is little reason to add our voice to the already noisy and merited condemnation of Red Kane's desperate attempt to add a third Pulitzer Prize to his shelf. There are few things that can be more contemptible than an attack on an aged and dying man. In the legal sense of the word, Harvard P. Gunther's final charge that Kane had murdered him is not valid, but in the moral sense, Kane is almost as guilty as if he had pulled the trigger on the Luger that World War II hero Gunther brought home with him from Germany. The *Herald Gazette* ought to be ashamed of itself for publishing such swill.

We hear that Red Kane is also a fledgling novelist. Possibly the dubious materials he has used against the late Mr. Gunther have been lifted from one of his novels.

We would suggest a possible plot for a future Kane novel: Why doesn't he tell us a story about a columnist who was so successful and won so many prizes that he thought that he was free from all obligations of human civility and decency?

Statement by Chicago's Mayor

The Mayor's press secretary announced today that the Mayor was deeply grieved by the tragic death of his good friend of many years' standing Harvard P. Gunther. "Harv was an old and true friend, a loyal supporter of the reform movement. Chicago won't be the same city without him. I'm sure all the people of Chicago join me in extending our condolences to Mrs. Gunther and her children and grandchildren over Harv's untimely death. I'm sure also that all good citizens of Chicago are dismayed by the journalistic irresponsibility which caused his death."

Statement by Shannon Armstrong, President,
Better Government Association

"All of us at the BGA are deeply grieved to learn of the death of our friend and colleague Harvard P. Gunther, long a supporter of better government in Chicago. Mr. Gunther will be sorely missed. We join all other responsible, civic-minded people of the Chicago area in extending our condolences to his family and in condemning the gutter journalism that cut short his life."

Statement by Cardinal Sean Cronin, Archbishop of Chicago

While the Catholic Church has traditionally believed that suicide is not a valid option, it also understands that, under the pressure of enormous stress and strain, some of us may make choices that in other circumstances we would find repellent. We lament the death of Harvard Gunther, even as we praise his well-known contributions to Chicago's philanthropy. We also regret that, by his own choosing, Mr. Gunther will be unable to respond to the very serious and well-documented allegations made against him. We shall pray for him and for his family that they may find in their faith both peace and hope.

Statement by Wilson Allen, Editor, *Herald Gazette*

The *Herald Gazette* deeply regrets the unfortunate death of businessman and philanthropist Harvard P. Gunther. If we had been aware of the precarious state of Mr. Gunther's health, we would, of course, have had serious second thoughts concerning our stories yesterday about Mr. Gunther. We wish to apologize to Mrs. Gunther and the family for any pain that we may have caused them.

Statement by Anonymous Reporter at Ricardo's Restaurant

Red Kane is finally where he belongs. Up Shit Creek without a paddle and without a boat. I hope the bastard chokes on his own turds.

58

The city room of the *Herald Gazette* was like a funeral parlor, and Red Kane was the corpse.

Either he had become an invisible man or the word had spread around the room that he was infected with a highly contagious disease.

Afterburner energies were still churning inside of him, fire, heat, light, power swirling around, devoid of outlet or direction. He felt as if he were, perhaps, an atomic reactor about to explode, a human Three Mile Island.

"I hope you're satisfied," Lee Malley said, standing in front of Red's desk, hands on hips, lips curled in contempt.

"So I'm not invisible." Red looked up at his friend dubiously.

"Everybody in this room wishes you were, fuckface," Lee said through clenched teeth.

"I don't understand it." Red thumbed rapidly through the pages of the *Tribune*. "None of the papers even mentioned that the police arrested the men who were trying to mutilate my wife and the man who was putting a bomb in my kids' car. Isn't that news?"

"The only news in town," Lee said contemptuously, "is that you killed Harv Gunther. Our circulation is the lowest of all three papers, Murdoch is coming to town, and you have to insult every right-minded person in the city."

Somewhere deep inside of Red there was a voice that said that John Madigan, the other editorial writers, and the heads of the civic federations did not speak for the people of Chicago. Rich Daley, who had a better feel for what went on in the streets than all of them put together, had said laconically that his investigation of the allegations would continue, even though Don Roscoe, who hadn't begun an investigation in the first place, now claimed that Gunther's death had made the whole issue "moot."

"I didn't kill him," Red said defensively. "He killed himself. No matter how old he was or how sick he was, he had no claim to immunity against the public's right to know."

"Right to know? Crap!" Lee looked ready to spit at him. "You'll never grow up, Red. But I never thought you'd drag the rest of us down with you."

The irony of it all, Red thought, as Malley walked away from his desk like a man escaping from a fire in a smelly garbage can, *is that poor old Harv didn't have this reaction in mind at all. He no more anticipated than I did that suicide would make him a hero. He died happy, though, because he thought Eileen would be horribly disfigured and Patty and Kate blown into a million pieces. My wife and kids are all right and my reputation seems to be destroyed.*

The first hint had come when his follow-up story had disappeared from the early edition of the *Herald Gazette.* Then the attempted attacks on Eileen and the kids were not reported on the ten o'clock news. Only the *Trib* carried the story the next day, buried on the back page of the first section. Police sources were quoted in the *INC* gossip column as linking the attack to Mrs. Kane's criminal-law practice. "Someone for whom she didn't get an acquittal."

"They're all guilty," Mike Casey had said softly, "because every one of them knew that Harvard Gunther was a vicious bastard. There was a conspiracy of silence to cover that up. There are others like him in Chicago about whom the press pretends. You broke the rules of the conspiracy, indicting not only Gunther but all of them. Small wonder that they're now turning on you."

Red was too busy trying to placate Eileen's furies to worry much about himself. As though she were trying to compensate for twenty years of patient, rational marriage, Eileen was hysterically, irrationally angry at him. He should never have taken such chances without telling her all the details first; he had risked her life and the lives of her children without even the common decency of a warning. It was the last straw of intolerable stupidity.

The column about her performance in the courtroom was vulgar, disgusting, male chauvinist; she did not know how she would ever be able to face a judge again. But that was minor compared to the danger to which he had exposed her and the children. Did he see what that acid had done to her desk? Could he imagine what it would have done to her face? Did he want to spend the rest of his years with a wife who looked like a circus freak? Was he prepared to walk down the aisle of St. Clement's behind two caskets? No, one would have been enough because Patty and Kate would have been charred fragments of little girls and not even recognizable corpses.

Despite all the practice with his mother, Red had no skills with which to respond to an emotionally distraught woman. He tried to argue. He had told her about the dangers and she had seemed to indicate that it was all right for him to go ahead with the story. Mike Casey and his friends on the police force had kept a careful eye on her and the children for the past several weeks. There never had been any real danger either to the kids or to her. Yes, he should have phoned; yes, he should have anticipated Gunther's suicide; yes, he should have realized that they all would now be humiliated together with him.

"You and the kids were never in any real danger, Eileen!"

"Never in any real danger!" she raged. "Did you see how close that acid came to my face? And that gun, which you so cleverly knocked in my direction. It almost blew my head away!"

"But the acid didn't get to your face and the bullet didn't hit you," Red pleaded, feeling that perhaps he deserved some credit for saving her life and her attractiveness.

"The only reason I'm alive and not a circus freak," she spat the words viciously at him, "is that Mike Casey had the sense to bring others to help him. HE was not a hot dog, grandstanding for a Pulitzer Prize jury!"

She stormed out of the parlor, rampaged up the stairs, and, as Red would discover later, swept into her arms clothes, makeup, and other vital material and withdrew into her study.

For the first time in their marriage, Eileen had deserted the conjugal bedroom in a temper tantrum.

His two daughters, whose lives he had also saved, were at their Aunt Nancy's and had not called him, presumably because they were angry at him too. What was going on? Where had he gone wrong?

He dialed Johnny's number at Collegeville. "I thought I owed you an explanation before the ten o'clock news," he began tentatively. "Have you heard anything? Have reporters been bothering you?"

"In Stearns County?" his son demanded curtly.

He explained briefly the Gunther exposé, Harv's suicide, the attempts on the lives of his mother and sisters, and that now everything was all right except some people were trying to make the dead man a hero.

"No big deal," his son said.

"Well, it was a big deal around here." Red wondered what was going on in Johnny's head. "Acid, knives, guns, car bombs."

"No big deal," Johnny repeated.

"Well, just so long as you don't get alarmed if it's on the ten o'clock news up there."

"It won't be," John said confidently. "Anyway, I don't watch the news. I'm in the darkroom usually at that time."

"Fine. . . . How's Lois?"

"None of your business," he snapped.

Red removed the phone from his ear and glanced at it suspiciously. Was that really his son, John Patrick Kane? "Pardon me?"

"She talks about you all the time. She's more impressed with you than with me. Why couldn't you have left us alone? I'm fed up with you prying into my private life. Everything I do you peer over my shoulder. And you had to interfere when Lois was visiting the family. Well, we've broken up. I hope you're happy about that."

"Not if you're unhappy about it, Johnny."

"As soon as she came into the house"—Johnny now sounded as angry as his mother had a half hour before—"you turned on that phony, shanty-Irish charm of yours. She thinks you're the greatest man in the world. That's all she talked about on our dates. How 'cute' my father is. I couldn't stand it, so we broke up. Nice goin'."

Red slid his tongue along his lips, which suddenly seemed parched and dry. "I'm sorry if I offended you, Johnny. You seemed pleased then. I thought she was a very nice girl...." He hesitated, not having the faintest idea of what else he might say.

"Mom says it will always be that way. My girlfriends will always think you're 'cute.'"

"Your mother said THAT?"

"She said it's because you ARE cute. That's all I need is a cute father. Please stay out of my private life. Leave me alone. Let me worry about my career and my friends and my sex life. Fair enough?"

"It's fair enough, if that's the way you want it."

"That sure as hell is the way I want it." Johnny slammed his telephone back into its cradle with such vehemence that Red winced.

He felt a strange burning sensation in his eyes like he wanted to weep. First Eileen, now Johnny.

At his desk in the city room the next morning, Red realized that this day was likely to be even worse. Something seemed to be cracking apart inside of him. The energies from his ecstatic experience—if that's what he should call it—were still churning around. In the image he'd been using for the last couple of days, the afterburners were going at full blast. But instead of driving the new Red Kane at Mach 2 speed, they seemed rather to be pulling him apart.

Eileen had approved of the story on Harv Gunther. Johnny had been delighted that he had charmed Lois. The city room had applauded his first story on Gunther. Winston had assured him it would mean another Pulitzer Prize for the *Herald Gazette*. Now Eileen would not sleep with him, Johnny had told him off, the city room treated him as if he had the bubonic plague, and Winston had killed the second story and printed a halfhearted apology instead.

Red opened his Gunther file and removed the unsigned note and Paul O'Meara's postcard. That was a story they would have to run, one of the most sensational stories ever. Even Wilson Allen would know that.

Sheila McGovern, secretary to Winston's administrative assistant, stood in front of his desk. "Mr. Winston would like to see you in his office, Mr. Kane."

"In his office?" Red asked incredulously. None of the working stiffs were ever invited to Winston's penthouse office on top of the Herald Gazette Building.

"Yes, sir, Mr. Kane," Sheila said sadly.

A raven-haired, creamy-complexioned colleen who looked as if she had just escaped from the bogs of the County Mayo, Sheila was a fourth-generation Chicago Irish person. The implicit sympathy in her voice suggested that not everyone had turned against him. Only those who mattered.

"Do you think they're going to throw me out one of the windows up there, Sheila?" He stood up, put on his jacket, slipped the note and the postcard into his inside jacket pocket.

"Of course not, Mr. Kane."

She didn't sound very confident, however.

59

"You really fucked us up this time." Wilson Allen was pacing back and forth behind Bradford Winston. The latter was sitting at a small antique desk in the center of the vast office. Windows faced the city, lake, and river. Next to the desk was a cabinet that seemed to match it, some kind of Early American oak, Red guessed. Three chairs, doubtless made by the same colonial craftsman, constituted the only other furniture in the room. The president of the Herald Company sat in one of them, a study in dispassionate self-possession. Red sat across the desk from him, gazing through the west window. Wilson Allen was pacing back and forth, a caged jaguar, behind the desk of the cool, faintly bored publisher. A few blocks away the 333 Wacker Building glowed in the cold, clear December sky.

Where are You when I really need You? Red asked of the

Cheshire smile that he thought had once lurked behind that building.

But that was not a fair question, for there was still an enormous, if terribly confused, love within him.

"How's your kid doing, Wils?"

"What the hell does that have to do with your destroying the *Herald Gazette*?" Allen spun on his heel and glared furiously at Red.

"I was just wondering," Red replied softly. "I hope he's still in remission."

"It's very good of you to ask," Bradford Winston said serenely, his steel-gray eyes unwavering. "I believe he's doing very nicely. Isn't that true, Wilson?"

"A hell of a lot better than I am," Allen shouted.

"Do I have to draw a picture for you, Red, or do you know why I've called you?" Winston tapped his letter opener lightly across the palm of his hand, a bayonet probably from the Revolutionary War.

"I expect, Brad, that you'd very much like to impale me on that deadly weapon."

"Not anything quite that violent." The president of the Herald Company smiled disarmingly.

"I suppose I'm going out the revolving door again," Red said, trying to match his nonchalant tone to Winston's.

"Only this time you'll never come back," Allen snarled, standing now behind Winston like a second at the beginning of a duel.

"Never say never, because never is a hell of a long time," Red cautioned him. *At least I'm putting my head on the block with dignity. A real modern-day Thomas More!*

"Harry Truman, wasn't it?" A faint frosty smile glinted momentarily on Winston's handsome, impassive face.

"I'll go, but I would like to know why."

"You killed Harv Gunther, that's why," Allen screeched. "You've come damn near to killing the *Herald Gazette* too."

"Strictly speaking, Wils, old boy, that's not true. He killed himself. He also killed Adele Ward, and he tried to disfigure my wife and kill my daughters. I'm sorry, but I think all of that is news. If you put the attacks on my family in tomorrow morning's headlines..." *my wife will never sleep with me again,* he thought "...you'll sell a quarter million extra copies. I think I should get a raise instead of being fired."

"John Madigan is right." Allen pounded on his boss's desk. "You are a spoiled child."

"Please." Winston steadied the desk. "After all, this little table is two hundred and nine years old."

"Sorry," Allen said penitently. "Why don't we just get rid of this guy? He'll hassle us all day with his blarney."

Winston sighed with mild impatience. "Really, Wilson, sometimes I think it might have been better after all if we had made Redmond editor of the *Herald*. He doesn't seem capable of letting his emotions interfere with the clarity of his thought.... Surely you must understand, Redmond." He turned away from Wilson Allen, who seemed now to be invisible, and looked toward Red. "You're absolutely correct, of course, it's one of the great stories of the decade. But Wilson is absolutely correct, too. We simply can't run anything more about poor Harvard Gunther."

Externally, Red was calm and cool. Wyatt Earp at the shoot-out at the O.K. Corral. But his thoughts and emotions were charging at full tilt. He had not eaten in twenty-four hours, and he had barely slept the last two nights. After an hour of fitfully tossing and turning the night before in his now-deserted bedroom, he had risen, dressed hastily, and walked for hours along the shore of the gray, truculent lake. His racing intellect examined and discarded a hundred answers to Wilson Allen. Finally, he settled for, "Would you mind explaining that, Brad?"

"Certainly." Brad tapped lightly on his antique desk with the forefinger of his left hand. "However vile Harvard Gunther might have been—and I'll concede to you that he was very vile indeed—he managed to buy his way into the Chicago Establishment. He was neither the first nor, I daresay, the last of the robber barons to achieve some respectability toward the end of his life. Still, he would have been a fair target for us if he had remained alive. The media, as you doubtless realize, consider any living celebrity a fair target. But if a person is old and reputedly sick, then one must be a bit cautious with an attack. When someone is recently dead, the old Latin proverb '*nil nisi bonum de mortis*' applies."

"'*Mortuis*,'" Red corrected him.

"Of course." Winston smiled faintly, as though grateful for the correction. "Two years, or even a year, from now, an exposé will be perfectly acceptable, but if Harvard Gunther wanted to end our series on him, he could not have chosen a better way than to put that Luger bullet through his head."

Red was conscious of his pounding heart, the blood rushing through his head, and his frantic ultrasonic mind. "I agree that we could not have written about Jack Kennedy's amatory adventures the week after his assassination, but this man wasn't Jack Kennedy. For reasons I can't quite understand—maybe it's guilt—the Chicago power structure is angry at us. But they don't represent the people of the city. We should elbow our way right through them and tell people the truth."

"Frankly, I'm disappointed in you, Red. Of course the people of Chicago are horrified at what appears to be our gratuitous attack on a dying man. We could argue with the utmost effectiveness, and we still couldn't win." He lifted his hand an inch off the desk and let it fall limply back. "My wife tells me that she has had phone calls all morning from friends who are terribly upset. Even her maid thinks we did a terrible thing to a poor old man."

Red Kane's brain churned in wild circles. He felt as if the top was going to blow off his head. The publisher of the *Herald Gazette* was telling him calmly and coolly that his wife's maid was representative of the people of the city of Chicago.

"I see," he said mildly. *Better get out of here before I lose my temper and make a fool of myself.*

"I'm really quite sad about all this." Winston sighed discreetly, a moderately disappointed prep school graduate. "You are, of course, perfectly free to try to sell the story to a competing Chicago news outlet. You'll find, I'm quite certain, that no one will touch it. In a way it's a shame Mr. Murdoch isn't in town yet. Our story is as dead, however, as Harvard Gunther."

"And you're dead at the *Herald Gazette*." Wilson Allen reappeared from the limbo to which Winston Bradford had banished him.

"A sacrifice to the wolves." Red stood up, struggling frantically to contain the violent thoughts and feelings that he pictured as laser beams about to burst out of his brain.

"There's really no hurry about removing your material from the city room." Winston rose with him. "And, of course, we will feel bound by your contract, which has three more years to run. Moreover, we will also pay you for those three years the present income from syndication of your column, which, unfortunately, we will have to discontinue. Consider it a three-year sabbatical, Red, with pay, in which you can do all the things you always wanted to do."

I have to escape from this room, Red thought, *or I may dive out that window. I feel like there is a prairie fire sweeping through my brain cells.*

"I'll leave quietly, Brad, but I think you're dead wrong."

"Of course." Winston extended his hand.

Red ignored the publisher's parting gesture.

He punched the button for the single elevator that rose to the penthouse of the Herald Gazette Building, but the explosive energy made him too impatient to wait for it. He bolted across the lobby and down the staircase. "Take care, Sheila," he said to the secretary of Mr. Winston's assistant.

"Good-bye, Mr. Kane," she called sadly after him.

Red ran down the fifteen floors to the city room, feeling as if he had lifted off the steps and was floating through space. He stopped in the lobby of the city room, took a very deep breath, and commanded his raging thoughts and emotions to be still. Let no one say that his departure from the *Herald Gazette* was devoid of class.

Casually he strolled through the silent room, well aware that every eye was on him, humming (he hoped not too loudly) "You're Irish and You're Beautiful."

No point in packing everything up, just the Gunther file, the O'Meara file, and his novel. He dumped them into the battered briefcase, as though he had all the time in the world.

Then he remembered the postcard and the unsigned note on Hyatt stationery. He had not used his insurance. Perhaps he had known that he wouldn't.

He tore up the note and tossed the pieces into the wastebasket. He considered the card briefly, wondered whether

Paul had watched the Sox in the play-off this year, and then tore it up too.

Leave Paul O'Meara to heaven's judgment.

The phone rang. A man with a cockney voice wondered if it might be possible to have a word or two with Mr. Kane the next day, an emissary of Rupert Murdoch already. Winston was a smart man, unlike his flunky Wilson Allen; but he had misread Chicago and he had misread the world of journalism.

Of course Mr. Kane would be delighted to have a word or two with him the day after tomorrow. The Ciel Bleu at the Mayfair Regent? Quite. "Just as a matter of idle curiosity, though, how did you know I would be staying at that hotel?"

"I'll explain the day after tomorrow." Red grinned.

His spirits soared. The story would be told after all. He would defeat Harvard Gunther and Bradford Winston and Wilson Allen and John Madigan and the *Sun-Times* and the *Tribune*, and the Better Government Association and all the other creeps.

Another phone call. This time from a high-level bureaucrat at the *Washington Post*. "Red, what the hell's going on out there?"

"What do you mean?" Red leaned back in his chair, hoping he looked the picture of contented innocence.

"There's a rumor floating around that the dummies have given you the sack because you blew the whistle on this crook ...what's his name?"

"Harvard Princeton Gunther."

"Good God, he sounds like a football game. Anyway, we'd be very interested in the story, if it's still yours."

"It's still mine."

"Moreover, the people in our syndication office think that the *Herald Gazette* has never really merchandised you properly, and our editorial people are open to the idea of a Midwestern perspective on the op-ed page three days a week."

"Oh?" Voodoo drums were beating in Red's ears.

"Basically, we think we can put together a package in which you sign on with us, do a column for us three days a week, and then we distribute it on our wires. We'll guarantee you whatever your total is with the *Gazette* plus, say, oh, somewhere between five and twenty percent more. Interested?"

"I might be." Red managed to sound remarkably casual. "Of course, the problem is I don't know how I can leave Chicago. The kids are still in school, my wife has her law practice...."

"Oh, that's the last thing in the world we would want," said the man from the *Post*. "The whole point would be that it's time for us to have a voice that speaks from the Middle West perspective and in a Midwestern locale. I'm afraid we need a decision in a day or two, especially since the Gunther story is apt to have a short half-life. Can you give me a ring tomorrow?"

"Of course," Red agreed. "I'll talk it over with my wife tonight, and be back to you in the morning. Don't call me here, though, because I suspect I won't be here tomorrow." They both laughed knowingly.

The Lord gives, Red concluded, *and the Lord takes away. Blessed be the name of the Lord.*

How about that!

Later, Red would wonder what would have happened if he had been in any condition the next morning to return the phone call from the *Washington Post*. He suspected that, like many other exciting offers in the world of the national media, this one would have evaporated in the harsh sunlight of contractual negotiations. But it was to be several days before Red was in any condition to lift a telephone. And by then he was doing all he could to forget Harvard Gunther and the Cheshire smile that had lurked behind the green glass skyscraper.

At that moment, however, Red was flying high, all jets going full force. He shrugged into his dirty brown trench coat, wondering why he had not worn an overcoat to protect himself from the fierce December cold. He picked up his briefcase and sauntered out of the city room of the *Herald Gazette* humming not "You're Irish and You're Beautiful" but "Waltzing Matilda."

That would show the so-and-sos.

He imagined that he felt the jolt of the afterburners as he rode down the elevator. Mach 2.

Any more speed and the engines that were driving him would blow up and disintegrate.

60

Red walked the three miles from the *Herald Gazette* to his house on Webster, even though the temperature was plunging toward zero and he was wearing only a thin coat. He was exhilarated, on top of the world, in full command of his energies and resources.

Later, the psychiatrist would say to him, "You were aware even then that your behavior was manic."

Red considered her suggestion carefully. By then he was ready to consider any suggestion carefully. The woman must be good. Had not Larry Moran recommended her to Eileen?

"I suppose it was kind of kooky to whistle the Australian national anthem as I left the city room."

She frowned impatiently. "You had just been discharged from a company for which you had worked for thirty years. You had been deprived of a certain Pulitzer Prize, you were in serious conflict with your wife and son, your colleagues at the paper were bitterly resentful of you. Your reputation in Chicago had been shattered; you admit yourself that it was unlikely that you could accept either of the positions that had been offered you. Moreover, you had scarcely had anything to eat in the previous twenty-four hours and had not slept for two nights in a row. It was very cold, you were wearing a light coat, and you walked three miles along the lakeshore. Does not all of that seem extraordinary?"

"Now it does," Red would admit. "It didn't then."

"You will concede that at that point your behavior had become manic even if you were not aware of it?"

"I was sky-high," Red conceded reluctantly.

"In fact, you had been sky-high for two months, had you not?"

"I suppose so."

"And now to your mania there was added a strong infection of paranoia. You were convinced that the entire Chicago Establishment was conspiring against you, and shortly you would be convinced that your family had joined that conspiracy, that indeed they had all banded together to destroy the new personality you had developed. Is that not so?"

"Yes," Red admitted. "That is certainly an accurate description."

"So you agree that clinical diagnosis of schizophrenia with incipient paranoia is appropriate?" She smiled confidently like a professor who has put down an empty-headed freshman coed.

"No, I don't think I agree with that at all," Red said slowly. "I think they WERE conspiring to destroy the new Red Kane."

It was then that the shrink left his hospital room to phone Eileen and suggest that he be transferred into the psychiatric unit.

When he turned off of Stockton onto Webster, Red felt that the afterburners had suddenly quit on him. Indeed, all four jet engines flamed out. He was cold, tired, hungry, lonely, and afraid. Something terribly wrong was happening in his life. What the hell was he doing walking home along Lake Shore Drive on a cold December evening when the streets were slippery frozen slush? He must hurry home to ask Eileen what was wrong. No, he couldn't do that. Eileen was furious with him. But it was unthinkable that Eileen would stay angry at him for more than twenty-four hours. He was already forgiven, of that he felt certain. In the light of their home and the warmth of her affection the world would sort itself out.

Eileen was waiting for him in the doorway of the house, shapeless in a long beige down coat, her face pale, lips tight, eyes dilated, an Irish warrior queen ready for battle.

"Where, may I ask, have you been?" Her voice made the windchill factor on Webster Avenue seem warm.

"I, uh, had some things to think about, so I walked home from work," Red said hesitantly.

"The coldest night of the year, you have to walk home from work! Red, have you lost your mind completely?"

"I'm kind of confused," he admitted, desperately needing a drink.

"Well," she spoke very carefully, spacing the words evenly, "while YOU were walking home pondering YOUR problems, your daughter Kate drove the family Volvo into another car and is in the emergency room at Grant Hospital with a fractured arm and collar bone and possible internal injuries."

Red collapsed into one of the chairs by the unlit fireplace. "Was anyone else hurt?"

"No, thank God for miracles. Only YOUR daughter."

Red tried to stand up but couldn't quite make it out of the chair.

"No you don't," Eileen said firmly. "I don't want you anywhere near the poor child. She's terrified of what you'll say to her. I only came home for a few minutes to calm Patty down. I'm going back now. You're useless. Stay out of everybody's way with your crazy fool exposés until we find out how bad Katie is."

Eileen slammed out of the house and down the street to Grant Hospital, only a block and a half away.

Red sat slumped in the chair, still shivering. Something was terribly fouled up. He was caught in a nightmare, only he was wide-awake. Kate had taken the Volvo and piled it up? The insurance company would love that. So would the cops. And it must have had something to do with the attacks on him in the media. Kate was punishing him for his notoriety. Dear God in heaven, what was happening!

"Do you want something to eat?"

"No, thanks, Eileen," he mumbled.

"Like I'm SURE I'm not Eileen."

He looked up. Patty. She sounded like Eileen, as angry and as contemptuous as her mother. "No, thanks. I'm not hungry."

"Are you going to sit there in that chair shivering all night like a geeky little grammar school boy?" She stood in front of him, hands on hips, another wrathful Amazon.

"I'll sit wherever I like," he said stubbornly.

"Boy, you really grossed out this time! Big Joe Hero!"

Red leaped up from his chair. "You keep your goddamn mouth shut, you stupid little brat!" he yelled. "Now get the hell to your bedroom and don't give me any more of your shit."

Patty fled the room wailing with outrage and humiliation.

His anger spent, he stumbled back to the chair. The circle was complete now. Everyone in the family—Eileen, John, Patty, Kate. He loved them all so much; he had tried so hard, and instead of making things better, he had only made them worse.

I think I am losing my mind, he told himself. *I am falling apart. I need a long, long rest.*

Luciano poked his black snoot around the corner of the staircase, sniffing suspiciously. "Luciano"—Red snapped his fingers—"one friend I have left in the family. Come here, boy."

Suspiciously, head down and tail up, Luciano crept toward him. Then, halfway across the floor, he snarled.

Luciano never snarled. The coal-black Labrador seemed startled at the guttural snarl that had escaped from his mouth. He paused a moment, apparently considering the possibilities of becoming a mean and vicious canine. He chased his tail in an excited circle, as though he were trying to figure out what came next. Then, satisfied with himself, he snarled again and bared his teeth at Red.

"Get out of here, you son of a bitch." Red heaved a maroon pillow at Luciano. It bounced off the Labrador's face. The dog yiped in protest, abandoned his brief career as a dangerous brute, and scampered up the stairs, doubtless seeking consolation from Patty.

For Red Kane it was the end of the story that had begun on the Feast of All the Saints at 333 Wacker Drive. Even Luciano, harmless, happy Luciano, a Labrador without an enemy in the world, hated him.

It was hilariously funny. So Red began to laugh, and the more he laughed the funnier it became. Buddy Hackett, Bill Cosby, Severn Darden, and Chevy Chase all rolled into one. Novel? Pulitzer Prize? Job? Friends? Family? Even Luciano!

He was now a spectator standing outside himself, watching the funny man in a trench coat and a Pat Moynihan hat slumped in a chair in front of an empty fireplace laughing hysterically. Dispassionately, he heard Patty on the phone.

"Daddy's cracked up. Yeah, like he's acting totally zonked, I mean awesomely! . . . No, he's sitting by the fireplace laughing. . . . No, he hasn't been drinking. . . . I think he's having a nervous breakdown. . . . Oh, Mama, come home quick. I'm so frightened."

From his secure vantage point outside of the deteriorating new Red Kane, the old Red Kane considered the possibility of reassuring his daughter: "That man in the chair by the fireplace really isn't your father, Patty. It's a counterfeit Red Kane who has been pretending to be me for the last couple of months. Let him go off the deep end. He's not worth worrying about."

Then Eileen was in the room, still in her coat and her cossack hat, kneeling next to the hulk of the new Red Kane, holding his hand, weeping and murmuring soft, reassuring words to him.

"No, Eileen, you've got it all wrong. Don't worry about that fellow. A day or two more and he'll be gone. There's nothing to cry about, everything's going to be all right."

Of course he could not communicate with her as long as he remained outside the hulk on the chair. So, to reassure Eileen, he moved back inside the disheveled and encumbered new Red Kane.

Calmly, as it seemed to him, he explained to her about the Cheshire smiles and North Korean tanks and dreams about Adele Ward and police guns on Memorial Day, about his new job with the *Washington Post* and Dav's last words to him in Saigon, and Harv Gunther, and Rupert Murdoch, and his long talk with Paul O'Meara.

"Oh, Red, darling," she pleaded with him, "Paul O'Meara's been dead for twenty years!"

"No, he's not," Red insisted, "I talked with him the other day, yesterday or the day before—it's all mixed up. Paul O'Meara's alive and Harvard Gunther's dead!"

And then, the incredible, mind-boggling incongruity that Harvard Gunther was dead and O'Meara was alive drove away all other thoughts. Red tried to stop laughing, but it was so extraordinarily funny he simply could not end his laughter, no matter how much his weeping and terrified wife begged him to be calm and trust her.

It was only when the men in white came from Grant Hospital, and one of them pumped something into his arm with a syringe that Red's laughter finally ebbed. Even as they bundled him up in a warm coat and led him, now groggy and almost asleep, out of the house, Red still thought that his joke was extremely funny.

Only he could no longer remember what the joke was.

Book SIX

Upon a gloomy night
With all my cares to loving ardors flushed,
(O venture of delight!)
With nobody in sight
I went abroad when all my house was hushed.
In safety, in disguise,
In darkness up the secret stair I crept,
(O happy enterprise!)
Concealed from other eyes,
When all my house at length in silence slept.
Upon a lucky night
In secrecy, inscrutable to sight,
I went without discerning
And with no other light
Except for that which in my heart was burning.

—San Juan de la Cruz

61

"Do you recall telling your wife that you had a conversation with a man who had been dead for twenty years?" demanded the psychiatrist. A lean, hard, triumphantly unattractive woman with thin hair, thick glasses, thin nostrils, and thick lips—a living refutation of Freud's assertion that anatomy is destiny.

"Did I say that?" Red rubbed his forehead, still intermittently a mass of pain. "That was pretty silly, wasn't it?"

"The point is not that it was silly, Redmond. The point is that it was wish fulfillment. You wanted this man who was your mentor to come back from the dead. So, as part of your exercise in religious enthusiasm, you brought him back from the dead."

As best Red could calculate, he had been in the hospital for two or three days, peacefully sedated, happily detached, and not quite able to separate his dreams from his recollections of what had actually happened during the first week of December. The psychiatrist wanted to commit him for long-term therapy, arguing that he was "a very sick man."

Eileen had insisted, however, that he be kept out of the psychiatric ward of the hospital and assured him that she was telling everyone that he was suffering merely from "complete exhaustion."

Even sedated, Red knew how that would be interpreted.

A really bad binge.

His wife and children were kind, solicitous, concerned, loving, just as they would be if Luciano hurt his paw messing with rosebushes.

Especially Katie, haggard and pale (save for two monumental black eyes), her arm trussed up in a complicated cast. "Gosh, Daddy, I hope my accident didn't make you sick," she said sorrowfully.

"What accident?" Red meant to wink, but he seemed to have forgotten how. So Kate looked even more sorrowful.

Eileen had told him, or at least he thought she had, that the accident might not have been completely Kate's fault. The other car had rammed the Volvo. The driver, a twenty-three-year-old medical student celebrating the end of his surgical clerkship, had been given a ticket for Driving Under the Influence. The police were being very understanding, probably because they knew about all the recent ... and Eileen hesitated ... "confusion" in the family.

Katie, of course, was charged with driving without a license. Their insurance company wouldn't pay. They would have to sue the young man and his insurance company.

The police, Eileen repeated, were quite nice.

Maybe Mike Casey had a word with them.

Red couldn't remember whether he had actually said those words or only thought them. And he was not altogether sure whether he really knew someone named Mike Casey.

Were all women psychiatrists ugly? he wondered, as Dr. What's-Her-Name (he never did find that out) badgered him. No, that couldn't be true. Mary Kate Murphy, Eileen's sister, was gorgeous. Why wasn't Mary Kate taking care of him instead of this witch? He would have to ask Eileen that the next time she came.

Had the *Washington Post* called while he was in the hospital? Or was he imagining their first call?

"You agree, then, that it's a sign of poor mental health to imagine the dead returning?" The doctor leaned over so that her face was only about a foot from his, her eyes probing his, her bad breath affronting his nostrils.

"I guess so," he said. "Especially if the dead are really dead."

That necessitated a long discussion of what he meant when he said "if they're really dead." He fended off her questions, trying to figure out whether he really had interviewed Paul O'Meara. On the face of it, it seemed highly unlikely. Paul O'Meara had disappeared in a snowstorm on the Wabash Avenue Bridge almost twenty years ago, before John

Kennedy's assassination, before the conception of John Patrick Kane, before his marriage to John Patrick's mother. Several years later the Superior Court of the County of Cook had ruled that Paul O'Meara was dead. What right did Red Kane have to claim that he had interviewed him in a deserted house on North Park—or anyplace else?

"What you say makes a great deal of sense, Doctor," he said agreeably. "I'll talk it over with my wife when she comes late this afternoon, and give you a decision."

Ah-ha, he thought. *I remember tape recording the conversation with Paul, and I'm sure I put the cassette in my briefcase when I left the* Herald Gazette. *If the tape is there and if when I play it I hear a conversation with Paul O'Meara, I'll know I'm not as crazy as this ugly broad says I am. If, on the other hand, there isn't such a tape, well, off to the funny farm with Red Kane.*

After Dr. What's-Her-Name had sallied forth to harass her other patients, Red surreptitiously dialed his home phone number. "Patty?"

"Dad."

"Are you home from school, or is it Christmas vacation already?" *Oh-oh, a bad thing to say. A healthy man would know what day of the month it is.*

"It's 4:30 in the afternoon, Daddy," she said sadly.

"I wonder if you could do me a big favor, honey. When I came home the other night I had my briefcase with me, didn't I?"

"Sure, Daddy. I brought it up to your study after..."

"After the men in white came," he laughed pleasantly.

"Right." She giggled with relief.

Obviously, if crazy old Daddy was laughing about the men in white, there was still some hope for him.

"Would you do me a very big favor and bring it over? Like right now? There's something in it I have to check."

Patty wasn't terribly enthusiastic, probably worried there might be something in the briefcase that might send Daddy into another fit of hysterical laughter. So Red Kane lied. "The doctor said it was all right," he insisted.

Thus reassured, Patty happily assented and said she would be right over.

Pretty damn clever lie, Red complimented himself. *But then, crazy people are good liars, aren't they?*

Patty showed up a half hour later, briefcase in hand, a red and blue scarf contrasting with her white down jacket.

"That was quick," Red said brightly, hoping that he looked bright-eyed and bushy-tailed and preeminently sane.

"Our new Bug started, thank goodness." She put the briefcase on the bed stand.

"Still cold outside?"

"Awesomely." She pulled off her gloves and loosened the scarf.

"Maybe it's a good thing Katie piled up the Volvo. It would have frozen to death in this weather. Are we going to get a new Volvo?"

"Really. When do we ever get like a NEW car? Mom has her eye on a Volvo that only has thirty thousand miles on it."

"It might freeze to death too." Except for Eileen, the Ryan family to a person were fixated on automobiles. Lancias, Renaults, BMWs, SAABs—you name it and some one of the Ryans had it. "I was kind of hoping we would get a BMW."

Red opened the briefcase, took out his Sony 510, and searched for a tape on which he had written the letters *POM*. No sign of the tape.

He unpacked the manuscript of his novel and placed it on the bed next to him. Again, he searched through the file folders, affidavits, photos, notes, and clutter of used and unused tapes. Finally he found it. "POM."

So I didn't imagine that conversation, or at least I didn't imagine putting those letters on the tape.

"Find what you were looking for?" Patty was watching closely.

"I dictated some notes to myself about revising my novel," he lied cheerfully. "While I'm here resting, I think I'll get back to work on it."

The lie satisfied Patty. She bundled up again in scarf, gloves, and down jacket—not covering her thick black hair, of course—and departed, doubtless to report to her mother that poor crazy Daddy seemed relatively sane today.

Fingers trembling, Red loaded the POM tape into the Sony and rewound it. What had he done with the copy?

A finger on the play button, he pondered. It would not do to have one of those tapes drifting around. He'd made a copy of it for Mike Casey, but there hadn't been a chance to give it to him. Now it didn't seem necessary.

Then he remembered that he had locked it in the middle drawer of the desk in his study. Fair enough. It would be safe there until he escaped from the hospital. Then he would pass it on to Mike—just in case. That is, he would pass it on to Mike if there was anything on the tape, if he had not imagined the whole interview.

Finally he worked up enough nerve and pressed the play button down to listen.

He only needed to hear a few words of the conversation to be reassured that he HAD spoken with Paul O'Meara. Therefore, Paul was NOT dead; therefore Red Kane was SANE. Well, more or less sane.

He listened to the whole tape, however, to make sure he remembered the details correctly. A nurse appeared toward the end of the tape and Red quickly turned the machine off.

"Eavesdropping on myself," he said lightly.

"You're really not supposed to work here, Mr. Kane," she reproved him. She jabbed two paper cups at him, one with water and the other with two pink pills.

"Entertainment, not work." Red gulped the pills down and reviewed the data again.

Paul O'Meara was still alive. He had helped Harv Gunther cover up the murder of Adele Ward. Red had destroyed the evidence of Paul's involvement in the cover-up. He still had evidence that Paul was alive, not to use against Paul but to reassure himself of his own sanity. Right?

Right. He turned the tape back on.

When he had finished the tape and rewound it, Red slipped out of bed and put the tape into the pocket of his jacket that was in the closet of his private room. He returned to the bed and began to think very carefully. He was glad that the shrink had him put on tranquilizers because his mental processes were working slowly and carefully, analyzing, searching, reconstructing, calculating.

Then it all made sense. "Damnation." Red pounded the bed in frustration.

Someone had been playing games with him, using him as a yo-yo.

Katie straggled in later in the afternoon, still looking guilty and bedraggled. But she was in a good enough mood to let him autograph her cast. And when he suggested, on impulse, that she take his novel along and read it, she seemed delighted. Of his three children, Katie was the only novel reader. The others, like their mother, "never had time for such things."

As the pieces of the puzzle fell into place, Red realized that he had to talk to someone. Certainly not the shrink; not Eileen, who couldn't possibly understand.

Larry Moran? Of course, why not? He phoned the rectory and was informed by a voice with a thick accent that "Father Moran, he no here."

Then Eileen arrived in a loving and solicitous mood of the "don't-you-worry-Luciano-I'll-take-care-of-you" variety. Before she had a chance to suggest that perhaps he ought to be moved to the psychiatric ward, so that he would get "better" treatment, Red began with, "Like I'm sure you REALLY, REALLY don't want to buy another secondhand Volvo!"

"You've been talking to the kids." She laughed as she unwrapped the vast beige scarf from around her neck and removed her female cossack cap. "Like really, those Swedish cars can't take cold weather."

When she left he had prevailed upon her to consider buying a new car, a Lancia, or even a BMW. He suspected that she would settle for a new Volvo. In the process he had also persuaded her, without having mentioned the subject, that the therapist had exaggerated the state of his mental health. If anyone had known what he was planning, they would have locked him up for months. He dutifully swallowed his two nighttime tranquilizers. He'd need a good night's sleep before he escaped.

When he awakened the next morning, he knew exactly where he would go. *Should have headed there on the Feast of All the Saints.*

Very carefully he studied the layout of the hospital corridor across from his room. Just two doors down there was a staircase. A fully clothed man, overcoat collar turned up, Irish hat pulled down, could slip out of his room and down those steps without anyone noticing.

When the nurse came with his midafternoon tranquilizers, he dutifully put them in his mouth and swallowed the assigned gulp of water. But he kept the two pills under his tongue, and as soon as she left the room, he removed them and flipped them in the wastebasket. *Two direct hits, four points!*

The routine of the floor indicated that no one would look into his room until just before supper. He closed the door so that it was only slightly ajar and shifted his clothes from the closet to the bathroom. He shaved and dressed quickly. The tall, broad-shouldered man in the mirror looked rumpled and a bit seedy. Some more gray had appeared in his wavy brown hair. But then, reporters are supposed to look rumpled and seedy and aging.

Okay. Now was the time for the break. Carefully, he opened the door a bit more widely and stuck his head out, hiding behind the door so that no one would see that he was fully dressed. He looked one way and then the other. No one in sight. Lucky the first time.

He was about to bolt from the door when he heard the rumble of a hospital cart. "Hi there, Mr. Kane."

"Hi there, Vanessa." He smiled at the nurse's aide pushing her cart slowly down the corridor. "You look lovely today, as always."

"You sure do go on, Mr. Kane." She smiled back at him.

Red closed the door and waited until he heard the cart rumbling in the opposite direction. He looked at his watch, giving Vanessa three minutes to make sure she had gone elsewhere on her appointed rounds, and then very slowly opened the door, peering into the crack as though he were a Peeping Tom in a girls' dormitory. No one in sight.

He opened the door a bit more widely, poked his head out, and looked around. Again, no one in sight.

He grabbed his hat, which reminded him of Pat Moynihan and hence of his first night with Eileen, and shoved it down over his forehead and then opened the door naturally and easily and sauntered into the corridor. Still no one in sight.

Carefully, so as not to panic, he ambled down the corridor and pushed open the door to the stairway. He heard the click of nurses' heels. Hoping that she was walking in the opposite direction, he eased through the doorway and then rushed frantically down the stairs, two, three, four floors.

On the second floor he halted, breathing heavily. It would not do to try to escape from the staircase. First of all, there might be a security guard protecting the entrance, and, secondly, if they did find his room empty, they would almost certainly set a trap for him. So on the second floor he strolled back into a hospital corridor and walked casually toward the elevators. No one even looked at him as he rode down to the first floor and walked out onto the street, confidently, as if he had every right to be there. *What the hell, I DO have a right to walk out onto the street.*

Where do I go now for help? he asked himself again. The answer was still obvious. The only institution in the world that could help him now was the Roman Catholic Church—the real Catholic Church. Send in the first team.

The 65-below windchill factor battered him the moment he stepped outside the hospital. They had not been exaggerating the cold. He signaled for a taxi. He had no money to pay for it. Regardless, they would have to pay at the other end of the line.

"Holy Name Cathedral," he told the driver.

62

"It reminds me"—Blackie Ryan peered quizzically at the Sony tape recorder—"of the cartoon in which a very haunted-looking creature says, 'I'd be all right if those paranoids would stop chasing me.'"

"Even paranoids have enemies, huh?" Red rewound the tape.

"Ah, the ineffable Mr. Bellow, quoting the equally ineffable Delmore Schwartz. Or, more precisely, in your case, some conspiracies are real, if implicit and unintentional. As I said earlier, Red, you should have kept off the Road to Damascus."

Blackie was wearing a maroon smoking jacket of the style and age of that affected by Sherlock Holmes's brother Mycroft. Eileen contended that, with the exception of jackets representing the Chicago sports teams (which he claimed to wear as a matter of liturgical propriety), her brother the Monsignor was still wearing the clothes he had bought when he graduated from Quigley High School.

"So I'm not crazy?"

"Oh, no." Blackie looked at him with mild surprise. "Of course you're not crazy. The combination of your intense religious experience and the resulting conspiracy against you combined to exacerbate the ordinary cycle of energy and discouragement which is characteristic of your personality. No, Redmond Peter Kane, you're not crazy. Oddly enough, everyone else is."

"Paranoids of the world, arise. You have nothing to lose but bitchy shrinks!" Red put the Sony back into its case and returned it to his jacket pocket.

"If you'll excuse me"—Blackie stood up, managing to convey that it was an action with which he was not all that familiar—"I will call my sister and reassure her that you are perfectly reasonable and normal. Moreover, I will urge her to consult with our mutual sibling, Mary Kate the Shrink, who will doubtless have strong words with her about her choice of psychotherapists. What is the point of having a sibling who is a psychiatrist if you don't consult with her in times of family crisis?"

Blackie shambled from his study to his office. Red heard only the mumble of his words, interspersed occasionally by a somewhat higher "Ah" or "Of course." Then he returned to the study, looking remarkably satisfied with himself.

"The woman would try the patience of a saint," Red suggested, "not that I'm a saint. Why does she think I'm crazy, Blackie?"

"As to the former, the Lord God seems to have other

plans. As to the latter"—Blackie blinked his nearsighted, watery blue eyes—"a woman, I have been told, is at best a mixed blessing; however, a mixed blessing is better than none at all."

"Rather chauvinist sentiments." Red rubbed his eyes. He would sleep for a month when this was over.

"Only if I do not say the same thing about men." Blackie Ryan settled himself comfortably in an enormous reclining chair that would have held a dozen vest-pocket monsignors.

"Not many brothers would dare interfere in a sister's marriage quite that definitively," Red observed.

"I am not most brothers." Blackie eased himself back into the chair, as though he had won the rights to its comforts. "As you have doubtless noticed in the Ryan family, many things are true by definition. Among them are the key truths that Blackie Ryan the Priest may discreetly intervene whenever he wishes and that his interventions are always quintessential wisdom. I must say..." He shook his head with some surprise. "...that your wife came perilously close at the beginning of our conversation to offending against those truths. However"—he smiled benignly—"the conclusion was that she's glad that FINALLY you and I are talking seriously to one another."

"Why does she think I'm crazy?"

"My dear man, you have reformed your life, you act like a thoroughly good man. So after a while, she says to herself, in effect, 'either my husband, the inestimable Redmond Peter Kane, is now a saint, or he's crazy.' The latter is by far the easier truth with which to live."

"A conspiracy to make me a saint?" Red was thoroughly alarmed. "You didn't tell her that, did you?"

"I didn't mention conspiracies." Blackie began to fiddle with the candle in front of the crib scene on his coffee table.

"Here, let me do it," Red intervened, taking the matches away from the priest's hands after several ineffectual attempts to light the candle. "Very pretty statues."

"Mexican-American, a gift from admiring parishioners. Lovely statues and inefficient candles."

"Inefficient candle lighter." Red lit the candle with a

single stroke of his match. "Now about this conspiracy. I know there was one and I know that I was the victim, but I don't understand how they put it together."

"Let's approach it from a different perspective." Blackie rested his chin on interlaced fingers, looking now not like a hurt leprechaun so much as an Irish Buddha. "Consider one of your colleagues, one of the more admirable and gifted ones of whom it is said, and of whom you yourself said, that he has enormous potential if only he ... Finish it yourself."

"The man that immediately comes to mind is Lee Malley, the editor of the Sunday magazine, and the concluding phrase is 'if only he weren't so much of a Sammy Glick....' Do you know who Sammy Glick is?"

"I am not unacquainted with Jewish-American literature.... You're saying that Malley would be a first-rate journalist and an admirable human being"—Blackie removed his glasses and began to polish them with the lapel of his jacket—"if he were not at all times and places ready to seize the main chance. But what would happen if he should abandon such self-serving ambition?"

"He'd be a hell of a guy and a hell of a journalist."

"Ah." The little priest grimaced with displeasure. The glasses were, if anything, dirtier than they had been before. "And what would this do to his relationship with you?"

"We'd be much better friends, wouldn't we? If a friend begins to live up to his potential, that makes the friendship better."

"Does it now?"

Snowflakes were falling again outside. It ought to have been too cold for snow, but snowing it still was. Doubtless a lakefront effect. Again the candle in front of the crib scene went out.

"I suppose I might feel a little threatened," Red said dubiously. "If a friend begins to live up to his potential, I suppose it represents a demand on me to live up to my potential."

"Ah!" Blackie bounded from his chair with a sudden display of energy and pointed an accusing finger at Red Kane. "And you would promptly join in a conspiracy with other friends to knock the unfortunate Mr. Malley back into line so he would not be a challenge and a judgment and a demand on you. Is that not so?"

"Oh, God!" moaned Red.

"Yes, precisely, God." Blackie was now standing in front of his bookcase, finger still pointing at Red. "Consider this situation: Redmond Peter Kane is a gifted, reasonably handsome, magnetic person who, with a minimum of effort, does moderately well as a journalist, a husband, a father, and a human being. Everyone looks up to him, admires him, laughs at his jokes, enjoys the cleverness of his writings. They lament, sincerely enough, that he has become something of a moth-eaten, down-at-the-heel character, hiding behind the mask of cynicism and aided in that project by consuming a lot of, but not quite too much of, John Jameson's magic concoction."

"I can hear them saying it," Red protested bitterly.

"Precisely!" Blackie's finger was now pointed skyward, as though invoking Divine Approbation on the rest of his sermon. "So then what happens? The Lord God, through an intervention, the precise dynamics of which we'll leave aside at the moment, activates these potentials. There is no more reason to say 'too *bad*!' And you yourself assert—quaintly alluding to Richard Nixon—that there is a 'new' Red Kane—crusading journalist, dedicated truth-teller, scourge of dishonesty and corruption, brilliant writer, sensitive and loving husband, sympathetic and helpful father, dedicated churchman. Do we all shout hooray for the new Red Kane? Or three cheers for Red Kane the Saint!"

"I'm not a saint . . . ," Red protested.

"Nonsense!" and, fingers still raised to heaven, Blackie returned to the coffee table, now preaching over the Mexican-American crib scene. "You are doing the things that a saint does—i.e., excelling in the demands of everyday life. I repeat: Do we cheer for the new Red Kane? Most assuredly not, for the new Red Kane imposes on us the obligation to change. If one party in a relationship undergoes a transformation, then the other party in that relationship must be transformed too. Three cheers for the new Red Kane? Again I say, nonsense! Rather, down with the new Red Kane!"

"People don't like us to get better." Red reached for the matches and began to dig wax away from the wick of the vigil light, lest Blackie's harangue be interrupted by the need to repair it.

"Or consider the case of that charming woman, your wife. Adore you she does, for reasons of her own—"

"The Ryan clan never liked me," Red interrupted.

"Don't distract me from the course of my sermon." Blackie's finger descended to point at Red's nose. "By definition, anyone who has the taste and intelligence to marry into the Ryan clan is in all respects admirable and virtuous. You know that. In any case, the good Eileen worships the ground you walk on and sorrows, doubtless daily, that she has not been able to bring forth the best of your affections and predispositions and abilities. The relationship between the two of you is unsatisfactory by the standards of her ideals, but tolerable in its daily course. It is defined, delimited, specified, controlled; yet she knows who and what you are; while she may protest that she wishes that you might be more, she has settled into a working relationship in which you are what you are and she is what she is. It is a *modus vivendi* and nothing more, but then what is life but an assembly of *modi vivendi*?"

"And then I change...."

"Ah." Blackie bounded out of the chair again and now stood directly over Red, pointing his peremptory finger down at him. "You comprehend! The good Eileen has found for herself a routine in which she, you should excuse my candor, can play the role of the affectionate and caring Irish mother to her brilliant but slightly wayward little boy—"

"More charming, perhaps, but not much more responsible than Luciano, the family Labrador."

"Yes, yes, of course!" Blackie's enthusiasm was rising. "I shall omit all details that may pertain to private matters. What does the good Eileen do, however, when she opens the *Herald Gazette* and finds a public love letter addressed to her, a charming, witty, tender, and touching love letter? Often, perhaps, she has wondered why she was never mentioned in your column; now she finds that she has been celebrated in one. A life in which such surprises occur, in principle and in theory attractive, suddenly becomes terrifying. Then the good Eileen finds that she is expected to respond with the same slightly daft enthusiasm. What does she conclude?"

"That I'm about to have a nervous breakdown," Red said sadly.

Blackie bustled out of the room and returned in a few moments with two bottles of Perrier water and two tumblers filled with ice cubes. "A reward for our virtue, Redmond." He filled both the tumblers and sipped at his own with a grimace of disgust. "You had to be done in, lest you force the rest of us to essay the same virtue which you so readily achieved. Your family, your friends, your colleagues, your enemies knew that with the unerring instinct that such implicit conspirators have. Moreover, they chose to do you in—about sixty-five percent convinced of their own sincerity—precisely when you were most vulnerable, when you had risked everything with the Gunther series.... And when, through a curious twist of timing, you were exalted by another one of your ecstatic interludes...."

"Why did God do it?" Red demanded.

"Why did God do what?" Blackie relaxed in his overstuffed chair, obviously satisfied with his sermon.

"Hit me over the head with His cosmic baseball bat precisely when everything else was going wrong."

"The Lord God, to tell you the absolute truth, is a comedian." Blackie held up his hands in a gesture of helplessness.

"Like Queen Victoria, I am not amused," Red said grimly. "What the hell does the Lord God expect me to do now?"

"Oh, THAT. Is it not clear what you must do, Redmond? You must continue to be the 'new' Red Kane, the resourceful platoon leader, brilliant journalist, fearless crusader, dedicated idealist, zealous Catholic, comforting and challenging father, and loving and demanding husband. What else?"

"They'll destroy me."

"They damn well will try." Blackie waved his hand in an indifferent gesture. "After a while they will give up. Perhaps they are only testing you to find out whether you are for real. Once so persuaded many of them may adjust, not without pleasure, to the new Red Kane."

"I may lose," Red said slowly, considering the implications of Blackie's strategy. "If I go back to being the new Red Kane, they may do me in permanently."

"The Lord God offers no guarantees. Your novel may be rejected again; no one may touch the Gunther story; you may not be able to find another job in Chicago; the children are likely to hold out for a long time, just to be sure that there is no other choice. . . ."

"I might lose Eileen."

Blackie sighed deeply. "How can I answer that one, Red?" The leprechaun and Buddha masks were swept away, and Blackie Ryan appeared as vulnerable as anyone else. "I certainly hope not. I'd bet on her, but I may be prejudiced because she's my sister. To be perfectly candid, however, you have to face the possibility that Eileen will not want to stay married to the new Red Kane. The grail is never fully possessed, but must always be pursued—that is the agony, the joy, and, to be candid, the fun."

"She's responsible for it all, Blackie." Red felt tears sting his eyes. "It was the similarity between the color of the skyscraper and the color of her eyes . . . then the emerald I bought her, and, Whoever it is Who's playing these crazy games with me, It, He, She . . . is more like Eileen than anyone else I know."

"So it works out in marriage," Blackie said wearily. "Husband and wife are sacraments of God for one another, the best hint each will ever have in this world of what God is like."

"I've never been much of a sacrament for her," Red said sadly.

"I'm sure she'd deny that," Blackie said as he left the room.

"I suppose . . . But, Blackie, the Lord God screwed me. . . ." Red shouted after him.

If the Lord God expects that kind of courage from anyone, then He or She would have to provide guarantees.

"What can I tell you, Redmond?" Blackie returned with the remnants of a six-pack of Perrier. "I should have brought all six bottles in the first place. You want guarantees that are simply not given to anyone. I quite agree that if the Lord God were a reasonable person, She would make those guarantees, but She isn't. It's understandable that we should seek them. Even Jesus in the Garden of Olives did. But they're not to be found. We grope ahead in the dark."

"If only I could be sure I wouldn't lose Eileen."

"That's the nub of it, isn't it? She is in her own way the chief conspirator on both sides—an agent of the Lord God and the chief of those who want to undo His work on you."

Red gulped most of the liquid in the glass in one swallow. His throat was drier than it had ever been, even after his worst hangovers. "She has the most to lose."

"And the most to gain, too." Blackie was now watching him intently over the rim of his glass. "No guarantees from the Lord God, Red, and no hassling from the rector of the Cathedral of the Holy Name. You must work out your own destiny by yourself in those moments of lonely silence that we all face when a loving voice says, 'Come on, jump!' And we say, 'Yeah, but the chasm is at least five miles wide.' Then the voice replies, 'Don't pay any attention to THAT!'"

"This has all been extremely helpful, Blackie." Red rose from his chair and stretched. "It's given me a lot to think about. I'd better get home now. I'm sure Eileen is worried."

"Take a taxi. I'll lend you ten more dollars. Don't walk this time." Blackie scrambled to his feet. "I'll come down to the door with you."

They walked in silence down the steps and through the corridors of the mausoleum-like Cathedral rectory. Blackie helped him on with his coat and instructed the switchboard operator to summon a cab.

Almost as soon as they were at the door of the rectory, a taxi pulled up. "There are still some advantages in clericalism." Blackie opened the door for him.

"I'm certainly very grateful for all the help," Red said blankly, shivering already from the intense cold.

"Redmond Peter Kane"—Blackie solemnly pointed his finger at him again, oblivious of the windchill factor—"I have an injunction for you."

"Enjoin away."

"I quote loosely from the Book of Job." The pointing finger waved in admonition. "Never, Redmond Peter Kane, I repeat, NEVER fuck with the Lord God."

63

The taxi in which he rode for the seven blocks from Holy Name Cathedral to the Old Town Ale House was toasty-warm; its driver mumbled in Iranian-accented English about the cold American weather in a way that implicated the Ayatollah in plotting against his archenemies, the Americans. Red fantasized about an Art Buchwald–like column on the two Red Kanes. Buchwald had chronicled the comedy of the struggle between the Old Dick Nixon and the New Dick Nixon until the comedy had turned into tragedy. How long had the New Nixon lasted? Certainly through the recognition of Red China, probably even to the beginning of the reelection campaign—three, three and a half years. The new Red Kane had lived for a little less than two months, and was now to be put out of his misery.

If God wanted to amuse Himself with cute little comic games at Christmastime, let Him find another victim.

The Ale House crowd was a curious mixture of far-out advertising types and reporters, along with business executives and blacks and Hispanics from the projects to the west. All were wearing their overcoats. The Ale House had not been insulated against the pre-Christmas deep freeze.

"Hey, man," yelled a burly black, who had once been a heavyweight contender if he were to be believed, "that old Redmond is back! Merry Christmas, Redmond. You come to warm us all up with your stories?"

"Came to warm myself up with some Jameson's. A powerful thirst is upon me!"

Three shots of Irish whiskey later, straight up as always, and the old Red Kane was alive, well, and prospering. Also, he was feeling very warm and mellow when Lee Malley, somewhat hesitantly, thumped down across the dilapidated table from him. "We'd all heard you were a little bit under the weather, Red." He examined Red's face carefully, doubtless searching for signs of manic-depressive psychosis.

"Just resting up." Red waved his empty glass. "Bartender, this glass seems to have evaporated. Could you moisten it a little?"

In truth, the whiskey was beginning to burn a hole in his stomach. It didn't really taste all that good.

"They're going to try to rehire you." Lee Malley's voice was neutral, his face expressionless. "With Royko leaving the *Sun-Times*, they're afraid Murdoch will hire you. Their circulation dropped twenty-five thousand the day after your column disappeared, and ten thousand more the next day. You've got them by the short hairs, Red."

"Ah-ha, isn't that interesting?" Red extended his shot glass in the direction of the bartender, knowing that he would not be able to sip any more than a few drops of it. Serious drinking required practice after two months of abstinence.

"They're terrified that you'll jump to the *Washington Post*. Either the *Trib* or the *Sun-Times* would pick you up from that syndicate. It could do us in pretty quickly." Malley managed to manufacture an expression of deep and sincere concern.

"Royko quit the *Sun-Times*?" Malley's earlier remark suddenly hit Red as if someone had heaved a brick through the window of the Ale House. "That's impossible."

"He said that Murdoch published papers that no self-respecting dead fish would want to be wrapped in. He's taken a 'leave of absence.' No one thinks he'll go back to work for Murdoch."

"A revolving door for all the columnists these days." Red considered carefully the rings his shot glass was making on the table.

"I hear from top sources," Malley whispered conspiratorially, "that if you promise to forget about the Gunther thing, you can have almost anything else you want."

"Oh, can I now?" Red dusted off his old leprechaun accent. "Well, we'll just have to see about that."

Lee Malley offered to drive him home from the Ale House. Red gratefully accepted, not so much because he wanted a ride with Malley but because it gave him an excuse not to drink any more.

While Lee negotiated the slush on North Clark Street in his Datsun sports car and babbled about the implications of the definitive deal between Rupert Murdoch and the *Chicago Sun-Times*, Red considered the possibility that he ought to call Mike Royko and compliment him on his courage.

No way. The new Red Kane would have done that.

He also pondered with satisfaction that the new Red Kane had only recently expired and already the old Red Kane virtually had his job back.

He unlocked the door of the house, noting that Eileen and the girls were chatting in the kitchen, and walked upstairs to his study without saying a word to them. He took off his overcoat and jacket, kicked aside his loafers, relaxed comfortably in his favorite easy chair. Then he opened the pack of Camels he had bought in the Ale House and lighted one. Terrible taste. How had he ever been able to smoke such things?

Nonetheless, it was necessary to smoke them, or at least to appear to smoke them, in order that the extirpation of the new Red Kane might continue according to plan.

Eileen appeared, particularly appealing in a beige sweater and matching jeans. However, the old Red Kane was immune to his wife's charms, for the moment at any rate.

"I called Mary Kate, as Blackie said I should." Eileen's green eyes probed at him anxiously. "She said our shrink was a castrating bitch with ideological horse manure for a brain."

"Sounds like a reasonable description to me," Red murmured, looking up with mild impatience from the collected poems of William Carlos Williams.

"She also said"—Eileen rubbed the doorframe nervously—"that you probably did have some kind of ecstatic experience."

"I always said that Mary Kate was a great psychiatrist." Red returned to the poems and Eileen drifted away, suitably rebuked.

The telephone rang. *Let someone else answer it. No, it was his private line.*

"Kane," he murmured, confident that he sounded drunker than he was.

"Hi, Dad, it's John." The young man sounded delighted with himself.

"Yeah?"

"I thought you'd like to know that the *Minneapolis Tribune* has bought a half dozen of my photos to illustrate a piece about winter in Stearns County."

"The *Tribune* is a fine newspaper. Don't let it go to your head."

"I just thought you'd want to know." John was suitably deflated.

"They pay much?"

"Twenty-five dollars a picture." Now he was even more deflated.

"Not enough to support a family on, John."

"I know," the young man said sadly. "I just thought you'd want to know."

"Thanks for calling." Red hung up. Now he was getting back into the swing of things. He crept down the corridor to his bedroom, removed enough clothes and toilet articles for the night, and went back to the study. As always, in a house over which Eileen Ryan Kane presided, the bed was freshly made in case an unexpected guest should put in an appearance.

The briefcase, which Patty had brought back from the hospital, was on his desk, having materialized during his brief trip to the bedroom.

He removed the files and the cassette tapes. Perhaps he ought to throw them away. No, the old Red Kane never threw anything away that might fit into a story someday. He dumped the tapes and the files into a cabinet next to the desk, locked the cabinet, and lurched back to his easy chair. *Thus ends the cases of Harvard Gunther and Paul O'Meara, until someday when I write my memoirs.*

He knew that he would certainly never write his memoirs.

He returned to the two Williams. The three shot glasses of Jameson's had made him sleepy, too sleepy to catch the elegant periodicities of Williams's lyrics. Still, it was essential to reestablishing the old Red Kane's ways.

Luciano, tail wagging, tongue hanging out stupidly, ambled into the room and curled up at Red's feet. The Labrador, sensing the equality of status that he and Red enjoyed in the household, would under ordinary circumstances park himself next to Red's chair only when there was no one else in the house. "Get the hell out of here, Lucky," he muttered.

The Lab struggled to his feet, favored Red with his most woeful, you-hurt-my-feelings expression, and, tail sagging dejectedly, crept out of the room.

Eileen, John, Luciano—three of the five members of the family had been given the message. Red Kane was back to his old ways. *Everyone can relax.*

None of them seemed very happy about it. *Well, guys, you can't have it both ways.*

"And that goes for you too, fella," Red informed the Cheshire smile that was being summarily dismissed from his life, all calm and curled or not.

Doubtless, Kate and Patty would check in before the night was over.

Patty came first. Standing at the doorway, a mirror image of her mother, though in blue, not brown. A prettier face than Eileen's, not as much starch in her spine yet, but the same cautiously probing eyes. "Adele's in heaven now, isn't she, Daddy?"

"I'm sure I don't know." Red pretended to be more interested in the book of poetry. "God, if there is a God, is the only one who knows who's in heaven. Isn't that what the Madames teach you over at Sacred Heart?"

"Daddy, they stopped being called that FIFTEEN years ago. Really!" That TOTALLY unacceptable word would have evoked a paroxysm of anger a few weeks ago. Tonight she thought it was a wonderful joke.

"Fine."

Katie was a different story. One arm still in a sling, the other clutching the manuscript of his novel, she bounded into his study as she had done when she was a three-year-old and he had come home from work. How long ago was that? 1971? Still in Nixon's first term.

"I think it's like totally heavy duty. MaJOR!" She flung

herself on the ottoman next to him. "A really bitchin' novel. I couldn't put it down!"

"Bitchin'?"

"Like a real killer. Like totally major, you know, way far out, great? Right?"

Katie seemed as thin and fragile as her mother and sister were strong and solid, the sort of young woman who could easily be swept away by a Lake Michigan wind. The same slender frame, pale complexion, and white-blond hair that made her cousin Caitlin look so vital made Kate look vulnerable, perhaps even tragic.

"My novel, you mean."

"Oh, Daddy, don't be gross. What else would I be talking about? Sure, it's kind of about you and Mom, but it's really about everybody, isn't it? Right? And it's totally funny, and the ending is just wonderful. Really!"

"I hope you haven't shown it to anyone else." He glanced up at her.

"Don't be a geek, Daddy. It's just our secret. Right? I'm not such a gelhead that I'd show it to anyone else. But all the kids will love it when it's published. I'll be so proud."

"Just put it on the desk," Red murmured.

"You ARE going to publish it?"

"Unfortunately, young woman, the publisher didn't share your enthusiasm. No, we're not going to publish it."

"Gross! Really!"

"One more thing, young woman." He spoke as if she were about to leave the study, which she showed no intention of doing. "You're legal, for driving that is, next month, aren't you?"

"Yes, Daddy," she said meekly.

"Did your mother postpone the use of the car because you took it without permission?"

"No, Daddy."

He glanced over the top edge of his book. She was slumped on the ottoman now, sad and dejected.

"June," he said firmly.

"Yes, Daddy."

She left the study, her frail shoulders sagging.

Well, that's that. He lifted the computer output from the desk where Katie had put it and dropped it into the wastebasket. *And that is that.* He smoked one more cigarette and then went to bed, quite satisfied with a good night's work but, unaccountably, sad over its success.

64

The road back was not without its potholes. Good habits, Red Kane discovered, were as hard to lose as bad habits.

He was rehired by Brad Winston with a twenty-five percent raise on the condition that nothing more be said in the *Herald* about Harvard Gunther. A possible story in another paper was not mentioned, most likely because Brad hadn't thought of that.

"Let the dead bury their dead," Red said.

"I beg your pardon?"

"It's from the Bible, Brad." Red stood up and extended his hand. "I think Saint Paul said it, though it might have been Jesus. It means in this context that I'm delighted to forget about Harvard Princeton Gunther. You and I have a deal."

The handshake was cordial enough, considering that Bradford Winston was a robot and not a human being.

Red ambled through the city room as though he had never left it, pretending not to hear the enthusiastic applause. Inside his cubbyhole he flipped on the CRT and began to work on a column. The applause died, as in the old days, because people were afraid to approach Red Kane when he was working.

It was a vintage Kane column, doing in, in six hundred terse words, John Madigan, Helen Slattery, the BGA, and the editorial writers at the other papers. Without mentioning Harv Gunther once.

To his amazement Red experienced some pangs of, well,

not exactly guilt, but regret at his revenge. It was kind of cheap. However, it was also what the old Red Kane would do.

Red assumed that at most he was only moderately more churlish than the average person. The average person, however, had slipped into the pattern of churlishness by which he defended himself from the world through long years of practice, scarcely realizing that he was churlish. The average person, a statistical construct, was not obliged to relearn consciously his modes of churlishness in a couple of weeks.

Particularly the weeks before Christmas.

Christmas presents were a problem, for example. Normally at Christmastime Red wallowed in his favorite blend of self-pity, guilt, and anger. But he would finally break down on Christmas Eve and buy presents for his wife and children and for the assigned member of the Ryan family from the St. Stephen's Day grab bag. (On December one, by ancient tradition, the youngest Ryan able to walk and talk drew numbers out of a cap to assign each member of the clan another member of the clan from whom a present must be delivered the day after Christmas—on the Feast of Stephen, the day on which according to the carol, Good King Wenceslaus went out. This year, as luck would have it, Red had drawn Caitlin's name, a young woman whom it was most dangerous to offend.) The shopping expedition was always hurried, the gifts inappropriate, and at the end of Christmas Eve Red would already be deeply into his customary blue funk. This year, however, his gut instincts told him not to buy Christmas presents, because he would all too easily slip into the delights he had experienced in his shopping orgy for Eileen during the month of November. *No Christmas presents this year even if it is difficult to be that churlish.*

I don't want to become a neo-Scrooge, Red explained to himself (not without some pride in the turn of phrase). *But if I am to get my family back, I have to stop being the new Red Kane.*

What if Eileen buys the presents, wraps them, and puts your name on them? She's capable of that, you know.

Damn right, I know.

I'll deny it to her face. That will teach the scheming bitch.

Moreover, he had been evasive when Larry Moran invited him and the family to assist in distributing Christmas packages in Larry's parish. Doubtless, as Larry had argued, it would have been a wonderful experience for Red and all the family. Just now they didn't need collective wonderful experiences.

It was also required, under the churlishness rule, to respond to the family in ways that might be objectively considered cruel. He justified such behavior with the argument that cruelty was necessary if the old pattern of relationships was to be reestablished. The alternative was to risk losing his family completely. Cruelty was therefore the Lord God's fault for refusing to provide guarantees.

Thus when Johnny had called from Collegeville to ask whether his father thought it would be worthwhile to take a course in creative writing from the great short-story writer J. F. Powers, Red had replied, "Who?"

"J. F. Powers," Johnny said. "You know, 'Prince of Darkness,' 'Presence of Grace,' '*Morte d'Urban*.'"

"Oh, yes, I think I remember him," Red admitted. Obviously Johnny was calling to brag a little. Powers only took the best in his tutorials. "Suit yourself. It's your college education. I hear the fellow only writes a couple of sentences a week. I'm not sure what kind of a teacher he'd be."

"He's supposed to be the best short-story writer in America." Johnny sounded hurt and deflated.

"That covers a lot of ground, John. Hardly fair to Updike or Cheever, even if they are WASPs. I suppose a course from him can't hurt. Remember, however, you learn how to write by reading and writing, not by taking courses."

"Yes, Dad."

He might just as well have said, "Yes, Polonius."

Kate bounded into his study one night in high dudgeon. "I think it's a real gross-out, the geekiest thing you've ever done. You're, like, totally a nerd!"

"Oh?" Red said mildly while he lighted a cigarette.

"Daddy." She stamped an angry foot. "Why did you try to throw out your novel? I found it in the trash can. I think you've turned into a real gelhead!"

"Did it occur to you, young woman, that that's word-processor output and that I have the whole manuscript up on disk?"

"I don't care." But the wind had gone out of her sails. "I still think it's nerdy to throw it in the trash can. I'm going to hide it so you can't throw it away again. I don't care if I ever get wheels! Really!"

Red devoutly hoped that she hadn't shown it to anyone else in the family. It would, however, have been unlike Katie to do that.

Luciano, with dogged determination, showed up every night after Red made his customary trek from the coatrack to his study, and parked himself at Red's feet. Just as doggedly, Red banished him from the room.

Patty asked him if he could read over her term paper on Charles Dickens. "I know that Dickens is one of your favorite writers."

"Not tonight, hon." He did not bother to look up from the collection of Harvey Shapiro's poems that he was reading. "I'm too busy. Give it to me over the weekend."

"It's due Friday."

"Well, that's too bad. Maybe the next one. Like I say, I'm busy tonight."

Dear God, I hate myself when I say things like that. But it's Your fault! If I don't act like a boor, they'll think I'm crazy and I'll lose all of them. I'll make it up to her later.

The Lord God had His tricks? All right. So did Red Kane.

He broke his churlishness rule, however, when Mike Royko called to congratulate him on his reappearance in the pages of the *Herald Gazette*.

"At least one Chicago columnist," Mike said gruffly, "is workin' for a living these days."

Red knew how cut up Royko was over the troubles at the *Sun-Times* and over what he took to be the betrayal of the paper by the Field family when they sold it to Rupert Murdoch. He had refrained in principle from sending his sympathies and best wishes to Royko because such behavior was clearly "new" Red Kane material.

"The two of us spend so much time in revolving doors, we're likely to bump into each other one of these days," he replied. And then he praised Royko's courage for walking out on the *Sun-Times* and telling the truth about what had happened over there. "Sometimes I think we ought to start our own paper, Mike."

"We'd fire each other the first day!"

Red justified this momentary lapse of virtue on the grounds that the old Red Kane arguably would have been civilized under such circumstances.

It was most difficult, of course, to be churlish with Eileen. They were still in separate bedrooms, she in her "office," he in his "study." The marital bedroom was quite undisturbed. The two of them were watching each other closely, maneuvering to find a safe level at which to renew their relationship, avoiding the risks of emotional intensity that might put the relationship in jeopardy.

Eileen had discarded her glasses for unifocal contact lenses, as she had promised. She had also permitted her hair to grow longer as he had suggested, and was now favoring pastel cashmere sweaters and matching skirts. The combination of unobscured green eyes, casually framed face, and subtly displayed womanly curves made her look younger and prettier. It was also a powerful if understated invitation to sex.

One night he left his study for a brief sojourn in the television room to watch the Blue Demons of De Paul begin another season in which they would doubtless skyrocket to the first rounds of the NCAA play-offs and then fizzle.

"I hope they win this year." Red had not even heard Eileen, bundled up in a maroon housecoat, enter the room. "Ray Meyer is such a nice old man; he's entitled to retire with a championship."

"They'll collapse again in the play-offs," Red said heavily.

"Do you want to come help me pick out the new Volvo tomorrow?" she asked casually.

"It's your car."

"No, the Volkswagen is in my name; the Volvo is in your name."

The Blue Demons were on a hot streak—ten baskets in a row. A bunch of hotshot alley kids for whom college was a brief transition between poverty and, perhaps, the promised land of the NBA.

"I suppose we can afford it," Eileen murmured, as Dallas Comygs dunked a leisurely shot from the left side of the hoop. "So do you want to come to the Volvo works with me and the kids?"

"That's not necessary. Whatever you three choose will be fine."

"You might want to referee."

"No, thanks." It was his turn to laugh lightly.

"I'm sorry, Red," she said in exactly the same dry, casual tone of voice. "I blew it again."

"Blew what?"

"I let you down." She sagged like an old woman who had just climbed a long flight of steps. "I lost my nerve and jumped at the first excuse to cop out. The German chocolate cake was too sweet, I guess. I would have had to face myself. So I ran. And betrayed you."

"No one betrayed anyone." He fled from the room, shivering with anxiety.

In his study, he poured himself a strong shot of Jameson's, sipped it, gulped at the strong taste, and set the glass aside.

The temptation to play Madonna to your wife was a dangerous aphrodisiac. If he had hesitated another half minute down there, alone with her in the house, he would have dragged off the housecoat, spread her on the floor, and asked politely if she was the same woman who had said that she was willing to try anything.

And then having enjoyed her spectacularly, he would be well on his way to losing her again, perhaps now forever. More baseball bats and warm breasts and ah! bright wings. And more afterburners and spinning paddle wheels.

I let her down, not the other way around. I was so confident of my own enthusiasm and love, I didn't bother to listen to her. Damn fool reporter. I listened to Lois, but not to my wife.

Then Red Kane saw the whole story, the whole *fabula* as the crazy Russian formalists would have called it. Until that instant with the mostly full whiskey glass in his hand, he had only known the *syuzhet*, the plot—and his plot at that.

But it had been her story all along.

Eileen was afraid of growing old and dying. She felt that she had messed up her career and her marriage; never mind that she was completely wrong on both counts. It was what she thought was true. She was approaching the age of her mother's death, a turning point that a husband with something more than a negative I.Q. would have recognized. So she would make a last, valiant attempt at intimacy.

Dumb, insensitive Red Kane had finally taken the hint and flipped out in some sort of weird mystical experience, quite possibly generated by an Ally of Eileen's. Then he'd acted even more insensitively. He'd heard what she said, but had not really understood or listened. He had seen everything as a problem of discussing their marriage—which meant clearing away the guilt he felt for his infidelities. He had thought the only response required to Eileen's problems was to offer affectionate reassurance to a child who worried about the wrong things.

He buried his face in his hands; tears of anguish strained to spill out of his eyes. An overwhelming urge to rush back to her assaulted his body. He pounded his head in frustration.

She had broken the rules. They both had agreed implicitly to bracket the last six weeks of their marriage. It had not worked. It couldn't work. Eileen had reached for intimacy. He had reached back. Perhaps she was capable of it. Certainly he was not. Intimacy of the sort they had sought was impossible—a trick, a deceit, a fake. If they tried again, they might lose the little that they had.

As Jacob had found long ago, it is tough to wrestle the Lord God.

But he did not want to lose Eileen.

Tears continued to sting at his eyes. *I am not a monster. I love them all. But if I want them, I have to be a monster for a little while. Then maybe I can slip in some of the less spectacular traits of the new Red Kane.*

Why won't the bastard stay dead?

The Hound of Heaven promised that if you yielded to Him (Blackie would have said Her), you had all else beside.

Red had tried that game and it didn't work.

Every day or two after that there was a slightly different encounter, innocent of the dangerous rule breaking that had occurred while the Blue Demons cavorted on the screen. In such exchanges he and Eileen reassured one another that their marriage was back on track, polite, civilized, dispassionate, marred neither by conflict nor intense affection. And Red, all the while protesting that it was the way it had to be, tried hard not to despise himself.

With considerable difficulty he suppressed the impulse to bring poinsettias home—banks of them—to turn the old house on Webster red and green with festivity. Nor was it easy to stay in his study for the Christmas-carol party during which Patty, Kate, and their teenage friends sang carols for several hours accompanied by Eileen on the piano. Eileen's sweet, clear voice seemed undiminished by time.

Finally, his body did not want to give up the habits—good or bad, depending on your perspective—that the new Red Kane had been developing. It resolutely refused to tolerate any more than two or three drinks at the most. It simply went to sleep when it was required to absorb more alcohol, a whole lifetime of carefully acquired drinking skills down the drain after six weeks of neglect.

Nor was it prepared to readjust to nicotine. Experienced smokers claim that even after three years of not smoking, they can reacquire the habit in a single day. Not so Red Kane. He was a sixth-grade boy sneaking cigarettes in the alley and choking on the damn things.

Indeed, so vigorously did his respiratory tract reject any attempt to ingest smoke into it, that Red smoked only at home and then did not inhale. He justified this aberration from the patterns of the past on the grounds that smoking was not essential to the persona of the old Red Kane, and that he'd always planned to give it up anyway.

The worst of the bad habits that the new Red Kane had created in his body was the need for Eileen. He felt a treacherous marital lust, which if yielded to would lead to a tidal wave of emotion that could easily shred the tenuous relationship between them. Red finally understood why there was so little passion between most husbands and wives. He was afraid of too much love—an unwieldy, unpredictable, and dangerous emotion, a brooding low-pressure area stirring about restlessly in the distant Caribbean of their marriage, threatening to convert itself into a dangerous and destructive hurricane.

Stay away from too much love, my friends, he mused, *it's bad for your marriage.*

65

On the Tuesday before Christmas, the Lord God launched a sudden and sharp counterattack, or so it seemed to Red Kane. Without warning. No ecstatic experiences this time. Red was playing against a new set of rules. The Lord God, it seemed to Red, tended to make up the rules as the game went along and as He—She, It, They, Whatever—pleased.

He had come home early the day before, without even a stop at Billy Goat's or the Ale House, and taken to his bed with a plea that he was coming down with a cold. He was not, in fact, feeling very well. The grimly persistent subzero weather, celebrated enthusiastically every night on the ten o'clock news, was wearing him out, along with everyone else in Chicago.

He also wanted an excuse not to attend the Ryan family preview of Mike Casey's first art exhibit. According to all reports, Annie Reilly's new husband was, if not a gifted painter, at least an extremely "commercial"—to use the agreed-upon Ryan adjective—painter. Red was delighted that his old grammar school classmate had acquired a glamorous new wife and a glamorous new profession in the space of a couple of months. Mike and Annie belonged together; even if it had required forty years for them to figure it out, at least they finally had. He wished them well, he wished Mickey well in his career as a painter, a hell of a lot better than being a Deputy Superintendent of Police under the present administration. But Red was afraid that the affection between Annie and Mickey, combined with the almost certain nostalgia that his paintings would excite, might provide the Lord God with the excuse for springing a trap.

So he stayed in bed and endured the bright-eyed, glowing-cheeked enthusiasm of the women in his family, who stormed into his sickroom when they returned from the gallery, quite oblivious of his ill health.

The next day, feeling better than he ought to, and indeed better than he wanted to, he feigned martyrdom and dragged himself off to his cubbyhole at the *Herald Gazette*.

Scarcely had he begun to work on his column, suggesting that "Merry winter solstice" would be a much better nondenominational greeting than "Have a good holiday," when the Lord God proved that He—She, It, Whatever—did not require an art gallery and a love renewed from long ago to spring traps.

The first call was from the man at the *Washington Post*.

"Red? I tried to get back to you but I guess you were under the weather. Hey, look, we're still serious about this thing. Damned serious. I've got authorization to go ahead with our original offer: three columns a week, written from Chicago, on national topics, more or less. We take over the syndication. We guarantee you a minimum of twenty-five percent over your combined income from the *Herald* and from the syndicate and we give you a five-year contract with a yearly option to end it on your part, not on ours. How does that sound?"

"You heard about my raise here at the *Gazette*?" Red gulped.

"Yeah, you'd be damned near the highest-paid columnist in the country. Grab it while you can, Red. If you look at your new contract, you'll notice that one of the little sweeteners that Brad Winston offered was the option for you to terminate with thirty days' notice."

Red had noticed that, indeed, when he glanced at the new contract. It was an extra little gift from Winston, who was serenely confident that Red would never leave the *Herald Gazette*.

"Do you guys have Deep Throat working for the Herald Company now?" he demanded.

"Ask me no questions, Red, and I'll tell you no lies. It suffices to say that we probably know your contract better than you do."

His income would now be solidly in six figures. Not quite as much as Eileen made, but getting up there, and only three columns a week—an hour and a half's effort! With that kind of money, perhaps Eileen might cut back on the law work. She looked terribly weary these last couple of weeks. The Hurricane Houston case had taken a lot out of her.

"I don't think, to tell you the truth, that I can make the change from being a local columnist to a national columnist. Too old a dog to learn new tricks."

"C'mon, Red; don't give me that bullshit. If Dunne could make the change, so could you."

"'Mr. Dooley' went national eighty years ago, and Finley Peter Dunne was a much more clever writer than I am."

"What's wrong with giving it a try? Even if it doesn't work, you're employed for five years. You have nothing to lose. We have everything to lose."

"If I left the *Gazette*, I'd be like a fish out of water."

"Red, get out of the *Gazette* while you can. It's a cemetery for you."

"I don't know...."

"Is there anything more we can offer you...?" The desperation in his voice was such to persuade Red that somebody at the *Washington Post* really did want a Midwestern voice. It had to be Kay Graham.

"Hell, no. Don't tell Mrs. Graham, but if I was going to jump, I could be persuaded to jump for a lot less."

"Look, I won't take no for an answer, not today. I'll call you back after the first of the year. Talk it over with your wife and family. You wouldn't have to come to Washington at all, not a single day of the year."

If he took the job, he would want to spend some time in Washington and New York. That would be part of the fun. With Eileen, too, perhaps.

"The answer will still be no then. Tell Mrs. Graham I am very appreciative."

"I can still call you back?"

"I'm not going to refuse to take phone calls from anybody."

"Thanks for listening, Red. Have a good holiday!"

"And a merry winter solstice to you," Red said ruefully.

"It's lines like that," the man from the *Post* chuckled, "that makes Mrs. Graham want you on board."

"And a fertile Saturnalia too." Red hung up.

He was sweating profusely. If the man from the *Post* had pushed him a little harder, he might have accepted. *You never give an Irishman,* he told himself, *a couple of weeks to think it over. That was a narrow squeak.*

He'd finished two more paragraphs of his column when the phone rang again. It was a Ms. Roberta Kendall from the publishing house of Fineman and Fichter. Ms. Kendall spoke with that intonation that only the top tenth of a Wellesley graduating class was able to achieve.

"Mistah Kane, we've heard from very good authority that you have a manuscript for an absolutely certain best-seller about the Chicago Irish. We understand, Mistah Kane, that your previous publisher has released you from all obligations with regard to this book. From everything we've heard about it, we're persuaded that we would want to publish it. Could you possibly send it to us, Mistah Kane, Federal Express today, and we would have a final decision for you right after the first of the year. And I mean, Mistah Kane, right after. No later than the fourth of January. We could talk about a six-figure advance."

"Is that all?" Red said ironically.

She missed his irony completely. "I am authorized to say that we could go quite high if the book is as good as I am told it is."

"I don't know, Ms. Kendall," he said. "Your offer is very attractive, but I'm afraid that I'm too far along in years to adjust to the demands of the novel-writing profession. I think I'd better stick to my last, and finish my life as a journalist."

"Oh, come now, Mistah Kane, I'm older than you are, and I don't feel old at all."

Well, that shoots my image of you, Ms. Kendall. "I really am terribly flattered," he said firmly, recognizing an ingenious trap when he saw one, "but I'm afraid I have to say no. In fact, I threw the manuscript out the other night and I don't have a copy of it."

"May I call you up again after Christmas?"

"I never refuse phone calls." Red felt now as if he'd been through a Turkish bath with an overcoat on.

"Well, I'm delighted to hear that and I hope you have a very holy and happy Christmastime too, Mistah Kane. I'll say a little prayer at Midnight Mass that you'll change your mind."

"And you have a good holiday yourself, Ms. Kendall."

You play dirty, Red Kane told the Lord God, of whose existence he was still not altogether certain.

He switched back to the command mode of the word processor and destroyed the file that contained the manuscript of his novel. That was that. One more temptation removed.

I would be utterly ridiculous on a promotion tour. Making a fool of myself on radio call-in shows is not worth a half a million dollars.

Satisfied? he demanded of the Lord God.

The third phone call came as Red finished his column.

"Gerry at the travel bureau, Mr. Kane. I remember when you made that trip to Brazil last spring that your passport was running out, so I thought I would check with you to make sure that it hasn't expired yet."

"That's certainly very considerate and efficient." He opened the drawer of his desk in which he dumped document certificate forms and other bureaucratic idiocies. "It runs till February first, Gerry."

"Oh, good. Then we won't have to have it renewed for your trip to Grand Cayman. The State Department can be dreadfully slow about these things, you know, and I certainly wouldn't want anything to interfere with that trip. God knows, with this kind of weather, I wish I were going to Grand Cayman."

"What trip to Grand Cayman?" Three fast pitches, right down the middle.

"Well, the trip you and Mrs. Kane are taking to Grand Cayman on January second." Poor Gerry was disconcerted. "Two weeks. Deluxe accommodations. First-class airfare from Chicago to Miami, and then Miami to Cayman. Mrs. Kane has made all the reservations."

The bitch. The conniving bitch wants to put me back in the hospital. Or worse. Force me to be the new Red Kane all the time. She never makes the same mistake twice. Probably devouring the literature on mysticism now. "I Was a Mystic's Wife." Great story line.

Red drew a very deep breath. For a moment all hung in the balance. "Oh yes, that trip, Gerry. We were planning to go because Mrs. Kane desperately needs the rest. Unfortunately, something has come up at the *Herald Gazette* which makes it essential for me to remain in Chicago. Worse luck! The two of us will try to get away sometime in the middle of March together. However, Mrs. Kane is still going to Grand Cayman."

"What should I do, then, about your reservation?" Gerry asked uncertainly.

"Cancel it."

Clever, he said to the Lord God, of whose existence he was still not certain. *But not clever enough.*

Epilogue

Lord, Lord, take me again out into the wilderness
I'll not be in terror of the wind.
Join me with the global spin
The better to wink at land and seas traveling with me.
Caught up in wonder,
fleeing from the everyman of my soul
towards my own creation—that new face, distinct—
and sharing with the universe our gifts
traversing terrain never seen by my eyes
but run through my sight—belief
Oh yes, get it—true seeing, humor beyond
mind and imagination
And more contagious than the common cold.
Ah, hold the flesh nestled into your air
cradle this baby born me,
double the sounds and send me off down the river rapids
bumping around,
blowing bubbles with the most ferocious wakes
Bake me, burn me, with sun so yellow
I feel for the shadow on my fellow man's back
and clap for the daffodils, thrill at the praise they give
living through the rainstorm
glorious again, lifting heads so rich with golden drops!
Flip flop—over there a pear, trying for ripeness
Eager for the bite
Reaching to be juice on teeth
Oh, never never land of Peter Pan
never was and never shall be but is
His!
Where war is a bore we have no need
except to breathe with the fuzz on the violets' leaves
kissing whiskered cheeks of loved ones
And know that something, everything is true
A bleeding joy in tears, that the secret lies open
and blessings are forever.

—Nancy McCready

Red Kane was feeling quite pleased with himself, like someone who had bet on all the underdogs in the New Year's Day bowl marathon and won on every bet. If he could only sustain the level of nervous tension that had built up in his family, it would be a perfect Christmas. In the past he had ruined Christmas for them without quite understanding what had happened. Now that he was doing it deliberately and consciously, he seemed to be much more skillful in disrupting the Joyous Season.

It was going to be a thoroughly melancholy Christmas for all the members of the Kane family, the kind of Christmas that Red particularly enjoyed; it would also doubtless mark the permanent demise of that resilient bastard the new Red Kane.

Everyone would be filled to the wassail-cup brim with anger and self-pity and guilt. Even the manic cheerfulness of the Ryans' Christmas festivity on St. Stephen's Night would not cancel out the anguish of Christmas Eve and the bitter disappointment of Christmas Day.

Eileen had tried on the phone the day before to begin a conversation with him about his "experiences," as she called them, in the tone of voice that one might have reserved for a discussion of a malignant tumor. She had obviously read the books. "I don't object to them, Red." She paused, doubtless looking for the proper legal label. "They're . . . well, a bit out of the ordinary . . . nevertheless they seem to have helped you."

Ah, a hint that he could have his cake and eat it too. Saint Redmond of Lincoln Park would not be turned out by his family as was Saint Francis of Assisi.

Bullshit.

"Woman, you'd try the patience of a saint," he had said as he hung up.

Nice turn of phrase, that.

Life was as it should be once again.

Midnight Mass at St. Clement's—he had adamantly refused to go anywhere near the Cathedral, thus starting the brawl with Eileen—was a temporary interlude, kind of a halftime pause in the donner and blitzen.

It was perhaps the most violent argument he had ever

had with her, all the pent-up resentments and frustrations they had both felt for the last two weeks exploding in obscenities in front of the children and Lois, who was visiting John for Christmas—a sign that the kids were serious about one another again.

Eileen almost never fought in front of the children and absolutely never used obscenities. Yet tonight she had called him a "vicious drunken prick," merely because he had stopped at the Ale House for a few quick ones before coming home and because he had rejected the family plans to go to the Cathedral. In response he swore at her in gutter language, something he told himself rather proudly he should have done long ago. Her green eyes filled with tears. Served her right.

"We are most like God," Blackie had said, "when we are aroused in passion and committed to the person who is the occasion of our arousal." Well, he wasn't very much like God.

Kate stormed out of the house; Patty shouted hysterically that he was a monster. He turned and shouted at her, raising his hand as if to strike her. John, confused and uncertain, stepped in to block the blow. Father and son shoved each other a bit until Red realized that his son was in much better condition, and left the Christmas tree, cursing bitterly, in search of another drink.

That the pretended blow at Patty was a fake did not make it any less effective in re-creating the old Red Kane.

Poor Lois watched wide-eyed, an orphan brought to Christmas among the nice people at the Big House only to discover that it was in fact a Mad House.

John, needing someone on whom to vent his powerlessness, must have turned on Lois. From his study, where he held a bottle of Jameson's in one hand and a Powerscourt tumbler in the other, Red heard John yelling at the hapless child.

God bless us everyone and thank you Tiny Tim.

Red returned the Jameson's to its cabinet. The point, he felt, had been made. He punched in Melissa's number on his private line to make sure that they had a date at the Doral Plaza in the afternoon of St. Stephen's Day. Her line was busy. Sex with her in the same bed in which he and Eileen had had their romps would wipe out all traces of the past two months. The only problem was that he was not sure he would be capable of any sexual feeling.

Still, the Lord God had been thoroughly and effectively turned off.

He was reasonably sober when he took over the wheel of the Volvo to drive to St. Clement's, more sober than anyone in the family realized. No one disputed his right to drive, willing martyrs to his drunkenness. Eileen's eyes were still liquid, with guilt now not pain. One fortunate outcome of his venture into sanctity had been that he knew that his wife was more easily guilted than he.

The car was as silent as a hearse as he drove up Clark Street in the lightly falling snow—what the cheerful meteorologists on TV called "lake-effect" snow. Another half inch on top of the four inches from the morning. And a windchill factor of seventy below zero. Perfectly appropriate.

The street was slippery enough for an accident if he had been as drunk as his family thought he was. Actually he'd had only two drinks, carefully nursed, at the Ale House.

It had been a pleasant Christmas Eve at the *Herald Gazette*. He had written a column suggesting that the Supreme Court abolish Christmas. If it is unconstitutional to have a Christmas crib on public property, he had argued, it is certainly unconstitutional to close government offices on a religious holiday and to suspend the delivery of the United States mail. Perhaps the crib is an embarrassment to the minorities who are not Christian, but hardly as much an embarrassment as having to take off work on a religious holiday.

And by abolishing Christmas, he'd contended, one could prolong the holiday buying rush, which is so important to American business. No one is embarrassed by making money off a religious feast, not even the heavy contributors to the American Civil Liberties Union.

Then he'd prepared and circulated a memo to Bradford Winston in which it was suggested that Wilson Allen ought to be transferred to the *HG*'s nonexistent London Bureau to obtain more experience with foreign news. No one signed the petition, of course, save for some reporters who had died in the late 1940's and Richard Nixon and Gerald Ford—fairly good forgeries that Red had done himself.

Give Wils something to think about over his Christmas dinner.

Eileen touched his hand lightly as she climbed out of the car, as if she were steadying herself against a fall on the icy sidewalk. He pulled away quickly. She didn't want him as a new man, she'd have to put up with the worst of the old man. Fortunately, disturbing memories of their ridiculous adolescent sexual escapades were fading. He had almost recaptured his sexual indifference toward her.

And the woman had been quite capable of sneaking over to Erinisle on Clark Street earlier in the day, buying Christmas presents for everyone, and labeling them as his gifts.

Indeed she would try the patience of a saint.

They entered the Romanesque church, which looked like a handsome dowager with a new dress and an injection of powerful vitamins—Christmas trees, candles, poinsettias, and banners that were disgustingly tasteful. Red and Eileen, after some vacillation, settled for a pew a third of the way down the aisle. For a moment it seemed that the two girls were going to another pew; Lois and John, caught between the two still-furious young women and their parents, were pulled in both directions. Then Patty and Kate shrugged their shoulders and filed in after Red and Eileen.

God rest ye merry gentlepersons.

Eileen's eyes were still glistening. *Damn, she usually has better control of her tears.* She had opened her fur coat (no mink for the lady lawyer), revealing a white knit two-piece dress with red trim. Christmas colors. She was wearing the damn emerald, which flickered dangerously in the soft light of the church.

She had yet to give him the Tiffany bill from her charge account for the gem. Martyr complex. Sexy Christian matron feeding herself to the lions.

He suppressed an impulse to touch her hand. He could postpone his sexual urges, almost undetectable now, until he saw Melissa the day after tomorrow. If Eileen wanted to be the Mother from Sligo, she could be just that for the rest of their lives.

The choir, disgracefully well trained, shifted from "O Little Town of Bethlehem" to "Silent Night," the church lights dimmed, candles blazed on the altar, their reflections bouncing off the poinsettias like shimmering waves seen from a vast deserted beach at sunset, a floodlight illumined the crib.

All the familiar Midnight Mass gimmickry, he thought, ignoring the lump in his throat. *Not much of a church but great theater.* "We're going to sing 'Adeste Fideles' as our entrance hymn," said the young priest in the sanctuary. "When Father Fahey and other ministers of the Eucharist come down the aisle, they represent all of us who are the faithful hastening to Bethlehem. The crib is Bethlehem for us at Midnight Mass of course, but we should remember that the altar is Bethlehem every day of the year, the place where the world is renewed."

Lois and John were holding hands. *When you're not married it's easy to heal lovers' quarrels.*

"'Adeste Fideles,'" the priest went on, "is the oldest of Christmas carols and one of the oldest hymns the Church has. It has suffered—like the Notre Dame fight song—from having been belted out too many times in bars...."

Sure enough, they'd been singing it over and over at the Ale House.

"Actually it is a very delicate hymn which should be sung lightly and slowly, as though we are walking across the hillsides with the shepherds, happy in the knowledge that we will soon see the Baby Jesus but singing softly so that we won't wake him up. All right, now imagine that we are on the outskirts of Bethlehem responding to the invitation to come, let us adore...."

Not bad; sentimental, but not gushy. Maybe we should have gone to the Cathedral after all.

The carol was indeed light and delicate. The procession down the aisle seemed to be on tiptoe. Next to him, Eileen was singing softly in her sweet, clear voice. Amazingly, Red was singing too.

Chaos swept through St. Clement's, blurring the whole church and the whole world. The cosmos once again dissolving. He reached for Eileen's hand, to protect her, no, to seek her protection.

Unaccountably her arm was already around him. She never made the same mistake twice. Exit Mother from Sligo, enter Daughter of Jerusalem.

There was another sound, overpowering the carol music, like hurricane surf at Grand Cayman, perhaps.

No, it wasn't surf. Not yet. It was a sound that was not a sound, a swooshing noise behind his head. Some warm-breasted, bright-winged Character swinging a cosmic baseball bat.

Again.

A Theological Note

This story is about falling in love again with your spouse, in its mixture of familiarity and mystery perhaps the most intense erotic experience that can occur in the human condition. Indeed it would seem that the evolutionary process has developed a uniquely human sexuality (as compared to that of the other primates) precisely to facilitate such intense eroticism. It might be argued that the rediscovery of mind-bending and body-wrenching mystery in the midst of everyday familiarity is what, specifically, human sexuality is all about.

This love affair in our story (as often in life) becomes "involved" with and possibly threatened by another Love Affair for which, the Catholic tradition believes, it is a cognate, a correlative, and a sacrament. The ecstasy of rediscovering physically and emotionally the intimate other and being rediscovered physically and emotionally by the other is a hint of the ecstasy of discovering and being discovered by the Other.

A priest, some few may still say, ought not to know about marital eroticism; if he does know about it he ought not to write about it, because such writing will shock the simple laity.

I am tempted to reply that only a priest can write about rediscovering and being rediscovered because he does not have to practice what he preaches in this dimension of human courage—no one can say to him, "When did you last take the terrible risk of falling in love again with your wife?"

How can you be a priest, it is objected, and know about such matters? To which I respond, How can you be a priest with any sensitivity to what happens in the lives of your people—the glorious opportunities foolishly squandered and the last-second triumphs seized from the jaws of certain defeat—and not know about them?

Be that as it may, the subject matter of this story would be inappropriate for a priest only if (*a*) human sexuality is base and vile and (*b*) priests are not part of the human condition and (*c*) human passion is not a sacrament—a manifestation—of divine passion. Since these three propositions are near heresies to the Catholic tradition, the objection is invalid.

(The allusion to the Song of Songs that appears in the first love scene is not an accident. Neither is Monsignor Ryan's theological comment on the nature of the sacramental as both "like" and "unlike." The use of such symbols and my emphasis on them in this note, I have learned from bitter experience, will be ignored by most Catholic reviewers, especially priests, just as it will be recognized by most lay readers of whatever denomination.)

One may wonder in passing whether the shocked laity do not exist largely in the minds of some Bishops and some priests. In an environment in which Cardinals die in houses of prostitution, Bishops are arrested for solicitation, priests are convicted in many cities for pederasty, the Vatican's lies about the death of John Paul I spawn conspiracy theories about the possibility that he was murdered, the various Vatican bank scandals and similar disasters in the American Church are well known, in which nine tenths of the clergy and laity no longer accept many components of the Church's sexual ethic, and in which a fifth of the clergy have resigned in order to marry, who remains to be scandalized, other than those whose emotional needs require scandal—if not in themselves at least in others?

It will be said by the same noisy few, who allege concern for the "simple laity" that are all but invisible in scholarly research, that priests have never written about marital eroticism before. Such a statement is simply not true. Celibates have ground out thousands of documents about marital intimacy, most of them negative. Given the renewed awareness of Catholicism that sex is sacramental, particularly after the historic Audience Talks on Sexuality of Pope John Paul II, a proper response to this second objection is that it is now time for priests to write positively and realistically about the crucial human experience of falling in love again.

Finally—the noisy few never give up—it will be contended that some simple faithful (numbers unspecified) will nonetheless be shocked by the erotic dimensions of this story and hence a priest ought not to have written it.

In the seminary we would have called this shock either

"pharisaical scandal" (hypocrisy) or "scandal of the weak" (unshakable ignorance). Even in those days, long before the Vatican Council, it was taught that such "scandals" could be ignored for "proportionate reasons"—in this case the development in story form of a positive Catholic theory of the agony and the ecstasy of being captured again by an obsession for your intimate other.

More bluntly, those who would be shocked or "scandalized" don't have to read the book.

A Sociological Note

I can make no claim to expertise on the theology or the psychology of intense religious experiences of the sort reported by William James in his classic *The Varieties of Religious Experience.* I do not know what (or What) causes them or how they occur.

However, the basic sociological research on such experiences, which Monsignor John Blackwood Ryan is good enough to quote in this story, was done in the 1970's by my colleague Professor William McCready and myself. The reader should be assured that the research is reflected accurately in this story. Such experiences are common in our society, occur especially in forceful and active men and women, often utterly transform their lives, not infrequently make them even more attractive, and correlate strongly with measures of emotional health and maturity. Occasionally, in the absence of proper support and understanding, these interludes can produce the "afterburner" effect Red Kane experienced—from which it does not follow that the experience itself is unhealthy.

Moreover, the reaction of Redmond Kane's therapist is not a caricature. Rather it is almost verbatim the position of the Group for the Advancement of Psychiatry in its booklet on ecstasy. One must say that their conviction that mystical ecstasy is merely an interlude of quasi schizophrenia occurring in an emotionally disturbed person is directly contradicted by the best national sample data currently available to us. Mary Kate Murphy's strictures on the GAP ideology are not, in my judgment, exaggerated, however colorful her language may be.

Some such experiences can be temporarily unhinging, especially when, as in this story, they occur at a time of emotional crisis, are not understood by the person's family, and are accompanied by an ideological psychiatric response. Nonetheless, the correlation between frequent ecstatic experiences and scores on various mental health scales is the highest ever recorded for these scales. Ecstasy ought not to be sought, perhaps, but it is certainly good for you.

I leave to the reader's imagination what will happen to Redmond Peter Kane once he escapes from the embrace of the "Cheshire smile, all calm and curled" that assaults him at Midnight Mass in St. Clement's Church. However, the empirical data indicate that many of those who have such experiences do indeed try to escape from the onus of transformation of life that the experiences seem to imply. Rarely are such attempts completely successful. Thus Blackie's solemn injunction to Red Kane is also supported by the social science evidence. Not that it needs such support.

—AMG

Chicago, Christmas Eve, 1983

Rio de Janeiro, Brazil, Mary's Day at Christmas (January 1), 1984

São Paulo, Brazil, Epiphany, 1984

Father Andrew Greeley is a priest, journalist and sociologist, as well as a bestselling novelist. Considered one of the top people shaping religious thought today, he is programme director at the National Opinion Research Center in Chicago and a Professor at the University of Arizona.

Also by Andrew M. Greeley

THE CARDINAL SINS
THY BROTHER'S WIFE
ASCENT INTO HELL
LORD OF THE DANCE
THE MAGIC CUP
VIRGIN AND MARTYR
HAPPY ARE THE MEEK
HAPPY ARE THE CLEAN OF HEART
DEATH IN APRIL
ANGELS OF SEPTEMBER